Fortune Favors the Sparrow

More from Phase Publishing
by

Rebecca Connolly

The Arrangements
An Arrangement of Sorts
Married to the Marquess
Secrets of a Spinster

The London League
The Lady and the Gent
A Rogue About Town
A Tip of the Cap

The Spinster Chronicles
The Merry Lives of Spinsters
The Spinster and I
Spinster and Spice

Fortune Favors the Sparrow

Agents of the Convent
Book One

Rebecca Connolly

Phase Publishing, LLC
Seattle

Phase Publishing, LLC first paperback edition
January 2021

ISBN 978-1-952103-21-6
Library of Congress Control Number 2021901028
Cataloging-in-Publication Data on file.

Acknowledgements

To Jane, the master of strong, vibrant female characters.

And to toast. For always being everything and anything.

Special thanks to Martha, Jennie, Lorie, Heather, and Jen for their insight and assistance in bringing this book about.

Want to hear about future releases and upcoming events for Rebecca Connolly?

Sign up for the monthly Wit and Whimsy at:

www.rebeccaconnolly.com

A Proclamation

By Miss Leonora Masters
Headmistress of Miss Masters' Finishing School

Forasmuch as it has been thus Ordained by the powers that be that the Rearing of gently bred ladies requires some assistance, and in Keeping with traditions long established, It has been decreed that such rearing Needs proper establishment for training purposes, Given the span and scope of such development.

As it pleases the powers that be, Never forgetting the honor due to her subjects, Development and education of young ladies shall be Courteously and courageously given.

Owing to the need for such establishment, Unto the finishing of the female sex, Nobility shall be thus encouraged, Their patronage much desired, to Relinquish the education of such female persons as aforementioned Yet in their youthful and less informed state Into such qualified care.

Nevertheless, with charity and succor, females of a Lesser status shall be generously and Indubitably sponsored in their similar attendance herein For the purpose of gaining appropriate Education as befits needs and station.

Occupied thusly, this establishment shall henceforth Render such superior instruction and care, Defending the virtue and honor of her pupils, Engendering appropriate accomplishment upon all, Avowing to maintain the standards and Traditions of her forebears, and shall Henceforth fulfil all other obligations as so indicated.

Given under my Hand at Miss Masters' Finishing School in Kent, the 1st day of March, 1790, in the Thirtieth year of His Majesty's reign.

God save the King
Leonora Masters

Chapter One
Kent, 1825

"*Comment dire 'say', Mademoiselle Harlow?*"

Clara Harlow turned with a smile to her student, a fond scolding in her expression. "*Comment dire 'ça,' Caro.* The word you are wanting to use is *ça.*"

The girl nodded obediently even as her brow creased with thought. "*Comment dire ça, Mademoiselle Harlow?*" she asked again, pointing to the passage in their assigned reading.

Clara came over to her, peering over her shoulder. "*Ah. Fourrure,*" she said clearly, emphasizing the difficult word as succinctly as possible. "*La fourrure. Que pensez-vous que ce mot est?*"

Caro returned her attention to the words and read the line again, her lips moving on each word, the barely audible breath of her voice still fumbling over pronunciation. "Fur?" she finally asked Clara aloud.

"*Très bien,* Caro," Clara praised, nodding in encouragement. "*Continue à lire.*" Caro beamed at her, then turned fully to her book once more.

Relief cascaded down Clara's spine as she turned away from the girl and continued to move about the classroom. Caro was one of the scholarship girls at the Miss Masters' Finishing School, which meant she had no fortune, no status, and no education beyond what she had been given since being brought into their fold. She was one of their star pupils for the rudimentary Rothchild Scholarship Academy and had exceeded anyone's expectations for what she might have accomplished.

At fourteen, she was still behind what other girls her age of a more elevated station were capable of, but in a year or two, that gap would close.

Educationally, at least.

It wasn't always easy for the parents of their upper-class students to accept that there would be students of lower stations receiving the same education and sharing the same meals as their daughters. There had been some rather disgruntled moments surrounding the principle, in fact, though Miss Masters had always intended the school to serve the spectrum of classes when she founded it. She certainly had never been intimidated by the complaints of powerful families and had never been ashamed of what they did for the less fortunate.

Miss Bradford, the current headmistress, was just as committed to the cause, and even less likely to be intimidated.

Clara, for one, always felt the desire to give a little more attention to the girls who had to overcome so much to gain their education. Having once been of high station, and then being forced into diminished circumstances, she fully comprehended just how vast the separation between stations could be.

Why couldn't a girl like Caro become one of the most educated women England had ever seen? She'd likely never be hailed for such things, but it would be a triumph, nevertheless. She could one day teach here or become a governess to the wealthy and powerful families who had objected to her education in the first place. There was a certain distinction that came with completing one's education at Miss Masters', and their placement of scholarship girls had, to this day, been perfect.

Not one girl had left without gainful employment.

Not even one.

Those of high standing, obviously, needed no such placement, but they were considered the most accomplished of ladies, there was no doubt.

It was an establishment Clara was proud to be part of, and she felt gratitude for her good fortune daily.

Her life could have been so much worse.

"Pardon me, Miss Harlow."

A voice from the door brought Clara around to see one of the most senior students at the school standing there, fingers clasped before her, the very picture of composed dignity.

Considering the girl had been quite a ragamuffin only a few years before, the change was astonishing.

"Yes, Martha, what is it?" Clara inquired as she crossed to her.

Martha bobbed a quick curtsey. "Miss Bradford has asked to see you, Miss Harlow. In her office, if you please."

Clara nodded at the request. "Class ends in a few minutes. Would you tell Miss Bradford I should like to wait to dismiss my class, and then I will come straightaway?"

"Of course, Miss Harlow." Martha curtseyed again. "*Je vais lui dire tout de suite.*"

The perfection in her accent warmed Clara's heart and she nodded in approval. "*Très bien dit,* Martha. *Merci.*"

Martha smiled and left.

There was no telling what Miss Bradford could want, but there was nothing to fear from her. It was customary for the headmistress to request to speak with any or all of the teachers at a moment's notice. While she maintained her position of authority, Miss Bradford also took great care that her teachers felt themselves part of a family of sorts. She insisted that any concerns regarding students, staff, or each other be brought to her at once, and, as far as Clara knew, it was done.

Over the last few years, Clara had come to value and respect Miss Bradford's insight and advice as she would that of a close friend, or even a sister at times. Miss Bradford was far younger than one might have expected any headmistress at such an establishment to be, but she had been personally tutored by Miss Masters for her position from the beginning, and there had been no question of succession when Miss Masters had decided it was time to retire. Miss Bradford was the only possible, equally qualified choice.

Nevertheless, Clara's curiosity was piqued. She'd only just had tea with Miss Bradford last week as a sort of personal interview, and she'd thought they had discussed everything pressing and pertinent then.

Unless the meeting was to discuss Miss Bradford's niece, Tess. She was the girl's guardian, which was a trifle unconventional, but

Tess did not seem to lack any support in her life. Indeed, being practically raised in a finishing school, Tess had more aunts than one might know what to do with, and the few men associated with the school had become uncles and brothers to her.

Now nearly fifteen years of age, Tess was a bright and engaging young woman, one of their more promising pupils. There was some question as to which station she properly belonged to once she left the school, but she floated easily between them all while here.

Such things mattered less in the safe confines of this place.

Clara glanced at the clock, then cleared her throat. *"C'est tout pour aujourd'hui, les filles. Vous pouvez ranger vos affaires."*

"Merci, Mademoiselle Harlow," the group recited in almost perfect unison. They rose from their seats and filed out of the room quietly, their soft words to each other a murmuring hum of sound that began to echo the moment they entered the corridor.

Clara sighed in the now empty room and patted her plain chignon to ensure its neatness before moving into the corridor herself. The vast array of students along her way to the headmistress's office was not lost on her. Each of the girls were instructed to wear plain gowns in shades of blue, gray, green, or cream, and identical aprons of neat linen were worn by all. The restrictions of gowns were adhered to by each of the girls, but the quality of those gowns varied starkly based on the fortunes of each individual student.

Some of the girls did not comprehend how senseless fine muslin was in the schoolroom, but at least the fashion of it was limited by the apron each wore. Still, it did not stop the girls from lower classes from eying such finery.

"Good morning, Clara," Miss Bartlett greeted as she passed, exiting her classroom with her usual quick pace, her unruly dark curls flying from their pins as usual.

"Emmeline! I didn't know you were back, how long can you stay?" Clara beamed at her friend, reaching out a hand to her.

Emmeline took it and squeezed. "Not long, I'm afraid. I'm due back in London on Saturday. My aunt…"

Clara shook her head sadly. "The poor dear. You are so good to look after her."

"I am not the only relation who does so," Emmeline reminded

Clara with an almost uneasy air. "My cousins tend her nearly as often, but she does seem rather fond of me."

"Who could help that?" Clara returned the squeeze of her hand. "Might we take tea this afternoon? I'm due to see the headmistress now, but I so want to have a chat."

Emmeline nodded. "I look forward to it." She released Clara's hand and continued down the corridor as Clara moved in the opposite direction. "Girls, not so hasty, please. Miss Edley will not appreciate a twisted ankle before your dancing class. Better tardy than injured, yes?"

"Yes, Miss Bartlett," the girls answered with the usual reluctance girls of their age tended towards.

Clara had taught the dance classes before Miss Edley had come along, with several instances of the same reluctance of spirit, and it had been a relief to give those responsibilities up.

Whatever Clara's gifts might have been, she was not an accomplished dancer.

She grinned now at Emmeline's natural attention to detail, and her quick instruction on her observation. It was so like her to do so, but she was still one of the favorite teachers here. Her demands in London kept her from being present continuously, but somehow, her classes never fell behind in their studies even when she was not present to instruct them.

Writing and rhetoric were her subjects, and Clara was convinced there was no woman more capable of instructing the girls in those matters.

Turning back to her course, Clara moved with a bit more quickness to her step, though, she noted with amusement, not with haste.

While she did not take Annette Edley's dancing classes, a twisted ankle would not help a teacher, either.

As girls made their way to their next classes, and the crowding of the corridors diminished, Clara felt herself breathing easier and looking more carefully around her. It had been some time since she had truly taken in the splendor of these walls she was so fortunate to inhabit. The sleeping quarters were simply furnished, but the remainder of the place was rather like a grand house in the countryside. It lacked the display of accoutrements and antiquities that one might see there, but in all other respects, it might still have been the home of the Beddingsfords, as it had been for centuries before.

The last Lord Beddingsford had sold the estate to Miss Masters for a laughably low sum, but he had been desperate to leave England and never return. Refurbishments had been made where safety or convenience required, but in all other respects, the place had simply been maintained.

The ceilings were adorned with vaulting and marbled moldings, gilded artwork, and carved beams, ages and ages of residential styles on display like a walk through history. Artwork hung on the walls without any familiar significance, the paintings being the work of former students, images of royalty, depictions of historical events, or landscapes of various counties of England. Strains of music could be heard from the classes now in session, some of it skilled while others were less so. Grand windows illuminated the corridors naturally, the views of the Kent countryside from them all too enviable. The day was fine, which was a blessing after what seemed to be weeks of dreariness.

Students would be clamoring to walk out of doors later, she had no doubt. Someone would have to notify Mr. Quinn that the gardens might be invaded. He tended to get quite finicky about such things.

Another corridor, and then Clara was there, the headmistress's office and quarters sitting in this part of the house rather than with the rest of the rooms. It must have been a lonely distance for Miss Bradford, though she had never made any mention of feeling so. Clara would not wish for such a position and thought herself very fortunate to not have the duties and responsibilities Miss Bradford must face on a daily basis.

She knocked softly on the closed door, brushing her hands down the front of her to rid herself of any wrinkles that may have appeared.

"Come."

Pushing open the door, Clara entered the large space, the once masculine study of Lord Beddingsford now bright and airy without becoming starkly feminine. The bookshelves were equally full as they might have been with previous tenants, though there were more than only books placed upon them now. Clara even caught sight of a small, framed watercolor on one, surely something Tess had done in her early art courses here.

A faint breeze crossed the room, and Clara felt one of her golden strands of hair dance across her brow. She pushed it behind her ear at once and forced her attention on the woman standing behind the desk, fair hair pulled almost severely back, dark gown neatly arrayed on her delicate frame.

"My apologies, Miss Bradford," Clara said with some embarrassment. "I forget how captivating your office is."

Miss Bradford smiled with her usual warmth and glanced about the room herself. "Is it? I sometimes feel as though it is rather cavernous for someone as small as me. And I hope you do not mind the breeze; I prefer having the window open a little when I am at work here. It is almost as though I am working out of doors."

"No, ma'am." Clara folded her hands before her, smiling. "You wished to see me, Miss Bradford?"

The woman tilted her head, her smile deepening. "My dear Clara, I do wish you would call me Pippa. And please, take a seat. This is a rather different sort of meeting than we have had before, and I do wish you would make yourself comfortable."

Clara nodded and sat, adjusting her skirts carefully. "If you like, Miss Bradford. Pippa, I mean." She smiled, her embarrassment returning. "Apologies. It is going to take some adjustment for me to call you that."

Pippa surprised her by coming around the desk and taking the chair nearest her rather than remaining behind it. "That is because you have excellent manners and a quality of breeding far above your present circumstances."

"You are too kind, Pippa." Clara looked down at her hands, the tips of each finger suddenly of great interest.

"Don't be ashamed of it, Clara," Pippa urged, placing a hand over her arm. "It is not your fault that your family came to such reduced circumstances. You were not hired on here out of pity, either. I consider you a woman of very fine conduct and hold you in the highest regard. Surely you must see that."

Clara's throat closed briefly with emotion, and she tried several times for a swallow before succeeding. "Thank you, Miss Bradford. I'd hoped... that is... I am very grateful to have been here for the time that I have."

Pippa raised a brow. "I hope you don't believe I'm about to release you from employment, Clara, and I desperately hope you have no intention of leaving us."

"No!" Clara cried before laughing. "Heavens, no. I will stay as long as you like."

"Marvelous." Pippa's smile returned, then softened shortly thereafter. "I trust you implicitly, Clara. More than that, I believe you to be loyal to your core. Do you consider yourself to be honest, trustworthy, and loyal?"

Clara blinked at the direct, almost heavy question. "Yes... yes, I think so, Pippa."

The woman's gaze intensified on her, smile still in place, though there was a hard edge to it. "I need you to be sure, Clara."

She took a moment to inhale and exhale even as her heart raced within her before answering. "Yes, ma'am. I am."

Pippa nodded once, and a corner of her mouth lifted with the answer. "And will a secret told to you remain in your confidence, Clara?"

"Of course, ma'am," she answered immediately. "It will never pass my lips or leave my heart."

"I need a promise, I am afraid. I mean no offence or implication on your character, it is just the principle of the thing."

Clara stared back at this kind, warm, remarkably influential woman who suddenly asked so much of her without any foundation or explanation. Could she blindly swear to keep in confidence whatever she would hear next?

"I promise, Miss Bradford," Clara vowed solemnly. "Whatever I am told, it will go no further."

Pippa's smile grew, and she moved her hand to Clara's. "I knew you would say that. I knew you were made of the strongest character. And for that, I thank you."

Clara shared her smile. "Thank you." When Pippa moved her hand away, Clara sighed once, steeling herself. "What is it that you need me to keep in confidence, Pippa?"

"That, I am afraid," Pippa told her, rising and moving to the second door in her office, further down than Clara had come in, and almost hidden in comparison, "is not something only I require of you." She knocked lightly on the second door, then stepped back.

A tall, well-dressed man with dark hair entered, and Clara rose in surprise, recognizing him at once. "Lord Rothchild."

He bowed with a grin. "Miss Harlow, good day. I trust Alicia and Eliza are behaving themselves in your classes?"

"They are, my lord, of course!" She nodded fervently. "And, if I may say so, they have their mother's gift for art."

"I am pleased to hear it. I was dreadfully afraid they might have my poor talents instead, and there would die all hopes of accomplishment." He glanced at Pippa, seeming to take on a different light as he did so. "Are we ready?"

Pippa dipped her chin. "I believe so."

Ready? What in the world would any of them need to be ready for at this moment?

Clara looked between them in confusion.

Lord Rothchild took pity on her. "You may wish to sit down, Miss Harlow. Just a suggestion."

Slowly, Clara did so, a feeling of dread nudging its way from her stomach up toward her throat.

Pippa gave her an encouraging smile. "As you know, this school was founded in 1790 by Leonora Masters."

"Yes," Clara said slowly, not entirely sure what the founding of the school had to do with any kind of secrets of such significance.

"The purpose was, of course," Pippa went on, "to provide a sterling education and accomplishment opportunity to the young ladies of England, ideally to become the most respected institution of its kind."

"A feat that I, for one, believe it has accomplished splendidly," Lord Rothchild interjected.

Pippa nodded at that. "There was, however, a secondary purpose to the founding of this school. I would venture to suggest that this secondary purpose was, in fact, the primary purpose for its foundation."

"As one who has been involved from the beginning," Lord

Rothchild added with a rueful smile, "I can attest to that."

Clara blinked hard. "Another purpose?" she asked, feeling rather stupid with the two of them sharing this same understanding and appreciation of which she was so ignorant.

Pippa inhaled slowly, then exhaled in a quick rush. "Clara, Miss Masters' Finishing School is England's primary training academy for female covert operatives."

The words pounded furiously against Clara's head, permeating somehow into the root of each hair on her scalp, setting the entire expanse on fire while the sinking feeling from before seemed to radiate to her entire body. It seemed a miracle she still sat in her chair when she had so clearly sunk through the furniture and the floor beneath it. Yet somehow, she had not moved in the slightest, her headmistress and one of their most important donors staring at her as though she might perish on the spot.

"Primary?" she repeated, though there were several other words she likely should have chosen out of the selection.

Lord Rothchild seemed to find amusement in her choice as well. "Yes. The only official academy, to be sure, but there are other private establishments elsewhere in England, Scotland, and Wales, and a rather promising one in Ireland, if you can believe it."

Clara wet her lips, the new information barely registering with her. "Covert operatives? As in…?"

"Spies, Clara," Pippa told her frankly. "We are training spies as well as ladies. We are training both. You must have wondered about some of the details of this place that never quite made sense. The Rothchild Academy, for instance."

"I beg your pardon," Lord Rothchild protested playfully, winking at Clara. "That is my pet project you speak of."

Pippa ignored him. "We fought a great deal of complaints about the scholarship program and that rudimentary establishment, but it was critical to the success of our primary purpose, and the only manner with which we could make it happen. A great many secret and noble donors have ensured that we have the funds to do so, and it has borne the country rather sweet fruit at times."

"We're not raising girls of a lower station for proper employment?" Clara asked, her heart cracking at the thought.

"Of course, we are," Pippa insisted. "Not every scholarship girl becomes an asset or operative. Only those that, when educated and trained enough, show a proclivity to that sort of work."

There was some relief in that, though the rest of the revelation still had her reeling.

"So…" Clara said slowly, her thoughts feeling twice as slow as normal. "Both of you are… spies, then?"

The pair of them nodded in an eerily calm unison.

"Miss Bradford here is the highest-ranking female spy in England," Lord Rothchild told her. "She also leads them and manages their missions, and only answers to the Chief Spymaster of England."

"And you," Pippa pointed out with a smile.

He inclined his head in modest yet playful acknowledgement.

How could anything be playful for any of them at this time?

Then again, only Clara had received news that altered the way she looked at everything that surrounded her. Everything remained unchanged for the other two.

There might have been something playful in what they said, when all was considered.

"Lord Rothchild is the second in command of covert operations," Pippa explained, as though somehow that was what had Clara so silent and befuddled at the moment.

She found herself nodding all the same, taking in the famed diplomat with a new consideration. There was nothing surprising in what had been revealed about him. She could easily believe that he was a spy, that he had been a spy, and that he was, in fact, leading all sorts of spies. He possessed the sort of charm that would be infectious to anyone, and the air of danger and mystery that made one somehow still wary around him. The blend of all three made him a captivating individual, and had he declared himself the most feared pirate on the seas, she would have been equally as nonplussed.

But Miss Bradford… this school…

Miss Masters…

Everything Clara had thought about any of them had been a lie. Yet none of it had been.

All that Clara had thought things to be truly had been. They had simply also been something else.

There was some sort of dishonesty there, but she could not identify the exact vein of it.

"Who all knows?" Clara found herself asking, though she doubted it mattered as much as the content of what she had been told.

Yet somehow, she cared enough to know if she was the only ignorant teacher in this school. She knew full well that parents would have no idea, and that at least a portion of the students would be unaware of what else was happening here. Who else was a spy in this place? Which of the girls were being trained to become operatives? Were there rooms used strictly for the operative training? Hidden facilities?

Questions spun and swirled like toy tops in her mind.

"I'm afraid I cannot tell you that," Pippa told her apologetically. "I may reveal my own status, but not that of anyone else. You are not the only one unaware of this other aspect, I will tell you that. And none of this was done with the intention of deception. It is entirely for your protection and the protection of those we are training and have trained. Nothing more and nothing less."

Clara nodded slowly, satisfaction with such reasoning filling her.

Lord Rothchild stared at Clara, no doubt seeing each shift of emotions play across her face. "Miss Harlow, you will have questions upon questions come to you the longer you consider what has been said here. I suggest you do not try to think of them all now and let yourself mull things over."

She nodded at the advice, thinking she would need days upon days of consideration for any of this to make sense.

But there was one question that absolutely required an answer before she considered anything else.

"Why are you telling me this?" Clara whispered.

Pippa and Lord Rothchild looked at each other before returning their attention to her. "Because we have received information about potential dangers in the area," Lord Rothchild told her, "and we need your help."

Chapter Two

$\mathcal{B}$oredom was a dreadful thing for a gentleman to endure.

There wasn't always something to be done about it, and those times only made the whole thing more maddening.

George Russell, Duke of Kirklin, hated boredom more than he had ever thought he did, now that he was fully and completely engrossed in the duties and responsibilities of his dukedom. The tedium of it all was more taxing than renovating the whole of it would have been. He'd been pleased a few years ago to discover that his uncle had taken such care during his tenure with the title, but he hadn't thought it would mean he had nothing to do.

Tapping his pen against his desk now, he pored over the perfectly noted ledgers with their perfectly ordered lines and the perfectly accurate numbers beneath them. There wasn't even anything to look at, but his estate manager had requested he look them over today and see that all was to his satisfaction.

Of course it was to his satisfaction. It always was. The estate was so well set up that it would have run itself with very little prodding from anyone.

Every passing day, it was becoming more and more clear that his uncle had spent the time he might otherwise have spent with children or a wife perfecting his estate and making it the most enviable, impeccable estate that could be found.

It might have been preferable that he had married and sired children, if for no other reason than it would have removed the present duke's boredom.

It would also have meant that Hawk would have had to go by

George instead of his near-permanent nickname referencing his position as Marquess of Hawkendale. What would that have done for him in this life?

He might have been trounced more at school than he already had been. Even his mother hadn't called him George when she was alive. She'd only ever called him Hawk, though it had been his father's title. They'd known he would have the title one day, unless his uncle managed to defy his lifelong pattern, and so it had been.

His father had passed when Hawk was only twelve, so it had come rather sooner than any of them had expected, but there was nothing to be done about that.

"Mr. Robinson to see you, Your Grace."

Hawk looked up in relief, though his butler maintained his placid expression of indifference. "Thank you, Hughes."

Nat strolled into the room with his usual lopsided, carefree smile. "Hawk! What the devil are you doing being so dull?"

Hawk gestured to his study as he sat back in his chair. "This is the life of a duke, Nat. Tedious doldrums of estate management, and duties without end."

"All the more reason to be grateful I am a peasant," his friend shot back as he dropped himself into a chair near the window, plucking a book irreverently from the shelf and thumbing through it.

"Ten thousand a year and the estate at Daveney hardly makes you a peasant." Hawk scoffed and initialed the page of his ledger to indicate it met his approval, then closed the book with a sigh. "What are you doing here? I thought London was your present hunting grounds."

Nat glowered at him over the pages of his book. "You make it sound so inelegant."

Hawk shrugged and laced his fingers across his chest. "Am I wrong? Are you or are you not specifically aiming to find yourself a wife of good breeding and more than adequate fortune?"

"You forgot exceptional beauty," Nat reminded him before returning his attention to the pages before him. "And yes, I am, but there is a great deal more craft to the game than a hunt, I can assure you."

"I see I have offended your skills as a sportsman; I do apologize."

Hawk rolled his eyes, marveling for the hundredth time this year alone that he was friends with this man.

"I heard that," Nat informed him simply.

Hawk raised a brow. "Heard what?"

"Your eyes. Don't strain yourself with the effort, we can't have you injured. Your prospects might suffer."

Now Hawk barked a hard laugh. "*My* prospects? Nat, I'm impeccable as a catch, but it's irrelevant."

"Is it? How fortunate for me, I do so hate being compared to you." He scanned the book with apparent interest, but Hawk knew better.

If Nat were actually reading a single word in there, Hawk would be most surprised.

He waited to see if Nat would prompt him to expound further, and when it was clear he would not, Hawk sighed. "You will not be lured, will you?"

"Not easily, no," came the reply. "You are not a pretty woman with distracting assets, and I am presently more enjoyably occupied."

"Well, Adrianna is not here, so there are no pretty faces to see." Hawk smiled with some satisfaction, knowing his friend rather enjoyed shamelessly flirting with his sister, despite the distance in their ages.

Nat snapped his book shut and rose with a startling efficacy. "Then I see no reason to be here at all. Good day." He turned on his heel and started out of the room.

"Have a nice ride," Hawk called, not moving from his present position.

By the count of five, Nat was back in the room, grinning shamelessly. "All right, Hawk. Why is it so irrelevant that you are an impeccable catch, as you say? I'm not saying you are, just repeating your own words."

"Thank you for the distinction." Hawk glanced out of the window and shook his head. "I need to see my sister secure first, if not my brother, as well. My mother would have been lost without my uncle to offer financial security when my father died, and I will not leave my siblings without means."

"Are you dying, Hawk?"

Hawk looked at his friend in surprise. "No."

Nat barely even blinked at the response. "Are you terribly unwell?"

"Don't be ridiculous, I'm in perfect health," Hawk protested.

"Are you needlessly reckless in your riding or prone to overindulgence of strong spirits?"

Sensing where his friend was headed with this line of questioning, Hawk scowled. "No, Nat, I am not."

Nat crossed one knee over the other and gave him a scolding look, his fair eyes hooded with the expression. "Then I fail to see why securing Griff and Adrianna's futures should prevent you marrying whenever you like. Don't you need an heir?"

Hawk made a face at the notion. "Yes," he grumbled, drumming his fingers on the surface of his desk. "Griff has said many times that he will not do it, nor will he truly take up being the marquess. I don't even think he's gone to Worsley Park since I've inherited, and it is supposed to be his now."

"Your brother is a nomad, Hawk," Nat reminded him without any hint of playful airs now. "Why else would he take every assignment the Foreign Office gives him on the Continent? Where is he now, anyway? Italy?"

"I haven't the faintest idea," Hawk admitted blandly. He managed a weak smile. "He writes every month or so, but whatever court he is involved in tends to take up most of his time. I think he writes to Adrianna more than me."

Nat snorted once. "Who wouldn't? So why not ask her what he's up to?"

Hawk waved off the suggestion. "She's far too occupied with her studies to pay much attention."

"Now that I cannot believe. She's intelligent and bright, I'll not deny it, but if I know your sister, she's far too occupied with other matters of accomplishment or forming various committees with her fellow students about something or other." He grinned at the thought. "Tell me I'm wrong."

As much as Hawk would have loved to tell his friend that he was being ridiculous, the truth of it was that it was a very likely scenario. Adrianna was as educated as any young woman of her station could hope to be, if not more so, given her insatiable curiosity, but she was vivacious and took to new challenges with an enthusiasm that worried Hawk at times. Were she a man, she would have been called driven and determined, if not ambitious, but as a woman...

Well, Hawk had felt at times that he may need to prepare various statements regarding his sister's behavior when it inevitably offended, concerned, or impressed Society.

"At what point do you anticipate her being finished, anyway?" Nat inquired while Hawk continued to draft imaginary missives in his head. "My sister is five years my senior, I know nothing about the process."

"Nor do I," Hawk admitted without shame. "I believe she is in her final year, but I would not be at all surprised if she has another year."

Nat's brow snapped down. "How old is the girl, Hawk? Sixteen?"

"Seventeen." He made a face and exhaled roughly. "I'd keep her at the school forever if I could."

"And what is your excuse for Griff?" Nat asked before Hawk could grow in any way sentimental, which was much appreciated. "He's of an age to mind his own life and concerns, the whelp wouldn't appreciate your interference."

Hawk only shrugged, not entirely certain why he pretended Griff had anything to do with his decisions. Griff would never be induced to settle into the life of tedium Hawk had taken on. He would likely never settle into any sort of life conducive to becoming Hawk's heir and leaving the freedom of his European tour of a life.

It wasn't as though Hawk had intended for his brother to actually be his heir in truth. He just... would have preferred not feeling utterly abandoned to his own responsibilities while his brother had all of the fun.

More than once, Hawk had found himself wishing that whatever court Griff presently found himself in was full of complete bores and a selection of the most uninteresting people Europe had to offer. Griff was inventive enough to have made any special setting one that worked in his favor, but there was nothing that said he should not have to put in a great deal of effort to do so.

Hawk had never possessed those skills.

Oh, he was social enough, and he certainly did his duty when it came to dancing, conversation, and patronage. He was a complete gentleman, well respected, and, he flattered himself, rather an appealing prospect.

But for all his boasting of being an impeccable catch, he had not yet managed to truly engage in any courtship worth maintaining. Easy flirtations in his youth, yes, but anything of promise? Never.

And for all Nat's playacting, he was shockingly devoted to the idea of a marriage for love and nothing else.

What a pair they were.

"Perhaps I should have you write to Griff next," Hawk suggested with a wry smile. "You might have better success in convincing him to come home."

"I daresay I would," Nat retorted. "I actually go to London from time to time, which is likely his only interest in England as a whole."

Hawk made a face. "I do what I must in London. I go every year for Parliament and the Season. I simply fail to see the need to remain longer than necessary."

"And instead you come out to Wiltshire." Nat gestured around them, eyes widening. "To Millmond. Where nothing ever happens, and nothing ever will."

The statement stung, partially because it was true.

"It's the largest estate belonging to the Duke of Kirklin, Nat," Hawk said with a sigh. "Where else am I supposed to go?"

"Oh, I don't know, one of your other four estates?" His friend looked up at the ornate ceiling above them, apparently disgusted with Hawk's stupidity. "One of the more exciting ones. Or at least a picturesque one."

Hawk narrowed his eyes at the impudent man who, he had neglected to point out, had come all the way out to Millmond himself without the provocation of an event. "You only fail to find Millmond picturesque because you're too occupied trying to keep up on a horse."

As he suspected, Nat's chin lowered as his eyes clashed with his, a familiar smirk crossing his face. "You think so? Poor, deluded fellow, I daresay it is time a reminder was set down in order to regain your sanity and grasp on reality."

Hawk rose and gestured for the door. "After you, of course."

"Yes, it usually is," Nat quipped as he started out. "You see? You're improving already."

Hawk chuckled and groaned as they moved through the silent corridors of Millmond towards the stables. "What are you doing here, Nat? Not that I am not pleased to see you, it is always a pleasure, but there isn't a particular reason I can think of."

"There isn't a reason I can think of, either," Nat told him without much concern. "Winter is approaching, so London is dull. I've no interest in visiting my godfather in York until Christmas, which is the only time I've any wish to see York."

"York is lovely," Hawk protested as they exited the house. "I'd sell my estate in Kent for one in York, if given a chance."

Nat gave him a derisive look. "I don't dislike York as a town or Yorkshire as a county. Only the prospect of an extended amount of time with my godfather."

The image was a laughable one, and Hawk would not deny it. Nat's parents had died while he was at school, and his godfather had taken charge of him, which was not an uncommon situation for anyone in England in the same predicament. The only trouble was that Nat's godfather was a crotchety viscount who grumbled incessantly about the departure of Society from its moral high ground, the ease with which baronies and the like were created, and how disagreeable it was that so much French influence had infiltrated London.

Nat had to dress very simply, yet very smartly when he visited Lord Rausten, or else he would never hear the end of it.

Even Hawk would admit that such a visit would be arduous.

"I never had such an experience when I visited my Uncle Kirklin," Hawk mused as they neared the stables. "He was a good sort, never quite seemed to me what a duke was supposed to be."

"How's that?" Nat asked, laughing as he loosened his cravat with a quick tug at his throat. "He *was* the duke, therefore, as he was, a duke was."

Hawk shrugged and nodded at the stable master currying one of the other horses while the hands prepared their saddles. "I see that now, obviously, but at the time, he might have been a country squire. He preferred that drafty old estate in Kent to any of the rest and spent nearly all his time there. I've been to Kirkleigh, of course, and when I visit Adrianna, I stay there, but once my sister is through with that school, I'll sell the whole estate."

They mounted their horses and started out of the stables at an easy trot. "You do realize the haughtiness of that statement, don't you?" Nat asked as they rode.

"Of what?" Hawk couldn't think how anything had sounded haughty when he had simply mentioned selling off one of his estates that was rarely used...

One of his estates...

Hawk muttered incoherently under his breath.

"There it is," Nat said cheerily. "I suggest you keep me as a friend, Your Grace, or you might lose anything that ties you to the average man."

"I'm not the only man with more than one house, Nat." Hawk shook his head and nudged his horse a bit faster. "Even considering selling one puts me on the outskirts among men of a similar standing."

In truth, it made him quite rare. It wasn't often that he met with other peers, let alone other dukes, as there weren't nearly as many as rumors and fanciful whims led anyone to believe, but those he had met seemed to view the idea of several houses and estates as rather commonplace, and seemed to collect more and more of them. Then, when the finances of the estates were strained too far to manage every house to its needs, the peer in question would make a fashionable retrenchment until the fortunes were restored.

Hawk couldn't live like that. He'd rather have one house as his main residence and perhaps just one other for the necessary retreat from normalcy. And one in London, of course, for when he was called there.

Three houses.

There wasn't much he could claim different from his present state when he could still say he had three houses, two of which boasted tenant farmers.

"I'd become a hermit of a duke if I could," Hawk grumbled to himself as his own hypocrisy irritated him.

"And how would that help your cause?" Nat asked at once, laughing as his horse began to stretch its legs more, its stride lengthening and pulling ahead of Hawk's. "It won't give you an heir, and Griff would have you killed in your sleep if you didn't even try to create an alternative one."

The mention of it in such business-like terms wasn't particularly palatable, but it was the way of things, and they both knew it.

But if Hawk hadn't become duke...

"Do you think my prospects are impeccable enough to give me leave to choose?" Hawk asked his friend, somehow missing the teasing note he'd intended his words to take on. "I mean really choose."

Nat sobered, knowing full well the sincerity behind Hawk's question. "I think so. Your fortunes are stable, your bloodlines are good, and your title waves a flag that any station would look for. Further than that, I think you could afford to stretch your scope, if you wished to."

Hawk raised a brow. "How do you mean?"

"Well, I think you could marry a poor girl, really." Nat looked at him in all seriousness. "It might raise a few brows, but if you can ensure your children are born on the right side of the sheets, you'd be a spectacular love match that way. Probably gain you a few more supporters."

Heat raced up Hawk's neck at the mention of legitimate children in such a way and he pretended to scan the horizon. "I've no intention of marrying a kitchen maid, Nat."

"Now *that* would be a scandal worth gossiping about!" Nat threw his head back on a laugh, then shook his head. "All I meant was you don't need to limit yourself where a potential wife is concerned. I think you're perfectly free, Hawk. Fortunate chap."

Nat could think that way, but Hawk knew it wasn't so simple. He couldn't marry just anybody, not with the bloodlines he now had to represent. There was some duty to his progenitors and the connections they had ensured in the family. He didn't want to be discussed over dinner with his hypothetical bride as though their relationship was something worth speculating over. Yes, he wished to marry for affection, but he would settle for the promise of it if he must.

All he'd intended by the question was to examine expectations of station and bloodlines.

He didn't need to be thrown out to pasture and told any mare would do.

Because the truth of it was, it would not.

"What about you, Nat?" he asked with far more lightness than he had managed to ask the first question. "What does your peasant status mean for your matrimonial prospects?"

Nat only shrugged his broad shoulders, his attention now forward. "You know my feelings on the subject. They have not changed."

"Still as devoted?" Hawk was impressed, he would not deny it. Nat had always claimed that only a love match would do for him, and, without the same bonds of duty tying him to expectations, his freedom was rather more than Hawk's.

Nat's parents had been the love match of their time and growing up under such influence had clearly shaped the man.

"Always," Nat said simply. "I may play the flirt, have my fun, but that will never change."

"And do you think you'll find it?"

The question surprised them both, it was clear from Nat's straightening in his saddle and tightening of his jaw. Hawk, for his own shock, felt the question to his toes.

Why? What had prompted such a frivolous question of sensibilities he had never held for himself? It was something Adrianna would have asked him after a night of too much novel reading, not something that a respectable duke asked his oldest friend on a whim.

It was on the tip of his tongue to take it back and challenge him to a race or something when Nat surprised him in return.

"I think so," his friend said slowly. "I'm fairly certain, in fact. I cannot say why, I certainly have no present prospects, but it feels right." He shrugged and looked at Hawk with a surprisingly open expression. "Fair enough?"

Hawk nodded. It was more than fair; it was revealing.

It was enviable to know something with such certainty. To know *that* thing with any kind of certainty.

And Hawk was notably envious.

For a man who had never truly considered much about marriage and the like, the notion was nearly upsetting in its stunning arrival.

He had all the time in the world to consider such things, and he certainly wasn't about to bother with them now.

"How about a race?" Hawk asked suddenly, flashing a grin. "I win, you have to go back to London and find a winter courtship for yourself. You win, you can come with me on a tour of each of my estates. I have to do so by the end of the year, might as well start now."

Nat's eyes narrowed at the challenge. "Agreed. But I want the lambskin on the carriage for the journey. I'm rather delicate, I must travel in comfort."

Hawk rolled his eyes, his smile helpless now. "I'll send a nursemaid to London with you after I win."

They shared the nod of gentlemen, then, on an unspoken cue, dug their heels into their animals and spurred the horses on.

Chapter Three

Clara sat on the edge of her bed in silence, staring off at nothing, shawl hanging limply around her.

Spies. The school was full of spies. The school was *founded* by spies.

The school was *training* spies.

She should have seen it, now that she knew the truth. There were too many questions that had occurred to her in the last few years that she had simply written off without examination. Too many inconsistencies that she had grown used to ignoring. Too many moments of the most bewildering sort with students that she had chalked up to the imaginations of excitable girls.

All of them revisited her mind from the vaults of her memory, taunting her with the now obvious reasons for them.

Poor little Clara, so naïve and blind she couldn't see what was right in front of her face.

Could she trust anything she thought she knew about this place? Or anyone?

Her interview with Pippa and Lord Rothchild had gone well enough, she supposed, and they had been particularly understanding with regards to her shock over the whole thing. She had taken his lordship's advice and pushed most of her questions back until she had time to consider them, but it had affected the remainder of her day quite strikingly.

Her afternoon classes had passed in a blur, and she was quite sure her lessons had been pitiful at best. She would have to make up for that tomorrow.

She would also need to give her answer tomorrow.

A knock at her door broke her stupor, and Clara blinked, looking at the door in confusion. "Come in?"

Normally, the statement was an invitation, not an inquiry, but nothing was as it should have been today.

Her surprise was compounded when one of the most senior teachers entered, smiling at Clara with the concern and understanding a mother would have worn.

Which meant she knew.

Clara couldn't smile about that. "Abby."

Abigail Charteris, with her eyes the color of the sky and her hair the color of a rich tea, came over to the bed, her telltale limp hardly noticeable as she did so. "May I sit, Clara?"

She nodded, limply gesturing to the spot beside her without a word.

"I know the context of your meeting with Miss Bradford today, Clara," Abby began without preamble.

"I thought you might," Clara muttered before she could help herself.

Abby, thankfully, ignored her comment. "I know that Lord Rothchild was there, and I know what they told you."

"Do you?" Clara asked, remembering belatedly that she had been told not to trust anyone without some proof.

"I know the world they told you about," Abby told her simply, "because it is my world, too." She handed a scrap of paper over to Clara.

In Pippa's neat, tidy hand, the words "trust her" were written, along with the seal of the ring Pippa wore on her left hand.

That seemed worthy enough as proof went.

"I was an operative for Seamstress before Milliner took over," Abby went on before catching herself with a smile. "I mean Miss Masters before Miss Bradford. I had barely begun my work under Miss Bradford when my injury occurred. I wasn't able to continue fieldwork when I recovered, my disability prevented me from any action. It was Miss Bradford who gave me the position I have here and allowed me to continue to serve, just in a different capacity."

Clara stared at this woman she admired so much, finding it easier to believe her former role in the covert world than Pippa's. Something about the fire that lived in her eyes but never in her tone, the determination and quiet fortitude she'd always possessed, made the image of her being a spy rather fitting.

"You said your injury was a riding accident," Clara murmured, thinking back.

Abby grinned at her, a soft giggle escaping her. "So it was. A riding injury while making an escape on an assignment and bleeding from several wounds." She blushed a little, lowering her eyes. "It sounds dashing and daring when I say it like that. The truth of the matter was that I was in a dreadful way, and my partner had to drag me into some nearby brush to hide from our pursuers after my fall from the horse."

"Heavens above…" Clara breathed as she tried to picture Abby in such a state, and in such danger, but as believable as Abby might have been as a spy, the scene would not fit. "And you still wanted to go back? After you healed, I mean."

"Oh yes." Abby nodded firmly. "Very much so. I loved my work, and it had given my otherwise tepid life such purpose and meaning… I was so brokenhearted when the doctors told me I could never be an operative in the same way. It had been all I wanted from the moment I began."

Clara shook her head slowly, marveling at such feelings about something so dangerous. She would not pretend that she was not moved and a little inspired by the idea of purpose and meaning, though she certainly had enough of both in her teaching here. It had always seemed a noble occupation, the education of women.

Could there be more for her in joining this other world? By all accounts, she would still teach, which was a relief, but to offer more of herself… To serve an even greater cause as well…

"I don't know what to think," she found herself admitting in a half whisper.

"About what they requested?" Abby pressed. "Or about any of it?"

Clara swallowed once. "Any of it. All of it." She shook her head. "I simply don't know. I apologize if this offends."

Abby's brows shot up. "Offends? Darling girl, I could not

understand you more. Pippa asked me to look in on you tonight because it falls to my lot to introduce our scholarship girls to this world. I have this same conversation on the regular. Ask me any question you wish, confide what you wish. It is safe with me."

Doubt prickled at Clara's mind, and she gave her would-be mentor a dubious look. "You aren't duty-bound to report it to Pippa?"

"Only if it relates to the safety of the kingdom, our operatives, or planned missions," Abby quipped. "Questions, concerns, and complaints are exempt."

Her cheerfulness was contagious, though Clara was not in the mood for it. Still, it brightened her spirits all the same.

Moderately.

"I don't…" Clara began, pausing to wet her lips. "I don't quite understand what my role would be. Should I accept, that is. I'm not very daring or brave, and I could never fight anyone."

"There are several roles to fill in the covert world," Abby assured her, reaching out a hand and placing it on Clara's. "Each with their own unique set of skills, tasks, and expectations. Would you believe we have individuals set aside specifically for filing and transcribing? They never see a dark alley or a weapon, but they are one of us all the same."

Well, that wouldn't have done for Clara at all, but it certainly did shed some light on the vastness of positions possible.

"What have they asked of you?" Abby asked gently with a squeeze of her hand. "What is your understanding?"

Clara's brow wrinkled briefly in thought. "They want me to go to a house on the coast and play a role, something that will enable me to stay, as well as come and go as needed. I am to use my artistry to capture every facet of the coastline and coves, observe goings on, and infiltrate local society. Also, I am told my… abilities in the French language will be an asset, though I don't know why."

Abby nodded slowly as she listened, her lips curving up more with each item. "Oh, say mastery, Clara, by all means. A Frenchman would envy your abilities, so marvelous are you."

There was no polite way to reply to such praise, so Clara only looked away.

"There's a terrible amount of pressure in this," Clara admitted in a raw tone. "I don't even know the context of this request, but I know enough to recognize that they would not recruit someone outside of the ranks if it were a whim."

"Yes and no."

Clara glanced back at Abby, whose wince she barely caught. "How so?"

Abby paused, no doubt needing to weigh her words for someone like Clara who might not understand. "Not on a whim, of course, but sometimes, the scope of something is too wide and too unknown to isolate appropriately with agents or operatives in the ranks. On those occasions, there may be a need for trusted, outside individuals to be brought in to assist in the gathering of information. It allows us to narrow down the details of a situation to better isolate it for the operatives and agents more equipped for the dangerous and complicated aspects."

Nodding, Clara leaned back on her hands, storing that information in her mind. "So, lives will not hang in the balance on my assignment?"

"Not yet, at any rate." Abby smiled at the irony, and, this time, Clara understood it.

Slightly.

"I'd wager," Abby continued, "that there are other houses and other areas of coastline that are being infiltrated and examined in the same way you are being asked to do. Some might be by existing assets we have, others by former operatives like myself who can no longer function in our previous capacities."

"It will not all be on my shoulders, then." Clara nodded again, this time exhaling deeply as relief rolled through her. "That's a comfort."

Abby chuckled to herself. "There's not much of comfort in this world, so I'd take that and hold on tightly, if I were you."

Clara sighed with a touch of reluctance. "It would be so much easier to agree to this if I knew the answer as to why. Why it has to be done at all, and why the stakes are so great."

"Alas, why is a question we rarely get answers for beforehand, I'm afraid." Abby nudged her gently. "But in your case, you may perhaps get some. I happen to know Pippa paces in her rooms nightly before bed, and we might be fortunate enough to find her in a giving mood. However…" Her expression turned serious. "She may require your consent before that information can be given. As a matter of security, that is sometimes required."

"I understand." And truly, Clara did. For the first time in all of this, she understood the need to agree to the task before a full disclosure could be made.

If she could understand that, might it be possible for her to understand more? She did not dare to hope, but there was an inkling.

"I should like to see Pippa," she heard herself say with a firmness she hadn't known since the morning. "Will you come with me?"

Abby rose, nodding and clasping her hands elegantly. "Of course."

Clara returned her nod, though it felt unsteady even as she made it.

The pair of them walked almost silently from the teachers' dormitory wing towards the main of the school and the headmistress's office. Her quarters were situated very nearly adjacent to them, though Clara had never understood why that had been.

Perhaps now she would.

Abby took the liberty of softly knocking on the door, smiling in encouragement at Clara.

How had she known Clara needed such encouragement? Was that something she would learn to detect in her training? Or was it written on her face?

How could she work in covert operations if her emotions were so obvious? She'd never be able to lie convincingly if that was the case…

The door was thrown open without any sounds from within, startling Clara with a faint gasp.

Pippa eyed them both without an iota of surprise in her features, her fair hair plaited and hanging long across one shoulder over her tightly cinched dressing gown. She smiled faintly. "I wondered if I would see you this evening."

Clara blushed at being so easily predicted. "I fear I have questions. I hope you don't mind."

A wry smile crossed Pippa's face. "I'd be most surprised if you didn't. Please, come in. I'll ring for some tea."

"Oh, there's no need!" Clara insisted as Pippa stepped back to let them in. "It's so late, all of the servants will be in bed."

"In a typical establishment, perhaps," Pippa allowed with a hint of a laugh in her voice. "At Miss Masters', however…"

Clara glanced over her shoulder as she moved into the room. "Yes?"

Pippa grinned outright. "I've just finished my summary of the day with Mrs. Allendale. She mentioned going to the kitchens for some tea herself, it will be no trouble to have some sent in. In fact, I do so on the regular."

"Is Mrs. Allendale…?" Clara began to ask before biting her lip. "That is…"

She could barely ask the question, but if the housekeeper were among the covert operatives in this place, it would not surprise her. Mrs. Allendale was more perceptive than any woman Clara had ever met and possessed a remarkable amount of influence for one in her position. Matronly and stern, kind and brisk, she was all contradiction and yet perfectly suited to any extreme.

If she were not a spy, who was?

"I cannot say," Pippa answered, her tone careful, but amused.

Clara glanced at her and saw an understanding smile there. "I have little trouble believing that."

Pippa laughed and waved her over to some chairs and a small table. "Yes, I'm afraid she has never been a housekeeper in a large estate, but her past did lend her to her present position quite well. Give me a moment while I send for tea." She smiled again before stepping out.

Abby sat and patted the place next to her on the divan. "Come sit, Clara. Make yourself comfortable. It will be much easier if you do."

"I don't know how easy any of this will be," Clara murmured, flicking the ends of her shawl anxiously and moving to take the seat indicated.

Thankfully, Abby made no attempt to soothe her further, aside from a small smile.

Clara had endured enough soothing that she could not be sure of nor understand, and simply wanted to get the information she needed so she could make a more informed and careful decision. She was not impetuous or impulsive, nor was she in any way daring, which made her all the more curious as a prospect for this covert world of secrets.

Then again, Clara did have a few secrets of her own…

"There," Pippa said as she returned to them. "Just a few moments, and we will have tea. I find I always sleep better after a warm cup of something or other, and it does not matter very much what the drink is so much as the temperature." She shared an amused look with Abby, and Clara looked at the two with bewilderment.

It was exactly the sort of conversation she would have expected to hear between them before she had learned of the secret life they lived. Almost as though there was no difference in their natures from who she had known them to be before.

Was that meant to be a sign? Was it intentional?

Confusion could only abound at a time like this.

"Clara," Pippa prodded with a gentle air, though there did seem to be an underlying note of insistence that forced Clara to look at her.

It was no wonder the woman had charge of female spies in England with abilities like that.

Yet Clara found warmth and a good deal of understanding in her countenance.

"You have questions," Pippa said simply, folding her hands in her lap. "If you'll ask them, I'll tell you what I can."

"Do I need to consent to the assignment first?" Clara queried, her eyes flicking over to Abby apprehensively.

Pippa hummed a quick laugh. "That would make this all rather neat and tidy, I daresay, but your questions probably keep you from accepting, do they not?"

Clara managed a smile at that. "Yes…"

"Then I cannot think why we should do the thing backwards, can you?" Pippa dipped her chin in a nod. "If it is something that will require some assurance, I shall tell you in advance, but anything I can tell you freely, given that I trust you without the confirmation, I will relate."

Was it really so simple? It couldn't have been, not when an entire world operated beneath the surface of the one she knew without detection. Yet here she was, being offered the answer to any question, within reason, without having to commit herself to joining anything.

There was something about the ease of such a thing that she did not trust a jot.

Now that she was invited to inquire, however, she did not know where to start.

She gnawed the inside of her lip, feeling foolish and stupid in front of these increasingly impressive women. "I don't..." She heaved a sigh and shook her head. "I don't even know what to ask, honestly. But... why?"

Pippa raised a trim brow. "Why what?"

Clara had known that was coming, and rolled her eyes, smiling in amusement. "Why me, first of all."

"Simple." Pippa straightened and smiled at her. "You are conveniently located for this assignment. You have a mastery of the French language that is to be envied. Your artistic abilities are splendid, and more than that, they are accurate. And you are someone I would trust with my life, should it ever be necessary."

"Is it necessary?" Clara asked with some mild alarm.

As though she had stumbled upon some private joke, Pippa and Abby chuckled. "Not this time, no," Pippa assured her.

The strangest sense of relief washed over Clara, just as it had when Abby had told her that lives would not be at risk over her assignment.

What a peculiar thing to find relief in.

Clara frowned slightly, moving on to her next question. "Why not have one of your operatives take on the assignment you put to me? Surely that would make more sense."

"It would," Pippa agreed, nodding calmly. "However, the information we have received indicates multiple areas requiring attention, and, with current assignments and activities, we simply did not have enough agents available. So, we have entrusted some areas to former operatives and trusted assets." Her smile spread and she gave Clara a pointed look. "Which is where you come in, should you accept."

"But if there's danger…" Clara bit the objection back, knowing that her friend and headmistress would never send her into an unsafe venture.

At least not intentionally.

As though Pippa could see Clara's mind spin and hear her thoughts, she sobered and sat forward, clasping her hands before her. "Clara, I cannot guarantee the safety of every person I place in a scenario. Not absolutely. But I do not put anyone in a situation without proper training and certainly not unprepared for what they might face. In your particular case, the potential for danger is as close to negligible as I have ever seen in this world. If that is of any comfort."

There was some satisfaction in knowing that Pippa had considered Clara's concerns before Clara had even had them. That her selection had not been simply convenient but something of real thought. That this woman, who held such power that was almost certainly unnoticed, saw something of value in Clara for that world.

How could she refuse that?

Clara blinked at such a clear decision on her part, given the turmoil she'd endured in the hours preceding this.

But now…

"I'll do it," she heard herself say. More than that, she felt herself smile. "I accept."

Pippa grinned, making her appearance years younger, though Clara would never have called her aged before. A smile such as this was rarely seen on the headmistress's face, but it brightened her entire countenance and heightened the underlying beauty that had so easily been missed.

And it made Clara's smile grow.

"I'm so pleased to hear you say that," Pippa said on a heavy sigh. "And relieved. To be perfectly frank, I didn't have another option for this particular setting."

Clara giggled, suddenly thrilled to be part of something so secret yet so unifying. "Where would you like me to go, then?"

Abby snickered to herself. "Steady on, she's not sending you to Bath."

"No, indeed." Pippa's smile became something rather knowing, her eyes taking on a new light. "We need you to go to Kirkleigh Park. It's only ten miles from here, and it's the seat of the Duke of Kirklin when he's in Kent."

Clara blinked in surprise, her newfound euphoria fading quickly. "The Duke of Kirklin? As in Lady Adrianna Russell's brother? Our student's eldest brother?"

At Pippa's nod, Clara felt the air rush from her lungs. "How in the world am I to do that? I cannot go without an invitation, and if the duke is in residence…"

"He isn't," Pippa and Abby said together.

Clara looked at both in turn. "Ever?"

There, Pippa winced. "Well, he may make a yearly visit, I suppose, or stay there if he comes to visit Lady Adrianna here, but he makes his home in Wiltshire at Millmond. We placed an operative on his gardening staff some weeks ago now, and it is quite certain he is not expected for the rest of the year."

"And how am I to stay at the house?" Clara pressed, the issue somehow larger than whether or not the duke was going to be at home. "What role did you have in mind? And when?"

She was startled to see Pippa grin again. "The late duke, the present duke's uncle, had a ward that spent a number of years at Kirkleigh during her childhood. Fondly, as it happens, very fondly. Her name was Alexandra Moore, and in appearance, she was a very fair child."

Catching the idea, Clara felt a new smile teasing the corners of her lips. "How convenient. Will there be an issue with my portraying her?"

"Not a bit," Pippa quipped eagerly. "She's settled in the south of France, and very willing to help us." She hesitated a moment, then continued. "Your cousin has taken great pains to help us there."

Thinking she might have meant a cousin of Abby's, Clara did not react immediately. When Pippa did not look elsewhere, or speak further, Clara's jaw dropped. "Mine?" she squeaked. "My cousin? You mean… Martin?"

Pippa rose and came to sit beside her, taking her hand. "Martin has been working for us for several years now. He's in Paris most of the time, but when we mentioned we were considering you for this, he insisted on being the one to find Miss Moore and get as much information as you could possibly need."

"I never thought…" Clara swallowed hard, tears flooding her eyes. "I never…"

"There is a great deal that Lord Rothchild could tell you about him when you see him next," Pippa told her with a surprising deal of warmth. "He cannot come back to England yet, as he is doing incredible work for us in France. He oversaw the operation that prompted the need for your assignment, as it happens."

Clara could not believe her ears. In all her life, she had only had one cousin, and he had been as close as a brother. Martin had been away for years, which had hurt her deeply, and, apart from a moving letter delivered only weeks ago, she never heard from him.

If he had invested and sacrificed so much of himself and his life into this world, how could she do anything less?

Sniffling, nodding through her tears, Clara gave her new superior a watery smile. "I'd like to begin my training at the earliest opportunity, please. Would tomorrow be possible?"

Chapter Four

"*Madrid*... Rome... Paris... Salzburg..."

Hawk shook his head as he eyed his brother's most recent letter before tossing it onto his desk. How was it possible for anyone to have been in four of the greatest European cities within the same month and genuinely have had any sort of sanity left? Perhaps Griffin had developed an inhuman level of endurance for such things, and for the amount of fine activity that would be required in the Society of those cities, he would have had to.

Nothing of the sort would ever be to Hawk's taste.

So why, then, was he so envious?

It was not as though he had never been to great cities on the Continent. Of course, he had in his earlier days, a younger gentleman widening his scope of the world. But it had not been for his own enjoyment, and he had not spent much time in any of the locations. Each had simply been a mark on a list of sorts, an item to accomplish rather than an experience to relish. Something he could add to his gentlemanly repertoire to fit in better among the others of his circle.

Now he was the duke, a respected man of property and fortune, with no little influence, and he could honestly say he would not have been able to tell the difference between Berlin and Milan.

Griffin was living for them both, it seemed.

Fortunate blaggard.

Once Hawk had secured all of his estates appropriately, once he felt himself entirely in possession of his title and his role within it, and once he was certain Adrianna was settled enough to not require his particular attention or concern...

He groaned at the thought. The only way his sister would ever be settled enough that he did not have to worry over her would be when she was married.

If she married.

She was an independent girl, and had been since she was old enough to speak her mind, and age had not brought maturity with it. Or, if it had, the maturity had not included a measure of reserve with it.

More's the pity.

He adored his sister and her vitality in life. It was simply that he was also terrified by it.

For now, however, Adrianna was at school, and others were tasked with her immediate care. When the day arrived that she would return to his guardianship on a daily basis, his life as he knew it would be at an end until he walked her down the aisle.

And his life as it was bored him. Everything about himself bored him. Sitting here in the study of his estate in Northumberland, scowling at his brother's letter, he was bored.

He felt… boring.

That might have been worse.

The world had enough boring peers, as well as scandalous ones, royal ones, and bankrupt ones. Every way he turned when in London, he seemed to find a new lord or earl or baron running about, none of whom were of any particular notability, let alone nobility.

If Society was so inundated with men bearing such titles, how was he to distinguish himself? He would be lost in the crowd by simply being respectable, honorable, reserved, and dedicated. He could not change his nature, he was too set in his ways. But surely there was something he could do.

Without having to be at a great many balls and standing aloof along a great many walls.

Hawk frowned at the thought and set Griffin's letter aside, then let his attention go past it to the window of his study. The day was fine, considering the chill they'd had recently, and autumn in Northumberland was typically particularly cold, though recently it had been quite perfect. But he wouldn't mind winter being slower to arrive, particularly if he were to spend much time at this estate.

If he stayed indoors nearly all the time, would it even matter?

But the stables at his Northumberland estate could not hope to rival that of Millmond, or even Kirkleigh, for that matter. There was a horse at his disposal, of course, but he'd have to rent horses from the nearest inn if he wished to use his carriage.

It was one of the things he aimed to have improved here, naturally, but that was undoubtedly a task for the spring.

Didn't help him at the moment, but it was true.

The clipped sound of boots on the floors in the corridor brought his attention around, and a rosy cheeked, windswept Nat strode in. He looked the part of a perfect country gentleman, and Hawk was instantly envious.

It was an all-too-common inclination for him these days.

Nat stared at him for a few moments, his steps slowing. Then he sighed and threw his hands up. "What did I do now?"

"You look refreshed and at ease," Hawk told him, his tone grumbling and petulant. "I should be feeling that in my home, not my guest. Or, at least, along *with* my guest."

"First of all," Nat said as he tapped his crop in one hand, "I hardly count as a guest. Secondly, would you prefer I be disgruntled and bored?"

Hawk barely blinked at the comment. "Why not? I am."

A too-smug smile curved on Nat's mouth. "Ah ha…"

Any time such a superior sound came from Nat was cause for concern, Hawk was instantly wary. "What?"

Nat tapped his crop in his hand once more and came closer to the desk. "Your problem is not with me, Your Grace, but with yourself. Despite being duke for a few years now, you have not decided what sort of duke you will be."

"What sort of dukes are there, Nat?" Hawk asked with amusement, more to deflect the sharp jab of truth that hit him squarely in the gut. "Please, enlighten me."

His friend was too wise to take the sarcasm as bait. "You seem to lack personality or motivation or something."

Hawk's brows snapped down. "I lack personality?"

"You lack identity," Nat amended. "You've become so focused on your responsibilities that you've forgotten to put yourself into the mix. You're the mold of a duke without the substance of a duke."

"I wasn't aware that dukes had substance," Hawk murmured as his expression eased back into its natural state.

Nat gestured towards Hawk as though that were obvious. "Not all of them."

The conversation was growing increasingly less enjoyable the more directed at Hawk it became, but a sense of discouragement had begun to seep into him the more Nat continued to identify the exact problem.

"What do I do?" Hawk asked before he meant to, the odd vulnerability of the question leaving him fairly exposed, even before someone he trusted as much as Nat.

Nat was less inclined to be sympathetic on the subject. "Don't sit there like a wallflower. Get out of the study and find something to do! And don't ask me for ideas, I can barely entertain myself. I refuse to take responsibility for you, as well."

Well, *that* was not particularly helpful, but he supposed that was fair.

Hawk winced playfully. "Does it have to be out of the study?"

"Leaving now," Nat announced as he turned on his heel and left the room. "Get out of the room, Hawk!"

Left alone again, Hawk pursed his lips in thought. What did he want to do?

Why did that feel like a stupid question?

But exploring his options was undoubtedly a better idea than sitting in his study and doing nothing, so he pushed himself to his feet and began to trace the path that Nat had trod just moments before.

That path, naturally, led to the stables, where he found his stablemaster and a few of his hands working on the dismantling of the existing structures and tossing the scraps of wood into a massive pile. He'd ordered the thing done, it was true, but he hadn't anticipated having it done so soon. Granted, destruction wasn't the end goal, but he had just approved the plans for the new stables, so it was rather delightful to see work happening.

An easy manner of gaining accomplishment.

Of being productive.

Of feeling useful.

Hawk's eyes widened, and he blinked at the epiphany that had begun and was still coursing through him.

That was it.

He wanted to do good, ultimately, and signing documents that brought good about was not good enough. Why not physically do the good that he could as well? He was a decent sportsman, always had been, and he prided himself he was not of a slovenly build or nature. He might not know what he would be doing, but he would still be active.

And he was open to learning.

He would be a most willing, eager student.

With a satisfied nod, Hawk strode forward, fixing his most welcoming smile on his face, despite the fact that he would be the intruder in this scenario. It was awkward to be so, given he was the owner and master of them all in the technical sense, and smiling would not rid them of that awkwardness. But, with any luck, it might help.

The stablemaster, who was perched on the roof, saw him first and paused in his work as he watched Hawk approach. The others followed suit until all eyes were on Hawk before he ever reached them.

There was nothing like making an entrance, he supposed.

"Good morning, Mr. Bailey!" Hawk called, raising a hand in greeting.

The stablemaster wiped his hands on his trousers and waved in return. "Good morning to you, Your Grace. Is there something we can do for you?" He gestured to the one part of the stable that was occupied. "Would you like Shadow saddled for you? Jones there can see to him, if you wish."

"No, thank you," Hawk replied easily, rubbing his hands together for no reason other than to look eager, if not at ease. "I rather hoped there was something I could do for you."

Mr. Bailey's thick brows rose, and he dropped a knee to the roof to kneel, which somehow only made him seem more incredulous. "Your Grace?"

Hawk's smile turned sheepish. "I would like to help you with your work today. If I may."

While none of the men at work looked at each other, the same expression appeared on each face as though they'd had a discussion on the subject he had somehow missed.

It was the expression of terrified disbelief.

Not entirely encouraging.

Hawk waited, uncertain as to his next step. He was in a position to demand he get his way, but in this matter, he was the novice and they the masters. He had neither position nor authority here.

"Has Your Grace any experience in construction?" Bailey asked, apparently without judgment. "Or demolition, as it were?"

"None." Hawk smiled without shame, praying it would help. "But I wish to learn and to be of use."

The expressions around him lost any hint of fear and took on more amusement, though it did not seem to be at his expense.

Bailey, for one, began to smile as well. "We are engaged in the work on your stables, Your Grace. Will you mind the use of your unpracticed hands in it?"

Hawk set his hands at his hips. "I trust none of you will allow me to err to the extreme that it would ruin matters irreparably. And I would be most grateful to learn everything I can to be a help and not a hindrance. Indeed, in all matters regarding the actual, physical activity on the estate."

Now the men looked at each other, and seemed to consider his idea with some interest.

Bailey grinned at Hawk as though he were his own son, though he couldn't have been more than fifteen years beyond Hawk's own age. "Then you'd best come on up, Your Grace. We'd be pleased to teach you the way of things."

"Excellent!" Hawk clapped his hands once, his excitement overruling his natural reserve at the moment. He strolled forward towards the ladder he saw leaning against the side of the structure.

"You may wish to shed your coat, Your Grace," one of the men suggested ruefully. "It gets rather hot despite the chill, and you'll want a better ability to move your arms."

Hawk nodded obediently and began to shed his coat without fuss, tossing it over a nearby fence rail.

"And your cravat, Your Grace. It'll only grow more cumbersome."

The winding strip of linen had never been shed with more gusto than at that moment.

Hawk glanced up at the group and held out his arms for examination. "Am I presentable for the task?"

"Good enough, Your Grace." Bailey waved him up. "Mind your step, and come on up."

Hours later, damp with perspiration and streaked with dirt, Hawk strode back into the pristine halls of the house, grinning from ear to ear, his coat and cravat slung over one shoulder.

"Your Grace…"

Hawk turned to his butler, still beaming. "Yes, Clarke?"

The stout man's eyes were fixed on the bottom half of Hawk's breeches and on his boots, which, admittedly, were caked in mud and scuffed to the extreme. "Your Grace…"

Hawk followed his gaze without concern. "Ah, yes. I do apologize, I am tracking filth into the house. Should I perhaps remove my boots outside?"

"No, Your Grace, not at all," Clarke insisted, his attention drifting now to the streaks on Hawk's shirt. "Your rooms will do just fine, it's just…"

When he didn't continue, Hawk prodded, "Yes…?"

Clarke's eyes snapped up to Hawk's then, the perfect butler, as always. "Nothing, Your Grace. Welcome home."

Clearly, that was not what he had been preparing to say, but if he were going to pretend as though nothing was amiss after his earlier display, Hawk was content to let him do so. "I've been on the estate all day, Clarke, but thank you all the same." He turned back and moved on, tempted to whistle, though it was a crime to all ears for him to ever attempt anything remotely musical.

But he was feeling content, and it had been so long since he had known the sensation, it almost called for its own aria in tribute.

The fact that he was even considering something musical was indicative of the victory.

Or of his madness.

Likely both.

Who would have known that he only needed to bruise his knees and irritate the palms of his hands in order to find satisfaction with his life?

"Who are you and what have you done with the Duke of Kirklin?"

Hawk chuckled and turned to face Nat, sliding his coat from his shoulder to hang over his arm instead. "Your humor does you credit, as always." He spread out his arms, looking down at himself. "Very dukely, am I not?"

"You look like a poorly treated farmhand," Nat said with the same sort of startled expression his butler had worn a moment ago.

"Your intelligence, on the other hand…" Hawk shook his head and continued walking, knowing Nat would follow like a curious puppy.

Amazingly, he got all the way to the stairs before his friend spoke again, though he had indeed followed. "What happened? Were you waylaid by gypsies?"

"I found something to do," Hawk informed his occasionally idiotic friend. "Just as you suggested."

Nat harrumphed behind him as they climbed the stairs. "I hardly meant for you to give yourself up to a gang of highwaymen. How much did they get?"

Hawk ignored that and continued into his bedchamber. "It was the most extraordinary thing, Nat. I was the worst possible set of hands for the thing, and yet the work went on. More than that, it filled me. I worked by the sweat of my brow and the strength of my hands, untrained though they were, and I saw the progress before me. The satisfaction in that…" He shook his head and tossed his coat and cravat on the bed. "Marvelous. Simply marvelous."

"You… worked?"

"I did." Hawk looked over at his friend, who had dropped himself into a chair just as Hawk's impassive valet, White, hurried into the room. "On the stables."

Nat gaped, wide-eyed and pale as he did so. "On purpose? Or were you atoning for some sin of which I am unaware?"

Hawk gave him a derisive look as White began to work on removing the offensive clothing items from Hawk. "Is it very bad,

White?" he asked in an apologetic tone.

White's jaw tightened, which was more emotion than Hawk had seen from him in years. "Not unsalvageable, Your Grace, but it will be a challenge." He huffed under his breath, which was another novelty for him. "Do you plan on making such activity a habit, Your Grace?"

"By heaven, I hope so!" Hawk told him and Nat. "It was the most gratifying activity I have engaged in for as long as I can remember. I've no intention of giving it up, so long as wiser hands can guide me."

"Then I shall send off for linen of a sturdier quality, Your Grace," White told him simply as he went about his work, tugging at his boots now. "It will be rougher against you, but better suited for the task. And for my own, for that matter."

Hawk found himself smiling slightly at that. "Well, we must do what is best suited for you, White. As always."

"I thought so, Your Grace."

Nat shook his head and sat forward. "I still don't understand. Tell me again."

Hawk snorted once. "You told me to do something. So I left the house and did the first thing that I saw needed to be done: the stablemaster and his hands working on the renovation project. I asked if I could be of help—"

"Which, of course, you could not."

"—and they agreed to teach me the way of it," Hawk went on, pretending Nat had said nothing. "I'd never used a hammer and nails in my life before today."

"Not sure that's something to be ashamed of," Nat told him without concern. "I don't think anyone of our station would say differently."

Hawk shook his head in disbelief. "I knocked down a wall today. I pulled fence posts. I mucked out a stable stall."

"What in hell's name did you do that for?" Nat exclaimed in disgust. "That is part of someone's employment, you fool, not a hobby to engage in!"

"I didn't mind it!" Hawk laughed, almost giddy with the memory of it. "The effort involved in such a simple thing… By Jove, I ache all over from that. The stablehands laughed, of course."

"Of course, they did. I would have, too, but not for the same reasons." Nat scoffed, shaking his head.

Hawk exhaled slowly as he slipped on a fresh linen shirt. "I stopped by the gamekeeper's cottage before I came in. He's going to show me his tasks tomorrow, are you interested in coming?"

Nat rubbed at his brow. "When are you doing so?"

"He wants to begin at seven in the morning. I had no idea there were early morning tasks, but it would seem—"

"No, thank you," Nat overrode, crossing one leg over the other. "I prefer to sleep the necessary amount for proper functioning, if it does not offend your newfound entertainment preferences. But you do as you like, and I wish you great joy of checking all the traps, feeding the hounds, and counting the pheasants on the estate."

Hawk lifted his chin as White went to work on his clean cravat. "I think you might be mocking me."

Nat raised a brow. "If you aren't sure, I am doing it wrong." Shaking his head, he rose. "Tell me, will the roasted pig we dine on this evening be one you slaughtered yourself?"

"Laugh if you will, Nat," Hawk told him with a severe look, "but I blame you entirely for it."

"What for?" Nat protested in outrage. "I've done nothing! I have literally not done a thing as regarding your secret desires to be a hired hand."

"Get out of the study and do something," Hawk quoted, raising a brow. "Your words, I believe."

Nat frowned at that, folding his hands in his lap. "That's not my fault. I was hoping you'd go to the billiards room and begin a game, myself. You could just as easily have gone to the music room to begin playing, and all of us in humanity are ever so grateful you did not. The kitchens to make pies, the ballroom to practice the waltz, the orangery to do... whatever one does in an orangery; all of those were just as easily viable for entertainment options. I simply told you to find one. Your choice is yours alone, and I will not be blamed for you falling off of a roof and breaking your back, thank you very much."

Hawk chuckled to himself, his friend's humor truly one of his most appreciated assets. "Well, I plan on helping with the spring

45

planting when the time comes, so perhaps that might tempt you."

"If it takes place after luncheon, I may consider it." Nat pushed to his feet, groaning a little. "Now that you do not smell of horse, shall we have a drink before dinner?"

Sighing as White tugged his cravat one last time, Hawk nodded, smiling at his friend. "Happily. I could use one after the day I've had."

"I was thinking the same thing myself." Nat shook his head, exhaling roughly.

"You thought I needed a drink?" Hawk laughed.

Nat gave him a bewildered look. "No, that I needed one. Why would I think that you need one? I don't think about you by first instinct."

"Why wouldn't I need a drink?" Hawk asked pointedly. "I've earned it!"

"Go have ale at the taproom with your people. I don't think you'll like the finer stuff."

"That humor of yours is getting worse."

"Have a drink or three. I'm hilarious after that."

Chapter Five

"*A*lexandra Moore. Alexandra Moore. Miss Alexandra Moore."

"Darling, you're going to tumble over your own tongue if you ramble on so."

Clara looked over at the woman accompanying her in the carriage, a stunning beauty of a woman despite her being on the other side of forty. "I cannot help it. I'm so dreadfully nervous. I've never told a lie in my life, and now I will be living one. Phoebe, what if I make a hash of this?"

Phoebe Jenkins, a sometimes advisor to the Rothchild Academy and their scholarship girls, and apparently one-time operative with the code name of Flora, gave Clara a severe look. "Then we'll be in trouble for certain, but really, you must call me Aunt Fern, dearest, or we'll never convince anybody."

"Right," Clara affirmed with a nod, more for herself than for Phoebe. "My dear aunt who could not care for me in my youth due to her own youth and inexperience, and who worked tirelessly to prepare a home for me as soon as she was able."

"Good heavens, child," Phoebe murmured in her crisp, cool tone that rang with the natural formality that always seemed to pervade her being. "Don't spout it all about simply because it's the truth we are living. There is nothing more obvious to an audience than an excess of information when it is not requested."

Clara winced and looked out of the window, raising an ungloved finger to her teeth to gnaw at her nail, a childhood habit she had long foregone. "Sorry, Phoebe. Erm, Aunt Fern. I haven't had any training yet, so I have not learned the way of things."

Phoebe sighed to herself and took Clara's hand away from her mouth with the same brusque motion a mother or aunt would have done. "Do not bite your nails, Alexandra Claire. It is most uncouth."

Strangely enough, the words and the action settled Clara in a way nothing had yet. Her newly adopted name in its full, precisely how they would explain her going by Clara, and the easy manner with which Phoebe had said it, were stabilizing to her. The fear began to abate, and just a dull twinge of unease curled within her.

Nodding to herself, Clara breathed slowly and watched as the countryside of Kent passed them by. It was ten miles from the school to Kirkleigh, and she'd packed her trunks for a visit of just a few days. They were simply establishing the connection, that was all. Then, once that was done, if all went well, they might be able to come and go from Kirkleigh at their leisure.

Clara suspected that word would reach the duke himself before too long, and then they might have reason to elaborate on this story of theirs. But until then…

"Does it get easier, Aunt Fern?" Clara asked softly as the carriage rocked them gently to and fro. "The lying. The pretending. Any of it, all of it."

"Of course it does, child," Phoebe replied with greater ease than Clara had expected. "It becomes quite second nature, and requires very little thought."

Her reply was not particularly encouraging, the thought of dishonesty becoming so simple and natural a distasteful one. Necessary, she supposed, given the line of work and the details that were involved in it, but for someone like her…

Phoebe sighed again, this time far more softly. "I was like you, Clara, when I started. Before I became Flora in truth. I learned that I could not think of it as the sin we have been taught it was. It is a protection that keeps us from losing our lives as we serve a greater purpose. To protect the kingdom, in some respects. We are not pretending so much as we are becoming, you see."

Clara turned to look at the older woman, transfixed by the perspective she offered, and of the glimpse she gave into the life she'd held previously.

Becoming, she'd said. There was something rather exciting, if not appealing, about the sentiment. She could easily become the exciting, engaging Alexandra Moore for a time rather than be forced to maintain the rest of her life as simple, boring Clara Harlow. Especially when it was for the good of the country.

"And you think I could become Miss Moore?" Clara asked with a smile, suddenly shy as she started this new adventure of hers.

Phoebe patted her hand twice before releasing it. "I think you already have, Clara, dear. And you'd best remember that, as we'll be there shortly."

Feeling that the ribbons on her hat were suddenly tight beneath her chin, Clara slid a finger between them, tugging gently. "Heavens…"

"Settle yourself, dear," Phoebe said. "The duke won't be there, remember?"

Clara didn't have the courage to tell her that it was not facing the duke she feared, but rather facing anyone. Her dress was too fine, her gloves too white, and her boots too shiny. The finery was beyond what she was accustomed to, and that alone was a reason to be uncomfortable.

She hadn't been in finery since she was a child.

Perhaps it would suit the recreated Miss Moore to be above the finery she chose to garb herself in.

Yes, why shouldn't it?

Would anyone at the house recollect Miss Moore from when she'd lived there previously? That would determine a great deal about the story she and Phoebe would have to tell, and how much freedom she would have with it.

"Oh, it is a fine prospect, isn't it?" Phoebe gushed, turning to look out of the window. "So delightfully situated, and such a pretty cliffside view! It must have been a joy to be a child here."

Clara stared out of the same window, the sprawling estate opening before them, the pale stone almost sparkling in the morning sunlight. "I wouldn't know," she said softly, her breath catching as the glimpse of the sea caught her eye.

"Of course, you would," came the unaffected reply. "You are Alexandra Claire Moore, and you were the ward of the late Duke of Kirklin. You lived here from eight until thirteen, so you must have many fond and happy memories of Kirkleigh that no one can take from you."

It took Clara a moment or two of reflection to fully comprehend what Phoebe was saying, without specifically saying it. But it occurred to her, and she brightened at the prospect.

"Yes," she said slowly, a smile spreading across her face. "Yes, I do. Several of them."

Phoebe looked at her with a quick smile. "Good."

It had seemed an age since Clara had grinned with real delight, but now she did so freely. There was excitement coursing through her, visiting this grand house and seeing if something might be accomplished there. She knew what to look for, but not yet why she was looking for it, which somehow made her still feel innocent in many respects.

Pippa said all would come in good time, and she had to believe that.

For now, she was going to enjoy being Alexandra Moore and exploring a grand house she was supposed to know well.

Kirkleigh was an older house, displaying some of the architecture more commonly seen during the reign of the Tudors, particularly with the elaborate work on the windows and the stylings of the roof. Yet the stone was paler than she had seen in buildings from that era, and the house itself was immaculate in its cleanliness and care. Even from the distance of their approach, she could see the glint of the sun on the glass panes of several windows. The trees along the drive were well manicured, and she could see a small grove of them behind the house on one side. On the other, however, was a vast expanse of land that seemed to drop into the ocean itself. The view of the sea was entirely unencumbered by nature or man, and Clara itched to explore the cliffside at once.

Surely there was a path down to the seashore, else why would the house be in such proximity?

She would find that path, and she would walk on the edge of that sea.

It was easy enough for her to forget that Kent was a coastal county, so much of the delights of visiting the seaside being attributed to places like Brighton, Eastbourne, or Bournemouth. Yet Kent had

Dover in her folds, and such beauty was rarely seen elsewhere.

How had she been in Kent all these years and never once ventured to places such as this?

"I think we may take a walk this afternoon, don't you, Clara?" Phoebe asked as she, too, eyed the coast.

Clara nodded. "Yes, Aunt Fern, I do."

Neither of them spoke as they continued on, the edifice of Kirkleigh looming closer and closer, the sun seeming to shine more brightly as they did so. The carriage rounded the circle drive and a pair of footmen sprang from the great mahogany door to wait upon them.

"Goodness," Clara murmured as the door to the carriage opened. "Are we expected?"

Phoebe only sniffed as she allowed the footman to help her down, then waited for Clara to join her. "Marvelous door, Clara. Such detailed work."

Clara had barely noticed the detailing on her first glance, but as she came to stand beside Phoebe, she blinked at it. Not only was the door immense and made from a very great, dark wood, it was also intricately woven with carved wrought iron that extended from the hinges outward in a display of ivy. There were even very small flowers dotting it, made of the same iron.

It was detailing fit for a looking glass in a lady's rooms, and never seen on something as ordinary as a door.

"Beautiful," Clara breathed, the artist in her wanting to sketch the pattern of it immediately. The whole of it. The entire door in its glory, but perhaps put it in a setting of a garden where the wrought iron ivy might weave into real ivy that then could continue on along walls of stone…

Phoebe cleared her throat very softly, bringing Clara back to the present.

"After you, my dear," Phoebe murmured. "The play is on."

Clara exhaled a very short breath before striding onwards towards the house, lifting her chin just enough. She'd done a few lessons with her friend Minerva Dalton at the school before she left, given that Minerva was an instructor in comportment, in the hopes that she might have more grace about her in being Miss Moore than she had as being herself. Whether she succeeded or not would soon be revealed.

A middle-aged butler stood in the doorway to the great house, a bland, anticipatory expression on his face as he watched Clara and Phoebe approach.

The thought occurred to Clara that this man was too young to have been the butler when Miss Moore resided here.

All the better.

"Good day, ladies," the butler greeted, bowing slightly. "Welcome to Kirkleigh Park. Were you hoping for a tour?"

Clara lifted a brow in what she hoped was a pert manner. "A tour? Well, I certainly don't remember any of those happening during my time here at Kirkleigh, but it has been twelve years."

The butler's brow wrinkled slightly. "I beg your pardon, miss?"

"Oh, you wouldn't know me, would you?" She laughed merrily, beaming at him and presenting her card. "Miss Alexandra Moore. I was ward to his grace, dear Uncle Kirklin, may he rest in peace."

"Bless me, Miss Moore!" The butler returned her smile, his entire countenance brightening markedly, making him seem years younger. "I heard your name so often in the later years of His Grace. It is such a privilege. Stafford is the name, please do come in."

Clara nodded and did so, relief pounding through her body with each beat of her heart like fire. "Thank you, Mr. Stafford. This is my aunt, Mrs. Daniels, who is travelling as my companion."

Stafford bowed to Phoebe as well. "Mrs. Daniels, you are most welcome."

"I thank you, Mr. Stafford," Phoebe replied in her most formal tone, her lips curving with just enough warmth to keep her from seeming cold. "If you did not know my dear niece yourself, what happened to the butler who did?"

"He took his retirement, ma'am," Stafford answered, not at all put off by Phoebe's tone. "Once His Grace was getting to be rather unwell and unable to manage his daily activities on his own strength, Chapman felt he could no longer serve him competently, given his own age. I was brought on then."

Clara let herself sigh sadly. "Poor Chapman. I was such a trial to him at times. And I was so far away when Uncle Kirklin took so ill.

By the time I received word…" She broke off, looking away. "I have not been able to bring myself to come back since his death. But enough time has passed that I thought…" She glanced back at Stafford with a sheepish smile. "Might we stay for a few days while my aunt and I are in this part of the country? I apologize for not writing in advance, I was undecided until we were near enough to come."

Blessedly, Stafford did not seem too perturbed by the suggestion. "Oh, I believe that could be arranged. Mrs. Clayton has gone to visit her daughter for a few days, so you find us without a housekeeper at present. The duke is not expected to come for his visit for another few weeks, and as this was your home for many years, it would be no imposition."

"You do not have to inquire of His Grace?" Clara pressed, ignoring his mention of the duke's visit in some weeks. With any luck, she and Phoebe would be back at the school by then, and all would be well.

"His Grace is very generous with visitors at Kirkleigh, Miss Moore," Stafford assured her. "Particularly with Lady Adrianna being just up at Miss Masters' so near to here. We have more than once accommodated her and a friend or two when on holiday."

Clara dimpled a smile, wishing she could force herself to blush. "But I am not family, Mr. Stafford. Even Uncle Kirklin was not a blood relation, only my guardian."

Stafford gave her a warm, if pitying smile. "My dear Miss Moore, as I am quite sure the late duke told you several times, you were very much family to him, and thus, I have no qualms about opening Kirkleigh just for you."

Though she was playing a part, though she was not Alexandra Moore, and though she had never set foot in Kirkleigh in her life, Clara felt her eyes well with tears and tenderness for this man who had known her all of five minutes. If this was what she could expect in this venture, she'd be Alexandra Moore for the rest of her life, covert operations or not.

"Bless your kindness, Mr. Stafford," Clara managed to eke out, blinking rapidly. "I don't feel I deserve it."

"Oh, child," Phoebe said with a slight laugh. "Speaking as your aunt, I can say with some certainty that you are most deserving. Now, won't you show me the rooms you slept in as a child?"

Clara stared at Phoebe with wide eyes, her smile becoming fixed. The woman knew very well that Clara had no idea what the layout of this house was, where the rooms were, how they were arranged, or which room would have been hers. How was she to show them to her?

What was she playing at?

"Of course," Clara told her, the smile beginning to strain her face. "But the house must have changed since my last stay, and I so wish to see those changes." She turned to Stafford once more. "Would you lead us there, Stafford? And explain all the improvements to me on the way."

Blessedly, Stafford bowed in acknowledgement. "Of course, Miss Moore. We've just had the work on the gallery finished, so we'll take the long way through it. I'm sure you'll be rather pleased."

Slowly, Clara let a breath escape her as she moved to follow Stafford to the magnificent staircase in the entry, the railings curling around in neat spirals as they became the balustrades at the base.

Had she slid on those railings and tried to race to the center of the coil? Had she slipped and fallen to the ground or the stairs and bruised herself? Or had she been too fine and proper for such behavior?

With a blink, Clara looked at the stairs again, remembering that it had not been her at all. It had been Alexandra.

Would she forget she was Clara throughout this playing? Would it be easier to do so?

A warm arm slipped around hers, and she looked at Phoebe beside her.

"Forgive me, my pet," Phoebe murmured, her lips barely moving. "What else could I say but that? You covered very well, I must say."

Clara nodded once, returning herself to the present, and to the task. "Such a beautiful color on the walls, Stafford."

He smiled over his shoulder as he ascended the stairs. "That was a particular request of Lady Adrianna, Miss Moore. She is a bright young woman who knows her own mind, and her brothers do indulge her whims regarding the houses, as there is no mistress to run them."

It was all Clara could do not to laugh at the kindly worded statement where Lady Adrianna was concerned. She was an independent girl with a willful streak that terrified every teacher at the school for fear that she might one day raise up the other girls in a rebellion against them, call the local militia to arms for her own ends, or become the greatest actress known on the London stage.

Heaven only knew what she might have been like in the walls of her own home or with her brothers.

Stafford led them gallantly through the first story of the house, and particularly to the gallery he was so keen to show them.

Once she caught sight of it, Clara wondered why Stafford had been so delighted about it, given there was hardly anything in it. Yes, the walls were lovely, and the wallpaper that had so recently been hung was very attractive and fine, but as for the art…

Half a dozen portraits and one childish watercolor, and that was all.

The disappointment was profound indeed.

"Is this it?" Phoebe asked primly, not bothering to keep the disapproval from her tone. "Mr. Stafford, I fear you have misled us cruelly."

Stafford, miraculously, only laughed. "Miss Moore, don't you recognize your own work?"

"Good gracious!" Clara exclaimed, truly having nothing else to say as she moved closer to see the watercolor he indicated. "What is this doing up here?"

"Where else should His Grace have hung it?" The butler laughed to himself and gestured to the empty wall space. "The rest of the artwork has either been sold or is being reframed. His Grace will decide what to keep and if he wishes to make any new purchases. Perhaps Lady Adrianna will send some of her paintings to us here to hang."

Clara grunted once. "Not likely, I'd say," she muttered.

"What was that, Miss Moore?" Stafford asked, coming to her as though she'd said something worth hearing.

The sound of hooves on gravel suddenly echoed up to them, and, like a hound, Stafford perked up, his attention facing the front of the house.

Clara looked from him to Phoebe and back again. "Is that an arrival?"

"Perhaps..." With a quick bow, he left them without another word, his duty seeming to nip at his heels.

When he had gone, Phoebe huffed quietly. "Well, I'd call that poor treatment, how are we to find your old rooms now?"

Clara turned back to the watercolor, fascinated by the loving care that had been given to such a childish and, by all accounts, unremarkable work of art. "Why do you suppose the late duke kept this? Not only kept it, but had it framed and hung up here in the gallery? This is a house for entertaining, I'm sure of it, and to have this among the rest..."

"What rest?" Phoebe chuckled dryly and moved to the window facing the sea, her skirts swishing loudly as they did so. "There is nothing else here, Clara."

"You know what I mean," Clara replied with a roll of her eyes, looking over at her companion. "You can see the hooks where other artwork has been. Why should this be among them?"

Phoebe glanced over, her naturally wide, blue eyes alight. "Because he loved the girl, Clara. By all accounts, she was as a daughter to him when he had no children at all. Many a parent has taken untidy works of art and treasured them long past all sense."

There was something in Phoebe's voice that made Clara turn fully to give the woman a more thorough look. "Did you?"

One corner of Phoebe's full lips quirked, but the emotion behind it was as unreadable as the reason. "I have no children, Clara." She returned her attention to the window, her slender shoulders moving on an exhale too heavy for her answer.

Curious. What could it mean?

"Whose trunks are these, Stafford?" a new male voice inquired in a too-loud voice, the irritation in it evident even from their position.

Phoebe turned from the window and came to stand beside Clara. "Oh dear..."

"What?" Clara asked, her knees already quaking in fear of the reply.

"Visitors, Your Grace. Miss Moore and her aunt. We did not expect…"

Phoebe hissed between clenched teeth. "Damn."

Clara swallowed hard.

Footsteps thundered on the stairs, and Clara could only grip Phoebe's arm hard as they waited for the fury that might lay ahead.

Chapter Six

The woman was stunning.

It occurred to him, belatedly, that both women could be considered great beauties, but the woman clutching her aunt's arm as though death were nigh was the loveliest creature he'd seen outside of a London ballroom, and indeed, within a great many of them.

His irritation very nearly abated at the sight of her, and his mind spun with new tactics.

He still was not particularly pleased at having guests in his home while he saw to the care of this estate as part of his tour, but given the appearance of said guests...

"Ladies, my apologies," Hawk said as he bowed, belatedly remembering that he ought to smile on such occasions. "I had no intention of intruding on the day-to-day activities of Kirkleigh. I believe I have the honor of being in the presence of Miss Moore? And her aunt, though I have not been given the name."

The aunt, a prim woman with a shocking degree of beauty, given her age, pursed her full lips as she curtseyed. "Mrs. Daniels. I presume you are His Grace, the Duke of Kirklin?"

Hawk nodded once. "I am, madam." He focused his attention on the young woman, whose hair somehow managed to be both brown and blond, a notion that distracted him immensely. "Miss Moore."

"Yes." She relinquished her hold on her aunt's arm and laced her fingers very properly before her, but made no other movement.

And, apparently, had no intention of speaking further.

Something about her name rang in his memory, and he found

himself staring at her with more intensity as he struggled to place her. "Miss Moore..."

One of her trim brows rose. "Yes, Your Grace?"

Hawk pressed his tongue to the back of his teeth in thought, then shook his head. "I pray you'll forgive me, but I'm afraid I cannot recall how I should know you. Would you have the goodness to enlighten me?"

Miss Moore smiled, and though it was small, there was something mighty and moving about it. "Miss Alexandra Moore, Your Grace. I was the ward of your uncle, the late duke. I lived at Kirkleigh for some years in my childhood."

She was... she was *that* Miss Moore? He didn't know why it hadn't occurred to him before, but he hadn't exactly been thinking about her as the years passed. Apart from fulfilling his uncle's final wishes where she was concerned, as laid out in his will, Hawk could safely say he had not given her one moment of thought since they had last met. He'd been all of fifteen and she perhaps ten, and, as he recalled, he had been more intrigued by his uncle's horses than his ward.

The years had been far better to her than to him.

"Of course!" Hawk said at once, relaxing as much as he was able now that he knew her identity, though the discomfiture of having her in his house and being such a beauty was still very much engaged. "I do apologize, Miss Moore, it has been several years."

Her smile spread, revealing near-perfect teeth. "It has, Your Grace, so I think you may be forgiven for not recognizing me. And I did rather unexpectedly present myself to Kirkleigh, which is hardly good manners."

The surprisingly low timbre of her voice was utterly charming and surprisingly natural. He felt himself growing more at ease with each passing word, though it should not have been at all shocking to be at ease in his own home. To be at ease before a beautiful woman of relative status, however...

"I presented myself unexpectedly to Kirkleigh, also," Hawk admitted, returning her smile just enough to be apologetic. "Poor Stafford, more than one set of unexpected visitors is really too much. And for Mrs. Clayton to be away, as well..."

Miss Moore's hazel eyes quickly flicked to the butler, who had followed him upstairs, her smile turning more amused. "I daresay he will rally."

"He usually does." Hawk gestured to the gallery, a rather embarrassing space of emptiness at the present. "You'll find the gallery rather lacking at the present, I'm afraid."

"Not entirely," Mrs. Daniels murmured, gesturing elegantly to the childish watercolor on the wall, neatly framed in a thin, gold frame.

Hawk nodded as he saw it himself. "Indeed, the best piece remains."

Miss Moore scoffed softly, surprising Hawk and bringing his attention back.

"You don't agree?" he inquired, fighting the urge to smile further.

"I have improved my artistic skills a great deal since then, Your Grace," Miss Moore said with a directness that startled him further still, yet without any hint of boasting. "The sentimental nature of this piece is, I grant you, irreplaceable, but as for the quality…" She shrugged her slender shoulders. "It can be improved upon sufficiently."

"Really," Hawk mused, curious in spite of himself.

Mrs. Daniels cleared her throat delicately. "I'm afraid, Your Grace, that we are now in an awkward predicament. My dear niece was hoping that we might stay a few nights here at Kirkleigh while we wait for friends to join us in Kent, but we would not dream of imposing on your kindness while you yourself are in residence. Unthinkable, and we shall remove ourselves as soon as possible to give you the peace of your own home." She looked at Stafford calmly. "Mr. Stafford, if you would be so good as to direct us and our things to the nearest inn, we shall make ourselves quite comfortable there."

One blink of his eyes passed, and then Hawk was shaking his head. "Nonsense," he said without knowing why. "Why shouldn't you stay?"

Both women stared at him with widened eyes. "Why, Your Grace?" Miss Moore echoed in a faint voice. "I am an unmarried and unrelated woman."

He indicated her aunt. "With a chaperone. And I defy the idea of being unrelated, under these circumstances. I may be the owner of this place, but it has never been my home. You, on the other hand, spent many happy years here. If anyone should be leaving, it is I."

"Don't be ridiculous," Miss Moore scoffed incredulously. "We'd never dream of forcing you from your own house!"

"Exactly." He smiled politely, the idea having more merit than he'd previously considered. "None of us should have to leave. How long would you like to stay? The house is at your disposal. I cannot say the same for myself, but as you came here for the house and not for me, I daresay you will recover your disappointment."

A faint crease made an appearance on Miss Moore's otherwise perfect brow. "Your Grace, we could not impose…"

"It's not an imposition if I have extended an invitation," he said simply. "Which I have." He clapped his hands together and rubbed them quickly. "Now, how long were you thinking of staying?"

Miss Moore bit her lip for a moment, just enough for him to appreciate the fullness of them before she ceased the action. "Just three days, Your Grace. Then we shall be out and about on our tour for a time, though…" She paused and exchanged a look with her aunt, who shrugged before nodding her encouragement.

"Yes?" Hawk prodded, intrigued in spite of himself.

The hazel eyes met his again, hesitance rampant in them. "Would it be an imposition if my aunt and I returned to Kirkleigh on occasion? We have a few ventures we'd like to take elsewhere in this part of England, but in between each, when we might prefer rest…

Hawk was nodding before she finished. "Kirkleigh will be open for you at any given time, Miss Moore. I only aim to be here a week or so myself, so please avail yourself of this place."

Again, those captivating lips pulled to one side in a small smile. "Then we shall, Your Grace. Thank you."

Why did her smiles make him want to smile also? He was not an overly jubilant person, and he was not prone to smiling without reason, but still the edges of his mouth began to itch with the urge to grin shamelessly.

He must have been more tired than he thought.

"Begging your pardon, Your Grace," Stafford broke in formally behind him. "Are we to expect anyone else to join you? Or any trunks?"

Right. That.

In all the fuss after he'd arrived, he'd completely forgotten about the manner of his arrival. He'd rode in from the coaching station, tired of the jolting around the carriage provided, little suspecting what confusion would arise. At least when a coach pulled up, there was a manner of expectation from his servants and belongings to see to.

A single rider was far more distressing to the natural way of things.

He glanced at his butler, somehow still amused. "The coach should be here shortly, Stafford, yes. And with it, Mr. Robinson. If you would please see the Aspen room prepared for him."

"Yes, Your Grace." Stafford turned to the ladies, smiling far more fondly. "We will have the Birch and Willow rooms prepared for you, Mrs. Daniels, Miss Moore, if that is agreeable."

Miss Moore seemed delighted by the notion, though her eyes did return to Hawk quickly. "You're certain about having us stay?"

He nodded. "Positive."

"And we won't be in the way?" she pressed. "What if your sister or brother should come for a visit?"

Hawk chuckled at the very idea. "Then we would be a full house indeed, Miss Moore, but still you would not be in the way. My brother's preferred room is the Cedar, and Adrianna refuses to sleep anywhere except the Poplar suite."

Something almost like a dimple, yet not entirely one, formed on her left cheek with her smile. "And what is the tree of your room, Your Grace?"

The question seemed somehow more significant and revealing than something as simple as trees of the woodlands. As though the tree his room was named for should somehow resemble him, should say something about his nature or his being; as though she could know everything she needed to by this answer alone.

Suddenly the conversation was one he'd prefer an escape from, and the meeting less than comfortable.

"Maple, Miss Moore. Sturdy, tall, and rather unremarkable compared to the rest of the forest." He bowed to them once more.

"If you ladies would join me for dinner, I would be most gratified. You need only change if it suits you, I will not stand on ceremony while you are here. Good day."

Without waiting for an answer, he turned and trotted down the stairs, pretending as though he had a great many things to do and a strict schedule to adhere to.

Truth be told, Kirkleigh was not, and had never been, his favorite house, and his newfound desire to see to repairs and needs, as well as participate in them, had not extended far into the care of this estate. He'd do his duty, of course, and discuss matters with the estate agent and his tenants. He'd ensure that all was prepared for the approaching winter, work alongside a few people, see Adrianna at the school, then scurry off to Elmsley Abbey in Wiltshire for the remainder of the winter. It was the last of his estates to see to, apart from the London House, and the one he felt most suited for the approaching holidays.

Even Nat did not see a point in remaining at Kirkleigh for long.

Though it was possibly the most aesthetically situated of his houses, it had never quite felt like his.

It was his uncle's house. Always had been, and likely always would be.

He hadn't been engaging in flattery or sentimentality with Miss Moore; the house was undoubtedly more hers than his. He'd sell it to her in an instant if it wasn't the traditional seat of the Duke of Kirklin. The moment he discovered how to circumnavigate that issue, he'd give her the first right of refusal for the place.

Perhaps he ought to start thinking along those lines while he was here. It was certainly worth a discussion with the estate agent, whatever his name was. The place was so efficiently run, he almost never heard from the man.

In that respect, perhaps Kirkleigh ought to have been his favorite of the estates.

In truth, once Adrianna completed her studies in the spring, there would be nothing to draw them to Kent at all. It would be wise to reduce the number of his estates in order to give better care to the ones he kept. He could find a buyer of means, and one who would be a responsible landlord to the tenants on the estate. It could be a particularly smooth transition, if he worked it all right.

The name of the estate should change, if he would be rid of it. How did one go about such a thing?

A laugh from the floor above him wafted down to his ears as he prepared to enter his study, and he paused a step upon hearing it. The laughter possessed the same low, natural timbre Miss Moore had employed, and the music of it struck him. He'd heard poets and lovesick friends describe laughter as musical, and his first inclination had been to think of an aria of sorts.

This laughter was no aria.

It was a gentle, favorite lullaby. A quietly hummed tune in unobserved moments. A playful melody one could recall on a carefree stroll. It was a sound of warmth and comfort, something that wound its way into his chest and settled there like a purring cat preparing for a nap.

It was the most soothing sound he'd ever heard.

What in the world was coming over him?

Shaking his head, Hawk strode into the study and shut the door firmly behind him, perhaps with more force than he should have, but it served the purpose of establishing proper distance from his guests. He moved around the large, open desk and shrugged out of his coat, draping it neatly on the back of his chair before sitting and staring at the vacant surface before him.

He was safe in his study, yet there was not much for him to do in here. He hadn't set up a meeting with the agent, had not determined when, or if, he would see his sister, if he needed to see to any particular estate matters...

Coming into his study might have been a pointless escape.

Hawk slumped back against his chair, pursing his lips in thought. He did not have tasks to accomplish, but he could identify his tasks... It would pass the time, and enable him to perhaps quantify the length of his stay with more accuracy.

As he was desperate to leave, having that in his mind could be rather motivating.

He pulled open a drawer and retrieved a sheet of paper, nodding in satisfaction as he then dipped his pen in the inkwell and began to write. He scribbled down the items he'd been thinking of, then began listing any and all ideas for how he could be of physical help to his tenants and estate. It was more difficult than he thought, given he had no insight as to what was needed, and he was not as familiar with the tenants. And as for the house…

Well, unless he wanted to be the one to hang the artwork back in the gallery, he wasn't certain anything truly needed improvement.

Perhaps he ought to meet with members of the staff, as well.

Surely he could help the gardening staff with weeds and pruning, if nothing else.

The duke who pruned.

That would be an excellent epithet for himself. He could hear Nat's laughter about the thing now.

He frowned as he realized he was actually hearing Nat's distinctive laughter, and it was echoing in the entryway.

Hawk glanced at the door, waiting to see if another person's laughter would join in. He wasn't entirely sure how he felt about the possibility, but he waited for it all the same.

The laughter came closer, still alone, and Hawk returned his attention to the paper before him, tapping the tip of his pen on a corner of the page in thought.

"Hawk! Hawk, where are you hiding?" The door to the study was flung open, and a disgusted snort rent the air. "You've been here less than an hour and you're working already? I thought you said there was nothing to do here!"

"I never said that," Hawk told his friend simply, adding an examination of the cove on his estate to the list.

Nat grunted once. "Yes, you did. You said you would have nothing to do."

Hawk gestured faintly with his pen. "You see? Not the same thing."

"Explain that to me." Nat pulled one of the other chairs over and plopped himself into it with his natural inelegance.

"There is plenty to do in Kent," Hawk told him, still not looking up. "And a great deal one might do here at Kirkleigh for entertainment, if one chose. But as for my present aims, and what I have found such satisfaction in doing elsewhere, I, myself, will have nothing to do here."

Now he looked up and found his friend scowling darkly at him.

"That was not an amusing trick, Hawk."

Hawk shrugged a shoulder. "It wasn't a trick. Just proper usage of the English language. Can I be blamed if you haven't mastered it as you ought?"

Nat shook his head in continued derision before jerking his thumb towards the rest of the house. "Who else is here? I thought you had no intention of hosting anything or anyone."

"I didn't, and I don't." Hawk set his pen down with a short sigh. "But when I arrived, I found Miss Moore and her aunt already here, so it seemed impolite to ask them to leave."

"Miss Moore?" Nat raised a brow. "Should I know her?"

Hawk shook his head. "She was my uncle's ward; she spent her childhood here."

"Did you know her then?"

"Yes, I did."

Slowly, Nat sat up in his chair and leaned forward, pressing the tips of his fingers together and drumming them at a maddening pace. "Really, Your Grace? You did? And she is… unmarried still?"

Hawk stared at the idiot across from him without emotion, almost without blinking. "She is. And I did. And that is an end of the vein of thoughts currently circulating in your mind."

"Oh, I can assure you these veins are heading for some vital organs indeed. Rejuvenated, they are." Nat laced his fingers and propped them under his chin. "Pity she's so beautiful, it will make resisting her quite difficult."

"I know, and it's…" Hawk clamped on his lips hard, narrowing his eyes at having been so neatly caught in the obvious trap.

Nat grinned like the mischievous lad he'd undoubtedly been, but said nothing else.

Best to move on under the circumstances.

"The point is," he continued, "this house was more home to her than it ever was to me, and likely more than it will be. As I intended to be here a very short amount of time, I saw no reason she could not use the house as she wished and remain, if she chose."

"Hold, sir." Nat straightened in his seat and matched Hawk's suspicious look. "Hold, I say."

Hawk held his hands up just a little above the surface of the table.

"Holding, sir…"

Nat dipped his chin in a superior nod of acknowledgement. "Intended, you said. Intended. Past tense. Do you not still intend to remain here a very short time?"

Bloody hell…

There was nothing to say to that, and Hawk did not even attempt a rebuttal.

Nat's smile was smug and intrigued. "Damned tricky thing, that English language, isn't it?"

Chapter Seven

*K*irkleigh was the most perfect house Clara had ever set foot in. She would even consider it a more beautiful place than the estate that the Miss Masters' school had settled in, though it certainly was not comparable in size. But the view from the Willow room was one of the coast and the sea, and she could have stared out of the window for the rest of the day and long into the night without finding a single moment wasted.

Had Phoebe not come in to talk a while, she might have done just that.

What she had seen of the house so far was no less exquisite. She had every intention of wandering tonight once all of the rest of them were in bed, determined to not only know the house as well as the real Miss Moore would have done, but to appreciate the work of art it was. And tomorrow, if the day was fine, she would explore that coastline she could see so clearly.

Phoebe had even told her she should draw it, as well as the coves thereabouts.

Let it never be said that Clara turned down a suggestion for her art that she herself found inviting.

But first, she must have dinner with the Duke of Kirklin.

It wasn't convenient to have him here with them while they were trying to do some preliminary investigating, but adaptation had given them an equal opportunity. The duke had known of Miss Moore's fondness for the place, so she might be permitted wandering and intrusion for the sake of nostalgia. She could move about without suspicion and without having to worry if she might be disturbing something or someone.

It really might have been more beneficial that the duke *was* here, all things considered.

Phoebe hadn't given her any insight into more specific tasks as yet, but Clara was sure she would say something before they retired for the night. Pippa had promised them both the exact details that had prompted this investigation of theirs once this first visit was completed, if it was called for. It seemed that she and the other superiors in the covert world wished to protect these early investigations, and the people involved, to such an extent that the larger issues facing them were not elaborated on unless required. Clara could easily see how that could be maddening, but she was grateful for it. She didn't want to know more at this point. She didn't want that window to the darker, more terrifying side of the world to be opened for her.

Unless it had to be.

She wouldn't back out now that she had committed to this project, but she would not be disappointed or upset if it turned out that she was not needed further.

Spending a few days here at Kirkleigh with the handsome Duke of Kirklin in her vicinity would not be a trial in the least.

Terrified though she was when he appeared, seeing the initial expression of irritation on his face, she had recognized that he was an exceptionally attractive man. Undoubtedly the most handsome one she had ever seen, which made imposing on his estate a worse crime. He had eyes darker than anything she had ever seen, and dark hair that, due to his riding in, had taken on a windswept look, though she suspected it was usually rather carefully kept. His clothing fit him perfectly, and while she would not necessarily have called his a muscular frame, she would be hard pressed to find anything lacking in it.

His glower was made more impressive by dark, thick brows, and having it turned in her direction was unsettling in ways she had never known. It shook her kneecaps and twisted her stomach, made her palms sweat, and caused the rims of her ears to catch fire.

Yet above and beyond all of that, he was a handsome man.

Once he had begun speaking with them, and his irritation had faded, he seemed a very good sort of man, respectful and a little playful. His insistence that they remain showed kindness, but anyone could be polite and kind upon first meeting. She refused to judge a man upon only the first encounter, especially after travelling and being faced with unexpected intruders into his home, so only time would tell what his true nature was.

If he showed such a thing to these two visitors.

It occurred to her that he would know Miss Moore from his youth, and the pair of them might not have had an agreeable relationship. Or they could have been the best of friends. Had Miss Moore fancied herself in love with him? Had he had any inclination towards her in the same way? Had the late duke had any wishes for the pair of them? Nothing official had been set up, she knew that much, but it said nothing about wishes and what might have been.

She had to play her part as Miss Moore carefully until she understood more.

The present duke hadn't said or done anything as yet that gave her cause for concern in that regard, and he had not addressed her by her given name, which she took for a good sign. But there had been several years since their last meeting, as far as she was aware, so it could simply be good manners there.

Dinner this evening could answer all of those questions.

Or give her more.

Clara stared out of the window of her room, exhaling slowly. She was fully dressed for dinner, having opted to change for the occasion as a show of respect, and one of the maids of the house had assisted her with her hair. All in all, she felt rather pretty, her borrowed green muslin fitting nicely and giving her eyes a brighter hue of green. It was perhaps a little plain, but that could be forgiven easily, as dining with a duke had not been on her, or Miss Moore's, agenda for the trip.

She prayed it would be enough.

"Clara? Are you ready, child?" Phoebe's voice called from the room adjoining hers, knocking softly.

"Yes, Aunt Fern," Clara called, smoothing her skirts with quick, anxious strokes.

The door joining their rooms opened, and Phoebe entered in an array of cream and pink, her complexion heightened by the pink sprigged rosettes dotting her bodice and extending into vines on her skirts. She was far lovelier than Clara could ever hope to be, regardless of age, and Phoebe's very small smile displayed nothing of whatever emotions lay beneath the pristine mask of her features.

"You look lovely," Clara told her, turning from the window and clasping her own trembling fingers before her.

Phoebe eyed Clara up and down. "As do you, my dear. Simple and unadorned, rather understated. When we return to the Convent, I'll ask for Tilda to be sent for. To continue this role, you must have more finery."

Clara had been told that the school was called the Convent in the covert world. She looked down at herself, then up at her faux aunt. "Truly? Why? And who is Tilda?"

Phoebe's smile turned far more mischievous. "Yes, truly, and because you are the former ward of a duke who was given a very handsome sum upon his death, and you must look it. And Tilda... Well, she is a dear friend, and you have need of her."

That sounded ominous.

"But why...?" Clara began, only to have Phoebe raise a hand, cutting her off.

"There is not enough time," Phoebe said without concern. "You'll understand when you meet her. Now, shall we go down?"

Tension surged within Clara, straightening her legs to an almost painful degree. "Is it too late to ask for a tray in my room?"

Phoebe gave her a sympathetic and knowing look, though there was an edge to it. "I'm afraid so. And it would serve nothing to do so. We need to be on good terms with the duke if we are to explore here, and if we want any hope of coming back."

"I know," Clara sighed, twisting one of her fingers a little. "I just feel so uprooted by having him here. It makes the pretending even worse."

"Why should it?" Phoebe inquired as she reached out and separated Clara's hands. "You're not going to be interrogated as to things you ought to know, and if there is a question that should have a very specific answer you don't know, be charmingly evasive. That should be simple enough, you must have much practice doing so for various parents of students, or the students themselves."

There was a thought. Clara hadn't considered that she might already have the training she would need for dealing with the sort of conversation soon required of her. It would not be pleasant lying to the duke directly, so if she could avoid doing such a thing in any way, she most certainly would.

Charmingly evasive.

That she could do.

Just how charming it would be was not for her to say, but evasive was manageable enough.

Nodding, she turned and moved to the door of her bedchamber, Phoebe following with only the swishing of her skirts as accompaniment.

"You remember the way down, don't you, Clara?" Phoebe murmured behind her as they moved out into the corridor.

"I do," Clara replied. She forced her pace to be sedate, trying to balance the tight ringlets alongside either ear. She preferred a looser style normally, but she hadn't the nerve to tell the maid when it had been done. She blinked, bringing herself back to the moment. "Though how we're to get to the dining room is another question entirely."

"Never mind that." Phoebe hummed a little as they moved down the hall, Clara's attention drawn by the paintings dotting the walls, each encased in gold frames. "Great families and houses enter the dining room from a parlor or sitting room, which should be sufficiently open for us to see well enough. All you have to do is seem confused and turned around, which would be understandable enough for anyone. Are you listening to me?"

Clara nodded, though she was far more interested in the intricate carvings on the wood beams above them, the artistry in the moldings and medallions. Even as they descended the stairs, Clara could not help but admire the tapestries, the grandeur of the windows, and the fine grain in the wood that had been selected for the railing of the stairs. There was beauty everywhere she looked, and yet she could not take it all in with the intensity she wished to.

"Clara, dear, I can see why you are so enamored by the memory of this place," Phoebe announced in a haughty, airy manner as she took her arm, drawing Clara's attention to her. "What an enchanting setting for a child to be brought up in. You must take time for yourself to wander its halls, revisit every nook and cranny. Do you think the duke will mind?"

It was on the tip of Clara's tongue to tell Phoebe that she hadn't the faintest idea what the duke would allow or mind, or what it was like to grow up in this house, when another voice answered first.

"No, Mrs. Daniels, the duke will not mind."

Clara restrained a gasp and turned to look below them as they descended.

The duke stood there, smiling politely up at them, still in his previous clothing, as he'd intimated, though looking a good deal neater and more formal. And he was more impossibly handsome thus than she'd imagined.

Swallowing with some difficulty, Clara smiled herself. "He won't? Are you certain?"

The duke smiled further still. "I think I can safely say so. But if you'd prefer, I'll inquire of him later."

Clara could not help but laugh at that, though the playful comment did not seem entirely natural to the man who had offered it. Why should that be, and how could she know it?

He did not say anything else as they finished their path down the stairs, winding around at last and presenting themselves before him.

His dark eyes took them both in without judgment, his slight smile still in place. "Ladies, you are looking well and refreshed, if I may say so."

"Thank you, Your Grace," Clara murmured, curtseying in greeting. "I hope you have not been waiting on us."

He inclined his chin. "No, Miss Moore, I've been waiting on another guest entirely. He arrived after we parted, and he's likely to get lost in his own house, let alone in Kirkleigh. I thought it best I escort him, for everybody's sake."

"Was he also unexpected?" she ventured to ask, continuing to smile at the memory of their previous exchange.

As she hoped, the duke's smile curved further still. "He was not. I was well aware of his coming, and when he heard I had other guests, he was far more interested in being here, I assure you."

A jaunty whistling met their ears, drawing Clara's attention up to see a striking, fair-haired man in a deep blue coat ambling down the stairs at an easy lope. The whistling stopped as soon as he saw them, and a quick, easy grin spread across his handsome face. "Kirklin, you should have sent for me in my tardiness. I would never have kept such fair ladies waiting on me."

"They had no idea they were doing so, Robinson," the duke drawled, his eyes tracing his friend's progress blandly. "And I don't believe they would have cared if they had."

Clara snickered at the droll expression on the approaching man's face as he reached the bottom of the stairs and hurried to them. "Well, introduce me, then, and we might have done with pretense."

The duke seemed to sigh without actually releasing the breath to do so. "Mrs. Daniels and Miss Moore, might I present Mr. Robinson? A very old friend, and sometimes unintended stowaway, of mine."

Mr. Robinson was mid-bow when that last comment registered, and he frowned at the duke for it. "Stowaway? My dear Kirklin, I was invited, and I never go where I am not wanted." He shook his head and gave Clara an apologetic smile. "I apologize for him, Miss Moore. I do not think his manners have much improved from when you last knew him."

Clara let herself laugh at that and smiled. "Our interaction was so long ago, Mr. Robinson, and I do not recollect a lack of manners from His Grace then. Indeed, politeness and manners were all we had."

"The manners of a boy are very different to that of a man, Miss Moore." Mr. Robinson grinned and offered his arm to Phoebe. "Mrs. Daniels, might I escort you into dinner?"

"I beg your pardon, Nat," the duke interjected without too much fuss. "As the host, I do believe that is my prerogative."

Mr. Robinson only raised a brow and took Phoebe's hand, looping it into his arm. "But you always say you never stand on ceremony. How was I to know you suddenly wished to?"

The duke blinked, his expression not changing. His eyes moved to Clara. "He's got a point."

"I believe he does," Clara agreed.

"Hmm." The duke smiled apologetically at Phoebe. "My

condolences, Mrs. Daniels. It would appear you have been claimed by my guest. Can you bear the unintentional slight?"

Phoebe's lips quirked, her eyes narrowing. "I certainly can, Your Grace. I never take offense when eagerness overtakes the rules of formality."

Clara coughed a small laugh and glanced back at the duke, who was nodding sagely.

"You are very gracious, Mrs. Daniels." He turned to Clara and offered his arm. "Miss Moore, I suppose that leaves us to lead the way, if you please."

Without hesitation, Clara placed her hand on his arm. "Lead on, Your Grace."

He smiled at her words. "I daresay you could lead me in this house."

The attempt at familiar humor made Clara's own smile stiffen as her pulse skipped. "I'll give you the honor, Your Grace. It is your house, after all."

"Yes, I suppose it is." His smile remained, which settled her nerves as he led the way into the dining room.

It was elegantly set, far nicer than anything Clara had been privileged to dine at, but not as elaborate as she would have expected a duke's table to be. Then again, the man had not intended to entertain, so there likely hadn't been time to enhance things with more finery. As it was, the room was almost luminous with so much candlelight, and it made her smile.

"Why do you smile?" the duke asked her suddenly. "Memories?"

"Mmm," was all the reply she made as he took her around to her place.

"Not painful, I hope."

She looked up at him in surprise. "No, not at all. Nothing could be unpleasant about Kirkleigh."

He gave her a gentle smile and assisted her with her chair, though she did not need it, then moved to his place down the table. Phoebe was situated across from her and Mr. Robinson sat on Clara's right. No one, she noticed, sat opposite the duke at the other end.

Mr. Robinson caught her staring. "Bit of a tradition, I'm afraid," he elaborated. "Kirklin's sister is mistress of all his estates until he marries, and she finds it all a very great joke if her seat is reserved for her alone."

Clara laughed at that, knowing Lady Adrianna well enough for that to be perfectly apt. "It is sweet of you all to humor her."

Kirklin shrugged. "It's not brotherly sweetness, Miss Moore. It's self-preservation."

"Amen," Mr. Robinson added.

Their food was brought in and served, creating enough of a diversion for Clara to find her bearings again. The gentlemen were engaging enough, and it would be only too easy to slip into her own nature and behavior rather than focus on being Miss Moore. If she were not careful, the two would blend all too well, and she would find herself tangled in knots.

"Mrs. Daniels," Kirklin said after a moment, giving her a scolding look, "I did say you did not have to change for dinner."

"I always feel better when I change for dinner, Your Grace," Phoebe said without effort. "More the thing, if you will. Clara, on the other hand, might not even remember to eat, let alone change for it, so engaged would she be in other matters."

Clara's cheeks flushed at the comment, which was more true than anyone could know, though it was true for Clara herself, not necessarily Miss Moore. Would Kirklin know that?

Mr. Robinson looked at her with mild interest. "Forgive me, Miss Moore, but I thought your given name was Alexandra. Was I mistaken?"

"No, you were not," she quipped even as her heart began to race with some anxiety. "My name is Alexandra Claire, named for my mother. Papa thought it too much to have two versions of Alexandra in the house, so he wished to use Claire for me, and Claire became Clara." She wrinkled up her nose on a laugh. "It's a silly convolution of a name, is it not?"

"Oh, I don't think so," Mr. Robinson boasted. He pointed up at Kirklin freely. "Kirklin over there has the given name of George, but he hasn't been called George since probably age three. His father was Marquess of Hawkendale, but it was Little Georgie who took on the nickname of Hawk. It suited once his father passed, God rest him, and he assumed the title, but when he inherited the dukedom, the nickname remained."

Kirklin raised a brow, no doubt at having his life so revealed. "Or there is Charles Nathaniel Allen Robinson, who prefers to be known as Nat, and thus align himself with a rather pestering insect of the same name. How apt."

The comment made all around the table laugh, including the man in question.

"When did you come to stay at Kirkleigh, Miss Moore?" Mr. Robinson asked, taking a sip of his wine. "How old were you?"

Clara chewed her bite of potato carefully, aligning her thoughts with the story she knew. "I discovered I had been made ward of the late duke after my parents died when I was seven years old, and shortly thereafter was sent for. I had been staying with my aunt, Mrs. Daniels, who was not yet married, when the duke himself came for me."

Phoebe smiled sadly, inclining her head. "I was an unmarried woman of no means. It broke my heart, but I could not take care of my Clara girl under those circumstances, and my late sister knew it well."

"I can only imagine," Mr. Robinson said sympathetically. "Very good of you to think of what was best for her in spite of your feelings."

"Thank you, Mr. Robinson," Phoebe replied, her voice breaking just enough. Her smile at Clara spread further. "And my dear girl was more than amply looked after."

Clara nodded in agreement. "I was. I never once felt anything other than cared for under Uncle Kirklin's guidance."

The present duke made a noncommittal sound as he chewed his own meal. "He certainly doted on you. Never inclined to marry or have children of his own, but I think you might have made him regret that decision later on."

"He would have made a wonderful father," Clara murmured, glancing down at her plate, wishing she had known someone as wonderful as the late duke in her own life.

What a difference that might have made.

Suddenly aware of the silence at the table, Clara looked up and forced a smile. "I was here at Kirkleigh until I was thirteen, at which time I began at Miss Masters' School. When I had finished there, my aunt wrote to Uncle Kirklin to request that she might take me abroad, as her circumstances had changed, and afterward see to my care herself."

"And he agreed," Mr. Robinson murmured, shaking his head in wonder.

"He agreed," Clara confirmed. "He was beginning to be unwell himself and did not like the idea of my tending him throughout it all, nor of my missing any experiences he would have given me had his health permitted. I could not refuse his wishes for me. It would seem so very ungrateful..."

Phoebe gave her a kind look, if a little scolding. "Dear girl, he sent you off with that lovely letter, don't you recall? You read it on our first night in Paris, just as he wished you to. He left you very clear instructions, did he not?"

Thinking quickly, wondering if that had been part of the notes from the real Miss Moore, and how she could have forgotten it, Clara nodded, swallowing hard. "Yes, he did. And he said I was not to harbor a moment's guilt or regret in pursuing that which would bring me joy."

"Hear, hear," Mr. Robinson said, raising a glass. "To that which brings us joy!"

They all raised their glasses in a toast. "That which brings us joy."

Clara glanced over at Kirklin as she brought her glass to her lips and found his eyes on her over the rim of his own glass.

What did he see there that kept his eyes on her? What did he think of this Miss Moore? Did he suspect her? Did he disapprove of her?

What would remaining in this house with him for the next three days bring?

"It's going to be damned confusing to call him Kirklin when, to you, Kirklin is your departed guardian," Mr. Robinson pointed out after drinking deeply from his glass. "Perhaps you might call him Hawk? What do you say, Your Grace?"

"Oh, I couldn't," Clara protested quickly, her cheeks flaming as she looked at Mr. Robinson in horror. "Such familiarity on so short an acquaintance is unthinkable." She turned back to the duke. "I will not become confused, I can assure you."

Kirklin shocked her by only shrugging as he set his glass down. "It won't offend me in the least, Miss Moore. I shall not feel slighted, disrespected, or in any way affronted should you choose to forego the use of my title here. As I said, consider these walls and everything within them yours. Whatever will increase your comfort will suit me very well."

The words were kindness itself, but his expression still seemed almost hooded as he spoke them. The paradox of it all left Clara uneasy, despite his saying she ought to be comfortable. Was he doing that on purpose? Or was he simply the sort of man who was goodness at his core but so wrapped in his reserve that one had to look for it to be sure?

Whatever it was, she would take advantage of what he offered, as he was indeed offering it.

"Thank you, Your Grace," Clara murmured, giving him a small smile. "I will not forego politeness entirely, it is not in my nature. But I will consider myself free to adapt as circumstances allow."

One corner of Kirklin's mouth curved, and with it, something in Clara's stomach turned to exactly the same angle. "As you like, Miss Moore. Just as you like."

Chapter Eight

There was something about Miss Moore.

He wasn't sure what, but it was certainly something.

For good or for ill, just something.

When she was in a room, Hawk had to look at her. Not constantly, not regularly, but repeatedly, as it happened, as though she would change from one moment to the next. She was captivating in every moment, there was no mistaking that, and her beauty was only part of the equation. Expressive features, enchanting eyes, an unassuming nature, and that laugh…

He could still hear it in his mind, though it had been a full day since he had heard it.

He hadn't even seen Miss Moore today, and he could recollect her laugh clearly.

Maddening.

"All right there, Your Grace?" the foreman called.

Hawk waved a hand at him and hefted the position of his hands on the two-man saw into a more secure position. "Ready," he grunted.

The burly man on the other side of the saw nodded, and the two of them began to work in tandem, Hawk's arms aching with the amount of work he had put them through already.

He should have come earlier in the autumn.

Not that Kirkleigh required much of him, but there would have been more for him to do if he had. Meetings with his estate agent the day before had proven just as he'd suspected, that all was in perfect order, but now that he'd acquired a new appreciation for the manual labor of his estates, opportunities to exercise those interests were at the forefront of his mind.

How could he have recalled that Kirkleigh was a masterful estate for hops gardens and hazel trees? There was a small fruits orchard as well, but it tended to be only providing for the families on the estate and for the local village markets, if there was a surplus. Being so late in autumn, all of the harvesting had been done, and there was nothing additional to do that might benefit the estate.

Which left winter preparations for his tenants.

Still good work, but hardly as satisfying.

His agent, Mr. Cole, had been baffled when Hawk had asked him to take him around to the tenant houses and cottages rather than the orchards and gardens on the estate. But, Hawk pointed out, Cole was an active man himself and could frequently be found at the smithy's working at horseshoes or axles, though he was no longer in that trade himself. Sufficiently encouraged, Cole had done as Hawk asked, and both men were now assisting laborers in mending cottages, fixing fences, and chopping firewood.

It was supposed to take Hawk's mind off of Miss Moore, but it had not.

Could not.

He'd not slept well the night before, not after the entertaining and engaging supper they'd enjoyed, even though all had retired early. Rather than rest, Hawk had racked his brain for every memory he could drudge up about Miss Moore, searching those moments for any sign of the woman now staying beneath his own roof.

He found nothing significant with which to compare the two.

Oh, there were moments enough with a young Miss Moore in them, but their interactions had been so fleeting that he barely recalled a word of their conversations. If they'd had any. He recalled one particular occasion where her ribbons had grown loose in her golden hair and he'd picked one off the ground for her, though why such an insignificant moment should remain in his mind so particularly he could not have said.

Why hadn't they come to his uncle's home more regularly than they had? Relations between the brothers had been cordial, and Hawk, as his uncle's heir once his father had passed, surely ought to have had some training at the hands of his uncle. Yet nothing of the kind had taken place. Letters from his uncle had arrived, very like the scenario Miss Moore had described with her own letter, but on no memorable occasion had he and his uncle broken bread together and discussed matters of the various Kirklin estates.

He had fond memories of the man, but they were few and far between.

In that respect, he envied Miss Moore, and there was a great deal of guilt for that. To envy an orphan girl, passed to a guardian she had never met rather than stay with her only living relation? To be relegated to the care of an aging duke with no wife and no children, brought up alone in a great house like Kirkleigh…

Yet envy her he did.

His thoughts returned to the present as the saw cut through the last of the log, releasing the tension he had been working against and raising him up from his slightly lowered position. He heaved an exhausted exhale and slumped his shoulders, the fatigue in them beyond anything he could recall.

It was a strangely glorious feeling.

A rumble overhead brought all attention heavenward, and Hawk placed his hands on his hips as he took in the impending storm.

"I think that's all for today, Your Grace," the foreman called out again. "The lads will just finish up on the cottage at the end of the lane, and we'll resume work again tomorrow, weather permitting."

Hawk nodded at him. "Agreed, Mr. Jacks. 'Til tomorrow, then." He shook hands with his fellow laborers, then started the walk back up the path to Kirkleigh.

There was a direct enough path through the village, but in his present situation, appearance what it was, he favored the longer, more private route along the cliffside.

It would not do for the Duke of Kirklin to be seen by the public without a coat, cravat, or waistcoat, let alone to be damp with perspiration and the linen of his shirt streaked with dirt from various tasks. White had procured him sturdier linen shirts, as he'd suggested, and it had proven both useful and frugal. His finer shirts would have been ripped to shreds or stained permanently, and he would have had to send out for more, which would have cost a greater sum of money.

As he was procuring various trinkets and accoutrements for Adrianna each month, he could hardly condone more expenses on trivial matters, though he could certainly afford it.

Adrianna, naturally, thought it was all coming from the pocket money allotted to her each month, but Hawk had decided very early on in her time at Miss Masters' that her whims and fancies, to a point, would come from his own funds. Her pocket money would be set aside and saved up so that when she completed her studies, she would have a sum of money for her own ends that was not tied up in her dowry or the estate.

He had not looked at the figures for some time, but it was certainly approaching a rather impressive number.

Hawk inhaled deeply when he neared the cliffside, the crashing of the waves prompting the action, as it usually did. The sea was restless at present, another sign of the weather turning, though no rain fell as yet. The path along the coast was well worn, though overgrown in parts, which shouldn't surprise him. There were no houses but his this far up, and only his staff would be in residence in his absence. Some of them might have taken the path on occasion, but they would be more inclined to take the path through the village rather than the coast.

No one came this way unless it was for the scenery, for playing as children, or to find their way down to the beach itself.

He had not done so in years, though it had been a favorite activity on the occasions when his family had come out to Kirkleigh. Even as a young boy, he had been drawn there, much to his mother's distress, and he and Griffin had made great use of the various coves and caves thereabouts.

But that had only been for a summer, perhaps two of them, and then there hadn't been as many visits to continue such adventures.

Come to think of it, he hadn't explored the caves and coves in years.

Perhaps he should do so before he left Kirkleigh. It might incline his heart more towards the place, which would undoubtedly do him good.

And he and Miss Moore could...

He paused a step as that thought went unfinished in his mind.

He and Miss Moore could what?

What did he want for himself and for Miss Moore?

Why should he want anything for Miss Moore?

What was Miss Moore to him?

That was the question, he feared.

In truth, she was nothing to him. The ward of his uncle. No relation, no remaining ties, and the only thing they had in common was Kirkleigh.

Kirkleigh…

He should dearly love to see the place through her eyes, and perhaps she might help him to eventually do so.

Hawk extended his stride as the path turned steeper, a turn in the path approaching a small plateau perfect for capturing the view, should one wish to. It was a place he knew well, as his mother had often walked to that very spot for just such a purpose. While he might not recall other aspects of this place, that image of his mother was one that had stayed with him for years.

Upon reaching the summit of it, Hawk smiled to himself and took a moment to look out over the beach and coves, watching for a moment as small fishing ships made their way towards land before the storm arrived.

"Incomparable view, is it not?" a soft, low voice said from behind him.

"Indeed," he replied, turning to face the voice.

A widened pair of hazel eyes met his, and Hawk's polite smile turned to one far more easy. "Your Grace," Clara gasped, rising quickly from a stool, a charcoal pencil falling to the ground.

Hawk smiled further yet. "Miss Moore, I did not mean to startle you."

Clara swallowed hard and gestured to his person. "I did not recognize you dressed as you are, Your Grace."

"Which is why I dress as such on days when I am to be engaged in labor." He stepped forward and bent to pick up the pencil, catching sight of the drawing on the page of a book held open by a white-knuckled thumb. "Taking in the view there?"

"What?" She glanced down at the book in her hand, her cheeks coloring a bright pink. "Oh." She brought the book up and swallowed hard, snapping the covers shut. "Just some sketching, really. Nothing too exciting."

Hawk handed her the pencil, surveying her embarrassment with interest. "May I see it?"

Clara's eyes shot to his, a lock of her golden hair dancing across her forehead while the rest remained pulled back in a loose chignon. "My drawing?"

"Yes, if you have no objection. Feel free to refuse me, if you wish." He smiled as gently as he knew how, a tactic that had worked on his sister on occasion.

She looked down at the leatherbound book in her hand, her thumb still holding the page. "Very well, though it isn't done yet." She stepped closer and opened the book, showing him her work.

It was an extraordinary likeness. Every craggy rock face in its exact form, every path perfectly illustrated as it moved down to the beach, every blade of grass in its proper place. Had he never seen this spot, Clara's drawing would have proved enough of an illustration that he should know the place even from a distance.

"I wanted to get as much of it done as I could before the storm, you see," Clara told him, her charcoal stained fingers tracing over hastily drawn marks on the beach portion of her page. "Then I would be able to paint it at my leisure later, knowing the details are correct."

"Not only correct," Hawk told her in shock, "but bloody perfect." He tugged the book gently, hoping she would release it. When she did, he turned and held the page out to compare it to the exact scene before him, his eyes flicking between each. "My word, Clara, you've captured it with such precision, I don't know that God himself could do better."

He turned back to her, holding the book out. She took it, her cheeks gaining more color still. "God certainly could, Your Grace, and has done. He is the Creator, and I only an appreciator of his fine work."

He indicated the book as she thumbed through the pages. "Do you have more like that?"

Clara's lips finally curved into a slight smile. "Like that? No, I rarely have a chance to sketch such nature. But I do have…" She flipped a few pages and showed him a portrait, the likeness equally uncanny.

"Your aunt," Hawk said on a light laugh. "Just as she is, I'd say. Did she approve of it?"

"She thinks I was too kind to her jawline," Clara admitted, her smallest finger tracing it. "But I'm fairly confident in it."

Hawk shook his head in disbelief. "You mentioned you had some talent in art, but I am used to that sort of claim from all accomplished women, so I admit to discrediting it. I never imagined... Clara, it's extraordinary work!"

"Thank you." She smiled up at him, a sudden heat catching in the center of his chest at the sight of it.

She did not protest against her skill, and she did not explain how she had gained such talents, or whom she had learned from. She simply acknowledged his praise for what it was, and left the thing at that.

It was utterly refreshing.

The sky cracked overhead, rumbling once more with the reminder of impending storms, a gust of wind whipping across them both.

"We'd better get inside," Hawk told her, moving behind her to pick up the stool. "We don't want to see your work destroyed by the rain!"

"Thank you," Clara said once the stool was in his hold and they began walking the path back. "And believe me, I've had more diaries of sketches ruined than I can count from one thing or another. Some were a very great loss, others not at all."

Hawk indicated the book with his free hand. "That, I can assure you, would be a very great loss."

Clara only shrugged, such a charming and natural action from a woman he would have thought so very fine in manners. "Perhaps. But I could do it again."

"Such confidence," Hawk murmured with a shake of his head as he looked up the path as they walked.

"I should have more modesty, I know," Clara mused, tucking the dancing strand of hair behind her ear.

"No, not at all." This time he shook his head more firmly. "I wasn't implying confidence with arrogance or bravado there. I was thinking only of your confidence in your abilities. You know that you can recreate something you have done, should the original be lost. That is a gift and a blessing, I think. The skill itself and the awareness of it."

Clara's brow puckered as she held the book to her chest. "Yes, I suppose it is. I wouldn't have said so before, but practice has proven that I can do so. What else could it be but confidence?" Her brow cleared and her smile turned wry. "I have so little confidence in other regards in my life, at least I can claim that one."

Hawk chuckled drily. "I'd say you're more fortunate than most to even have one. Who of any of us has confidence in our life?"

"Are you confusing confidence with certainty?" She stepped in front of him as the path narrowed for a few paces, then moved aside for him to join her when it widened. "None of us have that, you know."

"I am well aware," he assured her. "And I do mean confidence. Position and wealth have not given me talents in which I have confidence, only responsibilities to live by. For all of that, the only thing I can say I have confidence in is my ability to breathe in and out, thus keeping myself alive."

Clara made a brief humming noise he could not translate. "I don't know you well enough to protest your own knowledge of yourself, Hawk, or I would do so for fear of you venturing into melancholy."

He had to laugh at that, and at the strange tickling sensation her use of his name brought. It occurred to him that he'd been calling her Clara for the last few minutes without realizing it, though she certainly must have noticed. She had not reacted to it, nor had she reminded him of propriety.

There was some comfort in that, and in leveling the ground between them. It was so rare he could do so with anyone, let alone a woman, and he found it suited him well.

"Not melancholy, Clara," he told her, intentionally using her name this time, though he was careful not to emphasize it. "You'll not find me emotional as regards my own person. I am perfectly aware of the boredom I present to anyone, including myself."

Clara coughed a startled laugh that instantly prompted a smile from him, the sound somehow more delightful for being out in nature rather than in the walls of Kirkleigh. "Who would accuse you of boredom? I've known you all of a day, and I've not had wandering thoughts yet."

He gave her a scolding look. "A day, Clara? We've known each other a good deal longer."

She looked away quickly, drumming her fingers along the book she held. "You know what I mean, Hawk. You can hardly say we knew each other then."

"No, I suppose not," he admitted, wincing when thunder clapped again. "We'd best hurry, or we'll soon be drenched."

Nodding, Clara quickened her pace beside him. "What were you doing that required you to dress like this? Did a horse throw a shoe?"

Hawk grinned at the idea as raindrops began to fall. "No, I was helping my tenants with winter preparations."

Clara stumbled and Hawk was quick to snatch her arm to steady her. "What?" she squawked as she straightened, nodding her thanks. "Helping? How?"

"However was needed," he answered with a shrug. "Today, it was sawing rails for fences and mending cottage roofs. Tomorrow, it will likely be different, and had I been here a few months ago, I might have been a help in the harvesting."

"Do you know how few gentlemen of high station would be found doing such a task?" Clara grinned up at him, a sight he was entirely unprepared for. "What a marvelous thing! Do you do that often?"

The delight in her voice was unmistakable, and the warmth he'd felt in his chest before was now pulsing into his limbs. "Only recently," he admitted with a sheepish smile. "I needed an occupation while I visit my estates, and manual tasks not intended for one in my position have proven to be a most gratifying way to spend my time. And shocking my tenants and estate agents has been an added amusement."

"I can imagine so!" She squealed as the rain began to fall in earnest and, with a laugh, darted ahead, running madly for the house.

Hawk watched her go with a wild grin, then chased after her, reaching the now open door to the kitchens just before the drops of rain became large and furious. Mrs. Perkins, the cook, smiled in greeting, but made no mention of his appearance or Clara's.

He smiled at the breathless Clara, her hair now in complete disarray, though she was still as lovely as he had seen her yet. He turned to watch the water pound against the ground, and smiled when Clara came up beside him to do the same.

"That would have ruined your book," he said simply, inclining his head towards the storm.

"I would have gone to the bookshop and asked for another collection of foolscap to be bound in cheap leather," came her unconcerned reply. "Just as I've done for years. And then I would have gone out to draw again."

Hawk glanced at her, leaning his arm on the doorjamb to do so. "And what would you have drawn? The same scene?"

Clara narrowed her eyes out at the storm, as though she could see all the options through the falling rain. "No, I don't think so. If the storm had stayed away, I think I would have gone down to the beach next. Looked at the coves and caves, explored them until I could draw them from memory, perhaps walked in the water as it rolled onto the shore. Not that it would have added anything to my art to do so, but simply to say that I have…"

There was no helping the smile that crossed his face as she spoke, the scene she painted one his mind was only too happy to dwell upon.

"But even if I could only have my stool and my diary and my pencil," she went on, nodding to herself, "I'd be content to simply find the perfect spot on the beach and capture the whole of it to my page."

"I'll take you," Hawk said before he could think anything else. "Tomorrow, I'll take you down to the beach, and you can do all of that."

Clara smiled at him, her eyes brightening. "We couldn't go alone, Hawk."

He waved that off. "Your aunt and Nat can come, that is no obstacle."

"And your work with your tenants?"

That brought him up short. Above all else, he would insist upon being a man of honor who stood by his word. He could not go back on his commitment, and would not.

"I'll do a good half day of work there," he decided, flashing a quick smile at her. "The afternoon will be entirely devoted to the beach excursion."

Her eyes searched his, a frankness in them that he liked a great deal. "You're certain? You can spare the time?"

There was nothing to do but smile in the face of such a question, considering he wanted nothing more than to do exactly as she asked. "Quite certain. I will have all the time in the world."

Chapter Nine

"You clever kitten, I'm amazed you managed this."

Clara scrubbed at her fingers in the wash bin, grinding the bar of soap against the impossible stains she had managed to acquire the day before in her drawing efforts. "Managed what? To permanently stain my fingers with charcoal? Oh, blast this soap, it's useless!"

"No, silly girl, the seaside picnic with Kirklin this afternoon! A stroke of genius, Clara!"

Her scrubbing stopped, and she blinked at her still stained hands, the sound of water dripping into the bowl almost matching the beat of her heart. "Why is that genius? It doesn't mean anything, Aunt Fern, he's just showing it to me so that I may draw it."

There was a quick rustling of skirts and Phoebe appeared through the adjoining door, somehow pristine in appearance despite the fact that she was still in the process of getting ready. Her beauty was no less apparent for the disapproving scowl she wore for Clara alone. "I shall have to retract my declaration of your being both clever and a genius, my dear. I mean precisely that, getting down to the beach and coves so that you, with your talents, might capture them! What in the world would be the use in going down there if not for that?"

"Right," Clara said quickly, her toes turning cold as she realized the direction her thoughts had taken her rather than where they ought to have gone. "Right. Sorry, I'm simply distracted by these stains." She turned back to her fingers, hoping her blushing would be taken as a sign of effort rather than embarrassment. "This is why I rarely use charcoal. Were I at my leisure, I should paint these things, but alas…"

"The sacrifice of your elegant and nimble fingers will be much appreciated, I am sure." Phoebe huffed and turned back to her own room. "But this will work to our benefit regardless! And make it all the better for when we return home tomorrow."

Clara bit down on her lip hard, the thought of departing so soon exquisitely painful.

Kirkleigh had become something magical to her. A place where anything was possible, and warmth would abound in every memory. She had taken to wandering the corridors every night, and though she had not spent hours doing so, she felt she knew the house better than she'd known the house she was raised in. And there was still more to explore.

They could come back, she reminded herself. If her information proved useful, they would receive more information from the superiors and be able to return to Kirkleigh repeatedly, if not for an extended time.

Kirklin had already agreed they could come back without inquiring of him. But would Kirkleigh be the same without the present duke in residence?

Kirklin…

Hawk…

Thinking about the day she'd had yesterday, the interaction she'd had with the man before the rainstorm, she recollected that she had called him Hawk without intending it. Her face flamed at the memory, though in the moment, she'd not even recognized the thing. It had simply seemed the natural course of conversation.

He'd called her Clara.

That was too easy to ignore, given their history. They were practically cousins, she was sure, so why should he not defy the niceties?

He could forego them. She could not.

Alexandra Moore, perhaps, could do so. Clara Harlow could do nothing of the sort.

The fact that Clara Harlow presently *was* Alexandra Moore only made everything more confusing.

Clara shook her head now and moved away from the wash bin,

giving up on her fingers becoming clean in advance of their beach excursion. She was only going to get them more dirty, and the only people she would see were Hawk, Nat, and her aunt. No one would be kissing her fingers, and no one would truly care that they were stained.

She was hardly heading into the Marriage Mart like this. Or in any way. Not anymore.

Not ever again.

A sharp sting shot across her chest at the memories, years old though they were, and she sniffed, if only to distract herself from them. She refused to think about Louis, or her once-broken heart, or the scandal that had surrounded the whole affair, though nothing scandalous had happened.

Unless one counted jilting an innocent girl scandalous.

No one had seemed to find her faultless, let alone innocent, but that was the way of things.

She'd moved on well enough, and her role at the school was far more rewarding than she could have imagined life for herself after that.

Would Pippa let her teach for a week or two before she came back to Kirkleigh on assignment? She was almost desperate for a taste of her usual self, and to see the progress her students had made. Those teaching in her place were more than capable of doing so, but Clara did so love teaching the girls herself.

And she ached to paint freely again.

"Do hurry up, Clara!" Phoebe called from her room. "We mustn't miss the tide!"

Clara scowled as she shucked off her morning gown. "What in the world do you know of tides, hmm? Sailed much? Bit of fishing, perhaps? Or only fond of sea bathing? But no, no, no, we mustn't miss tides in the afternoon."

She shook her head and turned to her wardrobe, stopping short at the sight of Phoebe standing there, arms folded, brow raised.

"Bother," Clara muttered, her face flaming. "I am sorry…"

Phoebe actually smiled at that, and it was the most natural smile Clara had seen on the woman's face in years. "Irked you, have I? Lovely, always a pleasure. Come, let me help you find a suitable gown."

That was all? No scolding or offended airs? She found it… amusing?

Clara looked at her friend-turned-aunt in bewilderment. "Suitable?" she inquired, opting to continue the conversation Phoebe had begun rather than discussing her rant. "What must be suitable about it?"

"You'd be surprised, dear," Phoebe told her as she looked through the gowns. "Down by the water, there's bound to be a chill, so you will want something that is not too thin. You may find the hem gets damp in the water without trying, so you will want something that is not too sheer. And this is an informal occasion among friends, so you will want something comfortable. Given that there are two eligible men, it also would behoove us to put you in something fetching."

"Aunt Fern!" Clara protested, hands on her hips. "That should not come into it!"

Phoebe grinned at her over her shoulder. "That should always come into it, even if not part of the greater aims. Might as well have some fun with it, Clara, while you can."

Clara shook her head, closing her eyes in abject mortification. "I am long past that, Aunt."

"Until you've reached the grave, you are never past that."

Her eyes snapped open in surprise. "Not even you?"

Phoebe pulled a gown out of the wardrobe, holding it out to examine. "That should do nicely. Very seaside appropriate."

It was a cream calico with a blue striped pattern that extended into a blue ribbon band at the hem, a matching ribbon at the waist, and nothing extraordinary about it.

"That one?" Clara said, ignoring Phoebe's blatant avoidance of her comment. "Why?"

Phoebe glanced over at her. "Because I have a fetching hat to match, and you'll look a picture without intentionally looking a picture."

"Are we not intentionally making me look a picture?" Clara asked her, grinning as Phoebe began to undo the buttons on the back.

"Hush. Arms up."

Obediently, Clara did so, holding still as the dress passed over her head, her arms slipping into the sleeves. She turned for Phoebe to do up the buttons and tie the ribbon and fumbled aimlessly with the ends of her long plait.

She glanced at her hair, pursing her lips. "What about my hair? This is hardly attractive."

Phoebe turned her about, looking at it. "On the contrary, it's charming. The wind will undo too much finery, and the hat will hide too much intricacy. Nancy!"

The maid who had helped Clara with her hair every evening hurried in, though how she had anticipated being needed was beyond Clara's understanding. "Yes, Mrs. Daniels?"

"Might we pin up Miss Moore's lovely plait into something attractive at her neck, perhaps?" She twisted Clara's plait to demonstrate, offering the maid a questioning look. "Her hat would hide anything higher up, and it must be free from her face."

"Yes, ma'am." Nancy came around to join her, consulting in low tones. "Perhaps this way, madam."

Clara gave up being concerned about her hair, or, indeed, any aspect of her appearance for the day. It would not matter, at any rate.

She needed to get down to the beach, draw it, and breathe in the glories of the seaside before her life either became the enjoyable tedium it had once been or the uncertain encumbrance it had the potential to be.

It could very well be the last day when her thoughts could almost entirely focus on the experience at hand. Yes, she had a task to accomplish, but, for the moment, her task was entirely artistic.

And that was simple enough for her.

Clara glanced down at her skirts. "Nancy, will there be much difficulty in getting a charcoal stain out of this fabric?"

Nancy rubbed a bit of the fabric between her fingers. "I shouldn't think so, miss. I wouldn't advise staining it if you can help it, but it should be safe enough."

"Well, I don't intend to stain it," Clara told the girl with a laugh, "but it does tend to happen with this specific medium."

"Perfect!" Phoebe praised, clapping her hands. "Your hair is perfect. Now come, let's get your hat and be on our way!"

Clara shrugged and followed, shaking her head in amusement. Why Phoebe was so enthused about this outing, Clara couldn't have said. There was nothing in it for her but chaperoning Clara.

It was up to Clara to perfectly capture what they saw on this excursion.

Her supplies were all packed, and now she was dressed as perfectly as others deemed she must be, so there was nothing for it but to meet the men and walk down.

She could not help but to smile at that.

Hawk and Nat were the most companionable men she had ever associated with, including her former intended. Louis had taken her breath away, but, in retrospect, he had never been a real friend to her. She could never have just sat and had a conversation with him. Not really.

She'd had supper with Hawk and Nat twice now, and both times had been full of conversation without any effort. Nat was certainly the more social of the pair, but Hawk had an intensity to his engagement with others that Clara found particularly enjoyable. She could easily imagine a quiet conversation in a parlor with him or walking along a path together and laughing about something or other. None of it would have to mean anything, it would still be enjoyable.

Of course, if it *were* to mean something…

She shook her head quickly as she and Phoebe hurried to the back of the house, where they had arranged to meet the others. As attractive and kind as the Duke of Kirklin was, there was no use in taking meaning in anything he said or did. There was only harm in thinking anything remotely whimsical where he was concerned.

And she knew better.

"Clara," Phoebe hissed as they caught sight of the men on the terrace. "Your ribbons!"

Grumbling, Clara handed over her diary and her set of pencils before tugging at her ribbons and forcing them into some semblance of a knot. "Sometimes, it really does feel as though you are my aunt, you know."

"It is my pleasure, to be sure," Phoebe chirped, putting Clara's supplies under her arm to adjust the ends of her askew bow to make it seem less haphazard.

"That wasn't what I meant," Clara told her, though she had to smile at it.

Phoebe gave her a sidelong look as she handed Clara's supplies back to her. "Interpretation is an art, my dear. You'll learn that very shortly, mark my words." She turned her attention to the men ahead of her and brightened while also sliding her formal mask into place. "Ah, gentlemen! So sorry to have kept you waiting."

"Not at all," Hawk said in an almost rumbling manner, his smile slight, but undeniably present. "You are right on time." His dark eyes flicked to Clara, and he held up the stool from the day before as his smile quirked. "Shall we?"

Clara nodded eagerly, heat beginning to tingle in the tips of her toes and the backs of her knees.

"Excellent!" Nat boomed, gesturing for them to lead the way, an easel under one of his arms. "I am curious indeed to see your abilities in the flesh, Clara. Hawk has assured me he's never seen anything finer, and you had best believe the pair of us are rather sticklers where art is concerned."

Hawk rolled his eyes and nudged his head towards the stairs of the terrace. "We'd better start down or he'll grow too ridiculous for company."

Their joking, jovial manner continued the entire walk from the estate to the coast, laughter ringing from most of them repeatedly. Hawk did not seem particularly inclined to laugh, but his smile never wavered.

Clara desperately wanted to hear him laugh, if only she could determine how.

The path down to the beach itself was rougher terrain, though each of them managed well enough. Hawk led the group and Nat took up position at the end for safety, and both checked on the ladies with a rapidity that bordered on amusing. But Clara and Phoebe were not dainty women who feared a bit of dirt or nature, so no assistance was needed at any time.

When they finally reached the soft sand of the beach, Clara breathed in a deep gulp of the seaside air, the fresh, briny smell of it mingling with sunshine in a heady fragrance indeed. Even the sound of the sea rolling into the rocks was music to her ears, the chorus of waves receding after their crashing arrival something out of a fantasy, a great creature breathing in and out with such glorious songs.

"We may never get her away from the seaside, Your Grace."

Clara opened her eyes, not realizing she had closed them, nor that she had stopped and halted the progress of the rest, but all looked at her with varying levels of amusement.

Hawk looked the most blank-faced of the group, but that maddeningly small smile remained.

What in heaven's name did that mean?

"One would think you had never seen the seaside before, Miss Moore," Nat teased, the wind whipping his golden hair into slight dishevelment.

I haven't, she nearly said, biting it back just in time. "It's been so long," she told them instead, "it feels as though I haven't."

Hawk made a soft noise that she hadn't a hope of deciphering and gestured for her to go on. "The coves are this way. I'll show you the best spots."

More embarrassed than excited, Clara nodded, moving in the direction he indicated, slowing to let him lead.

He fell into step beside her rather than moving ahead, and she chanced a glance over at him. His hair rustled in the breeze, and somehow the coat he wore seemed unnecessary for the setting. It ought to have been more relaxed, more informal, and completely unadorned. He was not dressed in overt finery, but he could have entered the finest drawing rooms in London without raising any questions.

"How was your morning, Your Grace?" Clara heard herself ask, keeping her voice low so the others would not hear. "Did you accomplish all that you hoped?"

He cast a look over at her, expression as composed as ever, his smile quirking just a little broader than it had been. "I forgot we discussed that yesterday. Yes, we got a great deal of work done. There seems to be more to do, but it is all in hand." He looked down at his hands, his smile spreading further still in a wry expression. "I seem to have proven my lifetime of softness." He held up the palms of his hands for her to see.

In the center of each palm sat an angry, red, raw patch of flesh, not particularly deep, but certainly inflamed. There were two or three smaller matching marks at the base of some of his fingers, and each of them had peeling layers of skin at the edges.

"Hawk!" Clara winced, shaking her head. "Those look so painful, why aren't they bound?"

He shrugged, looking down at them again. "Eventually, they will toughen up, and it will take much more to injure them like this again. If I wish to continue working on my estates, and I do, the soft hands will have to go."

Clara had to chuckle at that. "No one will think your hands are those of a duke again."

He quietly laughed once himself. "When I meet someone who has made a study of the hands of dukes, I'll see what they make of mine. Until then, these are the hands of this duke, and I feel better for them."

What a statement to make. Clara would have given a great deal to press further into that, to understand what prompted such a feeling behind those words, but restraint pulled at her.

She was not the Miss Moore he thought she was. She had no right to his privacy, and her curiosity could not lead her. Not in this.

Before the moment could pass, Clara glanced down at her own hands, and smiled quickly. "Well, these are the hands of an artist, I suppose." She held hers up for his inspection. "Believe me, I've tried everything to remove the stains, but alas…"

Hawk's smile changed once more, this time something crooked and easy. He took her hand, surprising her, and eyed the smudged stains carefully. "It may not pass muster with high Society matrons," he told her, "but it suits you."

His thumb rubbed against the stain on the outside of her palm, setting fire to her skin and making her breath catch.

He looked at his thumb after for inspection, grunting once. "I'd have thought it would spread to my skin, but no, clean as can be." He released her hand, still smiling freely.

Clara's skittering heart slowly thumped back to its normal pace, her neck beginning to cool, though the skin of her hand was still painfully sensitive. He hadn't known what he was doing to her, he'd been examining her as one might a fascinating insect or flower. She bit back a strange jolt of disappointment for that and settled herself with the thought of his comfort with her being what it was.

He might not have realized it, but he had proven it.

"Ah, here we are," he announced before she could think of anything else to say.

Clara looked up and forced a smile at the sight.

Walls of white stone reached up to the sky, patches of grass dotting here and there before the summit, where grass and wildflowers hung over the edges. Within those pillars of stone, there were large caves and small caves, smaller rocks and pebbles dotting the ground around the entrances to each, accompanied by puddles and streams making their marks in the sand. It was a private nook of coastline, though the sand extended out past their pathway further down the coast. She could have walked along it, her feet in the water, and probably gotten to the next estate, however far away that was.

The temptation to do so was suddenly overwhelming.

She looked back at the present caves and cove, eyeing them with an artist's perspective. Setting her materials down on a flat rock nearby, she moved closer to the caves. "How deep do they go?" she asked, stepping on rocks and hopping between a few to get closer.

"Clara, be careful!" Phoebe called, content to hang back, as Aunt Fern undoubtedly would in this situation.

Glancing over at her, Clara grinned. "What, in case I should turn an ankle?"

She heard Hawk's low chuckle, and it rippled up her spine with a warmth that made her sigh. "Well, my brother and I did have our share of slips and falls on these rocks. More than one pair of breeches gained some holes from such adventures." He came over to her at the mouth of one rather shallow cave. "Did you never come down here yourself?"

Blast.

Clara shook her head, making a face. "Perhaps once? Twice at the very most. Uncle Kirklin did not care for this beach. We went to other, more fashionable beaches. Safer ones, he called them."

She waited, praying he would believe the blatant lie.

"That sounds like him," Hawk said at last with a sage nod. "I imagine he took you to the beach at Barcliffe instead. The Brownings have always been very open with their lands in that regard. Did you ever see the mass of fishing boats land there?"

Something about the statement piqued Clara's interest and she shook her head again, smiling broadly. "No! They land ships on their beach?"

Hawk grinned. "They do, though I'm hesitant to show it to you, since my own beach will apparently be found wanting by comparison. Never land any boats here, unless they are lost or part of a shipwreck."

Clara groaned and looked around her. "I shouldn't think anything is wanting here. This is so picturesque! Who needs ships anyway?" She continued on, heading for the next cave over, this one only large enough for children. "Goodness, did you climb in there?"

"Never. I left that for Griffin, and he used to hide in here often." Hawk went around her to the next cove, then turned and leaned his shoulder against the stone. "And if you turn right at this spot…" He pointed towards the beach. "You will find the perfect view of the sea."

Clara turned where she was, only for her arm to be gently pulled.

"No, no, right here," he urged gently. "This spot. Otherwise, the cliff is in the way of the view."

She let herself be tugged over and felt her heart leap into the base of her throat when he placed her directly in front of himself. His arm came over her shoulder, pointing at a very specific angle. "See there?"

Clara nodded hastily, though her vision was slightly hazy at the moment. She blinked to clear it, then blinked again when she truly saw it.

"Good heavens," she whispered, her breathlessness having nothing to do with the man behind her and everything to do with the scene before her. "It's perfection."

"Capture that, Clara," Hawk murmured, his hand sliding back by his side, brushing her shoulder as it did so. "The far end of the Barcliffe crags are there, and it's the only place on my property to glimpse it. I don't envy much on that estate, but if I could have their coastline on this estate instead, there would be no reason to have any other."

"I want to see it," Clara breathed, gasping with the desire to do just that. "I want to see all of this."

Hawk laughed softly again, the sound deeper and more delicious from this proximity than it was before. "Then you'd better get started, hadn't you? I'll walk you to as many locations as I can for you to draw before the light runs out."

Clara looked at him over her shoulder, leaning slightly for a more direct connection. "I'll hold you to that, Your Grace. And I'll not skimp on the art of each, either."

His eyes crinkled on a smile at her. "I look forward to seeing your efforts, then." He turned slightly, cupping a hand around his mouth. "Nat! Bring Miss Moore's supplies and the stool! She has work to do!"

Chapter Ten

Watching Clara work was nearly as satisfying as seeing the magnificence of her finished project. It was an art of its own, seeing her capture a scene on the page, and even if he were not looking at the page, he would still have considered the scene before him as art.

There was nothing remarkable about the way she was dressed, which he greatly appreciated, as it allowed the true nature, beauty, and essence of Clara to shine. She needed no adornment to be lovely, and the more he watched, the more he believed it.

She was on her third drawing of the afternoon, having perfected the Kirkleigh beach and Hawk's perfect view, and Hawk was fairly certain he was the only one paying any attention now.

Nat dozed on the sand, hands behind his head, cravat over his eyes. Mrs. Daniels sat on a large rock with a book. Neither of them seemed in any way perturbed by the lack of activities to entertain them at the present.

Hawk was glad for it, but the point was also irrelevant. He'd have stayed here to allow Clara her time to draw even if the others had demanded they return to the house.

He wasn't even certain what Clara was drawing at this point, not that it mattered. She was so talented, he'd have been fascinated by her taking the likeness of an open field. They'd moved further down the beach towards the Barcliffe property, finding a perfect view of the beach as a whole, with even the faint image of the house itself atop the cliffs visible to the naked eye. Clara's excitement about the scene had been just as evident, her teeth sinking into the fullness of her bottom lip as her bright hazel eyes darted here and there, taking in every particular of the cliffside and the beach before her.

Hawk did not blame her for such a reaction. Even he could admit that it was a beautiful sight, and with the day being so fine, it was something out of a dream. But he could also admit that he likely had never seen it with the same appreciation he had today. Everything was new, rare, and stirring, and while he might not have any artistic ability by any stretch of imaginations, he could see the opportunity for any hands that were so talented.

Clara's hands, for example.

He was not presently sitting close enough to watch her hands now, but he had been when she had drawn his beach.

Their beach.

Something within his chest leapt at the notion, finding a primal satisfaction in the statement, even if he'd only meant it in the most basic sense of the phrase. If he'd been thinking about the notion of Kirkleigh as a home, it would be both his beach and her beach. If he'd been thinking about use of the beach, it would have been his and Griffin's. There was not another way to look at it for now, but with the other two occupied, he could almost imagine that he and Clara were on this beach together.

Alone.

Why did that seem like such an appealing idea?

He'd only spent three days with the woman, and he'd been away for a great deal of the day working on the estate, as he had planned to. But coming home to Kirkleigh after had seemed somehow more glorious knowing she would be there. Dining with her had been easier than dining with his own siblings at times. There was never a lag in conversation, and yet there was never anything akin to chatter happening.

She was fascinated by a great many things, possessed an innate curiosity that ought to have meant she was bored to tears in his presence. Yet she never appeared so. Never once had she taken on airs or been in any way dismissive. She was always warm, always open, always engaged, and he was very much enjoying the sight of any smile she would give.

Each one seemed somehow priceless, despite the fact that there always seemed to be a smile of some sort on her lips.

When she was engaged in her art, as she was now, there was one particular smile that captivated him. It was soft, relaxed, and perfectly contented. Almost whimsical, even faraway, but she was perfectly present. No breeze unsettled her, no passing cloud made her frown, and it was rare that she even paused in her work.

Extraordinary talent, and an extraordinary woman.

Had he ever known this before? About her, or any woman at all? What was it that he knew?

What was it he felt?

He shifted his position against the nearest cliffside wall as Clara reached up and pulled her wide straw hat off, tucking the ribbons into it as she set it aside. She tossed her hair, though it was pinned up, and seemed to sigh at having her head unencumbered. Something about the action made Hawk smile, and the looseness of the pins in her hair became ever more evident when a gust of wind rolled across them from the sea.

Tendrils of deep golden hair began to wave on the air, the coil of plaited tresses sinking against her neck as a pin fell to the sand behind Clara's stool.

She did not seem to notice.

Her lips pulled to one side as she eyed her subject, and the end of one charcoal pencil tapped against the page.

Hawk waited a moment as he watched Clara, saw her brow wrinkle a little, noticed how her lips pulled in very slightly. She was considering something, trying to find a solution to whatever the problem was, and when her eyes narrowed, he chuckled to himself.

She heard the sound and glanced over at him, flashing a smile that caught him in the gut. "What?"

He shrugged, a rather new motion he'd adopted that seemed to come naturally in her presence. "You've decided something, and I'm intrigued to discover what it is."

"You noticed?" She tossed her head back on a dancing laugh, and Hawk forgot to breathe.

Had he ever noticed the turn of a woman's throat before? It seemed an odd part of any anatomy to focus on, but with such a laugh, her fragile setting of hair dangling precariously, her throat was on full and perfect display. It was impossible not to notice.

And it was lovely.

Hawk swallowed once and tried for his usual manner and sense. "I've been watching you work. I hope you don't mind."

She beamed, the laughter still dancing in her eyes. "Not in the least, though I don't know how it could be an enjoyable pastime for you." She looked at Nat, still sprawled inelegantly on the sand and attempting to sleep. "I've bored him into slumber."

"He's a man of minimal taste," Hawk assured her in as serious a tone as he could.

Clara scoffed a short laugh and looked over at her aunt, her smile softening. "Aunt Fern seems content. She's seen me draw often enough, the novelty is long gone."

"Pity," Hawk mused, not sparing a glance for the aunt, lovely woman though she was. "With the variety in subject and in medium, I should think nothing ever remotely repetitious."

Hazel eyes came back to his, full lips pursing just a little.

Perhaps he had gone too far in his compliments, making himself in some way a fool. The sting of it was that his flattery was anything but.

It was blatant, honest, raw truth.

And he had no manner of retreat, should he need it.

"Do you want to know what I was considering?" Clara suddenly asked, her voice lowering.

Holding his breath, Hawk nodded.

She waved him over, and he was moving with an attentiveness that he'd have called pathetic in any other man. He crouched beside her, putting his eyeline nearly of a height with hers.

"I have an excellent view of a great many things," she explained as she gestured towards the Barcliffe beach, cliffside, rocks, coves, and the wildflowers dotting various ledges. "But there is one aspect that I do not get where I am. Can you guess it?"

Being this close to her, feeling stray tendrils of her hair slap against his skin, inhaling the fresh, lightly floral scent of her, he couldn't very well guess his own name, let alone something she couldn't see.

Again, pathetic in anyone else.

Not pathetic now.

He blinked his eyes and forced himself to focus, to see the setting before him as an artist would have and wondering what would puzzle them.

It took long enough that his cheeks began to heat, but then at last, he noticed.

"The depth of the water," he answered with some relief. "The waves as they are make that unclear, and with the pillared island there, the perspective is skewed."

Clara nodded, leaning to the side to smile directly at him. "Very good, Your Grace. An eye for detail, I see."

"Depends on the detail," he muttered, pushing to his feet and setting his hands to his hips as he looked at the problem Clara had spotted. "The only thing I can think of to solve your dilemma is to get closer and get higher."

"Is that even a possibility?" She rose herself, tucking a few of her flying strands behind an ear. "It is your neighbor's property, after all."

Hawk thought about that, then shook his head. "I believe so. As I said, the Brownings are very generous with their beach. When they see your art, I'd think they'd be enchanted you'd take an interest in their land."

Clara laughed softly and peered up at him. "Remind me to have you do the talking if we happen to meet them."

We?

A rough swallow tugged at his throat, and Hawk found himself nodding. "I see a ledge not too far down the beach that should be high enough to get your proper vantage, and a decent enough path to get there. If you're feeling up to venturing." He glanced down at her, raising a brow.

Her smug smile was a delightful sight. "Let us venture, Your Grace."

Hawk offered an arm playfully, which was not an emotion he had known in some time, and Clara took it without hesitation. They began to stroll along the sand when Hawk looked behind them. "Should we not inform your aunt?"

Clara turned and waved to her aunt, then returned her attention ahead of them. "There. She knows."

There was nothing to do but laugh at such antics, and at the complete abandonment of strictly-adhered-to principles of Society and polite behavior. The two of them wandering away from their party without chaperone ought to have been scandalous and entirely unheard of, yet there was no sign of reluctance or reticence, and even Mrs. Daniels was not crying out in protest against it.

Of course, they would be in decently plain sight of her still, but she could not know their exact destination.

What a strange pair these two women were, and what a strange effect they were having on him.

Well, one of them, anyway.

Clara sighed and looked out at the sea, smiling blissfully. "I love the sea. I didn't know that before today, but I should be quite content to live by the seaside forever."

"Should you?" Hawk asked, more curious about the admission than he ought to have been. "What about it do you find so enchanting?"

She hummed to herself as she thought. "The near-constant breeze is refreshing, the sound of the waves soothing to my ears, and the cliffs absolutely stirring to behold. Look at the wildflowers." She pointed to various terraced ledges along the face of the cliffs where hardy wildflowers still lingered despite the approaching winter. "How can anything grow there? And especially how can anything beautiful do so?"

He saw what she saw, and again wondered that he had never seen it. He shook his head and had to look at her once more. "You have a perfectly refreshing view of things, Clara Moore."

Something about that made her laugh. "I have a very singular way of looking at things, Hawk, and that is all that can be said for me. A great deal of it is ignorance, but there it is. Oh!"

He paused as she pulled him to a stop and stooped, tugging at the laces of her boots. "Clara, what in the world are you doing?"

"I swore to myself that I would dip my toes in the water," she said simply, balancing on one foot as she tugged off a stocking. She tucked it back into her boot, then did the same with the other.

Hawk ought to have looked away, bare ankles and feet seeming an inappropriate sight on a lady, though he wasn't sure why, but he was so enchanted by her reasoning, he barely noticed the impropriety until she was standing before him in bare feet, a bit of her skirts held in one hand to keep the hem from the sand.

"Hmm." Clara frowned down at her boots, her drawing supplies in the hand looped through Hawk's arm, and the hand occupying fabric at the present. "I think I'd best leave those here for now."

"Nonsense." Hawk bent and picked them up, smiling at her freely. "I am perfectly capable of carrying a lady's footwear, I'll have you know."

She giggled and curtseyed as perfectly as any woman in a ballroom. "Thank you, Your Grace. Now, if you wouldn't mind escorting me closer to the water…"

He'd have escorted her to the East Indies on foot if she continued to smile at him like that. But he only inclined his head and steered them over to the water's edge.

Clara tentatively dipped the toes of one foot into the water, shivering against Hawk as she did so. She laughed very softly to herself and immersed her foot entirely.

"There," she murmured as she swirled the water around gently. "Now I truly feel as though I have been here."

Her words stirred something in Hawk, and he gazed at her with a strange longing that ached deep into his soul. There was a finality and farewell in her statement, and her imminent departure on the morrow suddenly loomed before him. She would be gone, and with her, the magic that had begun to inhabit Kirkleigh. The fondness he'd started to feel for a place he'd never truly cared about. The sense of belonging he'd felt lingering about his person of late that had been so lacking in much of his life.

There was nothing particularly enchanting about Kirkleigh, perfectly situated though it was.

Clara, on the other hand, was everything enchanting.

And he was so very enchanted.

His breath escaped from him in a rush, and he swallowed with difficulty. Slowly, not wanting to startle her, he moved his hand down to hers and pulled her diary and pencil set away from her, folding it beneath the arm holding her boots. Then, heart pounding, he returned his hand to hers, curving his fingers around hers with a hesitation that had him nearly trembling.

Clara's breathing stilled, and her eyes, still on her foot in the water, widened. He watched as she carefully wet her lips, as she blinked twice, then he smiled his way to a sigh when he felt pressure from her fingers against his.

The moment was so sweet, so tender, so exhilarating that it ought to have had a speech of sorts. Yet there were no words that came to mind, and certainly no words that he could speak.

There was just the connection between them, and, for a moment, he would swear that he could feel the beat of her heart through her palm.

He wondered if she could feel his, as well.

Clara lifted her head, careful not to look at him, and began to walk along the water as it rolled onto the sand. She kept a tight hold on Hawk's hand, tugging him along with her, and he was more than content to go. Nothing was said, and there was only the sound of the water, of Clara's steps, of the birds overhead.

It was a moment too perfect for words.

"Is that you, Kirklin?"

Hawk had never felt inclined to snarl at anyone or anything in his life, but the urge roared within him now. Had he not just thought...?

The irritated thought vanished when he caught sight of Mr. and Mrs. Browning walking along the beach towards them.

He forced his most polite smile and kept his hand closed around Clara's, more to steady his sudden burst of nerves than anything else.

If word spread around the established families in the area that he was in residence, invitations would flock towards him, and he still intended to leave in the coming days.

Especially when Clara was gone. What was the point of staying then?

"I thought that was you, Kirklin!" Mr. Browning crowed in jovial delight. "Oh, pardon me, I suppose I must call you Your Grace."

"Quite all right, Mr. Browning," Hawk assured him with a formal air. "You've known me since I was a boy."

"We have indeed!" Mrs. Browning squealed, the sound one belonging to a much rounder woman than she could ever be. Her eyes flicked to Clara. "And who might this be, then, Your Grace?"

Hawk cleared his throat. "Miss Alexandra Moore, Mrs. Browning, My late uncle's ward."

Mrs. Browning's eyes went shockingly round. "My heavens… Of course, it is! Oh, bless you, child, you've grown into such a beautiful woman!"

Clara blushed and curtseyed quickly. "Thank you, Mrs. Browning."

"You likely don't remember us," Mr. Browning blustered, smiling and giving Clara a wink. "We only truly met at the village festival in the spring, and your guardian rarely came."

"He had so many duties," Mrs. Browning added quickly, as though eager to defend the late duke, "and we know he would have come more if he could. But you were always a very pretty girl, Miss Moore. What brings you back to Kirkleigh?"

Hawk did not like probing, and he knew the Brownings were a good sort, but they were also notorious busybodies. That much he recollected.

"She is visiting the area and various friends," Hawk explained, squeezing Clara's hand in hopes of keeping her from having to answer. "Naturally, Kirkleigh is at her disposal. It was always more her home than mine."

"I hope you don't mind," Clara broke in, her voice taking on an apologetic note, "but I wanted to sketch your beautiful beach. Kirklin is helping me to find the best spot, but I don't wish to trespass."

"Not at all!" Mr. Browning boasted with enough volume to bring down rocks. "You are welcome to stroll and explore and sketch and do anything your heart desires. Our beach is at your disposal, Miss Moore." He winked again. "And you may stroll along the water's edge any time."

Clara dimpled a sweet smile that would have soothed a wild boar. "You are too kind."

Hawk nodded once and indicated the ledge they were heading for. "If you'll excuse us, Mr. Browning, Mrs. Browning, I must get Miss Moore up there to get some details done before we have to return to Kirkleigh. Our party is waiting for us, I'm afraid."

"Of course, of course!" Mr. Browning gestured to the cliffside as though they might wish to take turns at them all. "We'll just continue our daily walk, and you scribble away with all your fine accomplishment. Good day, Miss Moore. Good day, Your Grace." He tipped his hat and walked past them with his wife on his arm, the whispering beginning before they had gone more than a handful of paces.

Clara looked at Hawk, then the two of them burst into snickers, resuming their own walk with far more entertainment than before. The coiled plait of Clara's hair finally gave way, the plait now hanging loosely down her back in the same carefree manner Clara presently illustrated.

And it was utterly charming.

Hawk felt himself breathing easier, despite walking beside the captivating woman whose hand he still held, and whose child-like enthusiasm for walking in the sea somehow made him feel lighter.

"We need to go up," he told her, gesturing to the path. "Do you want your shoes?"

Clara shook her head and headed that way. "Not yet. I want to walk in the water on the way back to Aunt Fern and Nat. Do you mind?"

Hawk smiled at her, content now to let her lead them. "Not in the slightest."

Her smile back at him made him wish he'd offered something far more noble.

It was a steep walk up to the ledge, but not difficult, and Clara showed no trouble with it, nor hesitation. She released Hawk's hand when they reached their destination, leaving him feeling more chilled than the breeze off the water could have done, but her satisfied sigh and brilliant smile soothed him creditably.

"Do you see it?" she asked with an eagerness he loved. "Look!"

He came to stand beside her and found himself actually rather impressed.

The water was deceptively deep, for the most part, just a scant few yards from the shore itself. Not in a way that spanned the entire beach, but a good portion of it contained a sharp drop-off that would have been difficult to see from the surface.

"Remarkable," Hawk murmured, though he doubted he would have cared about any such thing before today.

Only with Clara's eyes could he have seen this.

"Thank you for bringing me here," Clara told him, her smile turning soft and almost shy. "The view is perfect."

Hawk looked at her for a long moment, the sight of her something wondrous and stirring, and heat began filling his chest, singeing a few of his ribs in the process. "Yes, it is."

Her eyes searched his, the meaning of his words unmistakable, and the slight quirk of her lips to one side nearly sent him striding to her and kissing her for all he was worth.

But something held him back.

Something he didn't understand.

And didn't particularly care for.

Clara reached for her diary and pencils, and he offered them up, their fingers brushing again as she took them.

The brief connection colored Clara's cheeks, and Hawk, for one, felt his throat tightening.

She turned back to the view to add the dimension of the depth of the water to her already perfect picture.

Hawk stared at her as she did so, admittedly with blatant interest, and also with some budding pain.

How could he bear having her leave tomorrow? How could she have come to mean so much in so short a time?

What was he going to do when she was gone?

He would have to find his reserve and restraint again by the time he bid her farewell. He needed to remind himself who he had been before, to some degree, if he wished to go on without feeling too much of a loss.

But he did not need to do any such thing right now.

For now, he would breathe in the sea air with her, and enjoy the stunning scene of this woman, fair hair dancing in the breeze, as she captured the beauties of nature with the skill of the heavens and the effortlessness of gods.

And he would smile at it.

Chapter Eleven

"*Miss* Harlow, Miss Bradford wants to know if you would be so good as to join her for luncheon today."

Clara blinked as she looked up from her blank canvas at the stout, pleasant-faced housekeeper of the school currently standing in the doorway of her unoccupied classroom. "Luncheon? Is it nearing that time?"

Mrs. Allendale gave her a pitying look, smiling a little. "Aye, Miss Harlow. Your last class has been done for over an hour now. Have you lost track of the time?"

Nodding, Clara reached behind her to tug at the strings of her heavy canvas apron, which she only donned for painting, and found herself amused by the slight emphasis Mrs. Allendale placed on the letter H in her speech. She'd never noticed it before, but now that she knew the little detail of Mrs. Allendale's connection to the covert world, it added to the colorful personality of the woman, and gave Clara additional questions to dwell on.

"I'm afraid so," Clara answered finally, setting her apron aside and coming over to her. "Thoughts elsewhere."

"Thoughts tend to go awanderin', I find," Mrs. Allendale told her, bobbing her head in agreement and gesturing almost abruptly to the corridor. "I'll take you to Miss Bradford."

Clara glanced at her curiously. "I do know the way to her office."

"I believe you would," Mrs. Allendale replied, completely unruffled and blunt in her tone, "but Miss Bradford is not eating in her office, so I'm to take you to her."

"Of course," Clara murmured, wiping her too-clean hands on

her simple skirts. "I apologize."

Mrs. Allendale gave her a bewildered look. "What for, Miss Harlow? You didn't know that, and I didn't say so."

With a light laugh, Clara shrugged a shoulder. "I suppose you're right, Mrs. Allendale."

"I usually am." She winked cheekily and strolled on, the cap on her head sitting askew, her arms swinging too determinedly.

What in the world had this woman done before coming to be housekeeper at the school, and how in the world had she convinced anyone that she could do it?

Just one of the many questions on Clara's ever-growing list, and those questions seemed to be multiplying by the hour now that she was back at the school.

It had only been three days, but to her, it might as well have been a month.

Leaving Kirkleigh had been even more difficult than she had imagined it would be, bringing her to the point of tears, though those had waited to fall until they were safely ensconced in the coach and driving away. Hiding those tears from Phoebe had proven a challenge, and if she had caught sight of them, she made no comment on it. Their entire journey back to the school had been one of silence, for which Clara had been eminently grateful.

Hawk had barely looked at her as they had departed. After a beautiful, breathless afternoon and a supper of almost unbearable attention at his hand, his silence was deafening. Blatant. Confusing. Heartbreaking.

She'd never met a single person who had affected her so immediately and so profoundly, especially over so short a period. She couldn't claim any feelings easily defined, certainly wouldn't have called it love, though there was attraction, affection, fascination...

It could have become love.

So easily, it could have become love.

He had been so very stoic as the carriage had been packed, ordering about the necessary tasks and seeing to details, but there had been no conversation with Clara. Plenty with Nat, with his servants, and even a few words with Phoebe.

He'd only spoken with Clara when the time had finally come to leave.

"Goodbye, Miss Moore," he'd said, his hands carefully at his sides as he bowed. "Remember, Kirkleigh is at your disposal."

The words were simple enough, but the tone...

It was exactly what an elderly duke would have said to a visiting extended family member. Or a one-time ward of a past duke. It was as though Hawk's father had inherited rather than Hawk himself.

It was as though the romantic and thrilling day before had never happened.

Her palm had burned with the memory of his hand in hers, which seemed almost imagined considering the man before her.

She'd thanked him with all politeness, ignoring how painful the tightness in her chest was growing, cinching against her ribs until she was growing almost breathless with it. Then she'd entered the carriage and looked away, not even bothering to watch the fading sight of Kirkleigh itself as they departed.

She could not bear to leave everything she had found there.

Returning to the school had been comforting, yet she still struggled to find the happiness she had once known there. Her students had been delighted to see her, and the rhythm of her teaching and routine fell back into place easily. The story had gone around of her visiting a cousin who had been in Sussex for a short period, and she went along with whatever questions she was asked, giving bland answers that ought to have satisfied without being pressed for more details.

She'd turned in her sketches the moment she had arrived, and Phoebe had done the same with notes she had been taking, though none of those notes had been shared with Clara. It seemed they had both had their particular assignments for their time at Kirkleigh.

Now, perhaps, she would understand why. And what. And who.

And then, if she was fortunate, she would learn how they were to proceed from here.

If she were to proceed from here.

To her surprise, Mrs. Allendale led her to the library of the school, a massive room that any lover of books would have adored. It was a room with a great deal of seating, walls of books on never-ending shelves, and very little space where a private conversation could take place. All the more curious, then, that it should be the setting Pippa would choose for a luncheon.

And a particularly sensitive conversation.

But perhaps the discussion of covert things was not taking place yet. It was entirely possible that this conversation would be related to the school itself rather than the world Clara had been so briefly introduced to.

She doubted she would be so fortunate, but it was possible.

Pippa sat at a small table near the one large window in the library, silently engaged in a book, giving no hint to anyone that she was waiting for Clara or anticipating a meeting. She might have only been in this library for her own amusement rather than a luncheon with one of her teachers.

There were no students to be seen.

Clara looked around the vast room to be sure of her suspicion, and it was quickly confirmed. They would be entirely alone in this room, and Clara could count on one hand the number of times she had entered the library of this school and found it devoid of students.

Very strange indeed.

Their approaching footsteps brought Pippa up from the pages of her book, and she smiled warmly. "Thank you, Mrs. Allendale. Clara, thank you for joining me."

Clara clasped her hands before her, dipping her chin in a nod, feeling a stiff formality seeping into her now that she stood here. "Of course, Pippa."

As though she knew what Clara was feeling, Pippa smiled more softly and gestured to the seat across from her. "Please, sit."

Moving to the chair, Clara sat and adjusted her skirts, her pulse beginning to speed up with nerves she did not quite understand. She felt as though she was going to be scolded in some way or some flaws were shortly to be identified. Perhaps she had not done the task the way Pippa and Lord Rothchild would have liked and had wasted time and a connection. Perhaps they felt they had been mistaken in asking her to do any of this and now needed her assurance of secrecy.

There were too many questions, too many unknowns. Did all covert operatives and assets feel this way?

"Mrs. Allendale," Pippa said, lowering her voice. "Would you kindly ensure that the room is secured? And then we may take luncheon here."

Mrs. Allendale nodded very firmly. "Right you are, Miss Bradford. I'll see to it." She left without another word, closing the great library doors behind her with a firm click of the latch.

Clara stared at the doors for a moment, then looked back at Pippa, her heart racing now. "I take it this is an official meeting, then."

"You would be correct," Pippa replied, somehow still smiling with a calm demeanor that Clara did not understand. She folded her hands together atop the table and gave Clara a very direct look. "I will be frank with you, Clara, because I feel that is the best way to proceed under the circumstances."

Clara found herself nodding at that. "I don't mind frankness," she replied.

Pippa's smile curved briefly, then returned to a stable easiness. "I have gone over your drawings and Phoebe's notes from your preliminary investigation of Kirkleigh and the surrounding areas. You more than proved yourself to be a worthy operative, in that regard. Your drawings were more accurate than several maps I have been looking at, and I cannot tell you what a help that is to us."

Relief began to seep into Clara's limbs, and she found herself relaxing into her seat, though she still did not loosen her posture in any way. Being in the presence of the headmistress had that effect on her, regardless of the topic of conversation.

"After consulting with Lord Rothchild," Pippa went on, taking a weighted breath that Clara wondered about, "we have decided that we would like to have you become an official operative for us and return to Kirkleigh to further investigate what we consider to be a great risk to the nation at this time."

The disconcerting sensation of her heart hopping over expected beats made Clara blink unsteadily, faintly wondering if she might swoon to the side shortly. Yet she remained fully upright, no indication of any faintness presenting itself.

"Investigate… Kirkleigh?" she managed, her voice squeaking. "Do you… do we… suspect the duke of…?"

"No, no," Pippa assured her hastily, "no, we never have. Your initial investigation was merely to see the coastline in the vicinity, as we had it notated on information gathered recently."

Clara frowned at the choice of words. "Notated on information?" she repeated. "From whom?"

Pippa slowly sat back, her hands dropping to her lap. "Earlier this autumn, an assignment took place in Paris. It was not designated as from my office, or from any other in an official capacity. We could not afford to have it owned in such a way. During that assignment, a map was found that had several points along the British eastern coast marked, the meaning behind each mark unclear. When this information reached us, we moved quickly to identify likely areas in more specific detail, and Kirkleigh was a conveniently located estate for our ends. We knew we could gain access without much difficulty, so we did so."

"Who was investigated in Paris?" Clara pressed, leaning forward and gaining confidence as her curiosity rose like a tide within her. "What are we facing?"

The weighty sigh that Pippa released told Clara a great deal without giving her any of the details she'd asked for. "It would take hours we do not have to get particularly specific, but there is a faction of secret rebellion in France who have been working since Napoleon was in power. They were not actively working against him, but his methods were not something they supported. The goals are the same, the means very different. They follow the likes of Sieyès, if you know the name, as well as Rousseau."

The names did not seem familiar to Clara, but she made a note to do some research in this library when Pippa was done with her.

"They have been working for years on undermining their own government," Pippa went on, "and governments all across Europe. There are sympathizers in England, supporters in the ranks of government, and a band of their number who are continually working towards their goals of building an empire."

Clara stared at this small yet powerful woman, so unassuming in appearance but with so much influence at her fingertips. She had just given her the sort of plot one might find in a novel, the quality of which would be questionable, and there was no sign of amusement in her features. Everything she had said was filled with the utmost gravity, and there was so much she was not saying between the lines.

The room was suddenly colder as Clara considered the implications.

"So they would overthrow the government, if they could," Clara murmured.

Pippa nodded firmly. "They absolutely would. We've lost a number of good operatives across the departments and contingents in our ranks due to their actions. They have used words of Sieyès to unite themselves. If you ever hear the phrase '*j'ai vécu*' spoken in your company, you will know they are aligned with this faction."

Swallowing, Clara returned the nod. "Does this group have a name?"

"Not that we're aware of," Pippa admitted with a disgruntled sigh. "For now, we simply refer to them as the Faction. It might aid us in our efforts if they did have a name. The Shopkeepers have been using every tool available to try and discover it, but we've found nothing."

"Shopkeepers?" Clara's head spun with the revelations, but that term was perhaps the most bewildering of all.

Pippa uttered a small laugh. "I apologize, I got ahead of myself. The leaders of the covert operations are collectively known as the Shopkeepers. Napoleon once said that England was a country run by shopkeepers, so those in power at the time decided to make it so. Our code names reflect such things." She smiled a bit more widely at Clara, her eyes crinkling a touch with real amusement. "Now that you will be joining us officially, you may refer to me as Milliner. Lord Rothchild, who is the second in command over all covert operatives in all departments, is Weaver. Anyone else you will learn as you need to, if you need to."

Clara nodded, the irony in the names not lost on her, but her own amusement difficult to find at the moment. "And what will my name be?"

"Sparrow," Pippa—Milliner now, she supposed—told her simply. "I think it suits."

She could have suggested Clara go by the name of Butter and Clara would have nodded numbly. Did it really matter what her official name was in this venture? She'd already pretended to be one other person, why not adopt the identity of another?

Except that Sparrow would be the persona Clara made her. Whoever she was, whatever she was, there was nothing else to base her on. Everything would be from Clara's own mind and own abilities. It was a name with position and responsibility, someone who answered to superiors and lived a life of secrets.

Perhaps Sparrow was simply the person of Clara Harlow after all.

"So what am I to do now?" Clara murmured, returning her eyes to Pippa. "I realize I am returning to Kirkleigh, but what is my task?"

"Barcliffe." Pippa reached down beside her and pulled Clara's drawing diary out, flipping open a few pages to the sketch she had done that magical day when Hawk had taken her hand as she walked along the shore.

Clara shook her head to clear the whimsical, longing reminiscence from her mind and focus more intently on the task at hand.

Pippa traced the shading that indicated water depth with a finger. "This was critical, Clara. It changed everything. A fully loaded ship could get closer to shore than in any other place we have found in the Kent coastline yet. We believe there are smugglers working with the Faction, though what is being brought into England, or who, is not yet known. This is what I need you to look into."

"I knew it," Clara whispered, staring at the shading in breathless wonder. "I knew that had to mean something; I didn't know what…"

"We believe it does," Pippa confirmed. "We have no way of knowing what connection the estate has to any of this, or if the family is involved, but we firmly believe this beach and cove are being used."

Clara shook her head, swallowing. "I cannot see the Brownings being involved. I met them, and they are… Well, I believe someone might consider them bumbling."

Pippa gave her a surprisingly scolding look. "Never be fooled by appearances, Clara. Skilled actors come in all shapes and sizes. No one is above suspicion. No one."

Suitably chastened, Clara nodded obediently. "When will I be going back to Kirkleigh?"

"Next week. First, we must have you undertake some training."

Training. What in the world would that entail? Visions of being handed an épée and being forced into fencing sprang into her mind, however unlikely it was. Would they train her to be a pickpocket? Would she learn the value of disguises?

The doors to the library opened, and Mrs. Allendale entered with a tray. She strode over to them with determined steps and set the tray on the table before them. "Will there be anything else you ladies need?" she asked, propping her hands on her hips.

Pippa eyed Clara for a moment, then looked up at the housekeeper. "Yes. Would you please tell them we are ready? Fifteen minutes should be soon enough."

Mrs. Allendale's brows rose, and she looked at Clara as well.

What exactly she was thinking while she did so was a terrifying prospect in Clara's mind.

"Right you are, Miss Bradford," Mrs. Allendale murmured, still staring at Clara. "Fifteen minutes it is." She left without another word, glancing back at the pair of them before closing the library doors.

"Who's coming?" Clara asked as she lifted the lid from the plate of cold meats and began to serve herself.

Pippa's soft smile returned, and Clara wondered faintly if the woman were ever angry. "A few individuals who will be training you before your return. I believe most of their faces will be familiar to you."

Clara gave her a questioning look, but Pippa only continued to smile as she helped herself to their cold luncheon.

Fourteen minutes and twenty-seven seconds later, the library doors opened once more, just as Clara had finished all she wished of her luncheon and was trying to think up topics of conversation to pass the time. She turned in her chair and gaped at the parade of persons entering now, all intending to assist her in preparation for her first assignment as Sparrow.

Every face but one was familiar to her.

Abby led the way, her arm linked through Phoebe's, which minimized her limp until it was barely noticeable. Minerva Dalton followed them, which was an unsurprising fact, and Clara was glad to see her among the group. Morna Lennox was with them also, and while Clara did not know the Scottish woman well, she liked and respected her very much. It would be intriguing indeed to discover what part she played in all of this.

What shocked her was the identity of the three men who followed the women. Mr. Quinn was the gardener at the school, Mr. Haigh was the stablemaster, and Mr. Fairfax worked with Pippa to determine the best candidates for the Rothchild Academy. Clara had enjoyed occasional conversations with each of them, and now they were revealing themselves to be among the covert operatives whose ranks she had now joined.

It was a force of people willing to help prepare her for the new tasks that would be required of her.

The sight was a stirring one, indeed, if a little intimidating.

"Good day, Clara," Abby greeted with her usual warm smile. "I'm so pleased to begin training with you."

Clara tried to smile at them all, but her nerves kept her from the ability to do so.

A tall, dark-haired woman with dark eyes stepped forward, her hair pulled back in the most elegant style Clara had seen on anyone who was not adorned for a ball. She narrowed her eyes at Clara, then nodded once. "Yes, I see what you mean, Flora. She is quite in need."

Clara blinked at that, then looked at Phoebe, belatedly recollecting what her code name had been.

Phoebe gave her a quick wink. "Indeed, Tilda. You will enjoy this."

Dread curled in Clara's stomach as she looked back at the woman she'd called Tilda. "I don't wish to look overly fussed," she warned weakly.

Tilda beamed as the others in the room chuckled knowingly. "My dear girl, no one I dress is ever overly anything except perfect. Now, stand up for me, I need to see you better."

Chapter Twelve

$\mathcal{E}$lmsley Abbey was a quiet estate, far removed from any great village or town, and the landscape one rich in rolling hills of green with glimpses of limestone scattered throughout. The tenants were pleased with their situation, the estate was thriving, and Hawk's daily routine had become a flurry of activity working alongside several of them as they prepared for winter, though the weather was mild enough that the concern was low. His estate agent had asked him to take some time in the next few weeks to discuss some ideas for changes in the coming year, and Hawk had yet to settle a time for that with him.

Mostly because the bustle of his hard labor was becoming increasingly important in his daily life.

How else could he avoid dwelling on a certain woman currently touring somewhere in England, if not already back at Kirkleigh?

Well, he knew it was not probable she was back at Kirkleigh already.

He'd asked Stafford to write to him at Elmsley if she returned.

That was likely a bit much, considering he had invited her to stay at the house whenever she liked or had need, and had failed to give any sort of conditions on the thing. He hadn't thought he'd needed any conditions, considering he did not even care for Kirkleigh. Why should he care if someone who loved the place should stay there in his absence?

He didn't care. She could live there for the rest of her days, if she liked.

He simply wanted to know if she did.

The day she'd left, he'd spent so long working with tenants, Nat had come to find him in the evening to ask if he intended on having any sort of supper. Hawk had deferred the reasoning for his intensity of work, claiming he had simply lost track of the time, but he was convinced that Nat did not believe it. Thankfully, his friend had not said anything on the subject.

The truth of it was that Hawk *had* lost track of the time.

Intentionally.

He'd never get Clara's downcast expression out of his mind. His reserve and stoicism, what had been so carefully reconstructed after the soul-stirring walk along the seashore, hadn't helped matters there. The connection between them had been undeniable for both of them, he refused to deny it, and felt Clara would say the same.

Yet to spare himself, he had refused to admit any such thing or leave her with any sort of clarity on his feelings, the future, or even that he was pleased to have met her again.

How selfish could he be?

It might have been for the best, eventually, given that Clara would be touring around England with friends and connections. She might even meet a well-situated bachelor who saw just as much fire in her as he did. That said, she might meet one who was all money and no manners. She might meet a fellow artist who hoped to make his living by his art and who would only be able to provide an attic over a business for a home.

Would Clara accept any of that for her future?

He realized that he hadn't truly spent private time with her during the few days they'd had together, so learning much about her tastes and her nature hadn't been possible. Of course he had not spent much private time with her; such things were not permitted, and he knew that well, but it seemed to him that it should have happened, given how much he had felt.

What exactly it was he *had* felt was less clear, but there was a great deal of it.

None of this made any sense, and Hawk did not appreciate things that did not make sense.

Walking back to Elmsley Abbey after a hard day on the largest tenant farm, Hawk shook his head, his almost-callused hands clenching and unclenching as they swung alongside him. Returning to his residence was not the same without the chance of seeing Clara sketching along his path, or without the opportunity of sharing a supper with her. He still found the work more satisfying than being a gentleman of leisure, but the rewards for his efforts were far less sweet.

He had to somehow break free of this lingering melancholy if he wished to function well in the foreseeable future, and if he did not wish for the holidays to be possessed of the same.

Even Adrianna had commented on his lack of enthusiasm when he'd gone to see her at the Miss Masters' campus. Receiving criticism at her hands was not uncommon, and it was always lovingly given, but there had been real concern behind her words this time. He'd done all in his power to persuade her that he was well and whole, and his new hobby simply exhausted his usual good spirits. As with Nat, his sister had not been easily convinced, but she had allowed him to shift the subject to that of her education and how she was progressing. Her answers were short, her stories long, and he was pleased to see that she was the picture of excellent health. He'd never had any doubts about sending her to the school, and as she had gone on there, he'd grown more convinced of it.

She had grown into a beautiful young woman and would likely be considered very striking when she eventually made her debut in Society. She had no desire to take part in the Marriage Mart, she had assured him, but she was very much curious about the rest of the Season.

He had wondered at the time just how long it would be before she received her first offer of marriage, and how she would respond to it.

It was a terrifying thing to be the responsible party for a young woman of means, beauty, intelligence, and breeding.

Those few hours he had spent with his sister had been the best he had known since Clara's departure, and the return to the too-quiet halls of Kirkleigh had been all the more jarring for it.

He'd left for Elmsley the next morning.

A thundering of hooves echoed from behind Hawk, and he shifted to his left to allow the rider room to pass, though it seemed a strange politeness to bestow when there was no path he had been walking on.

"You seem to be trudging, Your Grace."

Hawk groaned to himself, rolling his eyes and turning his head to glare up at the rider now pulling his horse to a walk beside him. "And if I am? What's that to you?"

Nat grinned at the cynicism. "I thought your new hobby was designed to give you more satisfaction and joy in your life, yet here you are, sour as lemons and twice as bitter. Somebody steal your hammer?"

Shaking his head, Hawk looked ahead rather than at the equine-mounted idiot following him and muttered incoherently under his breath.

"Come on, Hawk," Nat encouraged, losing some of his teasing air, though not all. "Misery loves company."

"I did not realize misery was a social creature," he grumbled moodily. "Makes one wish to reconsider hosting it."

Nat scoffed and tutted to his horse, who had begun snorting at his bridle. "Look, this estate of yours is perfect for a good ride, and taking one is marvelous for the mind. Do yourself the favor of doing so tomorrow, won't you? Might make your own company more bearable once you work through some things."

Hawk flicked his gaze up at Nat cautiously. "What makes you think I might have something to work through?"

"Because I have a set of eyes, am not an idiot, and have been with you while you darted from estate to estate," Nat snapped without spite. "You've not been downcast at any other place. On the contrary, you've been rather keen to start working on some project or other, and eager to learn the specific strengths and weaknesses for each estate."

"I didn't realize I had been so obvious," Hawk grunted with a swipe at his brow. "Or that I had been so closely observed."

"But we arrive here," Nat went on, clearly not listening, "and all is drudgery. I've never known Elmsley Abbey to be full of thunderclouds and chills, it's always been one of your most lively estates. Might as well be visiting a cave for all the life here now. Do you really need me to explain it more specifically, or have I made my point?"

Hawk scowled at his friend. "What I really need is for you to shut up and take that point of yours away from me."

"I shall take that as a no." Nat nodded and adjusted his hold on the reins, straightening in the saddle. "Clearly, you quite take my meaning."

Derision knew no better face than Hawk's at that moment, and Nat chuckled at seeing it.

Nudging his heels into the horse, Nat rode off at a trot, eventually moving into a full gallop towards the house.

Hawk did not bother to watch him go, knowing if he did not find something to brighten about, his friend would either continue to pester him on the same subject or abandon him to the gloomy estate entirely. What friend would wish to remain in his company if he were the picture of depression?

On the one hand, he might enjoy not having someone else always about when he rather thought sitting in a stupor of sorrow would be more worth his time. But on the other, he had never done that particularly well, and being without influences outside of himself could bring him to drastic actions that would be utterly out of character.

Better to live in the present than loathe to leave the past.

It might not be the end for him and Clara, though nothing had particularly begun. For as long as she wished to remain in England, and stay at Kirkleigh, he would have every reason and right to go there, as well. In point of fact, he could choose to make Kirkleigh his primary residence, if he was so inclined. It was, after all, his house.

It didn't feel like his house, but it was.

Hawk exhaled roughly, scolding himself for being so maudlin. It was a house, for heaven's sake, and if he hadn't any desire to live there for an extended time before this, it would make very little sense to do so now. As with all of his estates, he would see what the coming year brought for gains and needs, and informed decisions would be made at that time as to whether it should be kept or given up. If one of his siblings preferred any of the houses, he could see that it was written into their legacy or work out some sort of arrangement.

Other than that, he need not think of Kirkleigh at all, just as he rarely thought of the other estates, unless there were issues.

It was just a house.

Nothing more, nothing less.

And the Duke of Kirklin had several houses.

Hawk nodded, pressing his tongue to the back of his teeth in thought. Perhaps he should make an effort to go to London for the Season in the coming year. A bit of social engagement, establish worthy connections, perhaps even start the process of finding a wife for himself. Adrianna would take part once she had finished with school, and he would certainly need to be particularly present for as much of that as he could be. Why not turn the thing into something beneficial while he was doing his duty?

A pair of rich hazel eyes and a dazzling smile came to mind, but he was quick to shove the thought away. He could not continue to think of Clara when there was nothing there to tell.

He would not.

"A song? I have to break this code… with a song?"

"Yes. You can read music, can't you?"

Clara gaped at Abby without shame, then began silently sputtering as she struggled for an answer. "Well, yes, enough to plunk out a tune and be told that I need to practice more. Why in the world would anybody code a message that way?"

Abby continued to smile, no doubt finding Clara's distress amusing. "Because it is difficult, and no one will suspect it is being done that way. We've only known about this for a few weeks, Clara, and it's the best lead we've had in months, if not years."

Pinching the bridge of her nose, Clara groaned at the approaching headache. "Please tell me there are other people being forced to endure this ridiculously tedious deciphering who are not trained in the field."

"There are, don't worry." Abby patted her shoulder, as though it should give Clara some comfort.

It didn't.

Still, Clara nodded all the same. "Good. I should hate to be doing this alone." She dropped her hand and sighed, leaning over the table where her next task lay, her mind spinning as she took it all in.

It was her fifth day of training in between her classes, and while some things were coming easier, they continually gave her new things to work on or accomplish.

First had been a complete debriefing, as they'd called it, on the situation as it stood with this Faction, including everything that had been discovered on the Paris mission Pippa had mentioned the other day. She knew more details about past actions, present concerns, and future risks than she would ever have cared to know, yet now she did care a great deal. All of the gathering information now percolating in her mind had awakened a streak of patriotism and loyalty she had never really considered in herself before. She loved England, to be sure, but that love had never had cause to be tested, or really examined.

She was proving it now, there was no question.

After the debriefing, she'd been trained in information gathering by Mr. Quinn, infiltration and undetected entry by Mr. Fairfax, and riding by Mr. Haigh. Of course, Clara knew how to ride a horse, but there was a great difference between the gentle, polite riding one might expect of an accomplished lady, and what she was being taught. This was mad, reckless riding, sometimes without any saddle at all, jumping unexpected obstacles, sometimes while being pursued... It was a terrifying experience, but she had finally managed to meet Mr. Haigh's approval there.

Mr. Quinn and Mr. Fairfax had reached their satisfaction with Clara's skills far sooner, but she refused to consider the implication of that.

Then there had been training with Minerva for impersonation and blending in with any station of people, self-defense fight training with Morna Lennox, and a primer on encoding one's notes with Phoebe. She'd been given books to read on seafaring and on ships themselves, old reports on smuggling, and even some notes on military tactics. All of it was designed to increase her knowledge of the situation she would be entering, to give her a better sense of what she should be looking for, and to protect herself above everything else.

She understood all of that; her mind was simply exhausted from it all.

Now she needed to decode these letters using a song from some French opera?

This whole thing was madness, and no one would convince her otherwise.

Still, she had promised to do this, to devote herself to this assignment, and to return to Kirkleigh, this time as a true covert operative.

It sounded so silly when she said it like that. Of all people in the world, she was now considered a spy?

She, who had been forced to leave her own village due to rumors and perceived scandal, was now going to intentionally walk into a social circle and make connections. She, who had avoided anything even remotely intrepid, was now going to place herself directly into potential danger to root out any threats in the area. She, who lived the most uncomplicated life known to an unmarried woman, was now going to be living a double life in the most devious sense of the word.

How in the world had she come to this?

"Watch yourself, Clara," Abby told her, breaking into her thoughts. "You've missed a few there."

Clara's eyes darted up to where Abby's finger had traced and sighed as she quickly moved back and recorded the letters she had neglected. "How am I going to remember all of this in the moment, Abby?"

"You won't have to. We've given you several lessons on improving your ability to memorize, haven't we?"

"Yes…" Clara said slowly, wondering what that had to do with anything. She continued to notate the requisite letters of each word, the pattern becoming monotonous in its repetition.

"And Tilda has told you that she will outfit each of your gowns with hidden pockets, has she not?"

Sensing she was about to be neatly trapped, Clara scowled and finished her copying. "She has, and she was quite proud of that, though I hardly think we can attribute the invention of pockets to Tilda."

Abby laughed to herself, then said, "I would not put it past her, but you have a point. Those pockets will serve a greater purpose for you than simple convenience."

Clara glanced up at her friend, her curiosity unwittingly piqued. "Will they? How so?"

Reaching into the pocket of her pinafore, Abby pulled out the smallest book Clara had ever seen, and a very small pencil to match. "These will fit unobtrusively in any pockets you have. You may find opportunities to capture anything you see or hear, or happen to discover, should you be so inclined, on these pages when you are away from Kirkleigh. Should you happen to forget these, or, should an unfortunate situation prevent you from having access to them, your memorization skills will serve you well."

Believing what she was hearing was rather difficult for Clara at the present. It was as though some grand drama had been constructed around her, some bizarre orchestration of plots and ploys that were better suited to legends than to life. How could she be involved in anything that would require her to keep a constant record, or memorize things she may only get a moment of?

For what had to be the fiftieth time in the five days she had been training, Clara wondered how she was supposed to manage any of this. Her instructors had a lifetime of instincts to draw upon for their assignments, though most were not currently taking any, she understood. She had nothing of the sort, her instincts confined to a canvas or a classroom and rarely extending beyond.

She had been praised for her instinct in capturing the depth of the water on the Barcliffe beach, as it had made Barcliffe and the surrounding area a more likely target for investigation, which had apparently been difficult to come by. How could Clara tell them that she had not been thinking about her assignment, the potential for the covert world, or anything remotely related to ships at all?

She'd only been thinking of capturing the scene for her art, and of exploring more of the beauties before her with Hawk.

Hawk...

The passing days had done nothing to soothe the ache in her heart where he was concerned. When she considered the prospect of returning to Kirkleigh in a few days, the only image that came to her mind was his, and knowing he would not be there made the very idea of returning to Kirkleigh a distasteful one. She would not mind living in the lovely house once more, especially without a specified end to her time there, but Hawk had brought the place to life, made it the charming haven it had been, and given Clara the chance to dream when her life had forbidden any such thing of her.

Oh, how she had dreamed...

Even now, she could not admit to herself what those dreams had meant regarding her feelings for Hawk, and wisdom told her that she had only known the man a few days, and therefore could not feel anything worth trusting.

Wisdom did not hold any sway over her heart.

Worst of all, despite Pippa's assurance that Hawk was not under any sort of suspicion from the powers that be, Clara could not be so sure. Why would they choose Kirkleigh as the house for her residence? It could not have been so convenient when they had had to find the real Miss Moore and glean all they could of her life so that it could be portrayed by Clara. What had kept them from finding any kind of connection to the Brownings? Or any of the other families in the area, whose names Clara would undoubtedly soon discover?

Why Kirkleigh, and why Hawk?

All of these questions, as well as the discomfort of Clara's unclear feelings for Hawk himself, meant that facing Lady Adrianna Russell in any sort of capacity was impossible. Clara did not have any direct contact with the girl now, as she had passed Clara's classes, but there were still various chances for their paths to cross throughout any given week.

The day after Clara had returned to the school, Hawk had come himself to visit his sister, and, thankfully, protocols had been set in place so that Clara would be in no danger of meeting him.

It had taken all of her strength not to break those protocols herself and see him regardless.

Now she was expected to live in his house, continuing as Miss Moore, and serve her country.

Why did he have to come to Kirkleigh at all while she was there? This all would have been so much easier had she never known him, never felt anything, never known anything about him but that Kirkleigh was his. She would never have felt as though she was betraying him with the many lies, that she was ruining her happy memories of him by using Kirkleigh as her own personal fortress, or that at any minute he might burst back into her life knowing the truth and condemning her for all time.

She might never be free of these fears, but there was also no turning back.

The cause was too important, and the risks too great.

She only prayed she would not live to regret it.

"Clara…"

She paused in her absent work and glanced up at Abby, prepared to apologize for wandering thoughts, only to find Abby's eyes fixed on the page, their blue depths wide and surprised.

Clara frowned at the sight, looking back at her work in confusion. "What? Where did I go wrong?"

"No, Clara…" Abby leaned forward and jabbed a finger at the paper. "You deciphered the next layer without my giving you the key word. How did you do that?"

"How did I…?" Clara shook her head, lifting a shoulder in an imitation of a shrug. "I've been listening, I suppose. I know how important that phrase *j'ai vécu* is, from all that I've read and been told, so I thought it made sense to try it out once I'd gotten through the song. I'm not done yet, obviously…"

Abby laughed a bit breathlessly and grinned at Clara. "It doesn't matter. You did it. You'll be perfect, Clara. Utterly perfect."

There was something in that statement that did not sit well with Clara at all, but she could hardly say something when so many of her friends were part of this world. And they were still her friends, so she would never say they had lied to her or betrayed her. But she was not like them.

She might never be like them.

"How do you resign yourself to the changes in your life?" Clara murmured, sitting back. "How do you live a life not truly being yourself anymore?"

Abby sank down in the chair beside her and took her hands quickly. "Listen to me, Clara. You are not losing yourself in this. Yes, you are playing a role for a time, but only for a time. You have been chosen for this because you are you. You will succeed at this because you are you. I promise you, this will feel more comfortable to you very soon, and you will see that you never stop being yourself. You only find more facets of yourself you never knew were there."

Clara nodded, swallowing once, gathering her thoughts. Then she ventured, "Do you miss it? I know you're in training on a daily basis, but do you miss having missions and the like?"

"Every day," Abby told her without hesitation. "But this is how I can be of use now, and I accept that. However I can be of use, I will be."

Of all the things Clara had heard throughout her training, while at Kirkleigh, or since first learning about the covert world that existed around her, that rang the truest. The most real.

The most like her.

She found herself nodding repeatedly, mulling the words over and over in her mind. And when she was done, she looked her mentor in the eye and made the same vow.

"However I can be of use," Clara said clearly, "I will be."

Chapter Thirteen

"Why am I here?"

"Because we could use an extra hand."

Nat gave Hawk the driest of all looks and held up his hands for Hawk to see. "Do these look like the sort of hands you would like to have as an extra?"

Hawk squinted at them for a moment's consideration, then gave his friend a firm nod. "Yes, they do."

"Really?" Nat glanced at his hands himself, frowning. "I don't think so. They look useless for the task at hand."

"You don't even know what the task is," Hawk pointed out with a wry smile.

"I'm fairly certain any of the tasks these fellows would need help with would render this particular set of hands rather useless." He showed his hands to all of them as though to prove a point.

Hawk rolled his eyes and looked over at his estate manager and tenants. "Apologies. He's usually much more principled and much less fragile."

Nat coughed in apparent distress. "Fragile? I've never been fragile a day in my life!"

"I really thought," Hawk continued, still speaking with the others rather than acknowledging Nat's remarks, "that he might be more than the soft London gentleman that he appears. That he might relish a chance to prove his strength and his lack of pretension. I did not realize he'd disrespect you all in this way."

"Disrespect?" Nat's voice was nearly squawking now, and it took all of Hawk's energy not to break character.

Hawk exhaled heavily, forcing as much disappointment into the sound as possible. "After all, we're simply looking for someone to drive the team of horses as we load it up with our recently cut firewood. Surely even a soft gentleman can drive a team." He turned back to his friend at that, raising a brow.

Nat had opened his mouth to protest something else, outrage and indignation rampant on his face.

Then his mouth snapped shut, and he scowled darkly. "That was rude, Your Grace."

"No, it wasn't." Hawk looked at the others and held out a questioning hand. "Did I say anything that might be construed as rude or impolite in any way?"

Several heads shook obediently. "No, Your Grace."

Hawk turned back to Nat in triumph, though his friend's expression hadn't changed. "What?"

Nat waved dismissive fingers at them. "They work for you. They could not possibly be tempted to say anything contrary to your wishes, or to disparage you."

"Mr. Gentry," Hawk called without turning around. "What would you say about my help of late?"

"We've had worse, Your Grace," the man replied easily, "and we've had better, too."

Nat looked over Hawk's shoulder to give the man a bland look. "That can hardly be considered contrary or disparaging, Gentry. See me after class."

That brought good-natured chuckling from the group, and Hawk waved the entire group over to the wagon in question, grinning far more easily than he had done in some time.

It would have been easy enough for one of the men already gathered to drive the wagon while they loaded up all of the wood they'd cut on the land they'd needed to clear. There were certainly enough of them, and they had offered, but Hawk had grown tired of working alongside his men while his friend laid about Elmsley Abbey enjoying a fine holiday for himself.

If Hawk was going to work, there was no reason why Nat could not do so as well.

So Hawk had sent word up to the house that Nat was needed

urgently, and, as he suspected, his friend had come directly.

As he had not been panicked or in any way distressed about Hawk's health or safety, it was no stretch to conclude that Nat had been bored and in need of a task.

Now he had one.

The tree trunks had been split and chopped into neat piles all throughout the area, the men having habitually piled the logs together beside the stump they had been felled from. The stumps would be pulled out in the spring, then the ground turned into additional farmland. There was still a vast amount of forest on the estate, so Hawk had had no qualms with clearing a patch of it to extend the land of the most profitable farm.

And now there were several bundles of firewood they could distribute to tenants and other villagers before any of it was desperately needed. There was some satisfaction in being able to provide goods from their own lands, thus rendering the purchase of such items from outside sources unnecessary. Those funds could then be used for other, more needed items, and if Mr. Forbes, his estate agent, was to be believed, such things were needed by a few families in particular.

There was a great deal of satisfaction indeed, in that.

Hawk was already making plans to be as generous as he could afford with his poorer tenants this Christmas, both here at Elmsley and at his other estates. Letters had been sent just that morning to each agent for the express purpose of identifying the specific needs of families that would likely be unable to be met by their own funds and efforts. It was not a habit that he likely ought to fall into each year, as it might prevent his tenants from being as dedicated in their responsibilities, but he had no desire to see any of them starve or suffer, either.

Balancing mercy with wisdom would be key, though he could not see a fault with being considered generous.

That thought would have shocked him only a few months ago.

Working with his tenants, learning from them and speaking with them, had opened his eyes to the true nature of their life and their efforts, if not their needs. He no longer wished to be a distant master at any of his estates and was determined that he should work just as tirelessly on the behalf of his tenants as they worked to make his estates prosperous.

Such subjects of thought were doing wondrous things for his soul and relieving him of any formerly held concerns of boredom or inefficacy.

The Duke of Kirklin would be an active, generous, attentive duke, and one who commanded the respect of his tenants without demanding it.

It was as though the mantle of his identity had suddenly fallen upon him, and it had done so with the peace of a falling leaf, the weight of a boulder, and the magnanimity of being robed in a cloak.

Humbling, ironic, and stirring, this rebirth of himself.

And yet…

"Hawk," Nat called as he mounted the wagon and picked up the reins. "A message arrived for you before I left Elmsley. Not urgent, but it was from Kirkleigh."

Days of absence suddenly rushed together in a blink, and his heart leapt within his chest, smashing against his throat, then dancing along several ribs in a random pattern that made Hawk dizzy. He swallowed, fighting for the moderate indifference he would have felt had a note from Millmond arrived and been dubbed not urgent.

"Thank you," he said calmly, though there was a wavering note in his voice that he instantly hated, fearing Nat would hear it.

If he had, he made no comment on the subject.

It would appear it was a day of miracles, then.

He could not leave to fetch his message, not if he wished to maintain any sort of image of calm respectability, and save himself from an impertinent interrogation at the hands of Nat. He had to continue on as he had been, painstakingly fetching log after log and loading them into the wagon, then distributing them to those in need of them. Any change in that plan would have been suspicious, and he could not risk questions when he had no answers.

Legs twitching with the desire to run headlong towards Elmsley, Hawk forced himself to continue on with the others and see to the task at hand. He might be able to convince the group that distribution of the firewood could wait for another day, particularly if the hour grew late or any of them appeared fatigued. Perhaps Mr. Forbes ought to look at the figures for each family and make a list of priority, thus streamlining their efforts.

After all, one would wish to be efficient in such matters.

Pile after pile of logs were loaded into the wagon, one of the men jumping into the bed and making a rather neat and orderly structure to it all.

Excellent, that would delay things creditably.

It also proved a fine point, as it allowed them to stack more wood into the wagon than they might have been able to otherwise. With a few simple steps, they had maximized their space and created order in the midst of their rather physical, seemingly menial task.

Whatever notion man had made of a thing called intelligence, it certainly was far more multifaceted than one might expect.

Certainly more than Hawk had expected, and each revelation of it made him ever more grateful for having his eyes opened, belated though it was.

Perhaps Nat would have the same experience, if he could be coerced to join them.

Glancing over at him now, there was no sign that his friend saw any kind of distance between himself and the men around him, often jumping down from his post at the reins to load wood with the rest of them. He'd toss logs up to the wagon bed, clap a few men on the shoulders and joke about their efforts, then spring back up to the seat and drive the horses on to the next pile.

If Hawk were not careful, Nat would outwork him, gentlemanly hands or not. He shook himself from his musings and returned to work, forcing his anticipation to be home to the back of his mind.

Finally, the wagon was loaded, and without Hawk saying a word, the decision was made to deliver and distribute the wood at another time. Handshakes went around the group, and then they dispersed, the tenants walking together towards their homes, apparently going for a drink at the village pub before they did so.

Nat stared after them with a furrowed brow.

"What?" Hawk prodded, catching the expression.

"A drink at the pub sounds rather perfect," Nat grumbled. "I wonder that we were not invited."

Mr. Forbes chuckled beside them. "I think, Mr. Robinson, it did not occur to them that you might wish to join them. If you wish to pursue them, however, I am sure you would be welcomed." As though he might consider it, Nat looked at Hawk hopefully. Hawk shook his head firmly. "Not me. That would be a sure way to ruin their enjoyment. You go on, if you like. I'm for Elmsley." With that, Hawk shook Mr. Forbes' hand and turned on the path up to the house, not particularly caring if Nat followed.

Only a few moments later, Nat did follow, sighing dramatically. "I suppose you have a point."

"I do try to, when I can," Hawk said simply.

"May I partake of the spirits at Elmsley in place of the pub?"

"Of course, though I don't know why you're asking."

"Politeness, my dear fellow. Pure and unadulterated politeness."

Hawk shook his head in resigned disbelief, letting his friend ramble on in continued ridiculousness, without requiring much by way of response, until they reached Elmsley. At which point, Hawk immediately sought out his butler and the waiting message for him.

His staff at Elmsley being quite his favorite, the message was just as immediately produced, and Hawk broke the seal with a quick snap, his eyes tracing the letters before the page was fully at his eyeline. His heart pounded with an intensity that drowned out all else as Stafford's words took shape in his mind.

"Is Clara back at Kirkleigh?" Nat asked simply, no hint of amusement, teasing, or any sort of irony in his tone.

Swallowing hard, Hawk nodded. "Yes," he managed. "She is."

Nat grunted once. "Good. Send her my regards."

Hawk looked over at him quickly, then returned to the page.

He hadn't planned on writing her. Hadn't thought anything except wanting to know if she returned.

What in the world would he write to her about?

"Miss Moore, you've received a note."

Clara looked up from her watercolor in the gardens of Kirkleigh in surprise, staring at Mrs. Clayton without shame. "I did? From whom, pray tell?"

The dignified, graying housekeeper smiled kindly at her, quirking a brow. "I haven't opened it, Miss Moore. I believe that pleasure is yours."

Snorting a soft laugh, Clara grinned and rose, setting aside her paintbrush. "I suppose it is." She took the proffered note and opened it quickly, hoping for nothing and expecting nothing. She blinked as she stared at it. "It's... it's an invitation." She looked at Mrs. Clayton in shock. "I don't know anyone in the area anymore, Mrs. Clayton."

Mrs. Clayton smiled further and patted Clara's hand. "That is why one goes to such things, Miss Moore. To meet people and make friends." She winked and proceeded back the way she had come.

Clara watched her go, grateful that the housekeeper had returned from her visit with her daughter and was here for this stay of Clara's. She was a perfect match for Stafford in managing Kirkleigh, and she had been such a comfort to Clara in the two days she had been back.

There was a slight concern about how thick Phoebe and Mrs. Clayton were becoming. They had all taken tea together their first day back, and it was soon evident that the two women shared a similar commentary on the indecency of changing fashions, the inconvenience of stockings, and their growing intolerance for lack of musical ability, among other things.

Clara would not comment on their bizarre, budding friendship, unless they turned their bonding over disapproval onto her.

So far, she had been spared.

Time alone would determine if she continued to be so.

She looked back down at the invitation in her hand, the elegance of it rather remarkable, considering they were in a particularly quiet corner of Kent. It was embossed in gold, the writing on it particularly perfect, and it was distracting enough that Clara was content to admire them before actually acknowledging the content of the invitation itself.

When she finally did, her confusion was even more compounded.

Mr. and Mrs. Fleet requested her presence at an evening of dancing and cards next week.

Had she met the Fleets?

That was a stupid question, of course she hadn't met them. She had not met anyone since being at Kirkleigh. She knew the Brownings, she supposed, though that meeting had been entirely unintentional. If they were in attendance, she would at least have someone to converse with, and perhaps not have to resort to mere politeness. Given she was supposed to investigate their estate, speaking with them would be paramount.

If they were not at the Fleets', it would not be a disaster. After all, it was part of Clara's assignment to act for all the world, to create a fixture in their imaginations, and it would be so much easier to do so without any previous impressions.

But she would always run the risk of meeting those who had known the young Miss Moore, and therefore would think themselves acquainted with the adult version. She was practiced enough by now, even without her training, to make allowances for such things, and to pass herself off well enough that it should make no difference. She would have to put herself out into the local Society soon enough, especially if she wished to gain any sort of favor with her neighbors, so she might as well do so at the Fleets'.

That would be far worse than any other aspect of the assignment. Clara had never been one eager for social engagement, though she would participate without any difficulty. Her ideal evenings were spent in the quiet of whatever home she imagined for herself, drawing something or other in a garden or by a fire…

It would likely be what she opted to do here at Kirkleigh, when she was not engaged in some other activity for the night.

But there was the issue of making free in a house that did not truly belong to her and allowing herself the comfort of using it as Hawk had encouraged her to.

It still seemed a foreign place without him.

Beautiful, immaculate, comfortable while still being immense and fine, but foreign still. Entirely unfamiliar, and a place she could not see her footing in.

She'd have to overcome that soon enough.

Kirkleigh was her place now, at least for a time, and she owed it to her character to be as familiar with it as Miss Moore had ever been.

Still, she could not bring herself to act on her once curious inclination to wander the house after all the rest had gone to bed.

What would be the point of that now? She could wander the place during the day and claim simple reminiscence to any servant that wondered. After all, without Hawk...

Shaking her head, Clara returned her attention to the invitation again.

It would seem that the Fleets requested her Aunt Fern attend as well.

What a treat.

Phoebe would be delighted to go somewhere, to go anywhere, particularly if it meant that Clara would need to put on one of Tilda's fancier ensembles. Why she took such delights when she was by far and away the more beautiful woman, Clara did not understand. She could have snatched any man of any rank, station, or fortune, and of any age, as well.

Clara would...

Well, attention was not something usually paid to Clara, and she was all the more accustomed to that.

What was Miss Moore's life like in that regard? Did she have many admirers? Or any at all?

She'd have to go through the notes in her chest before the event, if not practice her dancing, as well.

It had been so long...

"Penny for your thoughts, Sparrow."

Jumping in fright and clasping her invitation to her chest, Clara whirled, the exercises she had been taken through for her self-defense springing back into mind.

One of the Kirkleigh gardeners sat crouched there, grinning at her easily, a far younger man than one might have expected to have had a position on the gardening staff that was not at an apprentice level.

She had never seen him before, as far as she could recall, and no one should know her as Sparrow yet.

Especially not here.

"Easy," he murmured, as though he were speaking to a skittish horse. "Milliner wrote me before you came back. I was placed here before your first visit in anticipation."

Clara swallowed hard, her throat parched in a painful way.

"Prove it," she rasped, her fingers sliding against each other as they gripped the air.

The man's smile never wavered. "Weaver took me from the Home Office fieldwork and bade me be of service to Milliner as needed. I worked at the Convent under Quinn, though I was out on assignment enough to rarely be seen. The day you started at the Convent, you wore a green muslin dress and a bonnet with yellow ribbon. Your first dormitory was the third floor, fourth window from the left. Miss Bartlett was the first window from the left on the second floor. Miss Lennox the third window on the second floor. After the first year, each of you rotated, and Miss Bingham—"

"All right," Clara overrode, cutting him off with a quick slash of her hand even as her cheeks tinged with color. "I believe you. For heaven's sake, it terrifies me that you possess such a memory. I half expect you to tell me the color of my petticoats on the third of October."

"Cream with pink ribbons, Sparrow," he replied without missing a beat.

Her eyes widened. "Now I'm only mortified."

He chuckled and waved his hand easily. "No need. I've been trained to enhance my memory, and now it will not go back. I do not mean to frighten, only to inform you I am here."

Hand at her throat, Clara nodded slowly, her fingers beginning to absently stroke and scratch at her skin in thought. "In what capacity? My protection? My watchman? My observer?"

His broad shoulders shrugged with a nonchalance that did not suit such a powerfully-built frame. "Yes, and a dozen other things, perhaps. If the need arises."

The sound of an approaching carriage disturbed them, and the man turned to work at some weeds at the base of a bush nearby.

Clara raised her chin and walked in his direction, sitting herself on a bench nearby and pretended to read her invitation again. "And what do I call you?"

"Brick will do," he muttered, yanking on a weed and placing it on the stone pathway beside him. "Mr. Brick if we're formal, plain old Brick if we're being official."

"That makes it rather simple, doesn't it?" Clara murmured as a smile creased her face.

He grunted once. "A rarity, you'll find."

Clara's smile slowly faded as resignation set in. "That does not surprise me a jot. Do you know Phoebe, then?"

"Flora?" He laughed to himself, a rumbling sort of sound that reminded Clara of pipe tobacco and whiskey, her grandfather's favorite combination. "Of course. I've known her for years upon years. We worked a number of assignments together in our younger years."

"You're not so old," Clara said before she could stop herself, and clamped a hand over her mouth the moment the words escaped.

Brick laughed far more heartily now, his attention still on his work. "I'll thank you for the compliment and swear not to tell her you said so."

Clara put her hand to her flaming cheeks. "*Now* I feel *very* mortified."

"That will fade," he assured her. "Listen, Sparrow. You must take advantage of that party. The Fleets are in thick with the Brownings, and have connections in Bristol, which could indicate interests in shipping. You recollect the reports of Barcliffe cove and its possibilities?"

"Yes, of course." Clara nodded firmly. "The first fair night, I intend to walk out and observe."

Brick paused, glancing over at her. "Do me a favor and don't venture there at night alone."

Clara huffed once. "Then when should I, Brick? If I have an assignment to fulfill, I have a responsibility to fulfill it at all costs."

"I said alone, Sparrow," Brick insisted, exhaling roughly. "I'll take notice of the tides and anything suspicious and leave word in your rooms. We will go down together, that way I may protect you from your own foolhardy judgment."

"I think I am supposed to thank you, but I rather think I won't," Clara said with a sniff. "But the plan seems sound. Back to the point: I should acquaint myself with the Fleets for potential connections to the cove at Barcliffe. Any particular note of how I might improve relations once I am known?"

Brick made a playful face of consideration. "Possibly. They have daughters, and daughters need accomplishment, do they not?"

Clara blinked at him. "And the daughters are not at school? With the Convent being so near?"

"Not everyone finds education outside of the home palatable." He continued to pull the weeds from the ground and set them into their pile. "I daresay a demonstration of artistic ability and a few lessons in improving theirs would set you highly in their favor."

"Would it?" Clara mused, eyeing the invitation in her hand one more time. "Well, well. We shall see what I can do about that."

"Miss Moore!"

Clara threw her hands in the air. "Now what?"

A maid hurried towards her, a note in her hand. She curtseyed when she reached Clara. "Begging your pardon. Mrs. Clayton asked me to bring this to you." She handed her the note, bobbed again, then darted away.

"My, my, when did I become so sought after?" Clara muttered to herself, shaking her head. Breaking the seal, she felt her heart give way and sprout wings, fluttering within her.

Miss Moore—

I do believe I have forgotten a pair of gloves at Kirkleigh when I left for Elmsley Abbey. Would it be a terrible imposition to ask you to send them on, if you find them? I shall be very grateful.

Kirklin

How had he known she was here? Why in the world would he send this note to her instead of Stafford or Mrs. Clayton? What sort of gloves were they?

Was that all he wanted to say?

Her mind spun on various questions, then she grinned without reserve or shame.

The Duke of Kirklin would never know one pair of gloves from another, and leaving a pair behind was a valet's concern, not his own. This note was useless, by all accounts.

Except one.

"Have you noticed an abandoned pair of the duke's gloves, Brick?" Clara asked almost airily.

"Have I what?" he repeated, not having any idea what she was saying. "Why in the world would anybody notice a thing like that? White doesn't leave things, and the duke rarely wears gloves."

Clara grinned further still. "Never mind, then. Must be mistaken. I shall have to write and tell him so."

Chapter Fourteen

"*Oh* dear, oh dear, how foolish of me."

"I beg your pardon?"

Hawk looked up from his letter, his laughter still echoing in his breath. "What?"

Nat blinked owlishly, a book in his hand and his pose in the chair growing more inelegant by the minute. "You said 'oh dear' and something about being foolish."

Had he really said it loudly enough to be overheard? Cursed idiot, having a friend always hanging about him was growing more and more inconvenient.

Hawk gritted his teeth, forcing a smile. "I thought I had forgotten something at Kirkleigh, but apparently, I did not."

"Of course, you didn't," Nat said with a scoff. "White never forgets anything, and he is famous for it."

Nat knew that, and Hawk knew that, but Clara wouldn't know that.

That was all Hawk cared about.

It was stupid and foolish, he knew that, but it was all he could think to do to get a note to Clara without being so blatant about it.

He was well aware that it was an obvious tactic, but at least it would have the appearance of legitimacy.

Whatever that was worth.

However ridiculous the note he had sent to Clara was, the note he received back from her was perfect and encouraging.

Your Grace,

Unfortunately, I have yet to find your mislaid gloves. I cannot think that they would be left behind, perhaps you are mistaken and ought to search your present lodgings again.

As an addition to this reply, I would add that Stafford wishes to know if you wish to keep the china stored here from the late duke. I have seen this china, of course, and find nothing in it to admire, if you need my opinion.

She had signed it with her name, a creative flourish taking place on the tail of the A ending her name, and he stared at that flourish longer than any pair of eyes had a need to.

How was even her penmanship full of artistry?

"Something's wrong with you."

Hawk looked over at his friend, belatedly recalling that he had been reluctantly engaged in conversation moments ago. "Is it?" he mused aloud. "I shouldn't think so."

"That's because you aren't seeing clearly," Nat informed him. "I thought you might be distressed today with the rain being what it is, and your inability to be a laborer, but instead, you have reduced yourself to reading ridiculous notes from Kirkleigh."

"This note isn't ridiculous," Hawk shot back, likely growing too defensive over the thing, though there wasn't much to do for that. "Mine was ridiculous."

"Your what?" Nat paused, then shook his head. "Never mind. I find I don't care enough to know."

That suited Hawk well enough, and he shrugged, looking at the fire in the grate before him rather than return to his simple note from Clara.

It did not matter what he was looking at, his thoughts would be the same.

"Have you heard from Griffin lately?" Nat asked without any sort of preamble, his attention returned to his book, interrupting Hawk before his thoughts could properly formulate.

But he certainly hadn't wanted to think about Griffin, and discussion of his brother in far distant fields was not entertaining.

"No," he said simply. "Nor do I expect to. We will see him at Christmas, and that is enough."

Nat only grunted, apparently absorbed in his book again.

Hawk hesitated a moment, then glanced back at his note from Clara, beginning the process of formulating his response to her. He would need to be as playful as she had been, even coy, though the word had a distasteful sentiment attached to it where he was concerned. Sly, perhaps. Innocuous in its content, but legitimate as well.

Something that would keep this conversation going and renew the connection between them.

Something to say without saying what he could not say.

Because he did not know what to say.

"Did your father grow up at Kirkleigh?" Nat inquired with mild interest, turning the page of his book. "Or was it one of the other estates?"

Rolling his eyes, Hawk looked at his friend with a sigh. "He did. Unless the family were at one of the other estates, much the same as I live now."

Nat hummed once, nodding to himself. "I'd have chosen Elmsley myself."

"Pity they didn't ask you, then."

"Indeed."

Hawk waited for another question to come forth, something about Adrianna or the art at Kirkleigh or the state of the roads or what was planned for supper, but shockingly enough, nothing came.

Nat simply continued to read his book as though it was his sole occupation.

Utterly ridiculous and simply pointless.

But that was Nat, he supposed.

Not much had changed from when they had been at Eton together. Serious when he needed to be, loyal to the end, and possessing an easy temperament that meant he was rarely ruffled. And he was the most irritating, witty, mischievous man Hawk had ever met.

What a choice for a friend.

Perhaps Hawk should tell him what he was beginning to feel for Clara.

"Do you think you could bear my absence for a time?"

Hawk closed his eyes, shaking his head in wry amusement. "I

think I could summon the fortitude necessary to survive adequately," he replied, opening his eyes again to look in his friend's direction. "Why?"

Nat shrugged, closing his book on a finger to hold his place. "I thought I might do as you're doing on my own estate."

"Sit in it and answer useless questions?" Hawk quipped with a quick grin.

"Of course not, I can do that anywhere." Nat tapped the side of his head with the book, eyes narrowing. "I've been considering the work you're doing at every estate you own. I have but one, and I would scarcely recognize a single tenant."

Sobering quickly, Hawk straightened in his seat and gave Nat a hard look. "Don't minimize your efforts. Daveney is a great estate, and you take excellent care of it."

Nat shook his head firmly. "I have a great estate manager, and *he* takes excellent care of it. I only sign my name to the paperwork. I may not wish to work a spade as you do, but I could certainly stand to plant my feet firmly on its soil and face my own workers. Perhaps drive a team when it might help."

Hawk chuckled at the image, knowing how Nat had enjoyed that particular task. It would not surprise him in the least if Nat did end up working the land himself, no matter what he said. He was just the sort of active man that would become bored and uneasy watching others in action while he sat by.

"I won't argue that direct attention to the estates is a satisfying change for my life," Hawk allowed, "and it certainly could prove to be so for you, but you are not me."

"A truth I am grateful for daily," Nat said with a satisfied sigh.

Ignoring him, Hawk went on. "It might not hold the same appeal. I applaud your desire to try, though. If you are determined."

"I am."

Hawk inclined his head. "Then I wish you luck. When will you leave?"

Nat shrugged his shoulders and slouched back down into the seat, opening his book once more. "Tomorrow? The next day? Perhaps even the next, we'll see what the weather does and how my inclination fares. I just thought I would take advantage of the situation at hand and inform you now rather than at supper or in the morning."

A scowl flashed across Hawk's face, and any sympathy or warmth he had felt for his friend in the last few minutes faded in an instant. He'd done it again, and Hawk had fallen right into his stupid clutches without a moment's hesitation.

More questions, inconveniently asked, purely to keep Hawk from doing whatever he was doing.

It was not fair, and it was annoying as well.

It was as though Nat knew exactly what…

The thought remained unfinished as Hawk looked back over at his friend with speculation.

Of course, Nat knew what Hawk held in his hand. Of course, he knew what it meant to Hawk to receive it. Of course, he knew that Hawk was behaving outside of his usual mannerisms and way.

And he knew why.

Perhaps Hawk should ask Nat if he could define these strange and flourishing feelings that were causing such havoc in Hawk's mind and daily life. If he had such clarity and introspection, he might be able to be of some use despite the irritation he produced.

Then again, why give the man more credit than he deserved?

"If you look at me much longer," Nat said calmly, "you won't have much time to compose a suitable response to your Miss Moore before the night is out. And I'd wager you're rather keen to get that message on its way to Kirkleigh. How else would you flirt with her so obscurely from this distance?"

Hawk shook his head in resigned wonder as what he suspected became confirmed by his friend's own admission.

His first instinct was to protest the suggestion, to insist that his friend was wrong, to deny any such inclinations or actions, and to reply that he had no need to send a response to any message, from Clara or anyone else. But Nat would know it was all a ploy to save his pride, and it would simply be a waste of words.

After all, Hawk wanted to do exactly what Nat had said, and it would be nothing to forego a little bit of pride in order to do exactly what he wanted.

"Very true," Hawk mused aloud, nodding as he looked back at

the fire in the grate. "You have a point." He pushed himself out of his chair and moved to the small desk in the drawing room, retrieving paper and pen. "I don't mind if I do jot this down now, thank you."

"Very good, Your Grace," came the bemused reply from behind him. "Shall I help you compose it?"

"No, thank you. I believe I have the task quite in hand."

Clara shook her head, swallowing hard and staring out of the window as the carriage approached the Fleets' stately home. "Oh, I shouldn't have come. I'm dreadfully out of practice in social situations, and I wasn't particularly accomplished at it when I was in practice. I'll make a hash of everything, I know it."

"Well, then we had best turn the carriage around, return to Kirkleigh, pack our bags, and return to the Convent before you bring down the entire fight atop our heads," Phoebe replied without any concern, her lips barely moving as she did so. "Clearly, they should have asked a more sociable girl to do your task. How silly of them."

The sound of the words, as much as the words themselves, made Clara sigh and rub out her brow. "I know, it's useless to say such things."

"It's useless to doubt yourself at all, Clara," Phoebe insisted, her voice now losing some of her prim formality. "You do not have to be more sociable, more accomplished, or more of anything to do this. You are not playing a part, aside from your name and very slight details about her life. I promise you, if you can be Miss Moore to His Grace, the Duke of Kirklin, you can be Miss Moore to whomever we will meet at this event tonight. You were so comfortable with him."

Clara swallowed and nodded, but her heart had given a terrible lurch to the left at the mention of Hawk. It was all she could do not to press her fingers against the now tender skin of her ribs from the internal collision that had taken place.

What Phoebe had said was true, but what she did not, and could not, comprehend was how painful it had been for Clara to be Miss Moore to Hawk, by the end of their time together. The tenderness in each small moment had been tinged by the lie woven between them, and it was beyond Clara's power to remove or mend it.

There was no denying the joy that each note from Hawk had brought her in the last week, though they numbered only two thus far. She had giggled, she had smiled, and she had spent far too long laying on her bed and staring up into the canopy above her bed as she constructed responses of varying wit. It was all a bunch of silliness, nothing in them holding any weight, and yet there was something in them that tickled the soles of her feet and made her flush in delight.

What in the world had come over her?

Hawk's last note had been delightfully droll, and she was still reading it repeatedly in an attempt to memorize its contents. He thanked her for searching in vain for his gloves, gave her full authority to dispense with the china if she wished, and asked if she would mind terribly directing the rehanging of artwork in the gallery, as he was presently away and unable to do so.

Then came the line that had made her sigh aloud in the most embarrassing manner.

I trust the vision in your eyes far more than I would ever trust my own.

It had taken her a full day to find a way to repay the compliment, and hours further to know how to word it as he had done.

The game they were playing was a unique one, and she loved it all the more for that. Oh, the delight in still feeling connected to him despite the distance, and without the inconvenience of fluttering hearts and tingling toes while trying to compose coherent conversation.

She still had a fluttering heart and tingling toes, but it was far more comfortable for them to be brought on by reading rather than his person.

Comfortable? There was nothing comfortable about having Hawk near her, pretending to be Miss Moore or not.

And yet…

She found herself craving his presence in spite of the anxiety it aroused. She wanted him back at Kirkleigh to make the place more exhilarating. She wanted to walk the shoreline with him, looking for clues to help her assignment while enjoying every moment of his company.

Except he could never know she was looking for clues.

He could never help her with the things she was searching for, or the questions she would need answered. He would not be able to give her insight into the things that puzzled her or protect her if she went too far.

For as long as she would remain on this assignment, this lie would hover between them, and many actions of hers would hold secondary motives.

He would be a distraction, if he had been here, and she would struggle to accomplish anything at all.

Well, one could not have everything, she supposed.

And Clara certainly could not.

Exhaling slowly, she nodded, her fair ringlets dancing with the motion. "We need to make connections to determine if any are involved in the smuggling, should it be happening here. I cannot think anyone will express particular sympathies that would be suspect, so I must listen for other clues."

"That is an excellent insight," Phoebe praised, the compliment seeming more genuine than patronizing. "There are a great deal of unknowns in this. Which, in a way, gives us some freedom."

"How so?" Clara asked with a tilt to her head as the carriage pulled to a stop.

Phoebe scooted to the edge of her seat in anticipation of disembarking, grinning at Clara. "If we do not know what we are looking for, we cannot make a certain plan for how to get it. So we may act freely and see what we stir up."

Clara pursed her lips, her eyes narrowing. "Why do I have the feeling you have some experience with acting freely and stirring things up?"

Her friend winked slyly. "I haven't the faintest idea what you mean." She stepped out of the carriage, the hood of her cloak staying perfectly in place against her exquisitely styled hair as she did so.

There was a masterful art of grace in Phoebe's every movement that Clara would never be able to imbue into her little finger, and she paused for a moment to appreciate the fact.

"Miss?"

Clara blinked, turning her attention to the footman extending a hand towards her. She managed a smile and placed her hand in his.

"Thank you."

He ignored her, as all proper servants would.

Once down, Clara looked down at the glimpse of pale green silks peeking through her elegant cloak and took a moment to compose herself. She was beautifully arrayed—Nancy, Phoebe, and Tilda had seen to that—and, as far as she knew, nobody here would have known Miss Moore when she was truly living at Kirkleigh.

Which meant this night held nothing she should fear.

Typical social anxieties aside.

Lifting her chin, sharing a smile with Phoebe, Clara strode forward towards the house. Their cloaks were taken by waiting servants, the height of the ceilings in the entry alone something of a marvel, and the way to the party was evident as all other doors were shut.

"Almost as though they have something to hide," Phoebe murmured beside her. "Not opening all of the rooms for guests to admire? Hmm." She eyed the corridor around them, rather neat in appearance, though hardly what she would call fine. "I'd say the Fleets are in financial difficulties at the present."

"Aunt Fern," Clara scolded through her teeth, keeping her smile fixed as they approached the rooms set aside for the evening. "What is the point in considering that tonight?"

Phoebe glanced at her, full lips quirking just a touch. "People will do a great many things for money. You would be shocked to hear some of the things I have seen occur for financial gain." Her lips pulled into a formal smile, her chin dipping in a prim nod as they reached their hosts. "Good evening."

"Mrs. Daniels," the petite Mrs. Fleet gushed eagerly, reaching her hands out to them at once, her slight frame belying the amount of enthusiasm she contained. "Miss Moore! What a delight to have you here, I am so pleased you have come!" She looked at Clara with a beaming smile, her mouselike hair curling limply on either side of her ears. "What a beautiful dress, Miss Moore! I declare, I have never seen such a lovely shade of green, and it does your complexion such credit. You look like a portrait in a gallery, I dare say. Pity we do not have many eligible beaux for you. The county is sadly lacking, just sadly."

The rapidly uttered bombardment of words made Clara's head

spin and her cheeks warm. How was she to respond to any of it? Or was she meant to? She opted to maintain her smile and nod as though she completely agreed.

"Thank you for the invitation," Phoebe replied, every word careful and pronounced, and, to Clara's ears, a little slow.

Perhaps that was intentional.

Mr. Fleet stood by and wore a frozen smile, no doubt meant to be welcoming, but now only appearing awkwardly overwhelmed. In his silence, that was only more pronounced, and with his wife rambling so often, it too might have been intentional.

"Come, come, come in," Mrs. Fleet insisted, not so much stammering as reiterating the command. "So many people for you to meet, so very many. We shall be along shortly." She gestured a waving hand to the rest of the rooms, and Clara, for one, could not have hurried more gracefully away.

"If the entire evening is to be like that," Phoebe hissed as she took Clara's arm in her own, "I will find myself unwell in exactly one hour, you have my word."

Biting back a laugh, Clara nodded and steered them both to a punchbowl as she took stock of any possible familiar faces in the room.

She hardly knew anyone in the county, and she was looking for familiar faces?

Did she expect to see the villagers that regularly came to the spring fête the school held? Not only would that have ruined her assignment, but it would have disappointed her, as hardly a one of them would have recognized her or recollected her name.

What an embarrassing impulse.

"Miss Moore!"

How in the world could she be hearing a familiar voice in a place such as this? Still, she turned and looked, smile in place.

The smile became slightly strained as she saw Mrs. Browning bobbing towards her, wiry frame swathed in lavender silks and lace. The woman's smile was warm, but somehow, she seemed more angular in her present appearance than she had been that day on the shore when Clara had met her. The attempted pile of her hair had not helped matters, as it seemed to be somehow melting from its heights into a coiled mass instead.

The urge to adjust her own hair made Clara pinch her thumb and forefinger together beside her. "Mrs. Browning, what a pleasure!"

Mrs. Browning beamed and tilted her head to one side, making Clara fear that her diminishing coif might slide from her scalp entirely. "You are a vision, my dear. What a pity Kirklin is not here to see it."

Clara's stomach clenched in distress. "The duke is very kind and was a gracious and generous host."

"But is he not missing you terribly?" Mrs. Browning pressed, her eyes narrowing slightly. "I could see how fond you were of each other that day, such a sweet pairing."

"I cannot presume to know His Grace's feelings, Mrs. Browning," Clara said as kindly as she could while the temptation to bare her teeth roared within her. "He was most considerate of my whims that morning, to be sure, but anything else is…"

Phoebe sighed loudly and returned to Clara's side with a disparaging look. "Mrs. Browning, how shall I bear to have such a polite and modest niece? She will not allow me to make any such claims myself, though it would be my dearest wish. Forgive me, I know we have not been introduced, but I truly feel that you might condole with me on this matter."

"Mrs. Browning, may I present my aunt, Mrs. Daniels?" Clara murmured, wishing she could jab Phoebe in the side with a pointy elbow without causing a reaction.

Mrs. Browning brightened markedly as she took in Phoebe's elegant ensemble and bearing and nodded rather sagely. "Indeed, Mrs. Daniels, I believe I do. Good manners on her part, to be sure, but really…"

"Really, Mrs. Browning, indeed." Phoebe smiled and gestured towards the room. "Will you take a turn with me, Mrs. Browning?"

"Of course!" The woman turned at once and Phoebe joined her, gliding in a way that only heightened their difference in comportment.

If only Minerva could see the comparison.

Clara got herself some punch, and began to meander on her own, content, for the moment, to not be forced into conversation. Phoebe might soon have Clara in an awkward situation by stirring up gossip, but it would all die down eventually, and with Hawk being away, what harm was there?

"My niece spoke so warmly of your beach, Mrs. Browning," Phoebe said loudly as she and Mrs. Browning reached the windows, "and of your generosity in permitting her access to it on such short notice. Might I have the pleasure of walking there myself on Thursday, if the weather is fine?"

"Thursday would be lovely," Mrs. Browning conceded without hesitation. "Indeed, I believe we are entertaining the Goldings that day, and it would be no trouble at all to have you, as well."

"The beach is always open on Thursdays at Brownings'," a gentleman in the room chuckled, overhearing them easily. "It is only on Tuesdays that one must face disappointment."

Clara's ears perked up at that, and she moved towards the women as casually as she dared. "Tuesdays?" she repeated. "Why is that?"

Mrs. Browning gave the man a playfully scolding look. "Mr. Francis would have you think it is always unavailable, but I assure you, it is not so." She smiled at Clara now. "Every second and fourth Tuesday, rather than host any friends or neighbors on our beach, we give it over to our tenants for fishing and for their own entertainment once the fishing has been done."

"Fishing for the markets?" Clara asked with unfeigned interest, though the question itself was not one she cared for an answer to so much as continuing the conversation.

The generous owners of the beach she was tasked with inspecting had specified days of closure? Whatever for? Why so regular? Why an entire day? It made little sense, and her curiosity was roused into full awareness.

"If they like," Mrs. Browning replied with a grand sort of magnanimity, "or purely for themselves. It has long been a tradition at Barcliffe, and they do so love it, we could not bear to part from the way of things. So long as it is not the second or fourth Tuesday of the month, the beach at Barcliffe is always available for all."

It was, was it?

Clara smiled and sipped her punch, the beginnings of a plan starting to form.

Chapter Fifteen

He'd grown so used to notes from Clara that notes from anyone else were more an annoyance than they ought to have been.

A note from his sister, for example, ought not to have sent him into bouts of irritation, and yet here he was, sitting moodily in his study.

Irritated. And pacing.

It was rare that Adrianna wrote to him to ask for favors. She wrote to him faithfully once a month, short details of her daily life, but other than that, only when forced. On occasion, she had been so forced and had to give him a report of her behaviors in said letters. She was not particularly poorly behaved, but he had received the odd note or two over the years informing him of certain behavioral quirks and actions that concerned her instructors. He had not had one for some time now, which was much appreciated.

This note, however, did not fall into any of his expected categories.

For some reason or another, Adrianna had developed a desire to do some volunteering with the rudimentary academy that was partnered with the Miss Masters' school and needed his permission to do so. Perhaps it was due to her position as the sister of a duke, and considering that the rudimentary academy, named for its benefactor, Lord Rothchild, contained some girls from the lowest class in Society. No doubt, the school had received some harsh words in the past when others had so volunteered and their parents wished for them to keep with their own station.

Hawk would never have done so.

That was not to say that he wished for his sister to marry across stations, necessarily, though he did not foresee himself cutting her off if she chose to do so. Rather, he thought spending time with such poor girls would be rather good for his sister, or for anyone of a higher station in life. It might grant her a greater appreciation for what she possessed, seeing what others did not possess, and heaven knew that Lady Adrianna Russell could use a greater appreciation for her lot in life.

Oddly, Adrianna had not included any form or instructions on the permission he needed to give, nor any details as to what her volunteering would entail. She had not asked him to come speak with the headmistress, nor had she expressed what exactly he would need to say in a response.

His rather tight-lipped sister had exceeded her previously set patterns there.

It was exactly the sort of thing he would have discussed with Nat, not that his friend had any particular insight into Adrianna, but simply because of his natural understanding of people in general.

But Nat had been true to his word and departed for Daveney shortly after stating he would do so, leaving Hawk without a single person to commiserate on the strange contents of his sister's request.

What in the world was he to do? Reply with some vague permission that said absolutely nothing at all?

He could hardly write, "I, George Russell, Duke of Kirklin, hereby grant permission for my sister, Lady Adrianna Russell, to do as she likes," or some such.

She might take over France if he wrote that. Or become a laundress, though that was hardly likely. Or commandeer a ship and sail to the West Indies.

He shuddered at the thought, which was not as far-fetched as one might think of her.

Adrianna had always had a wild, adventurous streak about her.

No, the fact of the matter was that he could not grant a general permission for such a task. He had every faith in the school, and in those charged with its running, to keep his sister safe and never compromise her reputation in any way, but there were too many questions he still held regarding something as varied as volunteering.

His sister had stated she wished to begin straightaway, which did not suit his present idea of replying to inquire further as to this project of hers. Knowing his sister as he did, she would have responded in rather agitated tones and found a way to forge his signature on whatever she wished. She would have her way, no matter what he said or how he said it.

Or when.

"Your Grace," his butler, Knox, intoned suddenly, making Hawk jump.

"Knox," Hawk managed to say without any strange inflections, moving towards him. "I did not hear you come in."

Knox's thin lips twitched, but, amazingly, he did not smile. "Apologies, Your Grace. A message for you. From Kirkleigh."

Heart palpitations stood in the way of Hawk's immediate action, and he stared with some abandonment at the tightly folded paper laying on a platter in Knox's gloved grasp.

He blinked twice, which seemed to settle his heart enough for his legs to function, and closed the distance between them to pluck the message from its platter and stare at the wax seal on the back.

There was nothing special about it. Not even an impression from a ring or a stamp. Stafford would have used the Kirklin seal, had it been from him.

Clara had no seal.

He turned the folded note over and looked at the direction. Sure enough, the hand was hers, and the very slight flourish on occasional letters made him smile freely.

A soft clearing of a throat brought his head up, and Knox raised a politely questioning brow.

Hawk would have flushed in embarrassment had he thought about it long enough. "Thank you, Knox," he said instead, turning away and moving to the window.

He did not wait for the door to the study to close, nor to see what his butler would do. He broke the seal and unfolded the paper quickly.

I wonder, Your Grace, if you could direct me to the location of a book on the history of Kent. I am sure there is one in the grand library at Kirkleigh, but alas,

I cannot find it. In return, I will relay the answer to your previous request, that of the Maple Room's bed hangings and their suitability in the room itself.

The hangings are lovely, and quite suitable. I find they complement the decor, and the wallpaper within. But I suspect, Your Grace, that you knew that already.

And I would take this opportunity to disagree with you on one point alone: There is nothing unremarkable about the Maple. Not in the room, not in the tree, nor in any other respect.

Palpitations resumed, and with a furious pace and unparalleled power. He thought a few of his ribs might crack from the force of it as the image of those words in her hand repeated in his mind like the flickering of a candle.

There was no mistaking her meaning, and the boldness of it caught his breath. He was not put off by her saying so, not in the least, and particularly not when it was so delicately hidden in a way that only he would understand.

He had likened himself to the maple once, just upon their first meeting, and called it unremarkable. Sturdy and tall, but unremarkable.

She refuted that now, and he'd have kissed her had she done so in his presence.

What an impulse to acknowledge!

He could not take much more of this correspondence between them across the counties. She was growing more engaging, more adorable by the day, and their conversation would have lasted all of five minutes had they done so in person.

Yet he felt as though he had been speaking with her for hours. Years, even. He felt as though he knew her in a way he had never known another living soul. As though their innocent, masquerading, silly notes back and forth had been a real courtship.

As though he could admit to loving her already.

His knees shook, and he gripped the ledge of the window to steady himself, the letter creasing with the increased pressure of his hand. Could he love her? Did he?

Would he?

He had to see her face again, had to feel the discerning power in her eyes on him, had to feel the touch of her hand. He would know the moment he was in her presence, he was certain, and then he would know what to do and how to act.

But how would he get to Kent and Kirkleigh? What would be his reason for doing so? He could not say he had been spurred on with the fire of hope from a line in her note, and he could not create some false calamity on the estate when he had recently been there and verified that all was well.

He began to pace again, tapping the blessed note into the palm of his hand as though it could send the answer to him through the connection.

What could he do, and how could he do it?

Elmsley was in perfect hands, and he was superfluous. It would be easy enough to leave now, and he could return with Adrianna for the Christmas holidays when the time was right.

Along with any other persons who might have an interest in joining them.

The letter hit his palm once more when he froze, his eyes widening as various words and ideas began to connect in his mind.

Adrianna.

He glanced over at his desk where the note from his sister sat, still open, her own neat hand on display as though given by heaven itself.

He could go to Adrianna.

She needed an answer straightaway, he needed answers before he could give his own, and the most efficient manner in doing so would be to go to her and ask his questions at once. He could assure himself of this opportunity she wished to take part in, and she would have a prompt answer from him.

And then he would be free to do as he liked.

It would make sense for him to stay at Kirkleigh while visiting his sister. It was what he had always done. That was the most expected thing of him, and anything else would have been cause for comment if anyone heard of it.

There was no need for him to create comment over this.

No, no, he had best go and see to his sister's wishes personally, though a letter would have done easily, out of respect for her apparently fervent desire.

It was exactly what a doting, kind, generous guardian would do.

And he might as well stay for some weeks and take the opportunity to see his sister more than once. Why, it would be a kindness for his horses and coachmen to remain until the holidays, rather than force them all to make the journey again.

Weeks at Kirkleigh.

What a prospect.

He grinned and clapped the letter into his palm again before turning to stride from the room, swiping his sister's letter up in the process. "Knox!" he bellowed, his voice echoing in the empty corridors of Elmsley Abbey. "Prepare my coach!"

"Why in the world are we doing this?"

"I've told you and Fern what I heard. Neither of you made any sort of protest when I did so."

"Her name was Flora, not Fern."

Clara rolled her eyes and hurried along, her dark skirts rippling against her legs in the cool night breeze. "I know what her name was then, but it does not change what her name is now. For heaven's sake, Brick, did you or did you not insist on accompanying me when I venture to the beach at night?"

The man beside her grumbled incoherently, which made Clara smile in spite of her irritating situation at present.

"I shall take that as a yes," Clara said primly.

"I did not mean for us to go out on a fool's errand," Brick snapped without venom. "Sparrow, you heard something, and that is all. You've no information to prove anything, let alone to presume this will give us anything. In this line of work, you need solid evidence to take action, not a whim or ideas of a grand discovery."

Clara glanced at him, annoyance and embarrassment rising in equal tides. "Would you do me the courtesy of speaking to me as though I am an equal and not a child? I may not have years of experience in doing any of this, and it may be my first mission, but do you really think I would leap to the conclusion of watching a beach in the middle of the night in late autumn during a rather cold spell if

I did not think it would prove useful? I may be a woman, Brick, but I am not an imbecile, nor am I prone to flights of fancy or grand ideals."

Brick walked silently beside her for a moment, and Clara felt her cheeks heat further still in the night, the temperature all the greater for the chill the air held against them.

Just when she thought she might have soured him for good, he exhaled roughly. "You're quite right. I never thought you an imbecile, and certainly know better than to think your being a woman is in any way a hindrance to your abilities. I've been tossed on my back more than once by one of the female operatives, and I'm not ashamed to say so."

The image made Clara smile, and she managed to look back at her hulking companion almost shyly. "I'd never be able to do that, Brick, nor are you in danger of it from me."

He flashed a quick, crooked smile. "With some training, Sparrow, I think you'd be surprised. But I should have known better than to make a senseless comment as I did. I beg your pardon."

Clara waved a hand, now embarrassed for an entirely different reason. "I give it, truly. And I cannot tell you why I feel so strongly about this, but I do. My mind instantly began to turn the thing over, and I could almost see the ships coming into the beach by moonlight. I just have a feeling, Brick."

"We'll work with that, then," he said simply. "Evidence is preferred, but a feeling with solid reasoning is enough."

Folding her arms against the brisk wind, Clara nodded. "I'll get evidence, I'm sure of it."

"And your friends, the Brownings?" Brick pressed as they started down the cliffside path at the edge of Kirkleigh lands. "Are you prepared to accuse them of treason?"

A shiver raced up Clara's spine that had nothing to do with the weather. "I'm not prepared to accuse anyone," she admitted with a rawness that made her throat ache, "but to suspect is another thing entirely."

"The difference between a feeling and evidence, that," Brick said with a sigh. He patted Clara's arm lightly. "Your instincts may prove right, you know."

Instincts. Such a strange word, something that made her feel as though she ought to have been far more experienced to possess. She had no experience or expertise to fall back on for impulses to be called instincts. She only had a feeling that something was suspicious, and had she not gone through the few days of training she had, she doubted she would have even felt that.

What if this was not the beginning of an instinct at all but the perfect example of naïvely running headlong into disaster with a foolish idea?

Only Brick would know her shame and embarrassment, and Phoebe would buoy up her spirits when it happened, but Clara knew she would never forgive herself.

She shook her head, scolding herself silently as she trudged down the path towards the sand below them. If she would snap at Brick for being so doubting and critical of her decision to be out here tonight, she ought to give herself the same credit. She was not harming anyone by being out here tonight, and it would allow her to look into the suspicious claim she had heard.

She'd have asked a Barcliffe tenant if the beaches were truly offered to them every second and fourth Tuesday if she knew one. But watching for ships to arrive or any activity to transpire on the beach would do just as well.

"Right," Brick whispered as they reached the sand and turned to walk towards Barcliffe. "Move slowly, stay silent, and tread lightly, aye? Walk in my footsteps, to hide our numbers."

Clara nodded and allowed him to go first, carefully placing her feet where his had pressed into the damp sand. It could have been far more awkward if he had been striding with his usual gait, but given the attempt to move slowly and with stealth, the steps were closer together than they might have been otherwise.

Almost silently, they continued on, the sound of waves hitting the shore doing a great deal to cover any audible aspects of their motions. The moon was hidden behind a cloud at present, but would soon reappear and cast light on them, and anyone else out and about.

Brick came to a stop without much warning, and Clara barely avoided slamming into his back in her concentration. She frowned up at the expanse of him, though he would not know, and waited. He pointed at an outcropping of the cliffside just ahead, and Clara followed the direction of his finger, nodding when she saw it.

It would be a perfect place for the pair of them to tuck in against the cliff and watch for approaching ships without being observed. Or, indeed, to see any ships that might have gone out.

She must allow for that, as well.

There was no telling what all could be happening here, truth be told.

A twinge of excitement began to curl her stomach, and she followed Brick over to the outcropping. He gestured for her to take the position nearest the rock and for them both to crouch down to hide themselves.

"And now, we wait," he breathed, his voice barely loud enough for her to hear.

Wait.

Clara frowned at the thought, considering her crouched position and the potential length of time she could be doing so. Without asking or checking for Brick's thoughts, Clara adjusted herself to sit directly upon the sand, arranging her skirts to accommodate the change and tucking her knees to her chest.

She could feel Brick looking at her, and, in the periphery of her vision, see him doing so. "We might be here a while," she hissed when a wave rolled in, "and I do not have your stamina."

He began to shake a little beside her, and she looked away, fearing his laughter might ignite some of her own.

It was a strange thing, having laughter during something that could be dangerous. She supposed people like Brick were used to such things, and life continued on in spite of missions and their danger. There was still amusement and irritation and boredom, even among their diverse activities. They still felt hunger while waiting for an arrival, still had to sneeze when there was too much dust, and longed for a rest when the day became too much.

They were much more likely to have more in their day than Clara did, but the impulse was the same.

She was not tired now, that was certain.

After the card party at the Fleets' home a few days before, Clara had set about setting this evening into motion. She'd spoken with

Phoebe and with Brick, and worked out the best time of night to go out. She'd studied her drawing intently, trying in vain to map out where a ship might go and what it might do. She had spent hours earlier in the day drawing the coastline as far as she could see while sitting as close to the edge of the cliff as she dared on Kirkleigh lands.

It was a fortunate thing indeed that she did not possess a fear of heights.

She had an invitation to go to Barcliffe for tea with the Brownings in a few days, and the idea of having a magistrate at her side to arrest them for treason floated into her mind.

What a horrid thing to take pleasure in! She ought to hope that her neighbors would be completely innocent of anything treasonous, that if there were any nefarious deeds taking place in their cove and on their beach, they were unaware of them.

That was what she ought to take pleasure in. Not finding satisfaction in seeing Mrs. Browning's angular face wreathed in shock and indignation as guilt was pronounced.

What had poor Mrs. Browning done to deserve Clara's suspicion and resentment?

Other than suspect her of having feelings for Hawk.

Despite the cold, Clara's heart warmed within her, beating a few fervent beats before relaxing into its usual pattern and tempo once more.

What would Hawk say if he saw her out here? Would he have joined her? Would he have laughed at her?

Laughed with her?

She could not have told him about the true task, but she could enjoy the stars and the moon above them in spite of that.

She glanced up at the sky, resting her chin on her knees with a soft sigh. There were a few clouds, as evidenced by the one obscuring the moon at present, but not enough to hide the brilliance of the stars. They twinkled and winked with their usual magnificence, though somehow brighter now that the moon was hidden.

It had been an age since she had looked at the stars for the simple pleasure of it, and she had never done so with any particular aims. No whimsy or wishing, no scientific aims, no romantic notions or ideas. It had always been simple appreciation and fascination of them, the light each possessed and what each did for the night sky.

There was something simply magical and beautiful about a star-filled sky.

A pang of longing lanced through Clara, and she laid her cheek against her knee, squeezing her eyes shut against it. She wanted Hawk to be beside her, not for an assignment or mission, but simply to look up at the sky and appreciate the stars with her. She wished for the stars to wring conversation from them both, stripping them both of vanity and pride, of pretense and propriety, leaving their souls bare to each other and comfortable to be so. Such nights could draw out secrets and heartaches, philosophies and musings, revealing more and more of a person until only the heart of them remained.

And she desperately wanted his heart.

She wanted him to want hers.

What a simpleton she was!

How could she have let herself get so caught up in something so fanciful? A few notes sent across counties, and she was a trembling mess of feminine nonsense? He was a duke, for pity's sake, and she had thrust herself into his life, not been invited into it. There was nothing here for her, not in the slightest. She was lying to him, of all things, and there would be no forgiveness for that whenever it happened to come out.

If it came out.

Not that it would matter, as the Duke of Kirklin would have no cause to think on Clara Harlow, or Clara Moore, once she finished her assignment. She would hide herself at the school for the entirety of the term after the holidays, would be absent from the annual fête, and rid herself of any and all opportunities to see Hawk ever again.

It was simple and straightforward, and after that, she would be returned to her equally simple life as Clara Harlow.

Why did that thought leave her not so much homesick as heartsick?

Her thoughts became less clear and more a swirl of images and art, rather like the sky at sunrise and sunset, filled with light and clouds, color and motion, taking her feelings along with it as though each sat on the sea itself. It was a marvelously relaxing sensation, and much welcomed after such pained self-reflection.

Clara felt her arm being shaken, and stirred in her place, turning her head to look at Brick, blinking when she realized there was a different light shining on him, and that his features seemed a little drawn. He said nothing, but the resignation in his face made her heart drop deep into the pit that had formed in her stomach.

She turned her attention to the sea and the beach, only to see that there was nothing there. Nothing but a faintly brightening horizon.

No ships, no people, no action.

Nothing at all.

"No," she breathed. She turned back to Brick, her eyes wide and aching even as the pit in her stomach swallowed her heart whole. "Nothing?"

Brick rose and brushed off his trousers, holding a hand out to her. "Come on, Sparrow. Best get you home and into bed before the day truly begins."

Sick with shame, eyes swimming in tears, Clara took his hand and let him pull her up, then silently followed him from the beach and back to Kirkleigh.

Chapter Sixteen

There was something markedly impressive about Miss Masters' Finishing School for Fine Young Ladies. He'd always thought so, but arriving through its grand gates and seeing its pristine grounds always brought the thought back.

Not even the finest houses he had seen of other dukes in the realm could match this place in appearance.

And his sister was learning how to be a lady within.

Apparently, wishing to assist poor girls who would only hope to ever even work in a house so grand as an upstairs maid.

The irony was not lost on him.

At least, he presumed that was what the girls from the rudimentary academy would go on to become. He'd never actually thought about it or considered such things. If Adrianna truly wished to participate in its programs, perhaps he would need to educate himself there. Not to protest or judge, but to properly appreciate.

It was a thought, certainly.

As the carriage rattled along towards the school, Hawk felt a slight twinge of guilt that he forced away with an almost believable grunt of disapproval. He had opted to go directly to the school rather than to Kirkleigh, more to see his task done than to be prompt in his attention to his sister.

That and he was not sure he was prepared to see Clara so soon. Nor to part from her once he was reunited with her.

He would rather face Adrianna and be done with his pretense for coming rather than try to fulfill both his aims at once.

It felt more complicated than it needed to be, but he could not help that now.

If Adrianna had the slightest idea that she was not his priority at the moment, he would never hear the end of it.

All the more reason to go to her first and ensure she knew she was the first stop he made upon his arrival.

She'd love that.

He did not wait for the carriage to come to a full stop before he opened the door and stepped out, setting his hat upon his head and tapping it to center. He had dressed smartly this morning, which would delight White when he arrived at Kirkleigh this evening, more to maintain an esteemed impression of his position than anything else. The fact that he might look well in it when he arrived at Kirkleigh and saw Clara again was simply an added benefit.

The giant of a butler appeared in the doorway, seeming to loom protectively there while waiting for Hawk to reach him. How in the world anyone had managed to dress the man in the proper attire befitting a butler was unfathomable, yet while he was the most intimidating specimen of man Hawk had ever seen, he was also one of the most congenial. Even now, he was smiling in greeting, the reddish glint of his slicked back hair almost off-putting in its discrepancy from his stature.

He'd never quite gotten used to Mr. Adkins in the years Adrianna had been a student here, and it seemed unlikely that would change this late in her education.

"Welcome to Miss Masters' School, Your Grace," Adkins greeted, bowing in welcome. "Always a pleasure to welcome you here."

Hawk nodded once. "Thank you, Adkins. All in order?"

Adkins maintained his usual smile, but something twinkled in his eye. "Oh, aye, Your Grace. Miss Ginny Gerrard did run away again, but she had only gone to the stables, so all was well."

Having heard all about the conniving girl called Ginny Gerrard from his sister, Hawk was well aware that containing her had become quite a feat. Surprising that Adkins would tell him about it, but he suspected that anybody known to the school would also know about the Gerrard girl.

"Good, good," Hawk murmured, entering the grand foyer of the house-turned-school and removing his hat. A plain-faced maid stepped forward to take it from him, and he tossed his gloves in there as well, smiling his thanks at her. He turned back to Adkins, presently shutting the door behind them. "I'm paying an unexpected call on my sister, Adkins. I don't need to have her fetched from her studies, but when she is free, I would very much like to see her."

"Of course, Your Grace," the butler replied amiably. He glanced at a grand clock standing near them and nodded fervently. "It will be just a few minutes until the present class is dismissed. Would you take a cup of tea in the drawing room while you wait?"

"Thank you." He followed as Adkins led him there, then found himself wandering the large room once the butler had left to see that Adrianna was fetched.

It was quite possibly the largest drawing room he had ever seen in his life, but Beddingsford House, as it had once been, was one of the largest houses in England, as well. The walls were papered in a faint yellow print, which added a brightness to an otherwise imposing room, and the furniture was neat and comfortable, but what drew his attention most was the art that hung within the room. Landscapes of the perfect English picnic, of a countryside so fine it was enviable, of a festival taking place in a rather familiar looking village all garnered his attention, though the finer portraits of flora and fruits were equally skilled.

He did not recognize the settings, nor the particular style of the artist. That was not so uncommon, he had never claimed to be a great purveyor of the arts, but it did seem a rather intriguing collection to have displayed in the drawing room of a school, a room in which dozens of parents and families had undoubtedly gathered over the years.

The selection of art would have been significant.

"A note has been delivered to Lady Adrianna, Your Grace," Adkins announced as he entered the drawing room. "She will be here presently."

Hawk nodded slowly, then gestured to the painting of the festival. "Tell me, Adkins, is this piece of something in particular?"

"Aye, Your Grace," Adkins replied, coming closer. "That is the end-of-year fête from a few years ago. Have you ever been?"

"No, sadly." Hawk narrowed his eyes at it, willing the scene to come to life in his mind, as it seemed capable of doing. "It seems a rather lively affair."

"Oh, it is, Your Grace," Adkins said with real fondness. "The whole village comes out for it, and several of the local families. I trust you'll come next spring, Your Grace, with Lady Adrianna completing her education."

Hawk considered that, nodding more to himself than in answer. "I suppose I will. I look forward to it." He cocked his head at the painting, a certain point occurring to him. "If this was done of the local fête, the artist must also be local. Was it one of the students?"

"No, Your Grace, it was one of our teachers." Adkins straightened beside him, his chest puffing up with pride. "Miss Harlow. She teaches art and French and is masterfully accomplished in both areas. All of the art in this room is by her hand, in fact." He gestured around with all the delight of a fond father.

In spite of his reserve, Hawk found himself more than a little impressed. He knew the quality of teachers in this school were impressive, but he had no idea that it also extended to their art. He would never have cared before he'd met Clara, but after seeing what her hands could create, he seemed more able to appreciate such works now.

She'd have had a great deal to say about the work of Miss Harlow, he had no doubt.

"May I speak to her, as well?" Hawk asked as he continue to stare at the picture, its quality impressing him further still. "I wish to compliment her work, and perhaps inquire if she might do a portrait of my sister."

"I'm terribly sorry, Your Grace, but Miss Harlow is away just now. Has a sadly ailing relative she is tending to, and we have no idea of her return as yet."

That was a pity, but hardly a tragedy. Her family situation undoubtedly was, and he was sympathetic there, but he already knew a marvelously skilled artist. One he would shortly see, and one whose hands he would much rather receive art from.

"What in the world are you doing here, George?"

Adrianna's biting tone lit the room and Hawk turned towards

the doorway, raising an eyebrow. She only called him George when she was cross or when she was teasing. Today, she was most certainly cross.

"Good morning to you as well, sister."

Her dark eyes flashed, and her hands settled on her hips, the school pinafore pinned to her gray morning dress and slightly streaked with dirt of some sort. She shook her head, sending her nearly black ringlets bouncing and swaying in a way that reminded him of the little girl she had once been. "George, I do not have time for this; answer me, please."

Adkins bowed, clearing his throat, and scooted from the room, his lips quirking at Adrianna as he passed her.

She did not notice.

"I see your manners are not yet accomplished," Hawk observed, clasping his hands behind his back and making his way around the sofa towards her. He indicated the streaks on her pinafore with his head. "What have you done there?"

His sister did not look. "I was in the gardens for a lesson in biology," she snapped, showing him the soiled tips of her fingers as proof. "And I would be washing now before taking my luncheon in those same gardens were I not standing here wasting words with you. What do you want?"

Hawk grinned, oddly loving how fiery his sister could get and how completely unimpressed she was with regards to anything about him. She would never blindly accept anything he set down, would never turn submissive and meek towards him, and would never do anything he ordered without a rousing fight of her own. Which also meant she would never be any man's plaything, nor take any abuses ill-advisedly tossed in her direction.

It might make her a terror to several men in all classes, but God help him, he adored that about her.

"I would not be disappointed in an embrace from my sister," he said with a playful wince. "Particularly since we are not observed, and it would not embarrass her to anyone."

Adrianna's mouth twitched, just as he'd hoped, and she marched towards him, hands returned to her hips. "I'll not hug you," she told him primly, "as it would be a crime to smear your excellent ensemble with this dirt."

"I thought you'd like it," he replied in delight, looking down at it. "I wore it just for you."

"Charmed." She went up on tiptoe and kissed his cheek, winking with a smile as she lowered back down. "What are you doing here?" she asked again, her tone far tamer now.

Hawk wrapped an arm around her shoulders, pulling her close and kissing her hair. "Seeing you, of course."

She jabbed a sharp elbow into his side. "I mean it!"

"So do I!" he protested, looking down at her. "You send me a letter asking for permission to volunteer, but don't say anything about what you will be doing or what I need to say in order to give it to you. Since I was doing nothing in particular at Elmsley, I thought I'd ask you in person what you will be doing and what you need from me."

Adrianna jerked to stare up at him with wide eyes. "You did? I mean, you are? I mean... you're going to give me permission?"

Her disbelief was a clear indication of her fervent desires, and he'd have given her whatever she wanted for such a touching reaction.

But he was her elder brother, and her guardian, so he knew better than to give in so easily.

"More than likely," he said with a cautious look, "but I need to know the details, Addie."

She beamed at the pet name, her eyes crinkling in a way they rarely did anymore, as she rarely smiled so broadly. "You haven't called me that in ages, Georgie."

He sputtered and tapped at her ear with the hand dangling at her shoulder. "And you've *never* called me that, for which I am most grateful." He gestured for her to give him whatever it was he had to look at. "Do you have a letter or something I'm to sign for this venture you want to be part of?"

Adrianna scrunched up her face in consideration. "In a way, though hardly so formal. I was simply to provide proof of permission, but I can fetch the description of the opportunity, if you like."

"Please do." He smiled, tapping her ear again, which made her squirm away. "I'll wait here, we'll talk about permissions, and then we'll have tea. Does that suit you?"

Nodding eagerly, Adrianna dashed from the room, leaving Hawk chuckling behind her. He sat in one of the nearby chairs, then rose again just a minute or two later when a maid brought in a tea tray, then sat when she had departed. He smiled to himself as he crossed one leg over the other, looking about the room again.

It was rather charming, now he looked at it more comfortably. Perhaps he ought to do one of his drawing rooms in a similar shade and style, preferably one that had a goodly number of windows. The natural light added much to the room itself, and with the right sort of scenery beyond those windows, it would be a lovely room indeed.

"Oh my…"

He glanced back at the doorway and saw his sister returned, staring at him with wide eyes, no hint of a smile in her features. "What?"

She blinked. "You look so relaxed and easy, so unnervingly like Griffin at this moment, I am not sure which brother is visiting me."

Hawk scoffed and pushed to his feet with a scowl. "I beg your pardon; he is a popinjay in need of a close shave and limited access to spirits. I barely resemble the man."

Adrianna blinked again, her lips curving into a smile once more. "Ah, it is you, George. What a relief."

He snorted at that and waved her in, gesturing to the sofa nearest the chair he'd chosen. She scampered in and handed the document to him before sitting at the very edge of the sofa, her hands tightly gripping each other in her lap.

Hawk smiled as he eyed the paper before him. "You really want to do this, don't you, Addie?"

"Yes!" she all but squealed. She scooted somehow closer, her eyes filled with a passionate light. "The girls that come into the school from the Rothchild Academy are so impressive, Hawk. You would never know they are lowborn, or cast-off orphans, or taken in from the streets themselves. One of my very closest friends here was a Rothchild-sponsored student, and she could do anything when she leaves here. I think she would make a rather marvelous woman of business, though she'll likely never get to do anything of the sort." She shook her head, her throat working. "I want to help, Hawk. However I can."

It was impossible to be anything less than moved by her words, and Hawk had trouble enough returning his attention to the list without emotion.

The items were simple and straightforward enough, but even if they had been more involved, had put Adrianna in more of a public light, he probably would have agreed.

As it was, there was no question.

"All right," he murmured, his voice surprisingly rough. "Where should I sign?"

"And in here, we have the library, which was not much before my grandfather inherited, but now I think you can agree, it is rather impressive."

Clara sighed in a show of delight, looking around at the shelves which were, admittedly, full of books, but the room itself held no distinctive features, no admirable architecture, and no indication of any recent use.

For an impressive room, it did not seem to be so for those that owned it.

"What a fine collection, Mr. Browning!" Phoebe praised, lying through her teeth, though her tone hid that perfectly. "Are you an avid reader yourself? With such a delightful collection, you surely must be!"

Mr. Browning hemmed and hawed, blustering with some show of modesty, though it was impossible to tell how much of it was genuine. "To my everlasting shame, Mrs. Daniels, I am not as avid a reader as I ought to be with such a collection at hand. I have not the patience for it, nor the inclination to spend much time doing so."

Clara moved to the windows, too small for the size of the room, but positioned well enough to give someone within a lovely view of the cliffside. Barcliffe was closer to the coast than Kirkleigh was, actually giving her a glimpse of the waves curling on the sea. Why, one could easily stroll from the house to the edge of the cliff without growing the least bit breathless or fatigued.

That was an interesting position, and one that not a lot of people would have enjoyed. Certainly, small children would not have done well in a house with such risks near it, but if anyone had interests in the sea…

Well, then Barcliffe was rather perfectly set.

She'd struggled with the disappointment of the night on the beach with Brick. Hours upon hours sitting there, falling asleep while waiting for ships to arrive or anyone to appear on the beach, and nothing had happened. She'd questioned Brick a number of times, ashamed that she had slept on her first assignment, and he'd repeatedly assured her that there had been no sign at all of anything happening other than night on the shore. No smugglers, no ships, not even any small fishing boats.

How could there have been nothing when she'd heard something so promising from the very person whose property she needed to explore? Had she jumped into this entire venture completely blind? Was she too naïve, too inexperienced, to do something of such importance as work to protect the country's interests?

These questions continued to swirl about her mind, though Phoebe had refused to let her grow melancholy or morose since then. She'd been the perfect mentor, taking Clara aside to commiserate on the uneventful evening, on the perceived failure, and what it could mean for her and for them. It might have been a failure, Phoebe had said, but that did not mean the mission had failed. Rather, it could simply add another aspect or dimension to the assignment, and it now fell to them to determine what the failure meant about the situation.

It had been an eye-opening experience, learning to view such a mistake in such a way. The discussion had gone on for several hours, long after either of them should have been asleep, but Clara, for one, had never felt her mind work so vigorously. It had certainly cured her of the despondency she had felt brewing, and she had quickly adjusted her thinking in the way Phoebe had encouraged her to.

Which meant this outing to take tea with the Brownings was more than just a social call.

It was an investigation.

So far, it had been rather uneventful, and downright boring. They'd come for tea, as promised, and Mrs. Browning had carried all conversation in her own hands, hardly granting either of them opportunity to say a single word. Neither of them minded, of course, but it had gone on so dreadfully long. Then she had insisted on their touring the house with her, taking them to each and every room she could. Mr. Browning had taken over when they had found him in his study, and Mrs. Browning had begged to leave them to discuss a few household matters with their housekeeper, leaving them to the effusive and longwinded explanations of her husband without any rescue.

Should she have had any rescue to give them.

Clara ignored whatever their host was saying now as she observed the scene from the window, the day growing far more dreary than it had begun. The distance from the house to the cliffs was the most exciting thing Clara had found about this house yet, and she could yawn at its discovery.

It was growing more and more evident that the Brownings were not involved in whatever was occurring at their cove, if anything was occurring there, and Clara could not say she was surprised.

They were both so completely ordinary that she wouldn't think them proper candidates for their own village's interest, let alone England's, and especially not France's. It was entirely possible that their shoreline and cove were being used by this French faction and its supporters without them having any idea of it.

Sympathy for them was not overwhelming in Clara's heart, and she could not rightfully say why. They had not insulted her nor offended her, and they certainly seemed to be fair enough neighbors, but something about their keen interest in everything and everyone irked her beyond polite irritation.

They were no simple busybodies, that was certain.

"Miss Moore, did I hear you in conversation with Mrs. Fleet the other night?" Mr. Browning asked, his voice booming needlessly. "Something about helping their daughters to increase their artistry?"

Clara turned from the window to smile at him with the kindness she ought to possess. "I promised to advise the girls on their artistic abilities in watercolor, Mr. Browning," she corrected with the gentleness of a dove. "I daresay each possesses her own version of artistry, as the word stands."

Mr. Browning blinked without comprehending. "Yes, yes, of course," he eventually muttered with a bland tone that proved his lack of understanding. "Well, you shall find them very accomplished girls. Might I persuade you to bring them here? They could paint our cove, and all!"

Really, it was as though Mr. Browning wanted her to discover something.

Smiling further, Clara nodded with an eagerness she did not need to entirely feign. "What a lovely notion! I am sure it would be perfect, Mr. Browning, if you do not feel we would be an imposition on your property."

"Not at all, not at all!" he exclaimed, the volume of his voice making her jump. "And you must stay for tea, all of you, and them as well. Mr. Fleet and I will be able to discuss tedious affairs of business while the ladies are at their art, and we might all walk the beach together once the tea is done! What say you to that, hmm?"

"I say perfection could not be more suitably settled," Clara praised, dipping her chin in a show of modest approval, tucking bits and pieces of his words into her mind to record in her diary later.

There would be much to plan and much to consider.

"Then I shall write to Fleet today!" Mr. Browning insisted, grinning so broadly his girthy cheeks strained with it. "Extend an invitation to them all. Shall we settle it for next Tuesday, hmm?"

"That would be the morning after the assembly ball, Mr. Browning," Phoebe pointed out with a severe look. "Are the Fleet girls out?"

He turned to give her a blank expression. "I haven't the foggiest, Mrs. Daniels. Pray, at what age do girls usually get out?"

Clara put a hand to her brow, now that she was out of her host's eyesight. 'Get out,' he'd called it. And this was a man who had raised children? If he was a spy for the French, she would call herself Marie Antoinette, never mind the poor taste in it.

Phoebe, thank heavens, was kinder towards him. "When did your own girls come out, Mr. Browning?"

"I haven't the faintest idea," he admitted without hesitation. "Before their marriages, certainly."

Clara looked up at the ceiling with a long-suffering sigh she could not hide, longing to be rid of their host, and to simply wander the unremarkable home to discover its more remarkable secrets. Enduring the tedium of his company was trying enough, but to investigate his home and his manners for the sake of the kingdom? She'd rather investigate the King himself and would not consider her efforts there in the least wasted.

The art upon the ceiling, however, was also not a waste.

Of all things, they depicted ships at sea, and a great many of them, in one place or another. They were positioned strangely, at odd angles and without much pattern to them. They varied in size, yet all were clearly schooners or clippers, with tiny rowboats dotted along here and there. It was almost as though they mirrored the stars in the sky, though the clusters of boats were too gathered to do such a thing.

"Ah, you notice our fine artwork above, Miss Moore."

Slowly, she lowered her chin to look at Mr. Browning, the change in position of her head making her a bit light-headed, though it cleared quickly enough. "It's magnificent," she praised without hesitation. "It perfectly captures the struggle man faces upon the seas."

He seemed impressed by her assessment and glanced up himself. "Yes, I suppose it does. All the waves and the winds... So many ships... yet the sea always has her way..." He nodded in approval and smiled at Clara again. "Very astute, Miss Moore. Perhaps you ought to be a teacher."

Her ears seemed to burst into flame at his words, and the backs of her knees suddenly lost all feeling. Tingling pains pulled at her stomach as she struggled to maintain her smile at him, and her mind spun with the attempt to answer appropriately.

Did he know? Or was he simply paying her a compliment with a secret irony he could not fathom?

"I was barely a passable student," Clara heard herself say, her smile aching. "I can only imagine how I should fare in attempting to teach any myself."

"I am sure you are too modest," he replied, his tone losing just a hint of the boisterous air it always carried.

Something was wrong here. It was slight, it was unclear, but it was there.

Something.

"Oh, dear me!" Phoebe exclaimed, looking at the clock on the mantle. "Is that the time? Mr. Browning, do forgive me. We have enjoyed our time here to such an extent, we have stayed far longer than we ought to have done. I am this moment due to call at the milliner's shop in the village for my new bonnet. Will you forgive a hasty departure from us?"

"Certainly, certainly," he replied, gesturing to the door. "Mustn't keep Madam Garlet waiting. She does have an eye, as I understand, so you shall want for nothing, Mrs. Daniels, though your beauty would make any bonnet quite fortunate." He offered her an arm and escorted her to the door, and Clara followed, breathing barely steady.

Retreating now was fortunate indeed, and she had much to consider, surely. An odd statement here, a particular drawing there, and that strange shift in Mr. Browning that was not at all called for, yet entirely unnerving.

Much to consider, indeed.

Whatever had passed, Mr. Browning was ever himself as he loaded them into the carriage, Mrs. Browning belatedly rejoining them for farewells.

Once they had safely rolled away, Phoebe groaned in an uncharacteristic show of emotion. "Had we stayed in that house one moment longer, and I would not have had to feign any sort of headache to beg our departure. Remind me to purchase a new bonnet before we see them again, will you?"

"Of course," Clara murmured, looking out of the window, still unsettled by her exchange with Mr. Browning. "I think they are hiding something, Fern."

"Good," came the calm reply. "I think so as well, and I look forward to discussing our individual reasons later this evening."

Clara smiled to herself, bemused by Phoebe's complete lack of concern for their situation, but also reassured by it. If the more experienced of the pair did not fear, why should she?

Kirkleigh was soon before them, as welcoming a sight as Clara had ever seen. They stepped out of the carriage without much fuss and Clara removed her bonnet at once, having left the ribbons loose and untied at their departure. She sighed as she entered the house, swinging her bonnet round by the ribbons as she smiled at the maid waiting for her things.

"Good day," came a deep voice of greeting before she could say a single word.

Heart skipping, Clara's eyes darted to the staircase, and her lips parted in utter astonishment as a gloriously handsome figure stood at the top of the stairs, grinning unreservedly down at her.

Hawk had returned to Kirkleigh.

Chapter Seventeen

$\mathcal{S}$he was more beautiful than he remembered, and it was a crime to admit it.

From the moment he'd set eyes on her again, swinging her bonnet around as though it were a child's toy and smiling at the maid with some inner joy he longed to know, he'd felt himself swept away as though on the tide itself, and they'd barely spoken a handful of words to each other.

Clara did not seem eager to do so, and Hawk, admittedly, could not think of many to say.

Wretched beginning, that.

Blessedly, Mrs. Daniels had no such restriction, and she had seemed truly delighted to see him again. The prim formality he had known in her before had relaxed, and he found himself thinking what a pleasure it would be to sit in comfortable conversation with the woman.

Not as enjoyable as it would be to do anything and everything with Clara, but Mrs. Daniels had an intelligence that made him curious and a steadiness he envied. He could see her as the perfect confidante for anyone, male or female, and did not have to be all that observant to see how she cared for and protected Clara.

Even now, she was keeping her niece from the trouble of having to converse, yet she did not ramble. She engaged with Hawk creditably, and somehow still included Clara in everything she was saying. It was an illustration in the mastery of the art of conversation, which would have served her well at any level in society, and in any situation.

It did not necessarily stop him from wishing she would be absent from this dining room at the moment, but that was not a personal attack on her.

It was only a reflection of the intensity of his feelings for Clara.

Whatever those feelings were.

Gads, it would have been easier if he could have just admitted he loved her, but he could not do it. His mind rebelled at the idea with as much passion as it embraced it. He was of two minds, and neither of them seemed willing to back down. All he knew was that he wanted to be alone with her in this room, or in any room, even if no words were exchanged and they did not touch. It would be enough to simply look at her with the freedom and frankness he craved, and to smile at her without fearing someone might see.

He wanted to walk along the seashore with her, perhaps even remove his own shoes, and take her hand again. His fingertips tingled even now with the memory of the touch of her skin against them, and that heady moment where her own fingers had squeezed his back.

Was his cravat too tight, or was the room simply growing steadily warmer?

He craned his neck, whatever the reason, and reached a slightly trembling hand out for his wine, being sure to sip carefully.

How could all of this happen so quickly, and yet feel so real? How could it exceed the depths of his soul and consume his thoughts when he had not even known her a month? Where was the logic in any of this?

He chanced a glance at Clara as he returned his wineglass safely to the table, only to find her looking at him, her eyes luminous, her lips settled in a soft, incomparable smile that seized his chest in a tight grip.

Instinctively, he smiled back, very slightly, but just enough.

He saw her shoulders move on an exhale, or was it a sigh?

Please, God, let it be a sigh.

He drummed his fingers against the linen of the table as he warred within himself, and Clara's eyes lowered to them.

Intriguing. Was she as intent on him as he was on her? To test the idea, he drummed them again, this time slowly, first forwards, then backwards, keeping the pattern going again and again, a simple and unobtrusive action that somehow kept her transfixed.

Her throat bobbed on a swallow, which somehow created a jolt of sensation in the little toe of his right foot. Then her eyes rose to his, the green of her hazel eyes so pronounced, he would have sworn it was the color of the earth itself. He could not look away, could not do anything but drown himself in their depths and let the warmth of them wash over him.

He would die where he sat if something did not happen soon. What exactly could, or should, happen was almost irrelevant.

Almost.

"Clara, shall we go through?"

Long lashes blinked over brilliant eyes, and the magic in them faded just enough for him to catch his suddenly uneven breath. "What?"

Mrs. Daniels cleared her throat, bringing Hawk back to the moment, and the recollection that there was another person in the room with them. Hastily, he slid his hand back from the surface of the table as though his intentional drumming of fingers had somehow been inappropriate and focused his attention on the handle of the fork nearest him.

"I said, 'shall we go through,' in order to keep with the politeness of things," Mrs. Daniels said in her crisp way. "His Grace likely wants his port and a few minutes of silence and privacy."

The idea of Clara leaving his presence was one that did not sit well with him, even if they did nothing but avoid speaking to each other directly.

Hawk shook his head calmly. "I've never cared for port, Mrs. Daniels, and I've had all the silence and privacy a man could need at Elmsley Abbey. I'll happily go through with you ladies, if you don't mind, and perhaps we can find the companionable relationships we enjoyed before."

His eyes darted to Clara as he finished, and the smile she wore prompted one of his own.

"If you like, Your Grace, of course," Mrs. Daniels demurred, rising gracefully from her chair. "We'd welcome your company."

"In his own house," Clara murmured with more than a hint of laughter in her voice as she rose herself. "We'd welcome him, of course."

Hawk hid a laugh with a brief cough, pushing to his feet and gesturing towards the drawing room, belatedly remembering that they had been living here for much of his absence and would know exactly where to go.

How had he turned into such a bumbling fool lately? Especially when he wanted to be the collected man he always had been. To be anything else at a time like this was all that was irritating in life.

Clara moved past him with a duck of her chin, her cheeks tinged with a shade of pink that made him mad to keep it there somehow.

What could he do? What could he say? With so much in his heart, so much on his mind, how could he possibly...?

He grinned as he recalled a token he had brought back with him from the extensive Elmsley library. He stepped closer to a footman and paused a step. "David, could you see that the book I had packed in my trunk is brought to me in the drawing room in the next few minutes?"

"Of course, Your Grace," the lad said with a firm nod, keeping his eyes forward in the perfect form of a footman.

Hawk returned the nod. "Thank you. Much appreciated." Feeling a little more comfortable, he strode into the drawing room and situated himself on the sofa.

Less than six feet from where Clara herself sat.

It was not intentional, only the most obvious choice. Mrs. Daniels had taken a chair, and her niece had chosen the side of the sofa nearest her. There was another chair in the room, situated similarly on the other side of the room, but the distance would have been more awkward than the close proximity. He could not have awkwardness, not now, not with her.

So perhaps his choice in seating was slightly intentional.

Or blatantly intentional.

He fought back a sigh of contentment, smiling as he allowed himself to be a little more relaxed in his position now, though he was still the picture of a gentleman. In fact, a gentleman in his own home ought to look and feel so at ease.

So content.

"It is a pleasure to be back here," he said as he looked at them both. "I hope it does not inconvenience either of you that I have returned unexpectedly."

"It is no inconvenience," Mrs. Daniels assured him, her smile gentle and far more natural than anything he'd seen of her before. Perhaps she realized hers was not the voice he was listening for. Then, blessedly, it came.

"Why are you back?" Clara asked, her voice soft yet unwavering.

Hawk looked at her without shame, the truth of the matter on the tip of his tongue, ready to admit that she had been the motivation behind a great many things he had done of late.

But the time was not right. Not yet.

"I had to make a visit to Miss Masters' Finishing School," he told them with some honesty. "My sister is in her final year there. Adrianna needed a guardian's permission for a particular venture, and there were some documents to sign, as well. As we are nearing the end of her term, I thought I might stay on at Kirkleigh until she is finished, then we would go to Elmsley together for Christmas."

"That sounds lovely," Clara murmured, her eyes darker and more captivating in the light of this room than they had been before. "Tell me about Elmsley Abbey. Where is it?"

"Wiltshire," he replied. "Very nearly in the center of it."

Clara bit her lip, a maddening distraction at a time like this, then shook her head. "I don't know Wiltshire at all. I've not been many places in England. What's it like?"

He hesitated, not out of reluctance, as he'd have talked about the virtues of toast had she requested it, but only to attempt, in his way, to do the subject justice. To romanticize the county first, and then Elmsley itself. After all, it would behoove him to incite within her a desire to see the place, to visit at first, and then, perhaps…

Well, he would not venture that far into madness without some encouragement.

"Rustic," he finally told her, smiling as he envisioned her there. "Charming. Peaceful. It is the very image of the countryside one dreams of when it is mentioned. Rolling hills in varying shades of green, and charming villages that all seem to be quaint yet bustling. The county is filled with chalk, which seems to give its nature a slight pallor that is simply fascinating."

191

"It sounds beautiful," Clara said without any hint of patronization, her smile the warm, easy one he had known before he'd left. "And picturesque."

He returned her smile without thinking. "I actually thought about you a great deal during my time there."

Her eyes widened, and he felt heat racing into his cheeks, his mind scrambling to add anything to the thought that would make it coherent and still flattering.

"The artistry of it all," he hastily continued, "which was something I had not truly noticed before, made me wonder what you could capture in a drawing or painting. You've trained my eyes to see things in a different way, Clara, and I don't believe they will go back."

She blinked at his words, and then, impossibly, she beamed with the glories of sunrise. "I would apologize for altering your vision, Hawk, but I am not sorry in the least."

He laughed, far more breathlessly than he'd intended, and found himself turning towards her more fully on the sofa. "Nor should you be. It is far more enjoyable to see things with more dimension and to notice their details. How else would one appreciate a simple field *after* it has been harvested?"

"Precisely," she quipped, her hands sitting almost childishly in her lap, "and you've got my fingers positively itching to draw all of Wiltshire now, just from your description alone."

"I think you'd have quite enough to be getting on with in Kent." He chuckled, then caught sight of David in the doorway, the book Hawk had requested in his hand. He gestured for him to enter and rose from the sofa quickly. "And to assist you in those efforts…"

He strode over to the footman and nodded his thanks as he took the book. Turning, and with Clara's eyes on him, he drummed his fingers on the cover of the book, which set Clara's cheeks to flushing slightly, much to his delight.

"I have brought you something from the library at Elmsley," he confessed as he made his way back to her, feeling rather playful now. "As per your request, I might add."

Her brow furrowed slightly, her deep golden brows knitting nearly together with it. "My request?" she repeated. "I don't recall…"

He handed the book to her, their fingers brushing with the

intensity of lightning and the sensitivity of fire.

His throat tightened, forcing him to attempt a swallow. After three attempts, he succeeded, and gestured at it. "Take a look."

Flicking her eyes up to him quickly, Clara opened the cover, her gaze darting back down. Her brow smoothed, and her lips formed a delicate smile that encouraged him more than anything else that day.

Clara looked back at him, those full lips almost dancing as they struggled to decide on the exact nature of the smile they would form. "This is perfect."

Yes, it was. He knew it, and she knew it.

And they were not talking about the book.

"*A Collective History of Kent?*" Mrs. Daniels read aloud, coming over to see the title page, her tone expressing all the confusion of one not hearing the true nature of the conversation occurring in spite of the spoken words. "What in the world was that doing in Wiltshire?"

Hawk shared an amused smile with Clara, his heart seeming to spring into bloom within his chest. "Waiting, Mrs. Daniels. For the perfect opportunity to be of particular use."

Sleeping was utterly impossible. She'd been trying for two hours and had only managed to form a headache somewhere above her left ear.

Why that should be, she could not have said; nor, she supposed, did it matter.

What did matter was that she could not, would not, sleep. Not yet, and not for some time.

Her mind refused to give her a reprieve, and she could not blame it.

When there was so much to consider, how could she possibly rest?

Clara sighed heavily, her eyes as open as they'd been at any point in the day and staring up into the darkness of the canopy above her. What was the point in this? If she was going to be awake and thinking, she might as well embrace it and make some use of the process.

Slipping from the bed, she padded over to her bureau, pulling out her wrap and a pair of thick stockings. She donned both, then ventured from her room down the corridor, the path familiar and well-trod by now. She'd taken several walks in the night while she had stayed at Kirkleigh, and each had proven worth her time, whether it be discovering more about the house or giving her time and space to ponder.

Tonight would be different, in a way. Her thoughts were competing with each other with a viciousness that spoke of the strength of her feelings for each. The determination to discover what was occurring over at Barcliffe and what part the Brownings played in it all was underlying everything. It occupied the corners of her mind and circled about with a repetition that was distracting, and the idea that there was a clue missing, or several of them, irritated her more than anything else.

And then there were thoughts of Hawk.

She'd barely managed a concise thought in his presence, which made speaking nearly impossible. He was even more impossibly handsome than she'd recollected, the dark of his eyes bearing the depth of the night, the shape of his lips one that would send any artist into insanity of delight. His voice rumbled pleasantly through her with every word, and the sheer cacophony of emotions in her body had rendered her nearly senseless.

Her heart had been wild within her, galloping freely about and sprinting madly when he'd said he'd thought of her in Wiltshire, when he'd spoken of how she'd changed his sight, when he'd smiled...

The moment he'd handed her the book on the history of Kent, she'd been sure a shower of sparks had begun to rain down across her entire body.

It could have been a confession of love for all the delirium it rendered. She'd not presume anything so extraordinary, but in that moment, she had learned something.

Felt something.

Hawk felt something. For her.

How was she to fully function when such a truth now lived within her? She had never been a girl prone to flights of fancy, and had certainly never been considered silly, but suddenly she had no control at all over her heart. It darted here and there at the very thought of the man, and her palms began to moisten, her toes tingled, and her neck burst into flame.

She had a mission to accomplish and having Hawk about had not been part of the plan for that mission. Yet she could not wish him away, and would not. She had longed for him to return, and now he had.

What could she do?

What should she do?

That was, perhaps, the more appropriate question at this moment.

What she could do opened up an infinite world of options. What she would do was uncertain. What she should do was entirely unclear.

Exhaling slowly, folding her arms about her in the chill of the house this late, Clara found herself arriving at the gallery, the large windows at the far end streaming in the light of the moon and casting stark shadows along the floor. It seemed she ended up in this room frequently on her nightly outings, and the windows there were large enough to allow her to partially sit on the ledge of one. It was a spacious yet simple room. Less of a corridor than one might have predicted for a gallery, but she could appreciate that.

Art was not something to simply be glanced at while passing through.

Still lacking in its art, the gallery was her favorite of all the rooms in Kirkleigh, partially because it had been the first room where she had seen Hawk. But also because her attention was ever and always drawn to the simple, childish watercolor proudly framed and hung within it.

What would Alexandra Moore have made of any of this? What had her feelings on Hawk been when she had known him? What had been her favorite room in Kirkleigh?

It was becoming more and more a regret that Clara had not met the woman herself, had not been permitted the chance to converse with her and share thoughts, ideas, and memories. That they had not become friends. That she could not now know what the person she was portraying would have done.

When all this was over, she would ask her cousin to take her there and meet Miss Moore herself. After all she had been through, and the truth she had known, Martin would owe her that much.

Her life had been miserable for so long, and he, her only living relative, had been gone for most of it. She knew now, of course, why that had been, and her painful feelings had faded, but the time that had been lost, the memories they could have shared...

She would go to France after this, and perhaps let herself cry upon his shoulder for all of it.

And all that was to come.

She was still living a lie, of sorts, after all. And if Hawk could ever come to love her, as she was coming to love him, he would not take her betrayal well. He was a gentleman of honor and respect to his core, all that was worthy and good in a man. Her being anything less than truthful would have been unacceptable.

She could not bear that.

Perhaps this all should end now. Her mission and assignment could not, she knew that well, but this connection she felt with him, these feelings he had roused, could not be anything worth indulging if she wished to vouchsafe herself from the agony that would surely come. It would be cruel to let herself go on too long in this, to indulge in a fantasy that could not, and would not, ever come to the blessed fruition she yearned for.

Why, then, did she yet linger in it?

"I didn't expect to see you here."

Her eyes closed on what would have been tears, had she let them form. Of all voices in the world, this was one she constantly craved, yet found wholly inconvenient at this particular moment.

Still, her heart burned at it.

"I couldn't sleep," she replied, letting her eyes open once more, rising to the slowly approaching figure in the dark.

He still wore his dark breeches, his linen shirt looser than she had seen and open at the collar. No coat, no cravat, no jacket, and his hair was disheveled in a way that tempted her fingers to toy with the locks. He was everything approachable, easy, and devilishly tempting like this, and she felt all of it with a fervor that numbed her whole.

His smile was slight, once he neared enough that the light illuminated it, and she loved the sight of it. "Anything the matter?"

"No," she whispered, shaking her head. "No, simply too much

in my mind."

Hawk nodded slowly at the words. "I suffer from the same tonight. Wandering in the dark helps."

"I know." She allowed herself to smile in return. "I've done so quite a lot in my time here."

"Have you?" His voice rang with amusement, warming the pit of her stomach. "I wonder we've never bumped into each other before, as I do it often."

Clara swallowed hard, tightening her arms in their still-folded position against her. "We've not been together often at night."

Something about those words seemed inappropriate somehow, or forward. Something intimate that she ought to have hastily corrected.

And yet...

"We've not been together often anywhere," he reminded her, his voice that delicious, low rumbling she so adored. "Nor at any time. Our recent acquaintance has been limited at best, if we're speaking only of being in each other's presence. Hasn't stopped us from anything yet."

"No," she said again, her voice barely holding weight. "No, it hasn't."

He cocked his head very slowly and came closer, her pulse skipping and igniting various points of her body. "Clara..."

"We shouldn't be alone."

Her whispered admission stopped him, the edge of them ringing not with disapproval, but with fear.

And panic.

And reluctance.

And...

"I think we'd be hard pressed to find a suitable chaperone at this hour," Hawk told her with complete patience and sincerity. "You're quite safe from me. Here." He gestured to the window beside hers. "I'll sit here. I'll keep to my window, and you keep to yours." He smiled at the window ruefully. "We are in perfect sight of anyone wandering to the east of the house, so that should suffice for observation."

Clara snickered to herself softly. "Who would be out in the night at this hour?"

Hawk shrugged as he took up the position he'd indicated, half-sitting on the ledge of his window as she was hers. "Poachers, night-fishers, watchmen... The possibilities are endless."

She gave him a derisive look. "Limited, at best."

His smile spread, his arms folding loosely across him as though in direct contrast to the tension in hers. "Nevertheless, there may be someone."

Good sense would have had her reply that it wasn't enough to take a chance on it, that the truth of the matter was clear and one of them needed to leave. Good sense would have her be mortified to be in this situation and to scurry off to bed like some proper miss.

Good sense had not accompanied her on this walk tonight.

"I've missed you, Hawk," Clara admitted roughly, looking out of the window at the night, watching the moon reflect off of far distant water. "It was strange to be at Kirkleigh with only Aunt Fern, and to not have a friend about for company."

"I'd have come sooner, if you'd asked."

The roughness of his voice sent shivers along her spine, raised bumps upon her skin, and she bit back a sigh of delight. "How could I have asked that?" she wondered more than inquired. "We barely know each other, and to be so frank wouldn't... It couldn't..."

"I'd do anything you asked me," Hawk told her quietly, ending her struggles to find the answer she sought. "That's the madness of this, isn't it? You could ask. Frankly and directly, you could ask me anything, and it wouldn't be anything but perfect."

Perfect. Such a word of power, yet so apt for their plight.

Everything felt perfect.

Yet it wasn't. Couldn't be. Would not be.

Clara leaned her head against the cool pane of the window and finally allowed herself to look at him, loving the open expression he wore and the comfort in this moment. "Perfect is a dreadful word," she whispered, her voice catching. "It only leads to heartache and disappointment."

"Have you been disappointed, Clara?" Hawk asked gently, not seeming in the least put off by her statement.

She allowed herself to nod, the confession rolling within her as on a wave. "I was to be married once. Years ago now. He met with the approval of everyone, and I loved him. I thought I was so fortunate to have found someone well situated that I felt so much for. He wasn't rich, but there would have been no complaints. It *was* perfect."

"What happened?"

Clara lowered her eyes, looking at the nails of her left hand as it rested upon her arm. "Scandal broke out. He was found amid efforts to compromise a local girl to such a degree that they were forced to marry in haste. And then word went around about a number of others who had been seduced by him, some compromised to the same degree, though he could not also marry them. I was surrounded by women who knew the man better than I did, and I had been the one he'd vowed to marry." She blinked and shifted her gaze back out to the night. "As you can imagine, rumors abounded about me as well, since it seemed he never treated a woman with respect. My virtue became a subject for gossip, even among... those I trusted most."

She'd caught herself before admitting her family had believed the rumors, as her identity now did not give her family to do so. One falsehood amid a confession of truth.

"Why did you not write us?" Hawk asked her, his voice filled with pain that ate at her. "You were my uncle's ward, we could have helped you."

She looked at him sadly. "I cannot rely on the goodness and influence of others all my life. I knew the truth, and that was enough. My aunt came to me shortly after to take me away, and I've never been back there since. It has not followed me, and I am as you see. No lasting harm done."

Hawk shook his head slowly. "I think you are a masterful woman, Clara. More than I ever imagined or knew." His lips curved in a fetching way. "And suddenly, I'm regretting my vow to stay in my window."

Blushing, Clara ducked her chin, but managed to keep her eyes on him as she smiled back. "So am I." Before anything could change, she rose and stepped away, adjusting a loose strand of hair behind her ear. "Good night, Hawk."

He rose as well, and, for a moment, she feared he might swoop in and take her in his arms, rendering her powerless and unwilling to resist. But he only stepped close enough to take her hand and bring it to his lips. Fire raced down her arm as the delicious sensation danced across her knuckles, somehow reaching deep into her core with it.

"Good night, Clara," he murmured, his eyes staying on hers.

Her breath caught at the dip in his voice, and she very much feared the words he conveyed were far different from the words he spoke.

Chapter Eighteen

There had never been much interest in attending a ball for Hawk. He'd done it, of course, and repeatedly so. But there was never much amusement or entertainment for him, and the forced enclosure with eager people to either make a match or forge a connection meant he had to endure all efforts at sociable encounters.

Such things were not enjoyable.

Usually.

Tonight, however, he could barely stand still as White put the finishing touches on his appearance for the evening. A point which his trusted valet was growing less than pleased with.

"Steady, Your Grace," White insisted with veiled impatience for what had to be the fifth time this evening. "I've no wish to strangle you as I style your cravat."

Hawk raised a brow at him. "Was that a subtle threat, White?"

"Nothing subtle about it, Your Grace," came the easy response. "If you keep shifting while I work this, it is very possible that you will become strangled, though it will not be my fault."

"Then I wonder at your taste, man," Hawk mused, lifting his chin with the assistance of his valet's palm. "What will anyone say if they should believe my cravat has the appearance of a noose?"

White hummed once. "None shall mistake this work for a noose, nor will they find slack to hang you by. Say collar, by all means, but rope was never worked so finely as this. You wouldn't want Miss Moore to find you lacking, would you?"

Hawk's attention snapped down to his impertinent valet with swift censure. "That'll do, White," he muttered.

The valet met his eyes with all innocence. "Pardon me, Your Grace. Are you not accompanying her and Mrs. Daniels to the assembly? It is the duty of a gentleman to be as much of a match as humanly possible for the elegant ladies he escorts, and with such fine ladies as these, I do have my work cut out for me, Your Grace."

Hawk narrowed his eyes in speculation at the man, not entirely believing his defense on his words, though he could not find anything erring in them, either. "Very true. I do wonder about your ulterior motive, though."

"That I shall be admired for my work and stolen away to tend to a man who appreciates my abilities?" White replied without pausing a jot. "Yes, I make no bones about that one, Your Grace."

This was getting nowhere, and quickly at that. It was clear his valet had no intention of addressing his speculation on Hawk's intentions, and it would be pointless to attempt to prod him further. But as he himself had been so neatly nettled without much effort, there was a great deal of curiosity about what was being noticed and said, and whether or not Hawk was lacking in discretion at the present.

None of these were questions for his valet, of course, but had Nat been present, he most certainly would have asked him.

The irony of it all was that, had Clara and her aunt not been at Kirkleigh, Hawk would not have dreamed of going to the assembly ball this evening. He had nothing against Gadsden and its good people, it just seemed a trifle simple. All attendees of fortune would be wise to render themselves a little less resplendent in appearance than they might have done for a ball on a fine estate, unless they were tactless enough to parade their wealth for all the world. White had not been pleased initially to be so limited, but he had gotten over it soon enough and taken up the challenge with enthusiasm.

Why in the world that should be was beyond Hawk, but fashion held very little interest or concern for him. It was quite simply the clothing upon his back and nothing more.

His own brother would have groaned at such a statement.

"Did you have flowers sent to Miss Moore and Mrs. Daniels, White?" Hawk asked as the valet finally smoothed the ends of the cravat and tucked them into his waistcoat.

"I did, Your Grace," he confirmed with a nod. "Mr. Brick had some very pretty blossoms in the greenhouses that he had cut for each and sent up. I believe they were received well."

A jolt of pleasure shot from Hawk's right hip into his left shoulder, neatly lancing his heart in the process. "Good," he murmured, nodding to himself. "Excellent."

"I should say so. Never underestimate the value of flowers in the eyes of God's females." He held out Hawk's jacket for him to shrug into, then brushed at the shoulders when Hawk did so.

"Is that so?" Hawk asked with mild surprise. "I had no idea. I thought it was simply a polite gesture."

White made a disapproving noise behind him. "Not at all, Your Grace. There's a full language of flowers, if you can believe that."

"What?" Hawk laughed, turning about and examining himself in the looking glass. "That is ridiculous."

"But true, Your Grace," White insisted. "I'll find the book for you and have it sent in. You appreciate accomplishment in language, do you not?"

Hawk gave his valet a sardonic look. "I hardly think this counts."

White only shrugged. "As you will, Your Grace. Will that be all?"

Returning his attention to his appearance, and, settling that it was as good as anything, Hawk nodded. "Yes, thank you, White." He tugged on his jacket sleeves, then turned from the room feeling far more prepared for the night ahead than he had only moments ago.

He felt the odd desire to whistle some jaunty tune when he looked further down the corridor, on the other side of the stairs into the additional bedchambers and saw two ladies in near-perfect synchrony floating across the floor towards him.

Well, towards the stairs, really, but he was also in that direction. He'd pretend Clara moved his way until the end of time.

She was nothing less than a vision, and his breath was impossible to find as she neared, and the details of her appearance became clearer.

A vision of lavender with a lace robe of white over the lot of it, bound by a lavender ribbon beneath her bodice, gathered and cascading from the left side of her skirts, leaving the hem of her dress visible, dotted there with the same delicate rosettes of lavender he could see scattered about the entire garment. The sleeves were small, and, thankfully, without the excessive billowing he had seen on garments of late. They captured her shoulders perfectly, echoing the white and lavender aspects of the gown in their folds.

Everywhere he looked, there was beauty, from the lace and lavender folds across the bodice to the string of pearls elegantly arraying her throat. Her golden hair had been curled to drape exquisitely at her temples and to frame her face, then piled back to flow in ringlets behind. Lavender gauze of sorts ornamented her tresses, and, as she reached him, he caught sight of a small bouquet of fresh flowers in one gloved hand.

He'd have gone to his knees for her had he felt them.

"I fear I am very far from my depth this evening," he managed when the ladies reached him.

Clara's cheeks, already tinged with a lovely shade of pink, deepened. "I do not think so, Your Grace."

Gads, was there a dearer creature in all the world?

He shook his head and reached for her free hand, bringing the surface of the glove to his lips. "I assure you, Clara, that I am," he murmured, wondering at the gravel he heard in his voice.

Her brilliantly full lips parted in a sweet smile, her fingers fluttering briefly in his hold. "We must disagree, Your Grace. Mustn't we, Aunt Fern?"

"Utterly, Your Grace," Mrs. Daniels agreed in her crisp way.

Hawk wrenched his eyes from Clara to smile at her, noting with all due deference that, had he not seen Clara, he'd have considered Mrs. Daniels at present to be the most beautiful lady in the world. Her choice of a bright blue made her eyes almost impossible to meet, so echoing in shade were they.

Suddenly, he wished White had put a greater level of finery on his own person.

Hawk sighed heavily and moved between them, offering an arm to both ladies with a shake of his head. "I shan't be comfortable all night, thinking of what the pair of you will suffer in excessive attention. How am I to protect my guests against the masses?"

Mrs. Daniels swatted him lightly with a fan. "Don't flatter so ridiculously, Kirklin, it doesn't suit us, does it, Clara? I must have you droll and sarcastic, or I shall think less of you."

He stifled a laugh and glanced down at the woman as they descended the stairs. "God forbid I should fall in your estimation, Mrs. Daniels. Should I call you agreeable, then? Fair enough for company? Tolerable?"

She laughed throatily, the sound pleasant, though lacking in the magic of her niece's. "Any and all will do, Your Grace, and in return, I shall consider you especially reliable company for the evening."

"Reliable?" he repeated. He looked at Clara in bemused disbelief. "Have you ever heard a more unappealing compliment in your life?"

Clara giggled, the sound dismantling four of his ribs in ecstasy. "I don't know, it seems rather akin to sturdy in my mind, and are they not both encouraging?"

His remaining ribs tumbled into the pit of his stomach, the urge to lean in and kiss the incomparable woman reaching an unholy tier in his mind.

Sturdy, tall, and unremarkable. Ever the maple, ever was Hawk, and Clara was again addressing his own description and praising it well.

The splendor of her eyes met his, and he saw her understanding and her meaning, saw his world in her hands, saw the heart of him beating with a fervency he dared not comprehend.

"I suppose," he murmured, wondering that his legs and feet were still managing proper motion in escorting them both.

He barely felt human at the present.

Thankfully, Stafford and a few maids met them at the bottom of the stairs with cloaks, and then they were shuttled into the carriage and soon rolling along towards their destination. He sat on one side of the carriage, the ladies on the other, which was undoubtedly a safer place for them all, though the distance felt immense.

He, for one, was content to simply stare at Clara, and, given their present positions, could do so without seeming improper, so long as he occasionally looked out of the window or at her aunt. Therefore, every count of forty, he shifted his eyes for a count of ten before bringing them back. Clara could tell, he knew that by the quirk of her lips each time his eyes returned. Which drove him mad and made him want to do it more.

What a game they were playing with each other.

Mrs. Daniels filled the drive with stories of balls she had attended in her youth, and her memory for detail was impressive, as was her skill in the telling of those stories. He found himself laughing along with her, despite his full attention being on Clara. He could still listen creditably and enjoy a fine tale to pass the time.

His amusement faded when he felt a small foot gently press against his, their shapes fitting together with a perfection that robbed him of thought.

He looked at Clara early, only having reached the count of five, and found her smile one of deep bemusement, if not delighted fascination.

Little minx, she'd upend his world in ten minutes if he let her.

Raising a brow, he increased the pressure against her foot, satisfaction surging as he caught a brief exhale on her part.

Oh, what a night lay ahead of them, if such things continued.

The carriage slowed and reached a stop far before he'd expected, making him wonder if time had a vendetta against his happiness, but he proceeded out of the carriage quickly and handed each lady out, following them into the Assembly Rooms. They handed their outerwear to the servants, then moved up the stairs to the spaces reserved for the night's entertainments.

Music was already underway, and, by the sound of it, so was a jig. The laughter of guests and enthusiastic clapping in time with the music echoed out to them, capturing the air of the event suitably. If one could say anything about the dances at Gadsden, they would undoubtedly say that they were full of spirit.

Hawk didn't care so much about that tonight as he did about one particular thing.

"Save me two dances," he murmured to Clara as they reached the top of the stairs and then turning, pausing before they entered.

She looked up at him in surprise. "Which two?"

"Any," he told her, taking her hand subtly, Mrs. Daniels' attention on the room ahead of them. "Whichever ones are longest."

Clara released a breath he understood well, and squeezed his hand, pumping his heart in the process. "They're yours," she whispered, her eyes bright. "A pity they will not have a waltz for us."

Us. The word held music in its single syllable. "I don't need a waltz," he said softly. "Any dance with you would hold the same pleasure."

She laughed once, almost as if to herself. "I was thinking the same thing. A waltz would only draw us closer, which sounds rather agreeable." Her smile spread quickly, then her hand slipped from his as she followed her aunt into the room.

Hawk stood out on the landing for a few heartbeats more, waiting for his lungs to engage in their proper function.

She'd finish him in two minutes, he amended, not ten.

His resistance was not nearly so great.

The two sides of Clara's mind had never been more at war, and the only thing she could say for herself was that she was distracted.

As they had readied themselves for the night, Phoebe had encouraged her to find an opportunity to be warm and friendly with the Brownings. On the rare chance that Mr. Browning had truly been in any way prejudiced against Clara the other day, such a thing needed to be resolved, and quickly. Tomorrow, they would be at Barcliffe with the Fleets and she would be helping the girls with their art, and it would prove quite beneficial if they could maintain the invitation to explore the shore of that estate.

Clara knew that, had been determined to find opportunity to do so once they arrived, but had been so terribly deflected by Hawk and his captivating manner.

She wanted nothing more than to engage in two exceedingly long dances with him, and she was quite proud of herself for the wit and frankness she had managed in their conversation. Why should she hide her feelings when she was already hiding so much from him? It was so blessedly freeing to allow herself to speak in this way, to give into the heady emotions she had felt growing within her for him. If she did not check herself, she would admit to him sooner rather than later that she loved him.

Her step paused and her eyes widened.

She loved him.

How could she love him? It had barely been time enough to

know him.

How could she not love him? He was everything good, noble, and true. He was charming and witty, generous and fine.

What use was time when there was such clarity?

She laughed to herself as she moved once more, smiling for the benefit of strangers around her. She hadn't thought she could feel anything remotely like love after the disaster with Louis, and yet she could easily see herself giving her heart to Hawk without hesitation, reluctance, or any remnants of fear.

Hawk had healed her from her hurts and freed her from the shackles of her past.

And she loved him.

"I do apologize profoundly for the rudeness of our departure the other day," Phoebe was saying, her voice wafting back to Clara's ears.

Her mind's haziness cleared as she forced herself to focus on that sound and moved quickly to Phoebe's side, smiling with warmth as she took in the Brownings.

They were over-trimmed in every respect, but seemed in good spirits, which was encouraging.

"Not at all, not at all," Mr. Browning insisted, his voice its usual volume of excess. "My lady here heard that your new hat is quite the thing to be envied, so it was a venture worth taking, I daresay."

Phoebe looked at Mrs. Browning in surprise. "How could you know, my dear? I have not seen you since."

Mrs. Browning smiled fondly. "Mrs. Guntrip saw you, and I saw her the day after. I can assure you, there are no secrets in Gadsden."

"Well, well," Phoebe murmured, smiling wryly. "Then I think it a very good thing I have no intention of keeping it a secret! What a fruitless effort that would prove to be!"

The Brownings laughed cheerfully, making Clara laugh as well, more for the ridiculousness of the sound than anything else. Was it a very great evil to join in laughing if it was not for the same purposes? She could not help it; they were such a ridiculous, mismatched couple, and the idea of them working against England still seemed equally ridiculous.

But that would have been a perfect disguise, would it not?

Her laughter faded as she considered that.

Focusing on the pair of them, she smiled again. "I do so look forward to returning to Barcliffe tomorrow. As a token of gratitude, might I do a painting for you? I have very little else to offer, I know, but it would make me so happy to give you what I can."

Mrs. Browning gasped dramatically in apparent delight. "Oh, Miss Moore! We should dearly love a painting, would we not, my dear? We are so very fond of art, and if you are skilled enough to help the Fleet girls, I can only imagine how very beautiful your own work must be. Oh, what a thing to imagine! Would you paint the house? No, the coast! No, the house *and* the coast! Oh, I cannot decide, you may paint anything you like, and it will be perfection!"

The rapid rambling was a bit much to take in, but Clara forced herself to remain polite and attentive, engaged in the silliness wholeheartedly. "I can hardly promise perfection," Clara demurred, "but I shall do my very best, I can assure you."

"I have no doubt your best is exquisite!" Mr. Browning boomed, winking at her and smiling widely. "I shall make a place for your piece in our gallery at once."

Clara laughed, not having to force it so very much this time. "Mr. Browning, you should perhaps wait until you see it! It might not meet with your pleasure and satisfaction."

He shook his head firmly, if a bit excessively. "Nonsense! We shall adore and treasure such a gift from a sweet girl like you, shall we not, Mrs. Browning?"

"Indeed!" she squealed in accompaniment. "Oh, indeed we shall!"

"There you have it, Clara," Phoebe said with a proud smile at her. "You should ever be so fortunate to have such ardent appreciators of your art."

Clara nodded in a show of modest demurral. "I am so very aware of my good fortune. And to have such beauty to choose from in your home and estate! How shall I decide?"

They began to debate the merits of certain scenes and aspects, which is just as Clara had hoped, the conversation having lost interest for her. She seemed to have regained her footing there, if it ever had been lost, and she was now in a pleasant position to do as she liked upon their visit to Barcliffe.

That was one aim done.

Now for the rest...

"Miss Moore."

A slow tingling began to ride the course of her spine, spreading into her neck and into the tip of every strand of hair on her head. She turned, barely breathing, and smiled, fearing her face might split with the intensity of it. She curtseyed politely before Hawk, allowing herself an additional depth of deference as might befit a man of his station and title. "Your Grace."

He bowed to match her, a twinkle in his eyes as he straightened. "Would you do me the honor of dancing the next with me, Miss Moore?"

"I would be very happy to dance the next, Your Grace," Clara replied, taking care that her voice was clear without being loud. "I pray you will forgive any errors on my part. It has been some time since I have danced in company."

"Then we shall be more aptly matched," he told her, smiling without reserve, which was quite the sight to behold. "I am no great dancer, madam, and extend the same advance apologies."

"Accepted, of course." Clara took the hand he extended to her, curving her fingers over the edge of his palm instinctively.

He nodded in acceptance, his eyes darting to Phoebe. "I'd be most grateful, Mrs. Daniels, if you would save the one following for me."

"As you wish, Your Grace," she responded, her pleasure evident.

Hawk led Clara away, and she heard his slow exhale as they left the earshot of the others. "I hope I waited long enough," he murmured. "Much longer and I'd have gone mad."

Clara could not help but smile at that. "Surely not mad. The prospect could hardly—"

"The prospect has not left my mind since breakfast, Clara," Hawk overrode with some insistence, his thumb brushing against the edge of her hand in a maddening graze. "I've not been of sound mind all day because of it."

A faint keening sound began to emit within her mind, and it was all she could do not to give voice to it. She looked up at Hawk, almost pleading for a reprieve even as she longed to lean into him for strength. "I'm sorry," she whispered, unsure what exactly she was apologizing for.

One side of his mouth curved. "Don't be. I've taken great pleasure in my relative insanity, and the reasoning behind it." His thumb pointedly ran along her hand as he brought her to the line of dancers, then backed away from her to his position.

How could a distance of a few feet suddenly seem a chasm? Her legs shook with the desire to run at him and fling her arms about him, clinging for her life and declaring her love in words without poetry or refinement.

Luckily, decorum had a hard rein on her, and she remained in place.

The music began, and the woman next to her crossed to Hawk in the pattern of the dance. He gave her the polite attention of a brief partner, taking her hands and turning about, as did other couples along the line.

Even that slight exchange made Clara ache for him to come back to her.

Utter foolishness on her part, and entirely nonsensical.

The man next to Hawk crossed over to bow before Clara, and she managed a smile for him, taking his hands and turning about, just as the others had done, before returning to her place with a glance at Hawk.

He looked as though he had not enjoyed their moment, either.

Oh, heavens, what were they to do?

They crossed to each other, brushing shoulders as they moved past, shifted around each other, which scorched a pattern exactly matching Clara's buttons into the tender skin of her back. Then they passed each other once more on the other side, again brushing shoulders, Clara managing to catch her finger against Hawk's hand in the process.

His eyes were nearly black as they met hers across the lines now, and it was all she could do to take a cool breath when she turned away to pass the line of two other ladies. She swallowed hard when she rounded the second, reaching out to take his hand as they met in the middle. His grip on her hand was hard, the pressure unbearable in the best manner she had ever known.

They parted as they returned to their original spots, then stepped forward with all dancers to take each other's hands, Clara fearing she had stepped too close when she could feel the heat of Hawk's breath upon her as they slowly turned about.

He dipped his head towards her, and, for a precious half-beat of her heart, she thought he would kiss her, and she longed for it.

"Almost," he groaned, his fingers sliding up to her elbows before grazing all the way back down to her fingers, then parting as they returned to their places.

Clara nearly swooned with the headiness of this dance, this moment, and what she so longed to have happen. "Almost," she murmured, though there was no sound to her voice.

They waited for the lead couple to proceed down the line of them, then joined hands to promenade along with the rest.

"Am I the only one who is on the brink of death in this?" Hawk hissed beside her, his hold on both her hands firm.

She shook her head, her throat dry. "No. You are not alone in that."

"You're with me?" he asked, a rawness to his question that nearly sent her swooning again.

She bit back a sudden impulse to blaspheme in yearning distress. "I am," she answered, feeling the answer deep within her soul. "Can't you tell?"

His fingers slid to find her wrist, exactly where her pulse was thundering wildly.

"Beautiful Clara," he breathed, his fingers stroking against it, rendering the fabric of her gloves irrelevant. "That's all I needed to know."

There was nothing she could do but sigh to that, and revel in the moment of insanity.

Chapter Nineteen

"Your Grace! Oh, Your Grace, I had not even dreamed that you would accompany our dear Miss Moore and Mrs. Daniels to our little tea today! What a delight, what an absolute delight to have you here! Mr. Browning will be so pleased when he finds out, simply boundless in his delight. Heavens, I'm so dreadfully flustered in this!"

Hawk tried to give the woman a sympathetic look. "Do try to calm yourself, Mrs. Browning, I beg you. I have no desire to cause any sort of fuss with my presence. I simply thought I should accompany my guests and be a better neighbor today than I have been in the past. Please, do not distress yourself on my account."

"You are so good, Your Grace," Mrs. Browning gushed, clearly not taking in anything he had said. "So very good."

It took all of Hawk's considerable willpower not to roll his eyes at the excesses. His neighbors were good people, but he suspected there was a reason his uncle had not been especially close with them during his life. He further suspected it was a very similar reason to the one Hawk was developing.

Oh, for a life of seclusion…

Were it not for Clara, he would not have even thought of coming out to Barcliffe today, but he had no desire to be where she was not, so here he was.

Even now, with her arm looped through his, his irritation at Mrs. Browning's behavior was minimal at best compared with what it typically would have been otherwise. Whether that was due to Clara's influence or her presence, he could not say, but there could be no denying that she was the cause.

"Mrs. Browning," she greeted now, looking lovely as ever in richly printed calico of green, though presently obscured by her blue pelisse. "It is so gracious of you to have us here. Have the Fleets arrived yet?"

Mrs. Browning took her free hand, patting it gently. "Dear girl, they arrived only minutes before you did yourself. I'll take you through to them. We've set up a very pretty arrangement for you all, easels and watercolors aplenty."

Clara let herself be pulled from Hawk's arm, and he mourned the loss of her as she and Mrs. Browning started on ahead. He bit back a scowl and instead offered his arm to Mrs. Daniels behind him.

She took it at once, patting his arm sympathetically. "Your restraint is much to be admired, Kirklin."

He quirked a smile at her. "Noticed that, did you?"

She scoffed softly. "Of course, but one would not have to witness your restraint to believe you possess it. I wonder very much if Mr. Browning does not speak at the volume he does simply to ensure his is the only voice heard."

Hawk snickered a laugh, looking away to find some sort of composure as they walked through the house. When he could, he returned his attention forward. "It is perhaps fortunate then that Mrs. Browning has sequestered Clara instead of either of us."

"Oh, very much so," Mrs. Daniels confirmed, nodding vigorously. "Clara has far more patience than I do and is eager to maintain a position in the good graces of everyone she meets."

"And you are not?" he inquired in amusement, giving her a wry look.

She met his look frankly. "My dear Kirklin, I no longer care."

Hawk grinned freely at this extraordinary woman, thinking his day would not be entirely wasted if Clara had to spend her entire time with the Fleet girls. It would not be the day he wished, but at least the company would be worth the effort. "I'm going to stand by you for the whole of the day, Mrs. Daniels," he vowed without shame. "Clearly, I am missing out on something by doing otherwise."

Mrs. Daniels now raised a brow at him, her mouth curving. "If you spend the entire day by me, Kirklin, I shall never forgive you. You have better company to keep, have you not?"

His eyes raced to Clara at once as they moved out onto the terrace, Clara and Mrs. Browning at the edge, pointing out various bits of scenery, plotting out the day's possibilities for the artists. Clara turned slightly, looking back at them, and smiled gently, amusement rampant in her features, delight underlying all.

"I believe I do," Hawk murmured, answering Mrs. Daniels' question. "Do you think…? That is, if I dared…"

He could not finish the question, or even a statement, regarding what currently pulsed through his veins. It was all he could think about after the ball the night before, and the exquisite dances he had shared with Clara. The moment where he'd almost kissed her in the middle of a crowded room. Every time their hands had touched, every heightened sensation that had distracted him, every smile she had sent in his direction had replayed continuously in his mind until they would be impossible to forget.

And he was falling headlong into an unknown sea of bliss but did not wish to make the journey alone.

"In order to have an answer, Kirklin," Mrs. Daniels murmured in a low tone, no doubt to protect his vulnerability from Clara or Mrs. Browning, "you will need to ask a question. No one can give you satisfaction until you do."

He nodded, hearing and understanding the unspoken truth in her words. "If I did ask a question of her, do you believe I would be pleased with the answer?"

A low laugh beside him did not help his uncertainty. "I would not wish to presume, as my niece does not confide in me on such things," she admitted, keeping her voice down still.

Disappointment curled a finger about his throat, and he managed a nod. He should have expected as much.

"However…"

He'd never clung to any word so fiercely in his life, though he kept his attention forward for fear of seeming too keen. "However?" he eventually repeated, forcing his tone to be bland.

Mrs. Daniels seemed to hesitate for a moment. "I have never seen Clara so happy, Your Grace. Never."

There was a shift in the way Mrs. Daniels spoke at that moment, and it took Hawk by surprise. Her usually crisp, formal, imperious tone had softened markedly, though it still held all the perfection in diction and accent. It had become warmer, gentler, far more relaxed, and rang with a loving sincerity that could not be denied.

That alone would have convinced him that what she had said was true, but given their conversation, he further believed that she had given him the answer she had not presumed to give before.

He nodded slowly, unable to help the smile that spread across his face. "Thank you, Mrs. Daniels. You have given me much to consider."

"Yoo-hoo!" Mrs. Browning called, waving.

"Oh, Lord," Mrs. Daniels groaned beside him, making him laugh. "When we are settled, fetch me a drink, will you? I shan't survive the day on tea alone."

"Absolutely," Hawk agreed.

Mrs. Browning took Clara by the arm and moved down the terrace stairs to the lawn, leaving Hawk and Mrs. Daniels to follow them.

When they had all descended, they moved out to the set of three easels and canvases prepared for the artists, Mr. and Mrs. Fleet and their daughters waiting for them.

Pleasant greetings were exchanged, and Mr. Fleet excused himself to return to the house and discuss business with Mr. Browning.

Leaving Hawk the only man among the group.

Under usual circumstances, that would have been a cause for concern, but as the Fleet girls were too young to be considered a match for him and everybody knew it, he was in no danger from anyone present.

Clara aside.

She was danger enough for him.

"Why don't we have you both get started on your painting?" she suggested now to the girls. "I'll watch a bit and see if I cannot make some suggestions that would be helpful to you."

"Yes, Miss Moore," they said in a dull unison.

Clara smiled at them warmly. "Have I made you feel like my students? I assure you, this is nothing like. I want you to paint and draw as you normally would, and I will only suggest something if I think it will improve what you are already doing. Your mother has told me you are already very good, so I am quite eager to see what you can capture from this scene before you."

"They will look the same," the younger of the girls pointed out stubbornly. "And Catherine is better than me because she's older."

The petulant protest did not affect Clara's expression in the slightest. "No, they won't," Clara told her with a shake of her head. "You will notice different things about the scene, which will be reflected in your work. That is the exciting thing. No two paintings will be exactly the same. Your technique might be different as well, which will give the scene a unique quality all your own. Does that make sense?"

Suitably consoled, the young Fleet girl nodded, as did her sister, and they moved to their respective canvases to get started.

Hawk watched Clara, marveling at the extraordinary manner in which she had spoken to the girls, how she had handled the natural jealousy between siblings, how she had already taught them more than he suspected their governesses had been able to. She was more than just a skilled artist, she was a patron saint of art itself. She believed in its beauty and richness, could see the brilliance in every piece, and gave sight to the blind in such matters.

Remarkable woman, and there had never been anyone like her in his life.

Nor would there ever be again.

He caught a relieved exhale from her once the girls had started their painting and smiled as she untied the ribbons of her hat, setting it aside. She patted the delicate chignon of her hair, a curling tendril dangling alone in its escape from the hold of the rest. Hawk envied that tendril, wanting to toy with it and wrap it around a finger for a time.

But he would stand here beside her aunt's chair and only observe for now.

Seeing him watching her, Clara flashed a quick and easy grin.

Astonishing how such a simple thing could move him so much and give him such delight. It was a comfortable exchange, all things considered, and he suddenly had a vision of doing so in other settings with a completely different set of people around them. A quick smile across a crowded room that at once filled him with pleasure and pride as well as set his nerves to a painful sensitivity that would take hours to subside. Always both, in his mind, and nothing especially simple about it.

Each would be extraordinary, unique, and powerful.

Which meant he would continue to be on the brink of death for the rest of his life.

If such a thing came to pass, of course.

Which he prayed it would.

Something both cold and warm nudged against his hand and he looked down in confusion. Mrs. Daniels held up a cup of tea, the china explaining the coolness while the freshly poured tea was the warmth.

"Two lumps with a splash of milk, yes?" She tapped the cup of tea against his hand once more.

He took it from her, bewildered. "How in the world did you know that?"

She winked, smiling up at him. "I'm observant, Kirklin. As you were." She returned to her conversation with Mrs. Fleet and Mrs. Browning, whatever it had been, leaving him to his fancies.

Clearly, she knew what those fancies were, or at least had some idea.

Fortunate to have such an ally.

Clara continued to watch as the girls painted, walking between the two with complete ease, and, true to her word, not stepping in or making any sort of suggestion unless absolutely necessary. And, as Hawk had suspected, it was blended with praise and compliments when she did so.

"You have marvelous control of the brush," she told one of them. "You could easily enhance the shading of the cliff in the same way. Just there." She waited as the girl did so, then beamed. "Yes, exactly! I knew you would see how. And look what that does for the entire cliffside!"

What was more extraordinary was how the Fleet girls responded to her manner. They turned from trepidation at such intervention to asking her to come and look, or requesting advice, or outright begging for her correction of something they had yet to master. Soon, all three were laughing about something or other, and the art began to improve markedly.

At least, it seemed to from his position. He did not see the need to throw her present situation into upheaval by bringing closer observation into it. Especially when he did not know the Fleet girls at all. He was a duke, after all, and having a duke observe any young lady's attempts to be accomplished would be intimidating.

Clara looked at him again, then, to his surprise, waved him over.

He was moving in the midst of his shock, the motion instinctive and completely involuntary. Just as it was instinctive and involuntary to slip his hand into hers when he reached her.

She looked at her hand in his, then brought her eyes to his, smiling freely. "I like this."

The feeling in his left knee vanished. "So do I," he admitted, exhaling pathetically and smiling with it. "Didn't even think about what I was doing, it just happened."

"Perfect." She laughed through her smile, her thumb brushing against his with a familiarity he adored.

He cleared his throat, more to keep his sanity than anything else. "Did you need something? I felt particularly summoned."

"That's because I summoned you," she quipped.

"Ah, I see." He nodded sagely, playing along. "And why doth my lady summon me?"

She shrugged her shoulders. "You were over there, and I was over here."

It was the best reason he had ever heard for anything in his entire life.

"Say nothing more," he replied, feeling certain he would have kissed her soundly at that moment had they not been in company. Then he twisted his lips to one side. "Was there anything else?"

Clara laughed that low, musical, natural laugh he so loved. "Well, if you wish to see what the Fleet girls have accomplished, you are more than welcome to do so."

He sobered, looking at the two girls with some concern. "Are you certain? I don't wish to make anyone uncomfortable."

"Of course!" she insisted, tugging on his hand in a way that her aunt and the other ladies would not be able to see. "I've already asked, and they are interested in your opinion."

"Mine?" he asked in some confusion. "Why?"

She smiled at him shyly as he began to come with her. "I told them you've recently developed a new appreciation for art."

Hawk returned her smile, each beat of his heart colliding with his chest. "That is very true. I have. And for one particular artist, too."

The color in her cheeks rose and her eyes lowered, but the hold on his hand tightened, and continued to remain so while they perused the art before them.

There was something so relaxing about being on the shore and able to breathe in the refreshing sea air. She had felt such strain on her mind for so long, being able to breathe deeply and freely was a powerful agent for peace.

She'd have removed her shoes and walked in the water once more, had she not thought it would scandalize all who were with her.

The paintings had gone so well, and the Fleet girls had been so grateful and pleasant to her, she could not feel the day had been anything but successful. Even Mr. and Mrs. Fleet had been full of praise about their daughters' work and the improvements that had been made. Clara had been very nearly sainted by them, which had not been comfortable, but she could appreciate the sentiment behind such effusiveness.

Mr. Fleet and Mr. Browning had finally joined them, having finished their business talk, and the party had moved down to the beach for a tour of the caves and coves, and anything else that could be shown to them down there.

It was difficult not to give in to insatiable curiosity and press them all for details, which was why she had paused to breathe for a moment.

Craning her neck from side to side, Clara let herself inhale deeply one more time, then exhale slowly, the fragrance of the sea seeping into her with a subtlety that soothed her.

When all of this was over, and her teaching days were done, she would have to be sure to settle by the seaside.

"You'd dip your toes in the water if you could."

Clara hummed a laugh, turning her head to look at Hawk as he came to stand beside her. "Of course, I would. I'd do so at any seaside I came to, and probably in several lakes, as well. If there is a new body of water, I'd want to dip my toes in and walk a while."

Hawk smiled at her, something easy, soothing, and understanding. Something that filled her with warmth and yet made her yearn. Something only he could give her, and only he had ever done. "I'd join you in doing so this time."

"Wouldn't that be a picture, Your Grace?" she mused. She sighed and looked towards the others, all chatting aimlessly as Mr. Browning said something or other about the trail they had just walked down. "Do we have to be with all the rest in this?" she asked, a scant tendril of hair dislodging in the breeze off the sea and dancing across her brow.

Hawk reached out and tucked the tendril back behind her ear, his fingers brushing against her brow, her ear, and her cheek as he did so. He gently rubbed his thumb along her jaw for a moment, creating a swirling pit of madness in her stomach. "I'm afraid it would not do for us to be exploring caves, coves, and beaches that do not belong to me without our illustrious hosts."

Sighing, Clara leaned into the soothing motion of his thumb, nodding against his warm skin. "I suppose so." She met his eyes, searching their depths for a sign that he felt something of the torment she was enduring.

She found every bit of it reflected back at her. His mouth curved in a slight smile, prompting one of her own. "Shall we?" he prodded, his tone deep and rumbling through her.

She nodded again, and he dropped his hand, both turning to join the others.

"Ah, at last," Mr. Browning near-shouted when they reached him. "I have just reached the extent of my knowledge of this trail, so your timing is perfection." He gestured with his walking stick for them all to move along the beach towards the caves, and he led them, strutting like a strange, rotund peacock.

When they reached a particularly expansive area of beach and sand, he turned to them, his arms open wide. "Here, you will see the loading area for the fishing boats of our tenants," Mr. Browning informed them all, his voice a cannon over the sound of the waves, "and several local fishermen, as well. Every second and fourth Tuesday, the beach is theirs to do as they will, be it pleasure, business, or both!"

Clara eyed the area, easily seeing the possibility, but not seeing proof of it. Not that it should be surprising, as it had been barely a week. She looked further towards the cliffside and saw what seemed to be a deep and expansive cave. It would have been perfect for storing boats, especially for the tenants and fishermen that would participate in the venture on those days, yet she did not see any boats within.

Curious.

"What is in there, Mr. Browning?" young Annie Fleet asked, pointing at the precise cave Clara had been studying. "Can we go in?"

Mr. Browning chuckled heartily, the sound echoing in the cave. "Of course, my girl. After you!"

The group traipsed over to the cave, and all entered easily. Clara trod carefully on the stone, though it was perfectly dry, and looked all around it in fascination. It was clear the tide did not reach the cave any longer, but at one time it had, and the impressions left by the water then remained.

Mr. Browning was droning on about something or other of his children's time playing in several of the caves, not just this one, and Clara had begun to tune him out when Annie cried out again.

"Look! Look, there's a hole in the roof!"

All looked up and, sure enough, there was a tunnel of sorts heading directly down to them. It was roughly the size of two men, but hardly bigger, and it would have been impossible to reach it without a very substantial ladder or rope.

"Ah!" Mr. Browning grinned at Annie, gesturing up at it. 'That is one of the few remaining hints at the life on Barcliffe and the surrounding area from long ago. Did you know there were once mines here, Miss Annie?"

The girl shook her head, looking doubtful.

"There were!" Mr. Browning insisted. "Dozens of mines, each of them creating tunnels while they hunted for precious ore. And those tunnels still remain in the ground, if you can find the entrance. Not all of them were closed in. This one…" He pointed up at the hole above them. "This one was probably such a tunnel, though instead of finding ore, they found this cave."

He went on, droning on about the merits of the ancient tradition of mining in the area, which aided in creating so many other caves, tunnels, and nooks in nature in the land round about.

Clara nodded at the surprisingly interesting fact, looking around the cave for any other signs she might find. If there was one mining tunnel in the area, there were bound to be more. And a cave this size…

"Where are the boats stored, Mr. Browning?" Phoebe asked with true interest. "Your own, or the tenants'. Is there a cave for that?"

"There is, Mrs. Daniels," he replied, calling out to her as though she were a great distance away. "It's a bit further down the beach, I will be sure to show you shortly. We used to store boats in here, but it was too in the way of other interests on the beach all of the other days. We could not have a passel of boats obscuring all of this magnificence, could we?" He chuckled as if the idea were ludicrous.

Surely a number of boats together were called a fleet, not a passel… It did not seem so great an error to make, but surely a man who had such an interest in maintaining his beach and water access and preserving the interests of his seafaring tenants and neighbors would know such a thing.

More curious.

Walking further into the cave, her fingers trailing along the cool rock of the side, she found her attention drawn to little valleys in the bed of the cave, probably from decades of water droplets falling onto it and etching a place for themselves, and now each had created a puddle filled with water. They were scattered here and there, no pattern to them, no arrangement that could be identified, and they simply…

She paused, a flash of something in one of the puddles catching her eye. It would require her to step away from the wall towards the center of the cave, and stooping down would attract attention if she did not think of something. She cast about her for some reason to have, should she be questioned. Without pausing to check for observation, she stepped over to the puddle, stooping down and reaching in.

Her fingers closed around an object, small and barely noticeable in the comparatively deep puddle, but certainly not an object of stone. She withdrew it from the puddle and stuffed it into the hidden pocket of her skirts, then returned her fingers to the water, as though that alone had fascinated her.

Footsteps behind her assured her she had been right, and she forced her heart to steady itself in its suddenly frantic pace.

"When you said any seashore or lake, I did not think you'd consider such a small body of water worthy of your touch."

She exhaled in relief and grinned up at Hawk easily. "I said my toes would go in the lakes and seas. I made no such claim for my fingers." She splayed her hand out in the puddle before her. "It's astounding that this crater is of such a size, is it not?"

"As you have very small hands," Hawk teased, "I should not consider it remarkable."

That earned him a scowl and she rose, holding her damp hand out to him. "For that, Your Grace, you can use your handkerchief to dry my very small hand."

He bowed, flashing a playful grin her way. "It would be my honor, Miss Moore." Reaching into his pocket, he withdrew a pristine handkerchief and wrapped it about her hand, then began painstakingly rubbing the fabric along her skin, his eyes fixed on hers. Somehow, what had begun as a game had become something so much more, something intimate between them, something that said so much more than what appeared.

As did everything with them, it seemed.

Would they never be frank with each other, and say what they truly meant rather than allude to it?

It was on the tip of her tongue to confess her feelings then and there, to be done with the pretense and let him know her heart.

But the murmur of voices nearby cooled her impulse, and she smiled sheepishly at them.

"Have you hurt your hand, Miss Moore?" Mrs. Browning fussed, nearly whimpering with it.

"She is quite well," Hawk answered for her. "Miss Moore has a fascination for water and must touch it when the impulse strikes. I simply had a handkerchief at hand to dry her fingers, that is all." He slid the fabric from her hand, drawing a gasp from Clara that she had to nearly swallow to hide. "Shall we move on, Browning?"

"Indeed, Your Grace, indeed!" came the pleased response.

Hawk inclined his head, gesturing for Clara to go before him. "After you."

She smiled at his simple politeness, wondering what endearment might be added to such a statement if he allowed himself to do so?

She stepped carefully about the small puddles once more, smiling at Phoebe, who had reached the sand and was standing there waiting for her.

"Watch your step, Clara," Hawk warned behind her. "There can be a drop from cave to sand in any of these."

It was on her tongue to thank him for his care, when something about the sand in front of the cave stopped her voice entirely.

Lines. Orderly, neat, and definite. They did not go far, and anyone would have missed them, had they not been looking for what did not belong. The simple answer was that the lines would have been from boats, but, by Mr. Browning's own admission, boats were not stored in the cave, therefore have no reason to come up so far. And the lines were the wrong direction for pulling boats into the cave in the usual sense.

This was a boat that had been turned in a horizontal direction and dragged. The planks of its construction had made impressions, and their unconventional angle in the sand puzzled her.

Why would a boat be dragged in such a way towards a cave that held no boats? Even if boats had been hidden further into the cave somewhere, they would have been turned so that bow or stern were pointing towards the sea, not the side of the boat.

But dragged like this, a boat could hide other things in the sand. Other impressions, other marks.

Such as footprints.

Clara gnawed the inside of her lip, wondering if her mind was leaping from stone to stone and clue to clue in her mind, or if, perhaps, she might have uncovered another piece to this bewildering puzzle before her.

Chapter Twenty

"It seems I shall have to go to London tomorrow." Hawk shook his head in disgust and refolded the message he'd just received, setting it on the table moodily. "Inconvenient time to meet with my solicitor, but he says it is important, so the choice is entirely out of my hands."

"What's so inconvenient?"

The question caught him off guard, and he looked at the only other person at the dining table with him at present.

Clara.

"What's that?" he asked, not sure what she meant by her question, as he had been rambling.

She chewed her present bite and swallowed quickly. "You said it was an inconvenient time to meet with your solicitor. Why so inconvenient?"

He blinked at that, then allowed himself to smile at her. "I did say that, didn't I?"

She nodded. "Yes. Why?"

He tilted his head at her, wondering just how to answer. "I think you know the answer to that question."

Her eyes widened, and she looked back at her breakfast with increased focus. "Oh."

Yes, oh.

Oh, indeed.

He continued to watch her for a moment, as he tended to do when she was about. She was simply dressed, which allowed her natural beauty to speak for itself, and it had a great deal to say. The pale shade of pink in her dress echoed her natural rosiness, as though it had been designed precisely for her complexion. Gentle curls hung about her temples, the rest pulled back into a mass of plaits and curls that seemed rather elegant, though he hadn't studied it enough to say.

He had better things to do.

"Will you stop staring, please?" Clara begged softly, shifting her eyes to him as she fiddled with the end of her unused spoon beside her plate.

Hawk smiled at the question, watching her still. "Does it trouble you?"

"It's embarrassing," she whispered, the rim of her ear turning a bright shade of pink. "I cannot bear it."

"You should bear it," he told her as gently as he could. "You should be accustomed to it. There should be nothing embarrassing about your being admired. Lord knows, I cannot help it, and looking at you is more satisfying than looking at the art you create."

Clara's lower lip tucked in slightly, and he smiled at the sign of nerves. She wasn't a shy creature, but she did not think enough of herself, of that he was certain.

It was the only thing he would change about her, were it in his power. She needed to understand just how beautiful he found her, how fascinating and marvelous, how incomparable...

She needed to fathom just how much he was coming to love her.

His eyes widened as he continued to stare at her, though at the moment his focus was lost.

Love her?

The moment he thought it, he knew he was right. That it was right. Loving her was right.

But he could not tell her so over eggs and toast, that was certain. It had to be perfect.

Perhaps he could do more in London than just meet with his solicitor. Perhaps his solicitor could, in turn, do a favor for him.

And perhaps he could find something or other to give to Clara. Accompanied by a particular question he was very close to asking.

"Have you heard from your sister at all?" Clara inquired, breaking him from his thoughts.

"Adrianna?" He shook his head, frowning in confusion. "No,

not since I saw her when I arrived. Why do you ask?"

Clara lifted a slender shoulder, her color returning to its more natural state with the length of silence they had passed. "You seem particularly close, I only wondered." She took a small, careful bite of ham. "Perhaps you should see her before you go to London tomorrow. If the suggestion is not too impertinent."

Hawk smiled at the recommendation. "Nothing you say will ever be impertinent to me. But why should you suggest it? Anxious to be rid of me sooner?"

She instantly turned towards him, expression wreathed in concern. "Oh, no, not at all! I'd rather you not go at all, I'm not sure how I shall bear..." She stopped herself, swallowing with some difficulty, and looked down at her hands where they sat on the table linen.

It was all he could do not to beg her to go on.

He turned and reached out to take her hand, holding the trembling fingers as though they contained a precious treasure. "Clara..."

She swallowed again, then raised her eyes to his, making no move to remove her fingers from his grasp. "I only thought," she said in a much stronger voice, "that a young woman of her age and station might desire something from London. There are so many shops there, and it is not likely that the school is in very near vicinity of shops of equal quality."

"Did you?" he asked, rubbing the hand he still held almost absently. "When you were seventeen, did you wish for trinkets from London?"

Clara's lips curved in a small smile. "No. I was content with what I had. Well..." She tilted her head, giving the question some further thought. "I'm changing my mind. Yes, I would have liked something from London a time or two. I'd never thought to ask, but the hope was there." Her smile grew, and she surprised him by covering their joined hands with her free one. "Ask her if there is something, will you?"

He returned her smile, laughing to himself. "My sister is, and always has been, a spoiled child. You still think she needs a trinket of some kind?"

228

"Yes," she replied firmly. "Or a new gown. A parasol. A pair of gloves. Something." She laughed to herself, the amusement finding its way to her eyes as well. "She might say no."

Hawk scoffed and shook his head. "It's Adrianna. She'll never say no." He sighed dramatically, letting his smile fade. "Very well, I will pose the question to my sister, though it may ruin me and devastate my fortunes."

"I'd think it would take a great deal more than that to ruin you, Hawk," Clara scolded in a playful tone. "No girl of seventeen is *that* fastidious."

"You don't know my sister," he grumbled, rubbing his thumb against her hand. He smiled at her for a moment more, then raised his chin a touch. "What would you have from London?"

She reared back, hazel eyes going round. "Me? Nothing, nothing at all!"

He nodded as though that answered the question. "I'm not familiar with the address of any shops that sell nothing, let alone nothing at all, so I'm afraid you will have to think of something else."

Clara rolled her eyes and tried to pull her hands away, but Hawk refused to let her, lacing his fingers between hers and giving her a more thorough look. She only turned more exasperated. "Hawk! I don't need anything from London!"

"Then it is a good thing that I did not ask if you need anything from London," he shot back, "only what you would have."

"Nothing," she told him firmly, over-enhancing every syllable. "Not one thing."

He shook his head slowly. "You can't have nothing. And if you cannot have one thing, I shall have to bring you more than one thing, which could get cumbersome, and if you do not tell me what to bring you, I shall have to guess, which I would be dreadful at, which might lead to my guessing wrong, which could send me to London all over again, and—"

"Very well!" Clara interrupted loudly, laughing at his excesses, just as he'd hoped she would. "Goodness, have you been spending too much time with Nat Robinson?"

"Unquestionably," he replied without hesitation. "It is a blessing to be relieved of his bad influence lately. So? What shall I bring you?"

He watched in fascination as her laughing smile turned into one far more shy and modest, which was a maddeningly fetching sight. She bit down on her lip, her eyes lowering to Hawk's cravat.

But she said nothing.

After a long moment, Hawk moved a hand from its hold on hers and pressed two fingers to the underside of her chin, raising gently until her eyes met his again. He smiled, stroking the skin there softly. "White will be delighted to know my cravat fascinates a young woman of such taste, but it does not do anything for this endless cycle we are engaged in."

Clara searched his eyes, her expression unreadable.

"What?" he prodded, stroking a finger against her skin again. "What is it?"

She shivered and took his hand, surprising him by holding it up to her cheek. He instantly scooted closer, cupping that cheek in his palm.

"What?" he whispered with a tenderness he did not know he possessed. "Tell me, darling."

The endearment tumbled from his lips almost clumsily, yet felt so natural he could not wish it back or find any regret in it.

And if Clara's reaction was anything to go by, she felt precisely the same.

"I cannot ask anything of you," she murmured, her eyes soft on his. "I cannot find the words to. I cannot… wish anything of you, nor expect it."

"Yes, you can," he insisted, taking her unoccupied hand and kissing the back of it tenderly, even as the fingers upon her face brushed lightly against the skin. "You can, Clara. I want you to wish, and ask, and expect… Ask anything of me."

She only shook her head, somehow near to tears, if he was any judge.

That would not do. He'd not seen her cry yet, and he felt sure he would go mad the moment he saw a single tear fall.

"Shall I tell you a very great secret?" he asked her, lowering his voice even though they were the only two in the room. "Something I swore no one else would ever know?"

"Probably not," she whispered, laughing slightly.

He had to smile at that but sobered quickly. "I came back to Kent to attend to business with my sister."

She nodded, no doubt recollecting that. "Yes, you were very kind to do so for her."

He accepted that with a nod. "But I could have done what I needed there without coming to Kent at all. I used that excuse to hide my true purpose in returning."

Clara stilled beneath his touch, barely breathing, as far as he could tell.

Reason would have had him stop there, wait for some encouragement, or maintain a polite distance that was safer by far.

He'd had enough with reason.

"I came back," he went on, heart pounding painfully within him, "because I could not bear to be away from you any longer."

Clara blinked once. "Really?" she half-gasped, somehow without truly moving.

He nodded more fervently than he had ever done in his life. "I had been in agony since the day you left Kirkleigh. Could you not tell as you departed?"

"No," she admitted bluntly, her air rushing out in a gust that spoke of his own struggles. "No, you were so silent and cool, I thought I had imagined… a great deal."

Scooting to the very edge of his seat, Hawk placed his other hand on her cheek to match the first, cupping her sweet face in both hands. "You didn't imagine anything," he insisted. "I simply couldn't bear the farewell, and my reserve protected me from it."

Her hands reached up for his wrists, her thumbs moving across his skin in a way that deprived him of feeling in both feet. "Did it work?"

"Not in the slightest." He smiled, letting his eyes trace across her features with all the adoration he'd longed to, loving the feel of her face in his hands, and this closeness between them.

Loving that he could confess such a thing to her without feeling embarrassed or ashamed. That she would take him as he was without wishing he were somehow more. That she was so completely without airs and made him feel so at home.

Home.

That was it, wasn't it?

Loving Clara, being with Clara, was home.

It would have been the same at any of his estates, or any place at all. It would be home so long as she was there, and he could love her there.

He did not need anything else.

Footsteps in the corridor broke the spell between them, forcing him to drop his hands and focus on his long-forgotten meal, now undoubtedly cold. He cleared his throat, his face heating. "So will you let me know what it is I can bring you?"

"Yes," Clara replied, her tone almost stiff. "I will."

"Thank you." He glanced at her and winked, making her giggle.

"What will you bring me?" Mrs. Daniels entered without any fanfare, her cap perfectly placed, her figure wrapped in a yellow and green striped gown that suited her perfectly. "And where are you bringing it from? I've really got very moderate tastes, despite what you might think."

Hawk and Clara shared another amused look and continued to eat in relative silence.

Clara exhaled very slowly in the garden, her fingers aching with the tension in them.

Gripping the stone bench beneath her with all her strength would do that to them.

All she wanted to do was dwell upon the glories of the breakfast that had passed, and how she would bear Hawk's departure. He had promised to return as quickly as possible, and she believed he would, but even so.

Her operative training had apparently been more effective than she had previously thought, for she had also considered his time away rather opportunistic.

She needed to get back into Barcliffe, and she needed to do so without invitation or detection.

Her right leg began to shake as she sat there, bouncing with an anxiousness that rippled through her entire frame. She had sent a message to both Brick and Phoebe, asking to meet them at this time and in this place. Hawk had been locked away in his study to meet with his estate agent about some matter or another, which was a blessed reprieve, as having him about created the most unfathomable fog in her mind.

She had a desperate need for clarity now.

Just a few days since their day on the beach and in the caves, and she had no more answers now than she had then. It had all been a waiting game, her clues sent away to those who had the ability to analyze them properly.

Thankfully, the Convent was close enough that she should not have to wait long. It was not as though London was needed yet.

At least, she hoped it was not.

Her relationship with Hawk was growing at such a rapid intensity, she could very likely find herself engaged before the mission was done, and then where would she be? Her betrayal would have been all the greater and such a scandal made over it…

She closed her eyes, leg still shaking, her heart cracking deeply at the thought. She longed to be Hawk's wife, loved him with a single-mindedness she had never known, and the knowledge that her dreams were at the tips of her fingers was one of exquisite bliss.

The reminder that her identity was a lie, as were her reasons for being at Kirkleigh at all, clouded those dreams with darkness that wove its way into her soul. A cavernous pit that would soon drag her down into its abyss, never to free her.

She could not live both lives much longer.

Something had to be done.

A whistling rather like that of a bird met her ears, and she turned at it, her eyes darting around the garden eagerly.

Sure enough, Brick was ambling towards her easily, as though he were only on an afternoon stroll. "I told you," he said to someone Clara could not see. "The song of a sparrow will call to her."

"As though she would recognize the song of a sparrow," Phoebe's voice replied, dripping with derision. "She's not studied ornithology, Brick. Hardly anyone has."

"There are a great many who have, Fern," he retorted without heat.

Clara rose, still not seeing Phoebe and looking for her.

Brick stepped to one side as he neared her and there was Phoebe behind him, wearing the hat and veil of a beekeeper and a pair of men's trousers.

What in the world?

The pair of them laughed at Clara's expression. "I am entitled to my hobbies, Clara," Phoebe told her lightly. "And it does make a masterful disguise for me."

Clara nodded, as it truly did hide Phoebe's identity perfectly. She hadn't known that Kirkleigh kept bees, but that was neither here nor there. She sat back down on the bench, still nodding, though it was not for any reason in particular.

"Something on your mind, Sparrow?" Brick asked, folding his arms.

She nodded just once more, then looked up at him. "Has Tilda told us anything about the cufflink I found in the cave?"

Brick reached into his trouser pocket and handed her a note. "She has. Expensive set, she says. Clearly fashioned specifically for our mystery fellow."

"Why's that?" Clara opened the note and scanned the few lines before giving him a look of complete disbelief. "Engraved? How in the world does one engrave cufflinks? There's hardly space for a monogram!"

"I haven't the foggiest, but it was enough for a few words." He pointed at the note, waiting for her to reach that bit.

Clara returned to the note, then frowned. "*Un lointain rivage*," she read aloud. "Foreign shore." She paused, then shook her head. "That's not any sort of motto, vow, or claim. Nor is it distinguishable." She dropped the note into her lap, groaning to herself. "It means something, somehow."

Phoebe sat down beside her on the bench, thankfully not offering Clara any sympathy or consolation after doing so. "Those lines by the cave," Phoebe said in a low voice. "You're sure they were from a boat being dragged sideways?"

"I cannot be certain," Clara confessed, refolding the note more to occupy her hands than anything else. "But it seemed the most logical, given the nature of the beach and the occupation of the shore."

"The cave is not used for boats," Phoebe muttered, her voice losing nearly all of its formal primness. "Yet it had to be a boat creating the lines. Nothing else makes sense." She glanced at Clara through the veil of her hat. "Do you think that cave could go far enough back to hide a tunnel of sorts?"

Clara nodded. "Absolutely. There have to be more tunnels about, especially given the one above. Do you think a boat is back there?"

"That would make sense," Brick agreed, his brow knitting in thought. "A boat being dragged will create a number of impressions in the sand, and, if done with enough force, could easily hide traces of all sorts. If the boat can be stored in the cave, it protects everyone. We'd never know the numbers, nor the number of times the path was travelled."

"Are you saying...?" Clara paused, wetting her lips, then looked back at Brick with a breathless smile. "Are you saying I was right? Ships are landing there and bringing items ashore?"

Brick grinned at her, creating lines on his face. "I always thought you were right, Sparrow. I just didn't know how we'd prove it aside from posting someone on the shore every night until something happened."

Clara could have laughed at the revelation, but the truth in it still hung about her. "We still don't know when, even if we know how they hide things and where the boat is stored."

"If the boat is stored," Phoebe interjected, "there could also be other things stored. Items, plans, or people."

"And if it's a tunnel, it could be one not closed off." Clara's eyes widened. "They could be escaping any distance away, which is why no one has detected anything on the beach itself."

"All of this could easily be smuggling, you know," Phoebe said with some reluctance. "No governmental ties at all. Simple smuggling."

That was true, but they could not stop the investigation now.

Brick whistled low, shifting his hands to the pockets of his trousers. "If they are not coming ashore on the second and fourth Tuesdays, when are they?"

Clara cocked her head as a new thought occurred to her, spinning about for a moment. "Foreign shore," she said again. "That was what the cufflink said."

"It did, yes."

She exhaled softly. "Agents. The cufflinks could be a symbol of those who are assigned to work outside of France. It's a bit ridiculous to hide such a thing in plain sight, but why would anyone examine cufflinks enough to see it?"

"Why, indeed." Phoebe shook her head, her eyes wide. "This is significant, Sparrow. It could make all the difference in so many places."

Clara nodded her agreement, swallowing as she considered the next piece of her plan. "I need to get into Barcliffe. Undetected. And in daylight, if possible."

The other two froze, though they had not been moving all that much, and looked at her after a moment of stillness. "What?" Phoebe asked in an almost hoarse voice. "You mean to steal into the house in broad daylight? It would be easy enough to manage at night, provided there are no security measures, but during the day? Whatever for?"

"To find her proof," Brick murmured, his eyes still on Clara, seeming less shocked than his counterpart.

Clara met his look, nodding once. "The library. There is something about that ceiling, all of the ships and their positions… I need to study it and sketch it. It may hold the answers. And then, if I can, I want to get into the study."

"Oh, is that all?" Phoebe sputtered, flapping her hands into the air a little. "The study that is in the precise middle of the house? How in the world do you plan to manage that, hmm?"

"Come now, Fern," Brick said with some amusement. "You've snuck into places just as improbable before."

She glared at him darkly, even through the veil. "I have, yes. She has not."

He lifted a brow at that. "So how do we make the situation a trifle easier to manage?"

Phoebe made a loud scoffing sound that did not suit the character she portrayed. "Take the people out of the house."

"That shouldn't be impossible," Clara said slowly, smiling a little. "All we'd need is an outing. I'll be unwell and insist you go without me. Hawk will be in London, so I won't have to feign anything for his benefit." Her smile spread as she looked up at Brick. "Think you can help me devise an entrance in the family's absence, Brick?"

He grinned back. "I may have an idea or two."

Chapter Twenty-One

*S*he was barely breathing, but her mind was clear, her attention focused.

It had to be for the next hour.

Unless she could do it in less.

One hour was all she was promised.

A late autumn picnic had raised a few brows when Phoebe had suggested it to all their friends, but when she insisted she had taken a great many of them in the south of France, the reluctance vanished and the excitement had blossomed. Clara had done her part to build up interest and excitement, had expressed her own delight in the prospect of the picnic, and had even made sure she had a particular ensemble prepared and described to those who would be in attendance. Aside from actually taking ill at the picnic, she was not sure how else to convince anyone about her intentions.

Phoebe had wished her well before departing to meet the other picnic goers and reminded her of a cardinal truth from her training: If you are caught, say nothing.

Clara could not think about that too much, or she would begin to shake in fear.

She would not be caught, she reminded herself. They had taken all possible care in this, and all that was left was for her to get into the house.

The rest would sort itself out.

Positioned as she was behind a tall bush, her back against the house, she could only wait. The servants moved like clockwork, Brick had told her, and the schedule was always the same. She did not have a clock to check, but surely it was near to time.

Before the thought was finished, the door a few feet to her right opened up, a pair of maids with a basket of laundry exited, turning immediately for the back of the house.

Clara moved quickly, grabbing the door before it shut and stepping inside. She let the door close behind her and waited for her eyes to adjust. She kept her breathing shallow, but slow, creeping along the narrow corridor just as she'd mapped out.

Brick had struck up a friendship with the gardener at Barcliffe, and a discussion about a greenhouse expansion had led to apt descriptions of the servants' passages at the back of the house, which should prove useful.

She passed one door, which ought to have been the kitchen. Which meant the next door ought to be for the stairs, and the one after should open into a corridor in the main of the house. She could get to both the library and the study by it, though they were in opposite directions.

She could only pray, as she had been doing, that the housekeeper at Barcliffe was lacking in her attention.

It was all she could do not to hold her breath as she reached the door she needed, though she did try to listen for any sounds on the other side. Nothing met her ear, however, so there was nothing for it.

She'd have to go through.

Moving her lips on a silent prayer, she turned the knob of the door silently, opening it only enough to see out. There was nothing she could see, and nothing appeared to move within. Taking the chance, she pulled the door open further, slipping through the opening and closing the way quickly behind her, taking great care to slowly return the handle back to its position, so as to avoid any sound from the latch.

Again, all was silent.

Clara moved as quickly as she dared, grateful she had taken Phoebe's advice and donned a pair of breeches. It had been monstrously uncomfortable at first, but the silence it afforded her now was well worth it. Layers of petticoats and skirts would have rustled, but the breeches and her slippers were soft enough to keep her safe. For now.

Replaying Mr. Browning's tour in her mind, Clara bit her lip as she reached the fork in the corridor. Her main objective was the library to her right. The study was another two rooms down on her left, and the possibilities there…

She closed her eyes, the decision more agonizing than she'd predicted. Phoebe had begged her to only go to the library, as that was her best chance. But if there was any hope of real proof…

Before she could change her mind, Clara moved down the corridor on her left, moving faster than she had before, as though she could outrun her doubts. Footsteps echoed along the marble from somewhere, though no one could be seen yet. She continued, praying she would not soon run into a trap.

The door to the study was ajar, which brought her up short. She flattened herself against the wall outside it, peering around the entrance of the room with caution. No sound, no motion, and yet…

Somehow, there was a murmur of voices, but too faint to be in the room beyond. She ducked into the study, an unnerving room without windows and wall-to-wall books, rather as a library should have done. Yet in this room, there was no dust, and it was well used, if the worn patterns in the rug beneath her feet were any indication.

Going on tiptoe, she moved carefully around the great desk, looking at the items on the surface quickly.

No papers, no notes, everything neat and tidy as any gentleman's desk might have been. Not even any ledgers nearby to see to his business interests. She moved behind the chair of the desk and crouched down, looking on either side. Valued items would likely be within arm's reach, or easily accessed, and a man sitting at his desk would wish to keep them in sight.

Still the murmur of voices continued, no louder or softer than before, and nothing distinguishable from one word to the next. Then there was silence, and the cause seemed unclear.

Footsteps in the corridor suddenly grew louder, and closer, and Clara crawled under the desk, keeping her body as close to the chair as she dared. She crouched on the balls of her feet, relieved that there was no rustling with the breeches or skirts to manage at the moment. She slowly shifted her feet further apart, just enough to balance in her coiled position. The fact that she could do so silently in her present attire was not lost on her.

The door to the study opened with a loud creak, and a man entered, his footwear clearly distinguishing him as a servant. Clara watched the feet move to a shelf to her right, then stoop down and turn down a corner of a rug she had not noticed as folded up before. She closed her eyes and forced her already silent breathing to slow, waiting for the man to leave. She was wasting her hour in hiding and limiting how much time she could have in the library. Provided she could get there after this.

Just when she thought her knees would lose all feeling, the servant turned from his spot and left the room, shutting the door firmly behind him.

Clara exhaled very slowly and counted to ten before slipping out of her hiding place. She moved immediately to the rug, turning back the corner.

A hinge in the floor met her sight, and the clear lines of a trap door.

Cautiously, so the floor would not squeak, she laid down and pressed her ear to the door.

The voices were clearer now. And they spoke in rapid French.

"The next shipment will be the largest yet. We've been given permission to go ahead with our plans."

"And the pieces?"

This voice was that of a woman, and it startled Clara to hear it. Her accent was not native to France, and it was not that good, but it was clear.

"In place. Ready for the command. Will you be ready?"

"We are always ready."

Then, in chorus, the pair of them said something that froze Clara's heart.

"J'ai vécu."

Clara had heard enough, given the time she had, and gently pressed herself up from the floor, turning the rug down once more. She glanced at the shelf before her, where the servant had been, and nothing was out of place. Yet in the center of the books sat a faded one with a worn spine, something about it nagging her.

She gingerly pulled it out of its place and caught her breath as she opened it.

Lines upon lines of French were written there, not quite a diary, but something of the sort. She flipped a few pages, wishing she had the ability to recollect such things with exactness. She briefly recollected Miss Henrietta Mortimer, a former student of the school, though before her time, who had possessed such a skill, and wondered if she had ever been considered for this life.

A loose-leaf page fell out from between pages and she glanced at it on the floor, eyes widening. It was a piece of music, though much too small to be properly played. She stooped to pick it up, and gaped at it, the notes and words familiar and engrained in her mind.

Suspendez à ces murs. The same song she'd need to use for any letter decoding she came across.

That was more than enough.

Shoving the music into her pocket, she returned the book to the shelf and tiptoed back to the door of the study, listening for any steps in the corridor. She had no idea how much time she had left, but it was not enough, she was sure.

She moved silently out of the study, closing the door behind her without a sound, then did her best to rush down the corridor with equal noiselessness. She paused at the break she had reached before, checked her surroundings, then darted towards the library. Her feet skidded on the marble floor as she reached it, and she barely avoided throwing the door open for herself.

Once inside, she took a moment, closing her eyes, panting and swallowing as her throat ached and burned.

She needed her artist's eyes now, not simple observant ones.

Moments later, she opened her eyes and looked up.

The same ships were there, in their random positions, and she searched the whole of it for any semblance of order.

She moved to the center of the room, laid down on the floor, and focused her attention on the ships, the illustration of the sky, the sunset, the waves… The number of boats varied, and the numbers did not seem to be increasing or decreasing, though the sizes of ships in each panel varied. One held two large ships and three small boats, the next showed large clippers, another had nothing but a handful of small boats. The meaning and the direction seemed to be chaos from the looks of it, yet Clara knew better than to assume that.

There was always some semblance of a plan in the mind of an artist, no matter what the result was.

She began looking at the other parts of the art, rather than the ships themselves. One panel held the sunset, another only water, one had the illustration of fish in its waters, one had a lighthouse…

She studied that lighthouse a moment more, frowning at it.

There were no lighthouses in the vicinity, yet this structure in the art stood tall and proud, its tip pointing directly at the largest window in the room, and out at the sea.

She did not have time for this. She did not have time for a full analysis, she needed…

Time.

Clara's heart began to pound as her eyes darted here and there across the ceiling, wondering if it were possible. The more she looked the more she believed it, and the urge to laugh bubbled up within her.

Time. It was a clock, not in the classic sense, and certainly not in an obvious way, but it was a depiction of time passing. Each panel held a slightly different color to the sky as well as a different number of ships. The lighthouse was a perfect top of the hour, and moving in the direction of a clock, she could draw very simple conclusions.

She reached into her pockets again, this time drawing out the small pencil and diary she had been given in her training. She held it up before her, her eyes flicking from ceiling to page with a rapidity that would have made her dizzy under other circumstances.

Not now.

Not here.

The sketch was rough and crude, and she created symbols she hadn't considered before to speed things along. Her hand flew across the page, and then paused when she reached the panel of the sunset.

Where did that fall in the scheme? She could easily see these panels discussing the smuggling of goods and agents, though the interpretation would take some time to understand, but the sunset… She had waited on the beach after sunset for something to happen, if it happened on the days she expected, and it had not.

What then?

She looked at the ships again, particularly in their order along the clock and their positions, and then looked at what followed sunset.

There were no large boats after the panel at sunset.

Her eyes widened as they darted back and forth once more. It wasn't sunset. It was sunrise.

The drop had already occurred when she and Brick were on the beach. The village fishing helped to hide any tracks left from the drop the night before, a perfect cover for the entire venture.

"*Bénissez-nous, doux cieux…*" Clara breathed, grinning up at the art. She finished her rough sketch, making sure her notations on the number of ships were exact, then took one last look about for any additional details.

When she saw none, she sat up, looking at the window with the perfect sea view. To one side of the center, rather unremarkable in its appearance, was a three-pronged candelabra.

The lighthouse.

She took a brief moment to sketch that on a separate page, then got to her feet, forcing her euphoria into the back of her mind.

Now, she needed to return to Kirkleigh undiscovered.

No small matter.

She crept from the library, more on edge now than she had been at any other part in the venture. None of this would do her any good if she could not get away, after all. She ducked into the corridor towards the servants' corridor just as she began to hear footsteps again. The hinges to the servants' corridors were clearly well cared for, as the door opened without a breath of sound. She entered the darkened, pokey area without a breath, pressing her back to the door as it closed.

There was no telling how often the servants moved through this part of the house, following the similar pattern or not.

Hearing nothing, she hurried down the long space and to the outer door, pushing it open only as far as she dared, squeezing herself out and back behind the bush that had held her before. She breathed there only a moment, waiting for any sign of servants or disturbance, then darted out at a sprint towards the hedgerow, her carefully worked opening still in place and now less carefully entered. Trees hid her next part, and she ran headlong in the direction of Kirkleigh.

She did not stop as she crossed the stream marking the boundary, and she did not stop on the hill leading up towards the house. She could barely feel her legs, but she ran still, images of pursuing servants forcing her on.

Strong arms caught her then, making her gasp, and she whirled in their hold, relief stealing her strength when Brick's concerned face floated before her.

"I did it," she wheezed in near delirium, clutching at his shirt. "I did it."

He grinned and scooped her up easily in his arms. "Of course you did, Sparrow. Come on, let's make you appear unwell."

Clara nodded blearily, grinning as she clung to her friend and ally. At last, she would be able to prove herself in this new role she had taken on, would have given something to her King and country, would have righted a wrong that could have disastrous consequences.

She could hold her head high, could make up for the blunder at the beach, and feel her assignment well spent.

She had done it.

Chapter Twenty-Two

*H*awk would have run the rest of the way to Kirkleigh had he thought it would get him there any faster. He was well aware that a team of horses would do the job far more efficiently but sitting here in comfort when he wanted to be racing was maddening.

He'd spent as little time in London as he could, but it had still been two full days there. Considering the day of travel prior, he'd been away three days, and had now been in the carriage for five hours.

They were due to reach Kirkleigh shortly, but it would feel much longer.

He desperately needed to see Clara. Needed to hold her. Needed to kiss her, finally. And then he would tell her he loved her, propose matrimony, and show her the special license he had been so fortunate as to procure during his time in London. It might have been presumptuous, but he would rather be presumptuous than regretting.

And then there was the ring.

He allowed himself a smug smile as he reached into the inner pocket of his jacket to pull the delicate band out for observation. The bright, pristine gold glinted in the light of the day, and the embroidery-like cannetille, design dotted with small diamonds around a larger, perfect amethyst gemstone, gave the ring a singularity he quite liked. It might have been overdone, but the moment he saw it, he had thought of Clara. Of her delicate hands, elegant fingers, and of feeling the hand bearing this ring weave its fingers through his own.

It had to be Clara's, and he prayed it would be.

Of course, he had also procured the drawing pencils she had relented in requesting, as well as a fine cameo brooch for her aunt. Adrianna had sent him with a list of items from a dressmaker he had never heard of, but he had been assured that the items would be delivered to her at school soon.

He had promptly ceased to care about her order after it had been submitted, and now he had only Clara on his mind.

Only Clara.

He tucked the ring back into his safest pocket, grinning out of the window as the road turned to more familiar sights. They'd actually be on the estate in a minute or two, and then he could get on with his plans.

He'd had enough of waiting, and unless he was grossly mistaken, all would go rather well.

What would his siblings and Nat have to say to that?

As though the horses knew of his haste to be home, their pace increased, sending the carriage bumping and jolting along like the mail coach. He grinned, not caring a jot for his comfort at the moment. He'd much rather arrive sooner in some slight disarray than later and pristine.

Clara wouldn't care, after all.

How would she respond if he simply swept her into his arms when he got there? He was suddenly rather keen to find out. For a man so in love, he did not have much contact to show for it.

He had not even kissed the woman, by heaven, unless one could count kisses upon hands. He had not embraced her, had not felt her arms around him, or anything of the sort. He could testify to the exact shape and size of her fingers, though, and how they felt clasped in his own. He knew the feel of her cheeks in the palms of his hands. He could tell anyone how her face appeared by moonlight, and which lock of hair would dislodge in a breeze off the sea. He could recount perfectly how the shade of her eyes changed from morning to afternoon, and from afternoon to evening.

But he did not know the feel of her lips on his, nor the taste of her.

And that was something he could not wait much longer for.

Did that make him so very savage?

He continued to watch from his window, more eager than a child, waiting for the sight of Kirkleigh itself to appear. Had he ever watched for anything so earnestly?

Then, at long last, it was there, gleaming in the sunlight, more beautiful than the house had ever been to his eyes, and more the appearance of home than anything he had ever seen.

His chest could have burst for all the warmth and delight swelling within him. What in the world was coming over him? The sedate Duke of Kirklin was fit to bursting over his own home because of the woman who was waiting there?

Yes, he admitted without shame. Yes, he was.

He frowned ever so slightly at the sight of a dark coach in front of the house, no crest or seal upon it to identify its owner. He was not in the mood for visitors when he had been planning a grand, almost histrionic reunion for himself. He'd have to see whoever it was away posthaste and find another way to accomplish his means.

Without waiting for the carriage to stop, he opened the door and stepped out, striding for the entrance in long paces, removing his hat in advance.

Stafford greeted him with wide eyes, his face drawn.

Stafford was never drawn.

Something was afoot.

Hawk handed the man his hat and shrugged out of his greatcoat. "What is it, Stafford?"

His butler swallowed. "The magistrate is in the Blue Room, Your Grace. With Mrs. Daniels and…"

He did not wait for Stafford to finish and marched for the Blue Room, his expression set with all the thunder he felt roaring through his veins. "What is the meaning of this?" he bellowed as he entered the room, looking around almost wildly in his fury.

Mrs. Clayton stood to one side, arms folded tightly, expression dark. Sir Henry Norris, the local magistrate, stood across the room from her, cool as the morning. He had a few lads with him, no doubt deputized to do something or other, though none of them seemed to be doing anything at the moment.

Then, there was Mrs. Daniels, fists balled at her sides, glowering with the murderous look of a far darker figure at the magistrate and his men. And beside her was Clara.

In shackles.

Hawk suddenly saw red. "What in the *hell* is all this?" he barked again, flinging his hand towards Clara. "I demand an explanation!"

Sir Henry turned to face him without emotion, bowing his bald head with apparent deference. "Your Grace. Your timing is excellent, I must say. We are in the process of making an arrest."

"In the process…" Hawk repeated, sputtering in disgust. "Have you a warrant? What are the bloody charges?"

"Yes, I have a warrant," Sir Henry replied, his tone infuriatingly passive. "See here. And as for the charges…"

Hawk held up a hand, looking over the warrant quickly. It did not say much, but what it did say confused him.

Clara Harlow was under arrest.

Who was Clara Harlow?

A faint familiarity rang in his mind, though he couldn't place it, and he looked at Clara in confusion.

Her eyes remained on the floor, her hair coiled into a crown upon her head. Or a halo. Yes, that's what it was. She could have been an angel standing there in chains.

And she was not looking at him.

A gaping hole opened up in the pit of his stomach, and it tugged at everything within him to sink. "Who," he ground out harshly, "is Clara Harlow?"

"For the benefit of His Grace," Sir Henry intoned gravely, "I shall begin again." He cleared his throat, the noise too lengthy for comfort. "I, Sir Henry Norris, do hereby arrest Miss Clara Harlow, known hereabouts as Clara Moore, on suspicion of burglary, forcible entry, conspiracy, robbery, and assumption of false identity of a living person. How do you answer these accusations?"

Hawk stared at Clara, waiting for her answer.

She gave none, never raising her eyes from the ground.

He couldn't even manage to blink, wondering why she wouldn't deny the accusations emphatically, preserve her reputation and her name, insist this was all wrong. Why was she just standing there doing nothing?

Except…

"Do you deny that you are Clara Harlow?" Sir Henry inquired, seeming almost bored now.

Clara did not move, nor did she speak.

"Do you deny taking part in any of these crimes by which you are accused?"

Hawk watched in horror as Clara only blinked, her face otherwise impassive.

"Do you deny entering the house of Barcliffe forcibly and without permission of its owners?"

What? The Brownings? Hawk looked at Sir Henry in shock, then at Mrs. Daniels, who had an arm around Clara now, but only glared at the older man calmly destroying her niece.

Even she was saying nothing.

Why wasn't anybody denying this? Why was it continuing?

Unless…

He slowly looked at Clara, tendrils of fury and betrayal unravelling.

As though she knew, Clara flinched.

That alone told him the truth.

His chest squeezed tightly, as though the walls of the room were closing in just on his heart. The weight of the ring in his inner pocket would have nailed him to the floor had he considered it too much. Had his indignation not been roused.

Had he been less sound of mind.

Another man entered the room then, moving past Hawk to hand a familiar, leather-bound diary to Sir Henry. "It's there, sir."

Sir Henry flipped open the book and eyed a page for a moment. "You've a canny hand, Miss Harlow. Pity, that." He turned several more pages, then murmured, "Ah, yes. Proof enough." He turned to show Hawk the page.

It was a roughly sketched layout of a house, more accurate than most, which followed, as Clara's hand had drawn it, but not enough to be actual designs. And it was undoubtedly Barcliffe, even Hawk could recognize that.

He returned his attention to Clara then. "What did you take?" he growled.

As he expected, Clara said nothing.

Then the pieces slid together in his mind, and he exhaled slowly. "Miss Harlow," he said slowly, nodding to himself. "Artist. Would you be the Miss Harlow employed at the Miss Masters' Finishing School?"

Clara clamped down on her lips hard, her eyes still on the floor. The last of Hawk's hopes dashed to pieces then and there.

"We are sure of that, Your Grace," the bland magistrate told him. "We've already sent word to the school; we anticipate her immediate termination. Never had any trouble with them before, and we'll do our best to keep their good name untarnished by this misfortune."

Hawk smirked at the word choice. "Misfortune," he repeated to himself. "Yes, isn't it just? Sir Henry, might I have a moment alone with the accused?"

"Certainly, Your Grace." Sir Henry came over to him, leaning close. "I'll keep your name out of this entirely. The real Miss Moore will be contacted, and there will not be so much as a smudge on the family or Kirkleigh."

Hawk nodded his thanks, beyond words of politeness now. One by one, the magistrate and his men left the room, followed by Mrs. Clayton. Mrs. Daniels, however, had not moved from her place beside Clara.

He had to admire that, he supposed, but he did not know what to make of her at this moment. "You, too, Mrs. Daniels," he insisted roughly. "Please."

She looked at him finally, her jaw tight. Then she brushed back a bit of Clara's hair and kissed her head, whispering something he did not catch. Ever graceful, she glided towards him, her pale eyes never wavering on him.

"If you wound her further," she murmured when she reached him, "I will cut your heart out."

"You'd have to find it first," he snapped, jerking his head towards the door, turning to watch her fully leave, shutting the door behind her.

He set his hands on his hips, lowering his head as he inhaled deeply, then exhaled the same. "I don't even know what to say to you," he told Clara, his back still to her. "I don't... I don't know how to look at you now. I don't know what to believe, not when the proof is…"

A faint sniffle, choked with tears, came from behind him, and he grimaced at hearing it, the sound somehow still ripping at the fibers of his being.

"I ought to be ranting," he went on, turning his head to almost glance behind him, but not quite. "I should be roaring in almighty fury and raining curses down upon your head. I should be enraged at you for dragging my name and the estate through the mud. I should be on my way to bloody high dudgeon over this. I have no doubt I will get there eventually. But I simply can't fathom why…? Why you would…? I just… I am actually at a loss for words here. Would you care to explain anything? Anything at all?"

"I love you."

Death might have taken him in that moment, for all the sensation he felt, but he was returned to life very shortly. Her voice, choked with tears, uttering those sweet words, would torment him until the day he died.

"Now you say something," he muttered, running a hand through his hair, "and that is what you say?" He shook his head, turning a little further, almost able to see her now. "Are you trying to change my mind about you, Miss Harlow?"

"No," she replied, sniffling again, her tears growing more evident. "No, I just wanted you to know. That part of me was real and true. I don't know what's going to happen now, or if I'll ever see you again…" She broke off, her breath hitching loudly.

He flinched at the sound, the pain of it reaching across the room to him.

"I love you," she said again, sobbing each word. "I never meant to hurt you, and I couldn't bear the thought of never seeing you again without knowing that I'd told you what I've felt since that day you took my hand on the beach. I don't expect anything from you, Hawk. I just… I love you."

The damned souls in hell could not know pain worse than this. His hands hadn't moved from his hips, though they seemed to be clamping down against them with an unsettling brutality. He'd lowered his head, whether from pain or to listen better, he couldn't say. He couldn't even move, wasn't sure if he was breathing, and he would have given anything to block out her voice.

Those words… How could he bear to hear them now?

"I'm sorry," Clara whispered again. "But I do love you. I always will."

I love you.

His head came up slowly as those words reached him, wrapped themselves about him, and something in him snapped. He turned sharply and closed the distance between them, his attention on one thing and one thing only. He seized her arms roughly and hauled her into his chest, his mouth finding hers in an instant, desperately plundering with a hot, aching need that pounded furiously through his veins.

Her shackled hands found his face, her lips molding against his with a perfection that shook the ground beneath his feet. She took everything he gave and curled into him with a willingness that unmanned him.

"Damn you," he whispered against her mouth as he caught her sobs, her body trembling with each one. He touched his forehead to hers, his breathing more ragged than hers, his eyes clenched tightly shut. He shook his head slightly against her, the stroking of her fingers against his jaw too much to endure. "Damn you."

He kissed her again hungrily, could taste the saltiness of her tears in their kiss, mingled with the longing surging through them both. Again and again, he kissed her, or she kissed him, the moments frozen in time while it lasted.

The doors to the Blue Room opened then, snapping Hawk from his frantic reprieve. He pulled her hands from his face, unable to meet her eyes, and stepped away, swallowing the sudden lump of emotion that had formed.

"We'll be taking her away now, Your Grace," one of the constables told him. "Sir Henry is making arrangements. We'll be sure to notify you of them when all is settled."

Hawk nodded, too ashamed and tormented to face anyone.

Footsteps told him they were moving now, though no one said a word. He could hear Clara's tears still, could taste them on his tongue, and the combination tore at his soul. He stood there, his head back, eyes closed fiercely, listening to her cry all the way to the carriage.

Then, he waited until the sounds of the carriage wheels could no longer be heard before he moved a single muscle, at which point he fell to his knees and dropped his head into his hands.

Chapter Twenty-Three

$\mathcal{I}$t was ridiculous how long it would take to prepare Kirkleigh to be sold. He'd gone over all of the numbers twice, and it would not do at all.

He could sell the place as it stood, and to hell with the fallout.

Nobody would care, would they?

Why should they? He didn't.

He didn't care about anything at the moment.

Could not.

Would not.

Since Clara had been taken away, he had no desire whatsoever to enjoy any aspect of the house, nor to keep it in the family. How could he continue to care for an estate that had never come to life for him before she had been there? Where so many moments had drawn them together, and stirred his soul in a way that nothing had before? He had fallen in love in this house, on the beach of its estate, in the gallery in the middle of the night.

How could he ever return to it after this?

Yet he could not bear to leave.

White had asked him the evening of the arrest if he wished to have his things packed to return to Elmsley.

Hawk had adamantly refused.

Even now, days later, he did not understand why. He did not want to be at Kirkleigh, not when every wall and chair reminded him of Clara.

Yet he did not want to leave. Once he left, it would be over. The magic would have ended.

Everything would become real.

She had lied to him. He had loved her. She had left. He had changed. She had cried. So had he.

He had loved her.

The truth of it was that he loved her still, and the truth of that made him ache deep into the hollow of his soul. How could he love a woman under these circumstances? How could he still care so much for the woman who had pretended her way into his home and his heart? How could he still long for the sound of her voice, the touch of her hand, the sweet taste of her lips?

Kirkleigh had become a prison, and he some half-alive creature haunting its walls.

He could not go on like this. He had responsibilities and duties that demanded his attention, and somehow, he needed to regain some sense of himself.

Today he would start. In order to sell Kirkleigh, he would need to take stock of each room. Mrs. Clayton had offered to make an inventory that he would only need to look over, but he did not want to ignore the trouble of such a task. He wanted to face the turmoil each new room would bring and force himself to reconcile with it. How else could he truly dispense with an estate that had been in his family for so long?

He would start with the bedchambers. Each of them. All of them. The whole bloody forest of trees that lined the corridors in each wing.

The first few bedchambers hadn't been occupied in some time, so the work there was minimal. No family history or heritage, no heirlooms, nothing he would wish to retain. A few of Griffin's belongings still lingered in the Cedar room, and several items remained in Adrianna's Poplar suite, as well. He would send them notes regarding their things, and any furnishings in the rooms that might have held personal meaning for them.

The Birch and Willow rooms were next, and he hesitated outside each. The Birch for confusion and shame. The Willow for the sheer agony of it.

Mrs. Daniels had departed Kirkleigh the morning after the arrest of Miss Harlow, though he suspected she would have done so the same day had she a place to go. She had taken a tray in her room and avoided any opportunity to speak with him or see him. As he had not sought her out, nor demanded explanation of her, there was not much to be said. Questions remained in abundance, more of them rising with every passing day.

Had she been the aunt of Miss Moore? Was she instead the aunt of Miss Harlow? Was she a relation at all? How much had she known of the situation? Why had she stood by Miss Harlow in spite of everything? What tied the women together, and how did such loyalty exist?

He had not bid her farewell in her quiet departure, but he wished now that he had done so. That he had paid her the courtesy of politeness. That he had looked in on her after such a distressing event. He might have known more of the situation had he done so.

But he had chosen to seclude himself in his own despair, and he would live with the consequences.

He stood in the room a moment, looking about its simple furnishings. Nothing remained of Mrs. Daniels' belongings, and one would never know the room had been lived in of late. The connecting door to the Willow room was ajar, and he stared at it for a moment longer than was wise.

He could almost believe Clara would be in the room beyond, if he entered from that way.

His feet seemed determined to try, moving him in that direction without much resistance.

A small dressing room filled the space between rooms, and Hawk stopped in the center of it. Some of Clara's belongings still remained within, and the sight of them struck him with more power than he could have anticipated.

Mrs. Daniels should have cleared all of this out. Should have seen all of Clara's things packed up and stored elsewhere. Should have sent some items along to the holdings that would house her until trial.

Hawk stared between a few simple gowns, something stashed beyond them drawing his attention. Fearing the gowns would fade into dust with his touch, he gingerly extended his hand and pressed them aside, reaching beyond in apprehension.

His fingers closed around a wrapped canvas, which startled him.

He pulled the item out, moving into the light of the bedchamber to see it clearly.

It was a painting, one done in oils and with such skill it could have been on display in a royal residence. The scene was one of a forest, the trees within a brilliant likeness to their living counterparts, and each bearing individual aspects and beauty to set them apart from the one beside it. Sunlight streamed between the trees on the canvas, wildflowers dotting the forest floor, and a small, winding path wound its way through the whole of it. There was something stirring in the landscape, whimsical and bearing an almost ethereal quality that captivated him.

When had this been done? He could not recall a single moment of seeing Clara with oils to hand, let alone sitting to create such a masterpiece.

He found himself smiling at the loveliness before him, a token that brought more fond memories than melancholy ones. He glanced at the images of wildflowers again, his eyes widening at the sight of a couple of leaves painted among them.

Maple leaves. Quite distinctly, and obviously intentional.

He blinked at the canvas, his eyes burning as they began to dart here and there, realizing with bated breath that what he was seeing before him was an entire forest of maple trees. Each bearing its own image, each standing tall, and each possessing a remarkable beauty.

Clara.

Hawk swallowed with some difficulty, wrenching his gaze away from the art to look about the room, only to find that he had ventured into the Willow room.

Of course, he had.

Sighing wearily, he turned slowly, scanning every wall, nook, and cranny for signs of her. Memories of her. Tokens of her.

His eyes fell upon a familiar-looking diary sitting upon the desk, wondering how it had made its way back there rather than staying in the hands of Sir Henry and those tasked with prosecuting her. He walked to the desk with trepidation, knowing he would not help matters by succumbing to the impulse of looking through it.

The only question he could bring himself to ask was if he truly cared.

His answer came swiftly enough.

No, he did not.

His fingers traced the simple black leather binding the pages, something about its worn surface easing the tension growing in his chest. He picked it up, flipping the first few pages open to examine the sketches.

Leaves and wildflowers filled several pages at first, followed by finer flowers in a garden or greenhouse, the detail noted in each incredible to behold. There were images of architecture, the buildings themselves unfamiliar to him until he caught sight of the shape of the Miss Masters' school and its expansive nature. This sketch had been painstakingly done, probably over time, and with a great deal of care.

He could see the love and effort in the rendering here, the attention paid to even the smallest feature. He had never quite thought of the grand house as being a home for those living within, but the feeling in the drawing spoke of such emotion and affection.

Clara clearly adored the place. Why then would she ever risk her life there by engaging in such crimes?

He frowned, flipping a few pages more. His lips curved into a helpless smile as the scene at his mother's favorite spot appeared on the page.

The first day, he had seen her draw, and could attest to her abilities. He could still see her sitting there, plain as day, a vision of loveliness he hadn't fully appreciated at the time. He could recall every moment of their walk back to Kirkleigh, and of their darting to the house as the rain had begun to fall.

Had he loved her then? Had it started so soon? Or had he needed more time to become so enchanted?

It was impossible to say, but he had felt something shift at that time, he knew. His heart had awoken, perhaps, to the possibility of her. Could he have known where it would lead?

His thumb began to peel back page after page, only glancing at their contents. A few sketches of Mrs. Daniels. The sketches of the beach. A profile of Nat.

Then there were drawings of Hawk.

His throat tightened as he observed several pages of his own likeness reflected back at him, his expression and position varying as much in the art as it did in his life. An image deep in thought, one of relaxed contentment, another as he might have appeared at the Assembly room, and one…

He forced himself to swallow the lump that had formed as his eyes fell on a portrait of himself laughing, full of joy as he so rarely was in his life. And she had drawn herself beside him, looking up in adoration and laughter, the pair of them almost dancing in their position.

How could he bear this?

How could he doubt this?

How could he doubt her?

Something cold and hard slammed against his chest, freezing the length of him with a slow crawl that resembled a London fog.

He couldn't doubt her. Couldn't doubt them. Couldn't believe…

He gasped in pain, gripping the chair before him, his knuckles turning white.

He was wrong.

Clara might have held a different surname while she was in residence there, but her heart had been true. Her nature had been true. She was not a woman of artifice and games; he had known that from the start. She was more open and sincere than any girl he had ever known, though she hadn't shared the history at Kirkleigh he'd thought. She'd still brought him to life. Still seen him in spite of the title and fortune he possessed. Had never schemed for his heart, only earned it through her goodness, loveliness, and warmth of spirit.

She had only ever earned it.

And he had turned against her. He hadn't stood in the way of those combining against her. Hadn't vowed to protect her or stand by her.

Hadn't done anything.

The diary fell to the floor as he strode to the door, flinging it open and marched down the corridor. "Stafford!" he bellowed, his voice echoing along the walls of Kirkleigh.

"Your Grace?" came the voice of his butler from somewhere below.

Hawk peered over the railing, gripping it tightly. "Where did Sir Henry say he was keeping Miss Moore? I mean, Miss Harlow?"

Stafford blinked up at him, brow furrowed. "Your Grace, I didn't..."

"The King's Arms, Your Grace," Mrs. Clayton replied, coming into view and folding her hands before her as she looked up at him, "but only until he could find room at the local House of Corrections. Being a lady, he wanted..."

"Fine, fine, very well," Hawk overrode, waving a hand. "It's only been a few days, so how long would they hold her?"

Stafford and Mrs. Clayton exchanged looks, then returned their attention to him. "Only until her bail was paid, Your Grace," Stafford told him simply. "Then she'd be free until trial."

Hawk grinned in abject relief, slapping the railing with both hands. "Excellent! Prepare my horse! Now!"

London was a dreadful place.

Well, what she could see of London from her present quarters, which, admittedly, was not much, but it did not seem to have much to recommend it.

Clara sighed as she pulled the curtain back in place, pushing herself up from the window seat and wandering back to the divan in the adjoining parlor, fussing with a small pillow there.

Four days she'd been here now, and she was prepared to go mad.

But, she reminded herself, at least she was not in prison.

She was particularly fortunate in that regard.

Sinking onto the divan now, letting herself lean forward enough to rest her elbows on her knees, she exhaled heavily. The day of her arrest had been one of nightmare, filled with dismay, shame, heartbreak, confusion, fear, and one brief, shining moment of glorious passion.

She'd clung to that ray of light often in the days since.

There had been no warning when Sir Henry had appeared, but Phoebe had immediately acted, sending Brick on Hawk's fastest horse to report it, and reminding Clara not to say anything before also adding that all would be well.

It had not felt as though all would be well, but she had kept to her silence easily enough.

Until Hawk had arrived.

Her mortification had been harshly compounded at being found in shackles by him, though she learned later that they had been wholly unnecessary, given the crimes of which she had been accused. She'd presume it was the ambition of Sir Henry Norris, justice of the peace and magistrate, though he had not appeared to have any feelings at all when he'd arrested her.

Hawk's words to her had cut through all willpower and strength, all sanity and pride, though she had very little left at that moment. She had seen how broken he had become, how betrayed and hurt by her actions. She would never be redeemed, she knew well, but at that moment, all she had left was her love for him, and it had rung so vibrantly through her quivering body. She had poured out her soul while she could do so, knowing it would never be enough, but praying it might make her less of an evil in his eyes.

She had not expected the rush of his passion, the fury in his lips on hers, nor the yearning she had felt behind it. Whatever her lies, whatever her sins, at least in that moment she could say that her heart had not been wrong. Her love had not been given in vain.

It had not been for nothing.

She'd cried through one night at The King's Arms, and then been whisked away by a man she didn't recognize under orders to take her to London. Sir Henry had conceded to the gentleman, nodding at some document he had been shown, and wished Clara well in her dealings.

Three miles out of Gadsden, the man had completely changed his accent, called Clara by her code name, and assured her that was the last of her experience on the criminal side of the law. Then he had fallen asleep, and they had continued on to London.

To Lord Rothchild's home, of all places.

And here she had remained.

Not as a prisoner, but as a guest.

Who could not venture outside of the house.

The irony was not lost on her.

To be fair, she had been in a number of meetings with various members of the covert world, discussing her findings in the library ceiling at Barcliffe, what she had overheard in the study, and her thoughts on what it could mean. Her opinion was valued in these sessions, which had been startling, to say the least. She had to be the most inexperienced member of the ranks in all of England, and yet she was an authority on this subject?

By the third session of the same discussions, she had grown far more comfortable with conjecture and venturing into the unknown, and her compatriots had seemed more than willing to indulge her there.

Lord Rothchild said little, smiled a great deal, and reminded Clara to make herself at home.

Considering his home was the finest of all homes she had stepped in, that was not likely to occur.

Perhaps more surprising in all this had been Lady Rothchild. She showed no surprise in Clara's arrival, displayed no reluctance in welcoming her there, and took great pains to visit with Clara when she returned from her daily outings. Being the wife of a highly respected and visible diplomat, she had a great many demands upon her time and person.

Yet she made time for Clara.

How bizarre.

"Clara?" the lady in question suddenly called. "Clara, are you up here?"

Clara rose quickly and moved to the door of her parlor, opening it wide. "Here, my lady."

Lady Rothchild paused at the top of the stairs, giving her a severe look. "Clara, what have I told you about addressing me that way?"

"I know, my lady," Clara admitted with a smile she almost felt, "but I cannot be comfortable calling you Emily. I simply cannot."

The beautiful woman smiled, her dark eyes crinkling with it. "We shall have to become better friends, then. After all, Sparrow..." She winked before tossing her fair curls on a laugh. "I understand the upheaval suddenly being thrust into this world can concoct."

Well. That answered that question.

"You know?" Clara asked, widening her eyes and coming closer.

"Oh, yes." Lady Rothchild nodded quickly. "Not all of the specifics, and certainly not many of the missions, but I know. I had a mission myself many years ago. Just one." Her eyes widened in apparent exasperation. "And one was trouble enough."

Clara laughed at that, her comfort with the woman reaching further now than ever before. "What were you called?"

"Vixen," she replied with a sly smile Clara wondered at. "Because my husband was known as Fox at the time, and I was his wife even then."

"You were his wife before the mission?" Clara gaped for a moment. "I would have thought you met during the assignment, or some such."

Lady Rothchild's smile turned soft for some reason. "No, we were already wed. Yet we did meet on the assignment, in a way." She exhaled briefly, then blinked, coming out of her reminiscence. "I digress. Would you come and take tea with my new friend and me? I think you will find her company most excellent."

Clara wrinkled her nose up at the thought. "I don't know, my lady. My company, such as it is…"

"Is much to be envied," Lady Rothchild finished easily. "I have told you, as has Fritz, that your name will not be marred by this once it is able to be cleared up. You need not stay cooped up in your room, my dear, when there is an entire house at your disposal. You are no victim, no criminal, no prisoner, and no great sinner, so please come and join me for tea?" She smiled warmly, her manner reminding Clara so much of Phoebe, yet without the same crispness in her speech.

She would be lying if she said she had not longed for company, and for a friend to confide in. Perhaps Lady Rothchild could be that person, and perhaps her sad retreat did not need to continue.

Perhaps.

"All right," she relented with a shy smile. She looked down at her dress, gesturing faintly. "Will my appearance do? I have other things."

Lady Rothchild waved that off at once. "You are perfect as you are. Come, you simply must meet my guests."

"Guests?" Clara repeated as she rounded the top of the steps and started down. "I thought you said it was your new friend."

"It is," came the airy reply. "Along with her gentleman escort. You know a young woman cannot gad about by herself in London, it is too improper!"

Clara had not known any such thing, having never been to London in her entire life, but she was not surprised by it. A young lady was not supposed to go anywhere by herself, supposedly, though the country did not seem to mind so very much.

Yet another mark against London, in her mind.

She would have been lost here, that was for certain.

Lady Rothchild waited for her at the bottom of the stairs, then looped arms with her when she met her. "I'll admit," she murmured, keeping her voice low as she started them walking, "this is a meeting I have been longing to witness ever since I learned your story."

Clara dug her heels into the ground as much as possible, her eyes widening and her breath hitching. Surely, she wouldn't have brought Hawk here. Surely, that interview was not one that needed repeating. She would run back to her rooms, pack her things, and lose herself in London, if he stood in the drawing room at this moment.

"Emily…"

Her hostess turned to her at once, her hands on her arms. "Such fear in your voice! My dear Clara, I assure you, I have only your best interest and care in mind. Will you trust me?"

Would she? It was a dreadful question, given the generosity of the lady and her husband, and the lengths that were being taken to protect her here. But so much had broken within Clara of late, and she could not bear to break further.

She searched Lady Rothchild's eyes, seeing a tender goodness there that settled her nerves. It did not mend the crack in her heart, but it did calm her fears.

And that was enough.

Nodding, Clara allowed herself to be pulled towards the drawing room, exhaling very slowly.

"There now," Lady Rothchild announced as they entered, a smile in her voice, "I told you I could coax her out. And you wanted to storm the stairs…"

A tall man at the far side of the room turned, hazel eyes and strong jaw as familiar to her as any of her own features, though it had been years since she had seen them. Her jaw dropped, and she barely noticed Lady Rothchild letting go of her.

"Martin?"

Her cousin grinned, a sheen in his eyes that prompted tears in her own. "Clare-Bear." He chuckled, sniffed, then rounded the sofa between them.

Clara was already running and flung her arms around him, laughing and sobbing in equal measure as the warm, strong arms encircled her almost painfully tight. "Oh my heavens," she eventually managed, hiccupping on the words. "What are you doing here?"

"What do you think?" he laughed, pulling back to thumb at her chin fondly, his eyes wet. "I've been getting updates on you for weeks, why would I not come for your first arrest?"

Her cheeks flamed, and she lowered her eyes to his lapels. "Let's not discuss that..."

He laughed low and embraced her far more gently. "Oh, darling, it's a common occurrence in our world! I've lost count of my arrests, I can promise you that."

"You've never said anything less surprising," she grumbled, pulling back to reluctantly smile at him, sighing as she looped an arm around his waist. "I have no doubt you cause a great deal of trouble."

"Just enough," he assured her with a wink. He looked across the room, nodding once. "Thank you, my lady."

"Of course!" came the teary response. "We love a good reunion, don't we, Miss Moore?"

Clara stilled, her eyes darting across the room quickly. "Miss Moore?"

Standing beside Lady Rothchild, dressed in elegant travelling apparel, stood a woman of about Clara's age and a very similar coloring. She smiled freely and inclined her chin. "Indeed I am, Miss Harlow. I hope you don't mind, your cousin allowed me to come along to meet you. I have a great many questions, but the first and chief of all is this." Her smile spread and she giggled lightly. "How did you find it, being me for a time?"

Chapter Twenty-Four

*M*oving heaven and earth could not be more difficult than what he was doing now.

And surely it had never been attempted on less sleep, or in such a state.

Hawk hadn't much choice to do otherwise, but surely his penance did not have to truly destroy him when he was working so tirelessly to redeem himself.

Everything had been hell from the moment he'd ridden from Kirkleigh in his joyous delirium. He'd dwelt on how heroic he would seem riding over to the inn or to the House of Corrections, paying Clara's bail and freeing her from her ignominious state. She would forgive him of his foolishness, and he would appropriately beg for it further, then she would agree to be his wife.

He'd pay whatever fines the courts thought appropriate, and to hell with what anyone thought. That would be the end of it.

How was he to know that she was not at the inn, nor at the House of Corrections? Sir Henry Norris had been called away to tend to other matters requiring his time, and the imbeciles at the House of Corrections knew nothing about where Clara had been taken or why. Finally, one less dim-witted than the rest suggested she might have been taken to one of the facilities in a larger town, given they had minimal accommodations for ladies.

There began his hellish plight in truth. He'd ridden to Canterbury, Ramsgate, and Dover, finding no information in any one of them. No sign of Clara, no record of her arrival or containment, and no indication of where she had gone. He'd returned to Kirkleigh only to inform them of his failures, and then had ridden headlong for the only other place he thought might be of use.

The Miss Masters' Finishing School.

His pacing of the drawing room he'd once so admired had seemed almost cruel, in a way. He took no notice of anything in it this time, wearing a path in the rug beneath his feet with his agitation. In what seemed more time than decency dictated, Miss Bradford, the stoic headmistress, finally met him, and, with apparent regret, informed him that she had very little help to offer.

Near to the end of his wits, Hawk had begged, rather pathetically, for any insight at all.

Miss Bradford had taken pity on him, and suggested Clara might have been taken to London, given the indignation of the Brownings and their insistence on seeing punishment doled out. It was not uncommon, and if she had been guilty of perjury as well, the judgment upon her might have merited a higher court.

Hawk had not managed to conceal his dismay at all of this, had run his hands through his hair, and asked how, exactly, he was supposed to find one wrongly accused woman in London.

Miss Bradford had sighed, then gave him the name of a very reputable women's prison in London. "Once I heard of Miss Harlow's plight, I sent a request to have her transferred here. I did not tell you because I am doing my best to protect her, and her reputation, and, quite frankly, I did not know if it would be permitted. Go there and ask for Miss Duncan. Tell her I sent you." She paused, shaking her head. "I don't know if she is still there. I have no influence in the law."

It was a strange thing to say, given he had not anticipated she would have any such power. He eyed her for a moment, wondering about the families who had sent their daughters there, many of whom might have had such influence.

"Do you know who I might call upon in London that could have influence upon the law?" he had asked.

She had nodded once. "Lord Rothchild."

Armed with such information, and desperate for any help, he'd ridden like mad on his horse, foregoing the politeness of a carriage or even a change of clothes. What did he care for his appearance or his reputation when he had literally lost the woman he loved and was growing more and more powerless to save her?

What charges did she face that rendered such security of her person? How could she be transferred out of local care when, if he recalled correctly, she was accused of relatively minor crimes? She was no fine lady, nor did she have ties to any, as she was not legitimately the late Duke of Kirklin's ward. There would be no interventions, as far as he could tell, other than his own.

If he could intervene.

He had to find her first.

His arrival at the Saint Martha's House of Corrections for Females had been eventful to say the least, given he had stormed the gates in the pre-dawn hours and demanded entrance. His signet ring had been the only thing to save him from being significantly bruised by a pair of burly guards with several missing teeth, and his less-than-polite request to see Miss Duncan at such an hour had been met with flat refusals. He could leave the premises and return at a reasonable hour, or he could hang about the gates with the London vagrants, it mattered not to them.

Duke or no duke, he would not be seeing Miss Duncan before she rose of her own accord.

Hawk had lost his senses at that. "I will not wait," he had roared, his fury towering with an intensity that could consume any living creatures near him. "I have ridden hellbent across two counties now, and when Miss Bradford told me to ask for Miss Duncan, I did not think that would limit me to the damned calling hours of London!"

The gargoyles of men blinked, then motioned for him to sit on a rickety stool behind him. Without another word, they had left him there, returning only fifteen minutes later with a woman in a dark calico gown, her hair braided over one shoulder, striding towards him without any sort of rancor.

"Your Grace," she'd said simply. "Miss Bradford sent you?"

"Yes." Hawk had cleared his throat, his emotions getting the better of him. "I am here to beg for the release of Miss Clara Harlow. I will pay her bail, and she will be in my care until the assizes in Kent. I will sign whatever documents required and offer one of my estates as collateral that she will be presented at the appointed date and time for judgment."

Miss Duncan's brow had furrowed, sending a frigid lance into his chest. "Miss Harlow? That's not a prisoner I'm acquainted with. Let me check the ledgers. Come with me." She indicated he follow and moved into an office space that would rival any solicitor's office anywhere, and far more orderly than any he had seen. She pulled a worn ledger from the great desk to one side and opened it nearly at the back.

He had watched as she ran a finger down three pages, shaking her head. "She was not brought in this week." Her eyes had met his with a surprising degree of sympathy. "I don't have her here, Your Grace. I am happy to inquire at our partner facilities, but they are much larger, and take in a greater number of prisoners. I can make no promises."

There had been no helping the swaying into her desk as his legs had begun to give out, and he'd braced himself upon the surface for stability. "What am I to do?" he'd rasped, not caring that she would witness his distress. "I have to find her. I have to…" He shook his head slowly, straightening up. "Thank you, Miss Duncan. I am sorry to have disturbed you so early." With a perfect bow, he had made his way from the room, from the building, and from the street.

He'd holed up at his London house until polite creatures of Society would start to move about, and then, shaved and changed, he pursued his very last hope.

The stopping of the carriage now signaled his cue.

It was now or never.

He stepped out and looked up at the grand façade, calling upon his politeness amid his madness, then moved forward to ring the bell. With brilliant efficiency, the door opened a moment later, a tall and long-faced butler appeared. "May I help you?"

Hawk handed over his card. "The Duke of Kirklin to see Lord Rothchild on a matter of some urgency." He waited a beat, then gave the man an almost smile. "He is not expecting me."

Apparently used to such things, the butler nodded and stepped back. "Please come in, Your Grace. I'll let his lordship know." When Hawk entered, the butler offered to take his hat and walking stick. "Would you follow me, Your Grace? His lordship prefers to meet his callers of urgency in a particular drawing room just above us."

"Certainly," Hawk relented, feeling encouragement for the first time in days. "I'm happy to oblige his lordship's preferences."

Silently, they made their way up the stairs, the eyes of several family portraits watching their progress. Hawk did his best to ignore them, the remotest sign of art now his greatest torment.

Entering the simple and unremarkable drawing room, Hawk moved to the window and clasped his hands behind him. "Excellent view," he murmured.

"Yes, I've always thought so," a new, deep voice replied.

He turned quickly, startled by the still taller, dark-haired figure of a finely dressed man entering without airs. He bowed quickly. "My lord."

"Kirklin," Lord Rothchild returned, bowing himself. "Forgive the unannounced entry. I heard the door and started down before I was notified." He held up Hawk's card with a brief smile. "Reeder handed this to me as I passed him. What can I do for you, Your Grace?"

Hawk dropped his hands and exhaled shortly. "I need your help, my lord. You are a patron of the Miss Masters' Finishing School, one of their greatest supporters."

Rothchild raised a brow. "I am. They named the rudimentary academy after me, which I take great pride in."

"Indeed." Hawk cleared his throat. "You may know, perhaps, a teacher by the name of Miss Harlow."

"One of my girls' favorites," he answered with a nod. "She teaches French, I believe. And perhaps dance?"

"Art," Hawk corrected without thinking. "She was arrested not long ago, on what I believe are spurious charges. I have been riding all over Kent trying to find her and pay her bail, free her, if I can, and, for the life of me, I cannot find her."

"Find her?" Rothchild blinked, though his lips twitched a little. "Is she lost?"

The hint of amusement was not at all appreciated, and Hawk scowled. "She shouldn't be. She was taken by the magistrate to an inn, there to be transferred to a House of Correction. Only she was taken on instead, we think, to London. I have some influence in Kent, and perhaps in a few other counties, but I have no personal influence to speak of in London, and certainly not in any realm of law, justice, or diplomacy."

He swallowed hard and took two steps forward. "I am desperate, my lord, and throw myself upon your mercy. I must find Miss Harlow, and I cannot do it without your help. Please."

Rothchild stared at him for a long moment, then exhaled and moved to the sideboard at one end of the room. "Would you care for a drink?"

Hawk nearly gaped where he stood, confusion running rampant. "What?"

The man reached into the sideboard for two glasses and a decanter. "I asked if you would care for a drink."

He was a menace and a boor, and Hawk would have stormed from the house had he anywhere else to go. "No, I don't bloody want a drink! I want your help!"

Rothchild set the glasses down and began to pour, sighing. "Yes, I understand that, but I am about to shock you in a way that you cannot possibly imagine, so I think you had better have a drink." He capped the decanter, then picked up both glasses, turning to face him. "In fact, I insist upon it. Please, sit."

Hawk did so as he watched him approach, utterly bewildered now, but took the glass when it was handed to him. "My lord?"

"Drink up," Rothchild encouraged. "Sip it, if you please. My wife does so hate a drunkard in the house."

The liquid burned its way down Hawk's throat as he obediently sipped, though the temptation to toss the beverage back and let the fiery punishment commence was a great one.

Rothchild watched him for a moment, then began to slowly pace. "I know more about your Miss Harlow than you think," he began, his attention more on the drink in his hand than on Hawk. "I know that she was jilted, rather fortunately, it turned out, and that her family chose to cut her off. I know how she came to teach at Miss Masters', and I know how she came to be at Kirkleigh." He paused to give Hawk an impatient look. "Your timing was rather inconvenient, Your Grace, if I may say so. We were not anticipating your being there."

"I don't understand," Hawk admitted bluntly, tracking the man's movements as though he were an animal likely to strike.

"I know all about her playing Miss Moore," Rothchild went on, not addressing Hawk's statement. "I'm responsible for finding the connection there and getting her the details that allowed her to portray Miss Moore believably in the role we needed her to."

Hawk shot to his feet, the liquid in his glass sloshing onto his hand. "You did *what?*"

Rothchild waved him back down, entirely unconcerned. "I and my colleagues placed her at Kirkleigh, along with an unnamed counterpart, and among the neighborhood for several purposes. The chief of these was to investigate the probability of rogue Frenchmen and their English sympathizers using the coast for their new smuggling enterprises, that of delivering agents and items strictly set aside to bring down the British government as we know it and furthering a long-held plan by several other rogue Frenchmen, and their English partners, to take control of all of Europe in a way only Napoleon has ever dreamed of."

Slowly, Hawk felt himself lowering back to the chair he had vacated, logic telling him to laugh at the plot he had just heard, while good sense told him that Lord Rothchild was in a position to know a great deal more about the goings-on in other countries and England herself than Hawk would ever hope to.

And he was not laughing.

Rothchild looked at him now, his expression almost severe. "I'll let you draw your own conclusions, Kirklin, about what such a position and role implies about Miss Harlow. Suffice it to say, I know exactly why she was arrested, and what she accomplished in doing those things. I know what our country owes her for that sacrifice, and I can assure you that she will never see the inside of a jail cell unless she develops an interest in touring one."

Relief ought to have washed over him, but he was too stunned to feel anything at all. If what Rothchild said was true, and he was inclined to believe it was, Clara would have been some sort of government operative during the time she was at Kirkleigh. Considering all that had happened, and how it had transpired, it would have to be something covert, else several others would know about it.

Clara was a spy?

Several phrases and words continued to circle Hawk's mind, when he suddenly seized upon one. "Never see a jail cell?" he repeated, looking up. "Do you know where she is?"

Rothchild's mouth suddenly twisted to one side. "Of course, I do. She's upstairs."

Clara stared at Reeder without blinking, her knees tingling rather unnervingly. "What did you say?"

"His lordship is currently speaking with the Duke of Kirklin in the green drawing room," Reeder repeated, unflappable as ever. "It was suggested that you may wish to know that and come down."

"What..." She swallowed very carefully. "What did the duke want?"

Reeder gave her a surprisingly sympathetic look. "I was not privy to that information, Miss Harlow. But what I would venture to ask is this: does it matter?"

Clara stilled further at that. Did it matter? How in the world had Hawk found her here? No one knew of her presence here, not even Pippa and the others at the Convent, Weaver had made that very clear. Yet Hawk was downstairs speaking with him?

No. No, it did not matter.

All preparations to receive Martin again vanished from her mind and she shot to her feet, bolting past the butler without answering his question. She thundered down the stairs without grace or decorum, nearly slipping when she reached the bottom as she rounded the stairs quickly. Her breath began to race in and out of her lungs in a desperate panting, fearing this would all end in a dream as had happened so many times before.

She tore into the drawing room without knocking, stopping stock still after doing so, her eyes finding a glorious figure standing just before a chair, an oddly empty glass in one hand.

Hawk's eyes widened as he saw her, the drawn nature of his countenance making her heart burn in agony.

"I stand corrected," Weaver mused in some amusement. "She is here."

Clara ignored him. She wet her suddenly parched lips, afraid to breathe. "Hawk?"

A sound somewhere between a laugh, a sob, and a gasp erupted from him, then he moved, rounding a table and dropping the glass to the floor, where it shattered. "Clara," he groaned. "Oh, Clara, my love, my darling girl..."

Dissolving into tears, Clara rushed to meet him, flinging her arms about him as he caught her up, crushing her to him. His arms spanned entirely around her, his hands nearly reaching his opposite shoulders, so tight was his hold. He buried his face into her shoulder and neck, ragged breaths rasping against her skin with a tantalizing heat as she drenched his cravat with her tears.

She trembled against him, racked by sobs of relief, of love, of shame, of utter release. At last, at long last, she was in his arms. Was encased against him with an intensity that thrilled through her. Was entirely, wholly, and perfectly his.

"Forgive me, my love," Hawk pleaded, his lips rubbing against the skin of her neck as he held her still, his hold never slackening. "Can you ever forgive me?"

"Yes," she gasped as her fingers curled into his hair, turning to press a frantic kiss along his jaw. "Oh, yes. Can you forgive me, darling? Do you forgive me?"

His arms moved then, his hands sliding to cradle her face, his fingertips grazing against her hair as his lips found hers feverishly. Again and again, he kissed her, deeply and tenderly, each pass of his lips weakening her legs and lighting her soul with fire. She clung to him with a desperation she had never known, caught up in everything he showered upon her and chased his passion with her own.

"There is nothing to forgive," he eventually breathed, his lips brushing against hers as he shook his head. He took her mouth in a long, lingering caress. "I've been lost without you, my love. Shattered and broken, and I haven't been whole until this moment."

"I know," she whispered, touching her brow to his, gripping his head as though it were all that kept her standing. "I love you so much."

He kissed her hard, making her whimper and sigh into the depths of him. "I love you," he murmured between kisses, incinerating whatever remained of her sanity. "I love you. Do you hear me? I *love* you."

His voice hitched on the word, and Clara cradled his face, tears streaming down her cheeks, her lips dancing across whatever part of him she could reach. "I love you," she whispered back, unable to say anything more.

Hawk shuddered in her hold, his arms wrapping around her once more, softly this time, tenderly and intimately, folding her against his body until they might have been one.

She could happily die thus, if she did not long for days and weeks and years of just such adoration.

Sighing once more, she nuzzled against him, weak and pleasantly languid in his arms. Could anything be imagined more perfect than this?

"I hate to interrupt," a deep voice intoned with a clearing of a throat. "Hate to intrude on a moment like this but, erm… National security, fate of the kingdom, destroying evil, so on and so forth… We need to plan. No rush. Only lives at stake."

Hawk stirred against her, groaning again as he pulled back. His eyes searched hers, one hand brushing gently beneath her chin before he tipped her face up again to slowly and thoroughly kiss her.

She'd have stumbled into him afterwards had there been space to do so. As it was, she followed and recovered by burying her face against his chest, fighting for breath.

"What sort of a plan?" Hawk inquired in a stronger voice than Clara could have managed, his hand running over her hair as she rested against him. "Can't I just take her away?"

Clara exhaled shortly and shook her head, raising it to meet his eyes. "No. I have to see this through, Hawk. I have to see it ended."

His thumb stroked against her cheek, his mouth curving in a smile as he nodded. "All right." He turned to face Lord Rothchild, keeping an arm firmly around her. "What do we do?"

She wrapped both arms around him, now standing at his side, leaning her head against him as she, too, looked at Weaver.

"Should be fairly straightforward," Weaver mused, a faint pucker in his brow. "A team of operatives waiting within the caves and the house. Wait for the ship to move back out to sea and move in on the arrivals. We could even use Barcliffe for the interrogation and containment, make the necessary arrests." He cast a wry smirk at Hawk. "Your eager Sir Henry would enjoy playing the hero. Pity this will never reach his ears, nor fall in his jurisdiction."

"I should not be there," Clara suggested reluctantly. "If they see me, they'll know, and it could all be ruined."

"Who?" Hawk pressed gently. "The Brownings?"

She nodded. "They are working with the Faction, smuggling in goods and people. Alexandra Moore says Mr. Browning's father had been engaged in smuggling for years…"

"You met Miss Moore?" he interrupted, laughing quickly. "What a strange meeting that must have been."

"I don't see why you shouldn't be there," Weaver observed with a thoughtful look, his dark eyes narrowed. "You certainly deserve to be. Perhaps you could assist in interviewing the French."

Clara brightened at the thought, nodding eagerly. "Could I? And I would love to see the ships and boats coming in. I've tried to picture it enough."

"Then see it you shall!" Weaver chuckled and winked at her. "If for no other reason than to satiate your curiosity. Very well, I will send out word and have it all arranged. It shall have to be soon. Second and fourth, yes?"

"Yes." Clara smiled wryly at this leader of spies. "The night before, if you please." She exhaled slowly, shaking her head. "Then there is the matter of my employment."

Hawk looked down at her in surprise. "At the school? What about it? I've seen Miss Bradford recently; she'll take you back."

"We can have that all arranged easily," Weaver agreed in a very nonplussed manner. "Nothing to worry about."

Clara still shook her head. "I don't regret what I've done for a moment, especially now, but how can we possibly recover my reputation enough for me to still teach at the school and expect the Society families to send their daughters there? My name is tainted in the neighborhood, no matter what Pippa or anyone else says. I'll have to tender my resignation."

"I've a rather different idea, if I may speak," Hawk broke in beside her.

Weaver waved a hand in encouragement. "Go ahead, Kirklin."

Hawk pulled away from her just enough to take both of her hands in his. He smiled the beautiful almost-smile she loved most. "Marry me, Clara."

All her breath vanished from her lungs, her eyes searching his in disbelief. "What?"

"Marry me," he said again, more firmly. "You know I love you. I know you love me. I was going to ask you before you were arrested, but I daresay I mean it more now than I ever could have then. Marry me. Then we can donate our own amounts to the school and get a program named after us."

"I beg your pardon," Weaver protested playfully.

Clara simply stared at Hawk. "How?" she asked weakly, her hands cold in his. "How can you marry me when the rumors will just—"

"With the special license I got when I first came to London," he overrode, grinning now. "And I have no doubt your friend here knows a discreet vicar who can accomplish the task creditably."

"I know three," came the helpful offer.

"And the best part of being a duke, especially a reserved one," Hawk went on, "is that I don't have to care that much about what other people think. But Rothchild and his cohorts can recover your standing in the neighborhood somehow, if you wish it. Say that you'll be my wife, Clara Harlow. Come and make every house a home, and every home heaven on earth."

Clara beamed with all the adoration in the world at the beloved man before her, squeezing his hands. "I will," she told him, winning herself a blinding smile in return. "Yes, I will."

He swept her up into his arms, laughing and kissing her soundly. "I'll adore you all my days," he vowed softly. "Every single one of them."

She put a hand on his cheek, sighing in contentment. "And I you, my love. With all that I am."

Epilogue

The ship slowly approached the shore in the dark of the night, with only a sliver of moon to guide her. A faint whistle echoed across the water, and three fishing boats appeared from the beach, rushing into the water and rowing out to meet her. When they arrived, goods were lowered into her, as were a dozen or so figures between the three boats.

There was no hesitation on the part of any involved, each piece efficient and well-practiced. Had she not been witnessing it, Clara might have thought it all impossible to occur in such a short space of time. Yet as the fishing boats rowed their way back to shore, she had to admit that there was a remarkable amount of skill and strategy involved in this venture. How else could it have gone on for the time that it had without any detection?

It was a marvel, there could be no doubt about that.

"Bloody genius," muttered the man to her left. "You have to give them credit for that."

"I do not!" the man to her right hissed vehemently. "Smuggling would be bad enough, but this? Treason is too good for them."

Clara exhaled in exasperation, shaking her head. "I'm beginning to regret bringing either of you along."

"I have just as much a right to be here as you," Brick replied from her left, his whisper doing nothing to hide his laugh.

She'd give him that. Turning her head, she gave an inquiring look to the man at her right.

He met her eyes without shame. "I'm your husband," he said simply. "I go where you go."

There was something utterly romantic and desperately sweet in that.

She grinned at him. "Yes, you are." Leaning in, she gave him a soft kiss.

"Now, now, Your Graces," Brick scolded on a rasp. "No time for that. They're nearing the shore. It's almost time."

Winking at Hawk, Clara turned back to their observation, raising up just a little more on her elbows, the rest of her still flush against the ground.

"Is the light out?" Hawk asked on a breath.

Brick glanced behind them. "It is. Signaling the clipper to leave, no doubt."

"And we're going to let it?"

There was no accusation, no outrage in his question. Only inquiry, and Clara adored her new husband for that.

He had taken her role in the covert world rather well as he'd learned more about it. The revelation of the school's true purpose had taken some adjustment, given his sister's attendance there, but when he'd realized the increased protection such a place had given her over the years, he'd accepted it well. His logic had proven valuable, and his gift for strategy almost unnerving.

Clara fully expected Weaver to approach *him* one of these days with a position among them.

She'd have a great deal to say about that, if he did.

"Yes," Brick answered, eyeing the beach in anticipation. "We need them to continue on the same schedule without suspicion. If they had any idea, they could change landings faster than we could identify it, and we'd have to start from the beginning almost."

"Almost," Hawk repeated, nudging Clara's shoulder with his own.

It might have been another kiss for all the thrill she found in it.

If there was one thing she could say about sharing the details of her covert life with Hawk, it was how much it meant to her that he had taken pride in her efforts. He would have boasted of her exploits and efforts, had it been possible. He never tired of the subject, and was ever telling her how impressed he was, how extraordinary she was, and how noble.

Perhaps one day, she would stop blushing at it.

Not soon, but one day.

"Who is positioned in the tunnel?" Clara breathed, watching the boats land at the beach and get dragged out of the water.

"Fists and Rook," he replied. "Perhaps Ivy."

She nodded, only knowing Fists, as he was really Mr. Fairfax at the Convent, but she had heard of Ivy. Perhaps she would come to know Rook and others by such names, if Pippa or Weaver could see a use for her as Sparrow in other assignments. But perhaps not.

Perhaps this would be all she would do for King and country.

She could be content with that. She would do more if asked, as she had vowed with all her heart to do all she could. But should her time at Kirkleigh be all that was required, it would be enough.

More than enough.

"Bit further," Brick murmured as they watched the figures begin to unload the boats. "Bit further."

"Is the ship far enough out?" Hawk breathed. "Could they see?"

Clara bit her lip, anxiety rising. "I think it's far enough. And the night is dark…"

Multiple figures suddenly appeared on the beach from either side, with a few streaming from the direction of the cave and tunnel. Brief sounds of scuffles could be heard, but it had all happened so swiftly and in near darkness that there had not been time for any great commotion.

"Excellent," Hawk praised under his breath. "Well done, all."

Brick grunted once and patted Clara's arm. "Better go now, Sparrow. They'll need you next."

"Right." She backed away from the cliff's edge, staying low to the ground and using her elbows and knees for motion.

Once safely away, she pushed up to her knees, brushing at her borrowed dark jacket and the tops of her breeches. Her husband's clothing would never fit her well, but until they got her properly fitted by Tilda again, she'd make do.

A hand extended out to help her up. "Your Grace."

She grinned up at the smiling face of her husband and placed her hand in his. "Your Grace."

Tugging her to her feet, he wrapped her in his arms, kissing her deeply and tipping her back a bit to do so, making her giggle.

"Shh," he insisted, laughing himself as he righted her. "Do you want everyone to know?"

"Many of them were there," she reminded him, swatting at his chest. "It was the most well attended discreet wedding I have ever seen."

"Your friends adore me, what can I say?" He laced his fingers with hers as they walked towards Barcliffe. "I have to admit, darling, this is not exactly how I imagined my wedding day."

Clara scoffed softly, looking up at him. "I did offer to marry you tomorrow instead."

"I'm not complaining," he replied easily, his thumb brushing against her skin. "I was rather keen to marry you, and sooner was undoubtedly better."

She covered her mouth to keep from laughing aloud. "With you prepared to forge all signatures, including the vicar's, to make it all happen in more haste? I should say so. A girl doesn't have time to breathe and enjoy a thing with you about."

He pulled her close, wrapping the hand he held around her back and turning her to face him as they walked. "Are you not enjoying it?" he murmured, his voice dipping with the sort of danger that curled her toes.

Walking backwards now, trapped between his arm and his chest, Clara fought to maintain a playful air. "I've hardly had time to reflect on the matter," she whispered as she pointedly rubbed her thumb against the hand she held, knowing how it would ignite him. "I really cannot say."

He growled and pulled them to a stop, pressing the small of her back until she was flush against him. Dipping his head, he dusted his mouth across her jaw, keeping a hair's breadth from truly kissing her as he moved, tracing her ear, the crest of her cheek. "Can you not?"

Her breath shuddered within her, arching her closer to him still, the soles of her feet aching uncomfortably. "I suppose..." she managed.

He chuckled against her hairline, her lashes fluttering in a sort of swoon at the sensation. "Suppose what, my love?"

Biting her lip, she nuzzled against him, swallowing back a

whimper of need. He complied, pressing his lips fully against her skin and dotting a path down to the corner of her mouth.

"Suppose what?" he asked again, his breath teasing the sensitive surface of her lips.

Moving quickly, she turned her face to mold her lips to his, using her free hand to press at the back of his neck and hold him in place.

When he was the one trembling, she gently pulled back and touched her nose to his. "I love it," she told him in a barely audible whisper.

He groaned and pressed his lips to her brow for a moment. "Hurry and talk to the French, will you? I've got to get you back to Kirkleigh before I lose my mind."

Clara chuckled, loving how he seemed to ripple at the sound of it. "Yes, my love."

He released her from his hold, and they continued their walk to Barcliffe, the house dark but for new candles lit in a rear drawing room. They moved up the stairs to the terrace, and Clara grinned at the figure waiting for her at the door. "Are they ready?"

Phoebe inclined her head in a sage nod. "They are, indeed. I have no doubt they'd rather speak with you than the others."

"Who wouldn't?" Hawk replied with a snort. "Evening, Fern."

She smiled in wry amusement. "Your Grace."

He shook his head and sighed. "We must do something about my name if I'm to keep doing this. How can I be the Duke of Kirklin himself if I'm skulking about in the dark?"

"I've seen stranger things," Phoebe quipped. She stepped back and waved them in. "Sparrow, on your way. Himself?"

Hawk coughed a laugh. "Yes?"

"You'd best enjoy a book," she suggested, sobering only a little. "I'm told they're not feeling particularly talkative."

Clara took his hand again, squeezing tightly. "I'm sorry," she whispered, torn between longing for him and the duty she had tonight.

He flashed her a quick grin and brought her hand to his lips. "Don't be. I've got my whole life with you. Go and be magnificent, my love. I'll be here."

Love for this man surged within her and she swallowed hard,

stepping close to cup his cheek and meet his eyes. "I love you so much."

"Good." He kissed her quickly, but with steady tenderness. "Now, *va sauve le monde, mon amour. Je sais que tu peux.*"

Clara bit back a giggle, giving him a scolding look. "*Va sauver le monde, mon amour. Va sauver. Il va falloir travailler ton français.*"

He quirked his brows. "*Merci, mademoiselle.*"

"Clara," Phoebe murmured.

Nodding, Clara stepped away from her husband, smiling a little, then made her way to the drawing room as she had been instructed. She heard a familiar voice within, barking particular instructions, and executing them in perfect French.

She managed a small smile. She'd hoped her cousin would join them tonight, and she was looking forward to seeing Martin in his role as Ruse.

Sobering, she fixed her expression into one of calm and pushed into the room. A few individuals stood within, comprised of both men and women. The blank faces were her allies, the angry ones her foes. All turned to look at her, expectation and reluctance wearing a variety of masks there.

But Clara was a teacher, and a teacher of young ladies of varying stations. She knew how to handle such things. She smiled at Martin, who stepped back in proud anticipation, then took in the others.

"*Bienvenues en Angleterre,*" she began, smiling around at them all and clasping her hands before her. "*Qui voudrait commencer?*"

Coming Soon

The *Ears Have It*

Agents of the Convent
Book Two

"All of London's a stage..."

by

Rebecca Connolly

About the Author

Growing up, Rebecca Connolly wanted to be Elizabeth Bennett, Mary Poppins, or British royalty, so it came as a great shock when she discovered she was an American girl from the Midwest. She started making up stories when she was young, and thanks to a rampant imagination and a fairly consistent stream of hot chocolate, ice cream, and cookie dough, she's kept at it. She loves a good love story, and a good swoon, and tries to share that with her readers. She still lives in the Midwest, has two degrees in non-writing fields, and dreams of one day having a cottage of her own in her beloved British Isles.

Rebecca is a huge fan of period dramas and currently writes in the Regency era, though she refuses to rule any other time period out. You just never know where the imagination will take you, and she'll write whatever story comes to her whenever it's set! There is always a story to tell, and she wants to tell them all!

You can find out more at www.rebeccaconnolly.com.